The First Book of Timothy

THE FIRST BOOK *of* TIMOTHY

A NOVEL

Robert Eaton Kelley

Dartmouth College
Published by University Press of New England
Hanover and London

DARTMOUTH COLLEGE
Published by University Press of New England, Hanover, NH 03755

Printed in the United States of America 5 4 3 2 1
CIP data appear at the end of the book

For Mary

and for all of our achievements together.
Everything began with her.

PART ONE

1

The New Frontier

He had stumbled upon the gathering but Timothy Brown King knew the face of John Fitzgerald Kennedy, President of the United States.

"George Washington, second lieutenant," a student said.

"No," said another, "Clark Gable, leader of the free world."

And then the picture disappeared. The television went blank. At first, the fifty or so male students in the lounge of Dartmouth College's eighteenth-century Hanover Inn groaned as one, and the rumble filled Timothy's body, pressed against his chest, burgeoned in his stomach. Scattered laughs followed, rolled across the room, and Timothy felt bereft as the wave of emotion left him, left the room.

He stared wistfully now as President Kennedy's face reappeared from another world. The voices of the students closed to a murmur and then became silent as if forced from the room by Kennedy's accent which again filled the lounge.

"We will not prematurely risk the course of worldwide nuclear war," President Kennedy said.

But as if the fate of the Western world depended upon his not hearing another word, Timothy stopped listening. His ears had been closed. In recent hours he had learned that it was his destiny to communicate with the unknown, to talk to strangers and ghosts, perhaps to spies everpresent. But first, the deepest of sleep. It was his overwhelming desire first to dream.

He picked up his suitcase and headed for the door. No one would stop him. He would leave the Inn. Not a single person would notice. Not a single soul on the earth knew what he was doing or where he was going. Was that not true? He thought to believe it. But given what had happened, he was beginning to waver. Given what had happened, perhaps he was to conceive of a different world. He was willing.

Timothy paused outside on the terrace of the Inn, stood there on a dark stage. On this still October night of 1962 he could feel the chill. A single cab waited across the street. The driver, his head tilted toward his lap, did not look up. Was he reading?

Timothy looked beyond the cab into the night. Across the campus green of colonial Dartmouth College in Hanover, New Hampshire, the white tower of Baker Library was lighted, outlined and gleaming in the black sky. Behind him he could hear muffled sounds from the television in the Inn. Rather than the distinctive tones of President Kennedy's clipped voice, they were just that, muffled sounds.

Did someone call his name? He turned to look back at the door of the Inn through which he had just passed. It was the very same door from which John F. Kennedy, the brash junior Senator from Massachusetts, had emerged more than two years before in March 1960, deeply tanned and displaying what a student reporter for *The Dartmouth* had described as that "famous Kennedy smile." Kennedy had come to the college late that winter campaigning for the upcoming New Hampshire Presidential primary to deliver what had been billed as a major policy address. He had just finished a press conference in the lounge of the Inn and he was moving slowly across the green toward cavernous Daniel Webster Hall for his speech among the pillars. A crowd had surrounded Kennedy, including photographers and reporters, faculty and students, local politicians and townspeople, even half a dozen mongrel dogs. The world had begun to take notice.

Timothy remembered that his father had been at Kennedy's side. John Brown King, Esquire, trustee of Dartmouth, Class of 1934, the token golden liberal on the College's Board of Trustees, and the probable next Democratic nominee for the United States Senate from the Grand State of Maine, proudly we hail, JBK, himself, The King. Maybe Senator King would later run for President, too. Hoop-de-da. Why not? March on, my man. JBK All The Way. Crown The King, President King, long live The King. Timothy was now beginning to recognize that he had not truly understood the dimensions of the fairy tale. The father as figure of history, not just his father. A phantom of American society. A chameleon in the family. The King is dead, long live The King.

And mother, where was his mother? You had to have a mother in America, did you not? Although some claimed that in the Soviet Union these days you did not necessarily remain with your mother, or your father, either, for that matter. Once born, that is. Before that you had no choice, of course. You stayed with your mother. Before birth. BB. But after birth, AB, after the most important liberation of all, you had to get on with it, get on with the socialist task. So where was Timothy's mother, Helen Eaton King? What transformations had she undergone?

Kennedy had not changed. The Senator had become the President. Timothy still remembered his own curious preoccupation with Kennedy that brisk March day in 1960, and his disappointment. When the campaigning Presidential candidate had addressed the college community there had been flashes of what would become known to the nation as the Kennedy wit. But instead of an enunciation of policy, there had been a series of disconnected one-liners. The students had enjoyed his chit-chat. Kennedy had spoken of the need for more "intellectuals" to engage in the political life of the nation, but Timothy remembered wondering if Kennedy regarded himself as an intellectual. He had not known what he had expected from Kennedy, but having seen him and heard him he had felt that there was little left to imagine. Flash and fizzle? At least the crowd had been excited, despite the fact that in those days the Hanover plain was Rocky and Dick country, that is, mostly the hunting ground of the warring Republican factions of Dartmouth alumnus Governor Nelson Rockefeller of New York and Vice President Richard M. Nixon.

In fact, Timothy at the time had been perplexed at the attention Kennedy had received, the aura of importance that had been bestowed upon him. After all, what had he achieved? What had he earned? And why were people so taken with him? What was wrong with them? The charisma. Obviously the crowd thought Kennedy had it. What was it? A pretty face? The gleaming, rakish, little-boy smile? American Irish rogue-royalty? Maybe the people just wanted a President with red hair. Yes, that was their secret, sinful desire. They were ready for a red-haired President. They just might risk it. Even if he was a Catholic. It was what JBK would have called a don quixote.

Not surprisingly, Timothy had been busily repelling the force, coping with the substantive presence on the Dartmouth campus of JBK that day while others had marked the glitter of the thespian JFK, the Saturday-afternoon matinee idol of the marquee, the celebrity actor. Despite the fact that JBK was Kennedy's strong ally, the son had thought the father should do battle with the pretender, should himself pretend. But Timothy had begun to feel contempt, not so much for Kennedy as for the scene, for the histrionic ceremonial play of politics. It had been one of those embarrassing, sickening, self-conscious moments for him. Nausea, vertigo. He had felt shame for himself and for his fellow souls, for the crowd of human beings that had surrounded him, pressing one and all, flattened together like a cheap sandwich. Neither the shame nor the contempt had attached to JBK, who for Timothy had been, in retrospect, by far the more successful actor that day, that day. The rich black long Cadillac limousine. A pipe-smoking actor for the season.

But what Timothy also could not forget was that months later, following the Democratic and Republican conventions, during the presidential election campaign between the two parties' nominees, incredible as it now seemed to him, he had begun to wish secretly—a secret above all to be kept from his father, no, JBK must not know, no, no, JBK—that Nixon would emerge triumphant, that Nixon would beat Kennedy for the Presidency of the United States. How perverse. Tricky Dick, whose person he found repugnant, whose most every motive he opposed. President Tricky Dick. Timothy had wondered about that, thought about it, except he had chosen not to dwell upon it. But why had that occurred? Perhaps it was simply in reaction to the fact that most of his circle of friends, mostly in spite of their parents' leanings, were predictably drawn to the handsome, stylish Jack Kennedy and jeered the awkward, ugly one, Richard the Louse. Timothy had always recoiled from being a part of the crowd, one of the boys. Yes, that was probably it, as simple as that. Or maybe in truth it was because Nixon was obviously evil and that had fascinated Timothy, fascinated him in the way that the character of Macbeth or Richard III fascinated one. Rather than Kennedy's candy-bar wrapper, however immediately and superficially bright and colorful and attractive that might be, Nixon was the genuine, exciting, malevolent, dank article. To dare to imagine him as President of the United States was to make your skin crawl, to make you quiver in a way you would never forget. What a way to go, what a way to dare to be. The President of the United States publicly, defiantly evil. Delicious. Exquisite. Magnificent.

Yes, Timothy had felt the curious corrupt allure of Richard Milhous Nixon. That which was utterly repellent attracted. There was something in that for certain. Something moldy. But something human? He did not know. He no longer knew what that meant. Human. But with President *Nixon* rather than President *Kennedy*—one, something apart from and more than a mere villain, belonged in a horror film, while the other belonged in the Sunday funnies, in a cartoon strip alongside Dick Tracy or Captain Marvell—he had felt for certain that the country would be radically altered. Except, he had not been able to explain exactly why . . . he had not been able to . . . what? . . . anticipate, envision the worst? Would Nixon have grown a beard in office? A five-o'clock shadow spreading from the White House across the nation.

Although there was no question that had Timothy been old enough to vote he would have voted for Kennedy—there was no question, was there?—nevertheless, he had been simultaneously disappointed and relieved when Nixon had been defeated, disappointed because a rare opportunity to alter the state of the world had been lost, but relieved as well because Timothy recognized that had Nixon triumphed, he, Timothy, would have felt personally responsible. Along with the secret delight, he would have been seared with guilt. A prison term would have been in order. Not the death penalty because, fortunately, he was opposed to it. Actually, Nixon belonged in a Dostoevsky novel and Timothy thought that he did as well, right there in a tale of light and dark beside Nixon, the furry-ferret Commie hunter. If there had ever been any doubt about that, there was not any longer. The worm turned. Commie hunter.

That day seemed so long ago. A movie. History lost. At present, October 1962, Timothy was twenty-one, but just two years earlier he might as well have lived in another century. Senator Kennedy had walked through the door of the Hanover Inn with JBK by his side and now President Kennedy was on television in the Hanover Inn. Whither JBK? Could he have been the next United States Senator from Maine? Maine's first President? That would have been a tale to tell, a tale of many tongues and multitudinous secrets. However, at this very moment, Kennedy was speaking perhaps as emcee of the end of this world, an ending which would silence forever many tales and render secrets moot.

End in sight or not, it seemed the world would shortly witness the metamorphosis of Timothy Brown King. Or fail to witness it. Maybe the question was not, what would he become, but when and how would he disappear . . . to reappear? In a puff of smoke, in the mist, in long lost youthful dreams. It would be a new version of, when I grow up I want to be . . . or, better yet, when I lay me down to sleep, I pray the Lord my soul to keep . . . if I still have a soul.

"Are you coming, Timothy?"

Charles Hamilton Jackson III had asked Timothy that on the telephone from Washington, asked him that very night.

"Did you get the ticket Dad's office sent you? It should be there. They sent it special delivery."

Yes, Timothy had said, he had received the plane ticket, but no, he was not coming down to Washington where, the *New York Times* had reported, there was an "air of crisis." The President and his advisors and the highest Administration officials were engaged in almost constant meetings. The steam was rising. The Navy and the Marine Corps were raising a storm near Cuba, forty ships and twenty thousand men on maneuvers, including six thousand Marines.

But, said the Administration, there was "no connection" between the actions of these military armed forces and the visible agitation of the civilian forces of government. Fifty to seventy-five lovingly named "Striking Force Jets" comprising the 19th Air Force, the swiftest fighting unit of the Tactical Air Force, had flown to MacDill Air Force Base in Florida and had been put on full alert. A flock of birds in the morning, chirping, anticipating full flight.

But a military spokesman had repeated that there was absolutely "no connection" between those arrangements and the "Cuban situation." And despite the fact that the airlines, in the finest, johnny-on-the-spot, opportunistic tradition of American capitalism, had taken out a full-page advertisement in the *Times* to announce that forty commercial jets flew south daily from Idlewild and Newark airports presumably straight into the heart of the tiny Caribbean island of Cuba—bring your own bombs?—he, Timothy, was not even going to fly to Washington. He was not going to be flying on anybody's airplane anywhere because not only had he, too, become disconnected, he had drifted into space on his own.

"What's that?" Charles Hamilton Jackson III had asked Timothy; Ham, his friend, debating colleague, drinking companion, and roommate of three years at Dartmouth, Ham whose father, Charles Hamilton Jackson II, had been a classmate of John Brown King's at Dartmouth, also class of 1934, had remained an intimate, lifelong friend to JBK and become an avuncular overseer to Timothy, was presently a special, secret advisor to President Kennedy, and was a millionaire, one of the country's many supposed hybrids, a Democrat who was a millionaire, Ham who was, himself, a very ambitious, privileged, fair young man of the present world. Sing his praises.

"You're not coming? You what? Hey, I can't hear you. Do we have a bad line or are you talking to yourself again? Timothy, you've got to get over that habit. You're way too young. It'll stunt your growth, man. What? You have withdrawn from Dartmouth? Hey, man, stop putting me on. This is no time for that. Mother has your room prepared. She promised barbecue, chicken and ribs. Everything is set. We'll go home to Richmond tomorrow night and Mother will drive us to the debate tournament at William and Mary this weekend. I can hardly wait. We are going to march right on through Jamestown and Williamsburg both. We will be victorious. It is ordained. The only question is, who gets the tournament's best speaker award, you or me? Remember, he who gets the glory gets the girl, right Timothy? And, oh boy, will there be some lovely Southern ladies there. Remember Brenda Fitzgerald? She of the golden thighs? Were you melting for her last year or what? Didn't you write a poem about her? Or was she the poet and you wrote on her? Come on. She was hot and bothered by your sideburns, Timothy. Remember how she called you Elvis?

"By the way, I've reread Kahn's *On Thermonuclear War.* Don't forget to bring our notes on him. Yeah, war is hell but, baby, peace ain't no picnic either. That's the rallying cry. As I said yesterday, Cuba does not change a thing. If they really have the weapons, if the Russians have really stoked them in there, we can make that work as an argument both for and against further development. Yes'm. Sure, it raises the stakes and increases the risk and we can use that as an argument against proliferation, much as it goes against my grain, but it can also mean that the U.S. needs to raise its ante to meet the challenge. Same old story. You have to know when to hold 'em and when to fold 'em, right man? We both agree that there's going to be a big bang one day, anyway. The question is, who's going to stick it to whom—and what we don't want is an indiscriminate gang-bang, right? Everybody gets screwed that way. Incidentally, remember again, this is all hush-hush. Dad would kill me if he knew I had told you anything. He doesn't even know what I know. Ha, ha. Don't worry, nobody can screw around with this telephone without my knowing it. Not without dealing with me and the FBI. They check this thing practically every other hour, I'm sure. I think I could call the President on this if I wanted to. Say, did you finish your paper on Dostoevsky? Look, man, get on down here. It's really exciting. This is the big time, baby. The President is going on television in an hour. If they don't play this thing right you might not get to D.C., let alone Richmond. Too bad you aren't already here, we could order champagne for our room. That way no matter what happens we would be in fine shape. The ladies would come to us. We could all die happy, fornicating for the flag. But make sure you watch it so you can tell me what you think. We can compare notes. We might get something out of it we can use. You know, an updated quote. And, anyway, we have to be prepared for how somebody else might use it, right man? No matter how ridiculous, you always have to respond. How can you manipulate the facts if you do not know what they are, right Timothy? Nothing but the facts and fiction, so help my bippy."

Ham was still talking when Timothy hung up. He had been so excited that he had probably not noticed until he had said goodbye that there was nobody on the other end of the line. Sweet dreams. Perhaps he had failed to notice the silence even then. Timothy had repeated with no apparent effect that he was not flying to Washington. No, not, never. Curiously, he had chosen to acknowledge that, yes, he did have a paper due on Dostoevsky's novel *The Idiot*, although he had not told Ham that he had been wondering all day if the subject of his paper was innocence or corruption. Actually, it was both. You could not speak of one without implicitly speaking of the other. Like good and evil. But he had wondered if there was any such thing as innocence. Or, if innocence was nothing more than ignorance, then what was corruption, wisdom? Had Timothy been innocent and was he now in the process of being corrupted? Was he now to be corrupt forevermore, forevermore? Was he now to relearn the truth? The truth of what? The truth of something. And if he ate of the tree of knowledge, of the tree of good and evil, would he surely die or would he become as a god?

For the moment, all he knew for certain was that he had finished a paper that he was not going to give to Professor Joyce. Maybe that was corruption. That rather than act as if the fate of the human race depended upon one's actions, depended upon his turning in that paper and regarding any interference by an outside agency as the hand of Satan, he felt that it did not matter whether or not he turned in his paper at all. Perhaps he was forevermore outside the chain of human endeavor. Long beyond recall. Or maybe this was only the beginning of the battle, the battle between good and evil, and his decision as to which side he was going to favor would resolve the issue for the ages. But, as yet, he had not decided to choose, if choice he had.

Yes, the Bible was a marvelous metaphor. It declared our corruption. Original sin. There was no innocence. We are born corrupt. It is in our genes. We were nothing but reproducing genes hopping along the chain of command. All was decided. Therefore, he would not worry about what he was going to do. He would simply enjoy doing it. Not that he had any choice.

He laughed. Create something out of nothing. It was not a drama if he di[illegible] not think it was. He had to believe. That was the problem. He had to believe, and why should he choose to believe any of this? Especially if he did not want to. Did he not want to? But how could he not believe?

He was unattached, but he was not free. And the truth shall set you free? The truth was a lie. There was a very important difference between being free and being unattached. All beings were not the same. In the United States, freedom was social and meant, for example, being free to make millions, and being in the outdoors. Being unattached meant being a grain of sand on the beach with the certainty of being pissed on by a two-year-old. Actually, being unattached meant being welded to the nameless, innocuous, common cycle of living to die in frustration and angst and anger. Obscurity. Would the Red Sox trade for pitching this year? Finally? Absolute freedom. Absence of commitment? Doing absolutely nothing? Because waiting for the perfect pitch which can never appear? Adrift. Absolute liberty. We can detach ourselves at any moment. The sense of never feeling attached. He was not a part of anything, he was free floating.

There, was that refreshing? Was that a Coke, baby, as Ham would say? No, it induced lethargy and paralysis. Fear and nausea. Thus, do merely for the comfort of engagement. Simply to be a part of something. Another expression of it: he did not know the answer to why. Nothing is necessary. He did not know what that meant. Stay tuned. Anti-society and anti-social, because to be otherwise was to be committed, to be identified, to define oneself, to say or reveal what one is, to make oneself. And what about overcoming lethargy, the flesh?

You think your life is your own. You are an individual. It was not somebody else's life. It was yours. They could not have it. Never forever. The heritage of America. And yet, there did seem to be a broad pattern to human existence, history. And it was not promising. Did this mean that he, Timothy, was simply a part of that predictable flow? If he was, and the freedom flow was down the toilet, what was the point?

When the Gila monster crawls it does not ask why it cannot fly. No, he would not accept the ugliness, the horror, the inevitability. Better artificial drama. Create it. The Great Mystery. Ghosts, boogie-man, vampires, the unknown fear. We need them. We must have evil. To some minds the existence of evil meant the existence of good, or, if there is a devil must there not be a god? Of course, other than nothingness, might there merely be evil? Given a choice, which would one take? Which would be more fun, more enjoyable, more exciting? Maybe he had already eaten of the tree of knowledge, the tree of good and evil, and he would surely die.

And, oh yes, he had neglected to tell Ham that he had already cashed in the airline ticket. If he had now become an alien, an invisible person, he thought he might need the money. U.S. legal tender. It was like carrying the flag. Showing the colors. If anybody questioned his being, his legitimacy, his existence, he could whip out his roll of bills. This is Yankee country, pardner, step aside.

The cab driver was still nodding. He was asleep or maybe he was listening to Kennedy on the radio. The radio. That was another time, yet another age. 1948. Nighttime, alone in a house on the Maine coast, a mile from the center of nowhere, from the center of a town that was not big enough to be called a town. Timothy, seven years old, listened alone to the slowly developing story on the radio of President Harry S Truman's dramatic victory over Republican challenger Thomas E. Dewey, the man with the moustache, the man they called the mouse, the guaranteed winner who lost.

Timothy could not remember why he had been left alone that night although that was not unusual, but he remembered his excitement, excitement that had lasted throughout the night. Give-'em-hell-Harry, the original big boppa of Hiroshima and Nagasaki. Soft on Communism, the Republicans had charged. Harry? Why, the best was yet to come with old Harry S, old Hydrogen-bomb Harry. Give-'em hell, indeed. It seemed like simple drama now in recollection. But in truth it had not been simple then either, simple only in the child's eye for whom there were centers of the universe. A radio, his radio, it had been a center of the universe, bringing him the thrilling tones of the announcer, the voice of H. V. Kaltenborn. Timothy had carefully and reverentially written down the town, city, and state election counts as they had come in, some in the hundreds, some in the thousands, bit by bit, every one of them, even when there had been no change from the previous tallies. He had felt order and security receiving and compiling the figures, excitement anticipating them. It had been as good as a fight for the heavyweight championship of the world. Blow by exquisitely punishing bloody blow, round by reported, imagined, thrilling, numbered, circumscribed, recorded round, unto fearful conclusion. Bop-bop-a-lua into extinction. Joe Louis vs. Billy Conn. Rocky Marciano vs. Jersey Joe Walcott. But, he reflected now, perhaps there were no heavyweights after all, not even any divisions. Had never been any. Only a child thought there had been. Had believed. Odd, but he had never forgotten writing down the figure of forty thousand for Henry Wallace. Forty thousand votes from where, Mars? When did this happen? Were they, one and all, Communists as charged? Even then? And why was that exciting? Forty thousand agents of the Devil, that's why. Oh, Daddy. Forty thousand votes from hell.

He looked beyond the cab again to where he imagined the center of the campus green to be. He could see nothing in the darkness. But he sensed that somebody was out there looking at him, taking his picture, observing his every step. You had to believe or all was lost. He thought he could see a figure moving away from him, moving toward Baker Library, perhaps to scale the two-hundred-foot-high Baker tower for the purpose of scanning the entire darkling plain. Absolute, all-mighty surveillance. After all, you could not be too careful. Only two hundred feet below in the basement of Baker Library was Quetzalcoatl, loose like a monster roaming the murals of Jose Clemente Orozco, lasting living proof that Orozco, the Marxist Mexican artist, had also been at Dartmouth in the 1930s. And over there, was not somebody, something coming toward him, slithering closer and closer? Timothy could not be certain. He squinted his eyes and began to imagine that he could see shadowy figures moving, wavering in every direction. Perhaps there were hundreds, even thousands out there in the center of night, gesticulating and acting in mysterious, magical ways, fauns with pointed ears, with tails and cleft feet, butting each other with their horns. He knew he had seen the students as they frolicked on the green under the bright noonday sun. He had seen them in the bright moment, bronzed bodies. Everything was promised. Everything had to be promised.

In 1952 Timothy and his best friend in grammar school, Johnny Knight, had participated for their very first time in the national-democratic-Godly-American-electoral-hail-fellow election process all by their little bitty selves on the elysian playing fields of Portland, Maine. The two of them had set up a loudspeaker on the school's playground so that during recess, for the glorious enlightenment of their beloved school-minimates, they could debate the relative qualifications of the two combatants, General Dwight David Eisenhower and Governor Adlai EEEEEEE Stevenson, to be President of these United States of America. Timothy and Johnny had floated their earnest tones over all of those frolicking, heedless little heads. And for that they had later received special credits in the subjects of speech and civics, kind of the Grammar School Medal for Good Citizenship.

Prior to that heroic battle of recess, Timothy and Johnny had polled all of their diminutive compatriots in all eight grades of the grammar school. But when the margin in favor of General Eisenhower had been found to be ninety-two percent to five percent over Governor Stevenson, everything had bogged down into the case of the missing three percent. It was a crisis. The world came to a stop, everyone forced to wait, breathless, while an emergency probe was launched. Vital questions had to be answered, the foremost being: at the time of the vote had all three percent of the non-voting been in the bathroom? Follow-up question: all at the same instant? True, such things were probably imaginable. But the timing? At the very least, the issue of sanitation loomed large, perhaps to explode during the general election campaign. And there was certain to slide under the door the side issue of hygiene. All of those bedwetters getting out of hand all at the same time. Perhaps there was a conspiracy to be uncovered. Something in the water. As a causal explanation, that in itself would have been exciting, a little dirty linen for the electorate, probable cause for a bloody nose or two among the combatants in the interests of patriotic fervor, truly an American touch. Much preferable to toilet training, which was the alternative, foreign explanation. Freud had only made it as far as New

York, which, of course, was not a part of America. On the playgrounds of Maine, principals and guidance counselors still set the rules and called the shots. Or so it seemed.

And then one of Timothy's long-time enemies, going back at least six months, had done the unthinkable, had cavalierly raised the possibility that Timothy himself had secretly destroyed the ballots in order to help his candidate, Governor Stevenson. Naturally, Timothy was outraged at this undeniable smear on his character with its thinly disguised stratagem of not only destroying for all time his good name, but of indirectly creating negative fallout for Stevenson.

Nevertheless, that dire threat had to be confronted later because, first things first, there was a school-wide demand that the election results be announced without further delay. Nobody could wait any longer. Everybody's legs were crossed. The electorate's trust in the integrity of the democratic process was at stake. It was like being ignored when you raised your hand to ask to go to the bathroom. The pressure, unbearable, mounted. Finally, a solution was discovered. Kind of a political compromise. It was decided that all three percent had indeed participated in the pre-election election, but that all three percent had abstained with notes from home. Perfectly plausible. That had been Timothy's idea. But, curiously, to deepen the mystery, Johnny Knight had further speculated that every single one of the abstentions had come from the third grade, which was uncanny. Of course, he could not be absolutely certain, but if that were true, a purge would be necessary. However, still another, bothersome question arose: why the third grade?

And then, with unerring political timing, Timothy had demanded a reconsideration, because, he wanted to know, what were eight-year-olds doing abstaining anyway? If it were true, he said, it might be thought to be subversive. And, surely, somebody would take it upon themselves to call the Committee.

"Eight-Year-Olds Abstaining,"

the headline would shout. Subversive, indeed, un-American. Yes, the notes from home were probably forged, and if their parents found out, they might all get in trouble. And, anyway, just what did it mean to abstain, to be an abstainer? And, worse, what else were the whole lot of them doing while they were abstaining? In those situations, everybody knew one thing led to another. They might be accused of something, anything. For example, to abstain at such a young age might be a sign of early impotence. Oh my, the best of an entire, new generation. What a predicament for America, particularly if it was catching, inherited even. What would the dear old U. S. of A do?

Nevertheless, Timothy would later boast that a little personal politicking on his and Judy Hough's part among their friends, backroom stuff, he said, had enabled him to rally support for the Governor, and after the broadcast-battle-of-the-recess between Timothy and Johnny, well-remembered by some as an oracular oratorical outburst, by others as an outrage, the General had barely eked out a fifty-two to forty-eight percent margin over the Governor. No abstentions allowed. Johnny Knight, whose father was a paper mill owner, had won the battle, but Timothy knew he had won the war by dissuading so many of his schoolmates from parroting their Republican parents. Before Edmund S. Muskie, the Grand State of Maine had been, as they used to say, rockbound Republican. Or rock-headed as the Democrats preferred it.

Timothy's status, already high at the school, had risen by a quantum leap. In recognition of his fabulous achievement, beside the Grammar School Medal of Honor, that is, the extra credits, even the school principal had patted him on the head. Knowing opportunity when he saw it, Timothy had quickly parlayed his triumph into a springboard to election as president of the eighth grade. It had all been very heady, indeed. Obviously, he had the stuff to become either a revolutionary or a politician or, failing that, at least a statesman. It was all a question of adjustment according to the guidance counselor, aided, of course, by the standard aptitude test.

But, although he had told no one, certainly not JBK, Timothy had been bedeviled at the time by fears and nightmares that he would never again enjoy such vertigo. He worried that he might be a fast starter, that he might have reached his zenith too quickly. All that remained was to hope that he might be a late finisher as well, that his strength would grow, not ebb. Eleven years old and he was already fearful of the end of growth, a euphemism for the first harbinger of death. The first year he failed to grow an inch someone would suddenly announce that life was over.

"Well done," JBK had pronounced afterward, as he had left home late one night on his way to the airport, destination unknown and unannounced, which, it had seemed to Timothy, was his typical journey. That is, in retrospect, most people would have said that his father's usual behavior was unusual.

But, later, Timothy had been demoralized when Stevenson had lost the presidential election by a landslide. He had not been able to fathom how the American people could have voted for Eisenhower over Stevenson. Guns over minds. Shoot and then talk. He had thought at first that perhaps it was because Stevenson was balding, but then he had remembered that Eisenhower did not exactly possess a thicket himself. Ah, but Eisenhower wore a helmet which was probably decisive. The perfect ruse. Old Dwight David Helmethower.

Later, JBK had not said a word about Stevenson's defeat. Silence from the mountain. And Timothy had felt partially responsible. Perhaps he had not campaigned hard enough and long enough. How dreadful. By association he had been marked by defeat at such a young age. Another premature sign of death. He had not even escaped grammar school and he had already fallen short of immortality.

But what had Stevenson been talking about? What was it that had led Timothy the younger to listen? That we . . . are . . . tempted . . . tempted to dissemble when we are asked to face, relate, acknowledge, confront the truth. Yes, that was it. Not so much that we spin our wheels as that we spin webs. That we falter when confronted with the truth. That it is precisely at that moment when we face the great temptation to dissemble. Timothy had always liked that. The great lesson of the election apparently was that safety and material security were more important than all else to the American people, most probably to the entire human race. Therefore, you voted for the general. Military might meant omnipotence: power preserved the American way, protected a nation of citizens from passing away. The people would follow a general anywhere. They would die for security in life.

And yet, yes, Timothy remembered, Stevenson had said something about the price we the people had paid for dropping the atomic bomb on Hiroshima. Something had changed. The price we had paid . . . price . . . cash? Did that have something to do with capitalism? No, Stevenson had not said that in 1952, but later, in 1956, when he had tried again to become President, poor man, when he had urged that the United States take the lead in stopping the testing of the hydrogen bomb. The hydrogen bomb was thousands of times more powerful than the atomic bomb. It was the Super Bomb. The first time the United States had successfully tested it, on a Pacific island in 1951, the island had disappeared. Should we try for the Pacific itself, those fathoms of fanciful water that had fashioned vast mushrooms of clouds centuries before the bomb? First the Pacific, then the Atlantic, and after finishing with the oceans of the earth, we could begin with the continents, and end, gloriously with the heavens. Kind of a ready-made puzzle, only this one you took apart, tossed in the air, scattered hither and yon. Even a child could do it. Perhaps a child unborn.

We extolled our virtues to the world, Stevenson had said, and yet we dealt with most of the world on mostly militaristic terms. He had said that in 1956. We had lost the moral initiative we had traditionally claimed. From atop the City on a Hill, from on high, it was our druthers to toss bombs rather than to mince words. Stevenson was not a big boppa, which was probably why he had lost the elections. The egghead. And another thing. The American people should be told, he had said, about our prospects for life or for death in this nuclear age. The context, the arena, had changed. We had the . . . the "freedom to know" those facts. That was it, another phrase Timothy had never forgotten, the freedom to know.

But, Timothy realized, that was the problem for the American people. Nobody wanted to hear that. Nobody wanted to even comprehend that freedom. My heavens, Americans did not want to be told about their new-found, new-age prospects for a second death. Deep down they all knew they were all going to die once and for all time, and they did not want to talk about it all over again. Certainly not something artificially contrived. Not by their own hand, by the hand of humankind. As children they had been reared with *it* in their churches and their temples and their cathedrals. They had first had intimations of death by being told tales of immortality. It was over and done with. Confined to sacred ground. Signed and sealed, if not delivered. Who wanted to be new-ly reminded a second time? Why be doubly morbid? The second death?

No. Actually, it did not worry us because we had already denied the fact of death before, the first death, that is, and to acknowledge this potential second death would force us to acknowledge the certain first death, which was buried, layered in our great unconscious, stored in Antarctica. Yes. We had faced death before, although we had forgotten that given of our condition, that we were all going to die. It was such an awful truth that out of necessity we, the human species, had created our religions, our gods, beliefs in forces beyond or more powerful than us, cartoons even. Or maybe we had already died and we had found a way to cope with that, walking the earth dressed as ghosts and all, and we could not redress. We simply would not. We had already died once and we would not face a second death. We just would not face it. Everybody wanted to live as if death did not exist at all, had never happened, don't mention it, not in this neighborhood anyway, and certainly not on this street. Only in Russia. Tra-la-la. Primitive forces at work. My time is your time.

Rather, there was a better, more realistic way to go. Tell the American people about their kill potential for the duration, about their killing force for the time they had to live, tell them that they had the power to be responsible for the deaths of billions, that they could make the earth disappear, reach the heavens with their explosive might, yeah, yeah, rearrange the universe, make big bangs, puffs of smoke, flares of colors everywhere. Our very own human rainbows and eruptions. Unfurl the flag, that was exciting, that had patriotic roots, that would make them bare their teeth. They would pass the hat for that. And, in fact, mixing his signals like a bona fide hot-and-cold-war liberal, one of the first and the best, Stevenson himself had lamented in that very same speech that Eisenhower the general had allowed the United States to lose its military superiority over the Russians. Oh, come on, Adlai. Say it ain't so or do not say it so. Do it or do not do it. Four years later, Kennedy had said and done the same thing. The missile gap. How boring these minds were. How American. Get it up and let you down. But how could Stevenson have done that? Good old Adlai with the hole in his shoe, the very same man who had said in that very same speech that the United States should be leading the world in a war against human want. Hey, Adlai, which is it? Do we feed mouths or close them?

In 1958 in his senior year in high school, Timothy had won the Fourteenth-Annual-Spring-Mud-Season-Key-Club-Northeastern-Oratorical Contest in, of all places, the granite mining town of Barre, Vermont. The title of his speech had been "Wage Peace, Not War," and he had prefaced his talk by telling his nonplussed audience that he was honored to have the opportunity to deliver his speech in a town of abandoned mines. Ready made homes. The way it used to be. Cave-dwellers. A return to roots, indeed. Or stones. Afterward, he had wondered what had prompted the judges to vote for him.

Ironically, Timothy's finest oratorical hour on the radio had occurred during that same Presidential primary season of 1960, when for an entire week he had gone on the Dartmouth College radio station to promote the merits of Senator Barry M. Goldwater and individualism. Timothy had decided to stake new ground for the illustrious author of the *Conscience of a Conservative*. The title of his radio speech had been "In the Name of Nietzsche Anything Goes." It had been his campaign contribution to Barry. What fun. What hysterics. Hysterical.

As a debator all through high school and college and, it had been assumed, for his future career as a lawyer, like father like son, Timothy had been trained to speak persuasively for any proposition, profound or ludicrous, or profound and ludicrous, regardless of whether or not he believed in it or supported it. And, speaking of truth, he had learned to have more fun when he did not believe, when he was truthless. He had enjoyed taking both sides of the same issue. There was something godly about that. Rather than human obligation, omniscience and omnipotence. Of course, most of the time he did not choose to believe. Belief, itself, was constricting, end of the line, terminal. Better to have the freedom to create and discard truths. A kind of conspicuous consumption of values. He had begun at that time to announce that his lifelong goal was to never ever believe in anything. Much more challenging, and exciting. Risk was involved. The great American freedom free-flow. You might get tarred and feathered . . . or hung . . . or elected. Oddly, for an aberrant few weeks, he had continued to speak out in favor of Goldwater's conservative extremism.

When Timothy's father, JBK, had found out about Timothy's rampage on the radio he had been furious. Timothy had known he would be.

"What in hell is going on with you?" John Brown King had shouted over the telephone. "What have I reared? Have you lost your marbles? How much publicity did this get?"

Timothy had never known JBK to react so strongly. Old stoneface. Man in the mountain. Nor had he, Timothy, been able to explain to himself why he had done it. The fact that he had enjoyed it appeared to be the only obvious explanation. Gratuitous titillation. Maybe that was sufficient. An important American lesson straight from our forefathers. Diddle yourself for yourself.

Oh, yes. He had also enjoyed . . . no . . . he had been exhilarated later that summer of 1960 listening one night on the car radio to Senator Eugene F. McCarthy's one-more-dance-please nomination speech at the Democratic National Convention in Los Angeles for the fading Adlai Stevenson.

McCarthy had seemed to whisper, *"Do not turn away from this man,"* to whisper over the crackling car radio before a suddenly wildly cheering Democratic throng at the convention in Los Angeles, cheers that in turn had lost to the cryptic static of the radio . . . before McCarthy's piercing voice had again stabbed Timothy's eardrums as he had strained one moment to hear with the volume of the radio turned full blast to silence and winced the next as clarion call, the crackling, and the crowds' cacophony suddenly blasted the cab of his car and his ear once again.

There was, intoned McCarthy, **"one man who did not prophesy falsely."** The legions had erupted, roared. Timothy was certain that they must have been prepared to march before losing their way over the airwaves. McCarthy had implored: **"Do not leave this prophet without honor in his own party."** *"Do not reject this man."* Tears on Timothy's cheeks. He, himself, had almost run off the road. Good old Adlai's death throe agony.

Timothy had wanted to be there, to be directly involved. Like being part of a roaring Fenway Park crowd in Beantown spilling popcorn and beer everywhere on everyone after Teddy Ballgame had hit a grand slam homerun in a losing cause. Although, was it not sacrilegious to compare anything with listening to the Red Sox on the radio at night with the lights extinguished, particularly alone on a summer night on your own back porch with only the sparkle of the radio and the fireflies, with a Pepsi and an Italian sandwich you had bought at the corner market after playing in a Pony League baseball game and going two for three, with lots of oil and extra black olives, onions and extra pickles, wearing your sweaty, dirty baseball uniform? On a summer night a ball game lasted forever. You had to have perspective. Lose that and anything might happen.

Yes, Adlai Stevenson and Ted Williams had been his childhood heroes. But why was it, why was there a greater outpouring of passion and emotion in a losing than in a winning cause? Because of grief and sorrow and loss. Loss of what? Hope. Stevenson had never become President, and, sadly, was currently playing out his last statesman's hours as the mouthpiece for the Kennedy Administration in the United Nations. Williams, too, had grown old. He had hit his last home run. The ultimate betrayal. Teddy Ballgame was no more. The summer of 1960.

The evening of McCarthy's speech in 1960, Timothy had been on one of his secret, mystical disappearances into the waterfront slums of Portland, Maine, alone, beyond the known, discovering what was impossible, beyond the tedium of his everyday world, a new, exotic end to every immersion in the unknown. From his very first foray into the mysterious new world of the darkening, decaying waterfront, there had been much for Timothy to encounter and discover and initiate. Eager for romance, dreamy love, heroic involvement, he wanted and would have the searing touch of flesh. Late in sex, but not in love or fearful, imagined perversion. Moonstruck early, in all ways. A great deal of experience in pining and posing and pretending. Doris Day and True Love, and fateful love. A great deal of desire, consuming, thwarted, bursting passion. Innocent. Appearing innocent, and he was, sincerely believing in his innocence, his ideals, his best intentions, and he was innocent, idealistic, dreamy-eyed, well-intentioned, but he was also undefined, susceptible of any action, open to suggestion, subject to experimentation, intense, eager for adventure and mystery, wanting enchantment and excitement, capable of absolute ruthlessness, my god. Oh what would his mother say, Helen Eaton King, oh what would mother say?

First love, fell into bed with an already pregnant beautiful blonde delicate girl who later yearned to lie to him, to tell him the child was his, believing he was sufficiently naive and nice, and innocent. But she could not do it. She could only be very gentle with him when she realized it was his first time, and eventually tell him the truth. When he did not know she was pregnant, he had not understood why she had cried. The first had cried.

"You got a freedom lay," Ham had said when Timothy had reverentially and secretly confided his primal moment. Timothy had never forgiven him that comment.

Second love, he had slept with a middle-aged, dark-haired, full-bosomed Abenaki woman from Boston who had passed out in the middle of coitus, their limbs intertwined. Timothy would never forget. The second had passed out.

"You didn't even know what tribe she was," said Ham, taunting him.

"That is not true," Timothy had lamented. "It was her name. I did not know her name, her name. She would not tell me."

It had not been his first night, that night on the Portland waterfront. Not his first foray. There had already been many encounters in a brief span in his short life. But it was that one night in particular he would remember most. He had gone to the seedy Hotel Amsterdam for the first time. Had a couple of drinks, and then danced. What was her name? He was never certain. It began with an A. Anita? Adelaide? Aurora? She never gave him the same name. At least that is how he remembered it in his dreams. She was older, at least ten years older, and she had kids, lots of them. Had he exploited her? Why was it that he had felt from the onset that he was taking advantage of her, that simply to know her was to take advantage of her? He had known from the outset that they would end the evening in her bed? No, and he had felt guilty about it. No, and he had felt depressed. She had seemed so worn out. Tired. Perhaps it had been her last chance at love. Her only chance. He had thought she might die in his arms. The last love. Oh, what, what would his mother have thought, oh what would mother have thought?

All in all, it had been an evening of great emotion. It was well after midnight when he had returned home to be told by the police that both his father and his mother, John Brown King and Helen Eaton King, both the male bronze sculpture of Timothy's life and the surviving femme fatale of his birthing barrage, both had died. Both had died in a spectacular, flaming automobile crash with a Security Oil truck. Both bodies had been burnt beyond recognition.

Timothy remembered the irony of that. Security Oil. He had inherited a lot of stock in that company. He also remembered wondering why both of his parents had been out so late and where they had been going. Nobody had been able to tell him. In fact, Timothy had not understood why his father had suddenly decided not to attend the Democratic National Convention in Los Angeles. After all, he had been a delegate from Maine. It had been his partisan, patriotic duty to attend that convention. He should have been there with the confetti and flags and balloons and portable toilets.

If JBK had gone he would have voted for Stevenson. He would have been there to try and prevent the last hurrah. And who could say what the world would be like now? He would have been alive. She would have stayed home. Charred beyond recognition, as though a meteor had burned through space and fallen to earth.

"Leaving just when the bombs are falling? Ha ha. What sense is there in that? What sense is there? Ha ha. Here, let me take it."

It was Falstaff, a little old man from the town of Hanover who was a favorite of many of the Dartmouth students. Timothy smiled softly and sadly and let the old man take his suitcase. It seemed the natural thing to do under the October skies. He had seen Falstaff many times, although he had never given him more than a passing thought. And it had never occurred to him that the little old man had ever paid any attention to him, that he had ever even recognized him. Yet, at this moment, Falstaff acted as if he knew Timothy and there seemed to be a feeling of warmth between the two of them, of understanding, as if Falstaff had been waiting there for Timothy's departure.

Falstaff had been . . . around, always in town, except Timothy had never seen him coming or going. And Falstaff was always well-dressed, not what you would expect from a town character. Which was what Falstaff was. He was different, not normal. Not like anyone else in town. A well-dressed, weird little old man. He was always there, just smoking a Camel, the only normal thing about him, sitting on a bench in the middle of town or leaning against a building while the town went around him. It seemed he was there morning or night and Timothy had briefly wondered whenever he had passed him where Falstaff had come from or what he was doing or if he did anything and if he did, what was it? Was he the Director of Life? The Conductor of the Official Chorus? The Chronicler of the Age, perhaps?

This much was known, that the old man was called Falstaff because he often bought spirits after hours for underaged Dartmouth students at Tanzi's general store. A secret agent for Tanzi's. At least that is what was always said, what one was told. Local lore. The tradition. Freshmen were told that and the word was passed on from year to year. Not that anyone ever seemed to know for certain. You could never find that one person who knew, who had been there, who had seen, and who had drunk. But the little old man radiated a sense of knowing exactly what he intended, and his presence now reassured Timothy.

They walked without a word toward the cab and Timothy saw for the first time that one of the old man's legs was shorter than the other, that he walked like a see-saw. Timothy had never before seen Falstaff walk. To the left, to the right, to the left, to the right. Up and down, up and down. The cab driver opened the trunk and old Falstaff put Timothy's suitcase in it. At that moment Timothy sensed that Falstaff and the cab driver had performed this ritual many times before. What would they call it? Sending one more sweet prince, one more son of old Dartmouth off into the wide, wide world?

"See you, son," Falstaff said, and he moved away, teetering first right and then left, up and down, moving more or less in a straight line back toward the center of town. You had to wonder how he managed to do that. A lifetime of practice? Except that his practice had probably begun in Buchenwald where he had been interned as a German Jew and which he had survived. That too was known. That too was passed on to freshmen. Silent knowledge. Silent symbol.

As the cab drove away, Timothy thought of his grandfather, the Reverend Hezekiah Brown King. "Go out to the length and breadth of the land and it shall be yours," saith Hezekiah, the king of the pulpit. "God said to Abraham, 'I will make nations of thee, and Kings shall come out of thee.'" That had always been his, Hezekiah's, basic message. He had preached it and practiced it. A dynamic, flamboyant, dramatic man. Conquer the world, see the world, discover the world. Just so many travel posters? Once, Timothy had been told that when he was two years old, Grandfather Hezekiah, eighty-eight going on three hundred and eighty-eight at the time, had attempted to tie his shoes for him. Someone had come into a room and found both the old preacher and little Timothy sitting on the floor, Hezekiah fumbling with Timothy's shoelaces, making no progress at all, the boy staring at his grandfather in fascination. A three-hundred-and-eighty-eight-year-old man who could not tie the shoes of a two-year-old child. What had happened in the preceding three hundred and eighty-six? Years later, Timothy was certain that he could recall that moment, certain that he could remember his grandfather's hulking helplessness. Truly a legacy.

It was a traumatic moment, but for whom? Hezekiah or Timothy? That was the question. And it was an important question. You had to get the answer right or everything, everything got screwed up. For whom was the shock of revelation? Children learn of the limitations of their capacities quickly and spend the remainder of existence recoiling. Unless they have imaginations. Or was that the other side of the coin, the positive reaction to the horror? Was insanity an aspect of this? An act of recoiling, certainly, but positive or negative? How much can you shuffle the deck? Were there really any secrets? Maybe he was about to find out once and for all. Go out and conquer and discover and make over, absolutely. That was it. Make. An illusion? A cruel, crushing burden? More than human beings were capable of? Make out of what and for what? That was the question. What had already been made and could not be undone? John Brown King and Helen Eaton King were his biological parents, were they not? That was it. After that they were people, were they not?

He remembered coming home after eleven at night, a young teenage boy in a Maine country town coming home from the Friday-night movies, walking along that dark country road, that stretch of rises and dips, of few houses and fewer stores, and then no street lights and rarely a passing car, four miles at night up and down long hilly wooded country roads. He always heard, imagined people, animals, something, stirring, rustling, following him, following beside him in the woods, behind him on the road, waiting, waiting in front of him. His eyes could never penetrate the darkness. He would feel his way along the road with his feet, tripping occasionally, slightly, scuffing, hearing the noise he made, thinking it gave him away, exposed him, exposed him to attack, from what he did not know. He would want to run, at least walk quickly, get out of there, but he never dared to move too quickly for fear that he would stray off the road, downward, and end in the woods, in a large black hole, never to emerge. And there would be the accompanying temptation, the tug to drop to his hands and knees and feel the invisible tarred road, the covered earth, the urge to crawl so that you would not deviate, so that you would get it right every inch of the way. But what would he meet with on that level, another crawling human being?

A country boy who had not been taught anything by his immediate elders, he had grown up a street kid, having learned everything about the world initially on the streets, only problem being that the streets of Maine were non-existent. The woods? Nature? No, he had not communed with nature. Only with himself. And now, with a new word, a seemingly different word, what who when why was himself?

Timothy had not learned to tie his shoes until he was five.

"Or learned to tell time until I was six," he muttered again.

He had been stumbling, trying to catch up ever since. At least that is what he had thought for a while. Maybe he had not really been behind at all or even out of step, but headed in a different direction. That cliche. A different drummer. He and Henry David. It was the world that was out of step. Problem was, there was no other world to choose. If you rejected this world, there was only one other step to take.

"Maybe all of this time I have been merely trying to catch up on time."

And that was impossible. That much he knew.

"Time?" asked the cab driver, who spoke around biting a cigar he had just finished lighting. "It's ten-forty. Don't worry, you won't be late. You'll catch it. The bus for Boston leaves at eleven. God willing you'll be on it."

The time of day. Whose time? The world's? Timothy's? The time of former President Dwight David Eisenhower, old Helmet-hower? Actually it had been reported that Ike, while campaigning the very day before for Republican candidates in Boston, that "I-like-Ike" had said, referring specifically and imminently, of the very moment, to Kennedy and Cuba but, heroically, heroically for Ike, attempting at the same time to speak in a historic context of the pulpit of the Presidency, even if he had no idea that that was what he was attempting to do, that Ike had said that whenever a President of the United States had a pronouncement to make regarding a current foreign-policy crisis, well, that was "sacrosanct," that was the time for the old rally-round-the-flag-boys knee-jerk kick-in, a kind of patrio-historico wad of gum to dam the dike.

But good old happy boy Ike did not leave off speaking of the pulpit of *The President* while meandering through the historical ages: "If anyone argues with him," said Ike of *The President,* "and the bigger the following this opponent gets, the more it has divided our country." That was it. Pure Ikeism. If one gets it one has it? Yes, that was a problem all right. And who was this opponent? The enemy within or without? Which? Neither? It was 'who's on first' all over again. Good old happy Ike. The only individual who had unknowingly figured out how to be both dull and funny at the same time and wildly entertain the unsuspecting American people who did not have a clue. The straight man for his own accidental jokes. A one-man comedy show for an audience that did not know enough to laugh.

As the cab drove out of the hills of Hanover, headed for the bus station in White River Junction, Vermont, Timothy remembered hearing on the radio that President Kennedy, Vice President Lyndon Johnson, and Secretary of State Dean Rusk had cut short campaign trips and returned to Washington, the President and Vice President because of reported colds. Timothy wondered if perhaps the country had a cold. At least he wondered about the truth of the matter. However, with vampires around, it was even more important to wonder about the truth of time and after a few more heartbeats on this historic date on the calendar, the hour of the clock had to be changed from Daylight Saving Time to Standard Time. With vampires around, it would be in one's interest to know whether it was the upside or the downside of time. To make a mistake could be fatal or something else. And what about the Prince of Darkness?

Monday, October 22, 1962

2

s god dead is god dea

Right now he was Angus Anguish. Only one of his code names. A great name in history, except who knew it? He should have been in Russia in 1917. Dream casting. Having been conceived, it was not inconceivable. Maybe China, 1925. Not altogether improbable. Spain, 1937. A very nice romantic likelihood. Pretty bloody. The best credential. And the most likely. China again, 1948. Quite possible, if improbable, yellow journalism in America, but the most recent. Unrecognizable, forgotten places in between and since. A cook's tour of conspiracy, a hornet's nest of horrors, a laborer's labyrinth, a tangled, gnarled ball of thread to be unraveled, crazy and clandestine. It did not matter. Even the United States. New York City, this morning of October 23, 1962.

A Tuesday at dawn, Angus Anguish broke from the door of the elegant Washington Square townhouse on Macdougal Street, west of Washington Square Park, the beau quartier, or it was an adjoining boarding house, a slum unto itself, a poor bohemian latent pre-revolutionary chaos amidst the surrounding palaces, started from the door like a bull from a pen, an aged bull, down the front steps, falling, drunk or ill, stumbling down the stairs like a man who had lost his faith or had just lost, he hit Macdougal Street. Actually, he hit the Macdougal Street gutter, hit it as if thrown, tossed like trash. There was no one to pick him up and no one to hear his insistent, rambling, interior monologue, if monologue it was. With his face in the gutter it was probably impossible to understand him anyway, if there was anything to understand. Had someone discreetly bent over to lend an ear, the flowing noisefroth from his lips or rather his throat, guttural, might have sounded something like . . .

"sgodeadisgodeadisgodeadisgodeadisgodeadisgodeadisgodeadisgodeadis"

Not exactly words that were

STREAKING ACROSS THE SKY

Once he struggled to his knees, he definitely added,

". . . Wagner . . . tonight . . . have to . . . ofcourseyouhavetobastard."

Or something like that. He was mumbling. Grunting, wheezing, and mumbling. Maybe he was referring to the Mayor, the honorable Robert F. Wagner, Jr., of New York City. An assassination plot? Had it come to this? Not exactly a global assignation, maybe a disciplinary exercise to prove that he was still a good soldier.

Ironically, perhaps the shock of the impact in the gutter cleared his head, ordered it. Perhaps the clearing of his head was like cleaning a stovepipe, a basement, a dirty, gloomy, dark, depressing hole, a clutter of junk, the dusty filth of his soul, like clearing tunnels in his lodgings that wormed through scattered piles of bedding, dishes, newspapers, butts, and ashes, so much excrement piled high from his solitary excavations.

Fury, the Fury, demonic, sexual, or whatever, that one could enter into: why did those moments seem separate or contrary or stand in opposition to what one envisioned, dreamed, to ideals, decency, civility, good judgment, morality, to everyday life? The beast? Divinity? The walking symbol, focus of the overt, covert, latent, raw, unsocialized, primitive, everpresent, blind, driving, murderous, furious, frustrated force of life. The Isolated Fury.

Anyway, he moved on again at another dawn, moved on maybe like a street sweeper mindgone in his early morning, daily ritual, sweeping with his broom in total command, aggressively, determinedly sweeping down the gutter as if leading an advancing, unstoppable army, angrily, viciously sweeping down the gutter, wielding a broom like a long spear, like a rifle and bayonet, like a rapier, the long handle of a broom plunged into a horizontal three-foot brush like a knive plunged into a piece of meat, liver.

"Sonofabitchyoubethere . . . tonight . . . wehavetomove."

Huge, ponderous, heavy, gaining only in pounds and years—he was not a young man—with a big head, a large nose, thick fleshy but still powerful arms, maybe he precariously skirted the gutter of the street, shot straight ahead for fifteen or twenty feet, then crossed to the inner sidewalk, breathing heavily, nearly colliding with the steps of brownstones, and darted ahead again for another fifteen or twenty paces, lurched from left to right and back again in the early morning hours. Or he skulked entirely on the inner sidewalk, appearing as if he were about to flatten himself in frightful flight against each and every building facade, to fall on each row of steps in supplication, to lurk in alleyways, searching for crevices, for hallways, trying to hide, to move unseen at dawn with few to see him, moving as if he sought to avoid detection among the city's millions, fearful but certain that no one in fact did see him, as if in effect the millions were not there, fearful certainty. Moving and twisting in agony, turning halfway to the left, partially to the right, sometimes completely to the right, suddenly, at undetermined, unexpected moments, he stopped, wheeled around, looked back and shook his fist, cursed.

"Goddamnit . . . be there . . . havetodoit . . . sonofabitch."

The possibility was that he sought to project a false, misleading image in order to disguise himself, or that he had once aspired to a grand stature in the public eye, dressed in a rumpled slept-in green corduroy jacket with brown leather patches on his elbows, wearing a red-checked woolen smelly hunter's shirt, grimy khakis, loafers without socks, topped by a dirty brown beret, or he was attired in a purple velvet suit, black silk ascot, white lace shirt with ruffled sleeves flowering, growing, a powdered white wig beclouding his head, rouge bejewelling his large puffy cheeks.

A figure not unlike that of an utter fool, a ridiculous fop, as he reached Washington Square North and turned right toward the great Washington Square arch that marked the entrance to the urban verdure. An idiot anywhere else, maybe. A small town in Indiana, perhaps, but not in Greenwich Village, not in Washington Square Park, that stage of extravagant poses, intense, hysterical, desperate, hilarious, uproarious, lethal. Nearing the triumphant arch, no one would have thought him a conquering general, despite his size, or a revolutionary, despite his language, or an erstwhile member of a privileged class, whatever his attire, or even a uniformed employee of the New York City Department of Sanitation, even if he carried a broom. But whatever his profound desires, he presented to whoever might have been watching in the early light a spectacle of uneasy madness, even if no one was watching, even if not a single soul saw him as he passed, mumbling, passed through and under the arch, George Washington's, into Washington Square Park.

"City Hall . . . fuckeryes . . . tonight."

It would have been more fitting if Angus Anguish had waited until nighttime, as souls often did, to take his walk in the park, to prowl, grouse, smell, scratch, and squat, waited until nighttime when the city's buildings became quivering, shuddering animals, its lights those of a swamp or bog, when he might have been mistaken for a silent water buffalo, powerful, brooding, unapproachable.

As it was, as he passed under the arch, nearly colliding with its base, in Indiana he would have been judged a bum, a broken man, a wino. No one would have thought him a revolutionary marching under a triumphant arch, oh no, heavens no, not in Indiana, America.

He may have imagined the park as his, his royal preserve, his hunting grounds, except that he would number no victims. Or he may have regarded it as his courtyard of entertainment and pleasure, complete with buffoons, magicians, harlots, actors of every description. But if he was a revolutionary in disguise, a disguise totally successful because no one would have feared him, no one would have taken him seriously, the park was ideal for clandestine meetings. Although large gatherings would undoubtedly be dispersed by New

York's blue marauders, small groupings were expected, tolerated. And individuals were guaranteed free play, free enterprise. Just disguise it, anything goes.

Upon entering the park, Angus could roam to its farthest reaches, to the northeast, northwest, southeast, southwest, roam, if one could judge by his movements, in systematic fashion, as if he had previously divided the park into sectors, or, if he had not surveyed and laid the divisions himself, as if he presumed that someone else had and, having done so, had forthwith named them, what? China? France? Spain? Russia? More. Poland. East Germany. Hungary. Cuba. But not united states.

Whatever, Angus would appear to talk, talk to anyone, none of whom would be of a kind, except that they would be possessed of a common status, refugees of the city, both transient and permanent, who were forever rediscovering the park at varying hours, passing through, having left a quickly forgotten encounter, going to the unforeseen, not of the worrying kind, speculators in time and emotion. He would talk in the early morning to a sleeping, oblivious, bedraggled heap, stretched full-length on a bench or simply on wet greenbrown grass. Speaking as if on a platform before the entire world, impatient, intolerant, angry at the thought that some might not think so, might doubt, that anyone would dare walk away from, by, through the park, standing before the figure of a reluctant follower, Angus would implore or berate with wildly waving arms.

"I've tolyouantolyou . . . no time to lose."

And having delivered his message, confident of its acceptance, he would turn and point to another sector.

"You be there, bethere."

And leave. Move on, anxious to deliver other messages, involved with his world, Washington Square Park, as if it were the entire world, perhaps impatient, intolerant, angry with any who did not see it that way, move on to find a podium, a bench for himself where he could hold court, conduct a meeting, engage in the first personal, soul-searching consultation of the day with a single representative, a single traveler, adventurer, with anyone who came, for most of the morning, do not disturb. Angus would talk with any of them and none of them would listen, which would not stop him from talking.

He would talk with, say, Johnny Chessman, black and in his seventies, who came every morning to win chess games at fifty cents a shot. With Irene the Slink, who would do to you whatever she wanted at any time of the day for five dollars on down. With Jeremy the Jobber, who would take you, male or female, to his haunt, The Fat Black Pussy Cat underground cafe, where he would let you buy him soup and drinks in exchange for any stories he could imagine, favorites he repeated, good moneymakers, lengthy, worth several drinks, three bowls of soup, thick bread, and shelter for most of the day.

To all of them Angus could have talked and they would never have listened.

"You know that bastard . . . I've tolyouantolyou . . ."

He could talk to Johnny Chessman only when Johnny thought that Angus's chatter, his wildly waving arms, bothered Johnny's opponent more than him. Johnny came to the park for his chess games dressed for the occasion in an unimposing simple shiny brown suit, frayed white shirt and pale tie, and worn but polished black shoes. Johnny would do anything to win, but he won mostly with a good, solid, mechanical, unspectacular game. Most of the time he won. When he did not, he could blame Angus.

"Cussed man, you taking bread from my family," his family being himself. "Yuh leave me alone today. I gotta livin ta make."

When Johnny won with Angus, he would praise him, convinced Angus's chatter was distracting to his opponents.

"Keep on blowin. I take care of yuh, I do that."

Jeremy the Jobber would sit and nod his head at Angus until he spotted a visitor to Washington Square.

"I see a visitor who needs my immediate entertainment. I deeply regret my forced departure."

"He's coming tonight . . . thistheday . . . bethere."

"I'll tell 'em, man," Jeremy would say, waving as he walked away, "I'll tell 'em, pretty boy of mine," laughing and clapping his hands.

"At it again, honey?" Irene the Slink would ask him directly. "What are you saying? You need Irene today? I can't waste it with you, honey. I can't be repaid for the time I lose. You ain't gonna repay me. What I have lost, I have lost," she said urgently to him, walking on by.

Johnny chalked up his chess games, Jeremy lived his liaisons, Irene joined her johns. All the while Angus held his seminars, they ignored him, and it was as if it had never happened.

Except that from high above the eastern border of Washington's preserve, the cohorts of Angus Anguish were ordinarily observed for most of the day and evening, oh, of course, frequently, hourly, by the minute, even verily to the second and beyond, although admittedly not at that precise, exact moment, by a newly engaged inquisitive adventurer, the Slayman, Slaymunster, Slaygood, by name of Associate Professor John Darnell Slamunster, professionally known by some as AP Slamunster, the young, confident, and aggressive high doctor who instead of gazing from his office window or from a window or windows or, for that matter, from behind a tree, was ordering his students from his perch in his fourth-floor classroom at Washington Square College, New York University, to be mum, to maintain solemn silence, decorum, immobility. Actually, annoying as it may have been, had Associate Professor John Darnell Slamunster been struck by an ardent desire, by the necessity to spy upon Angus Anguish during the hour to be, it would have been impossible for him to do so personally, as the windows of his classroom opened to the east while Washington's Park Preserve, of course, lay to the west. It was a distressing arrangement, and he had done wartangle with the University housing bureacratici, buildings and grounds collective forces, heating plantation aficionados, and with whoever else eschewed responsibility, in a furious campaign to have his classroom switched in the interests of partisan surveillance, all to no avail. But in the meantime he had his messianic messengers, his growing gang of followers, former students, his secret force of esprit de corporals encircling and infiltrating Washington Square Park. It was convenient for keeping his and others' eyes on the world.

Presently, however, and unfortunately for his peace of mind, Associate Professor Slamunster, or AP, was deeply absorbed with saying to his class that he would speak today on Dostoevsky's novel *The Idiot.* This was not necessarily a revelation to the students, as this was the very date, alas, that the novel appeared for discussion on the syllabus, although, unlike the mainstream mundanity of many classes, Slamunster's classes kept to schedules rather than to a single schedule, variability being the desirability, because Slamunster was a very busy man, very much in demand, pulled by many threads in countercultural directions and times. But AP John was always in control or, rather, he always insisted upon being in control, insisted that he was in control because it was necessary to be in control, on time, precise, definite, or, in this instance at least, it could be said that his syllabi were not the usual fictions. He would have sworn to that, put his hand on the Bible, so help him God, mother, and powerful country.

As always, AP would announce with a furious flourish that it was his intention to begin with a few introductory comments. The preliminary announcement, this prologue of the soul, of the gods . . . well, his tone of voice commonly assumed that the students were in full cognizance of the fact that his comments, nay, not mere comments, that his pronouncements were of the grandest significance, uttered at great personal cost to him, that they were to be recorded, cherished, and preserved, treated, certainly not as ordinary classroom lecture notes but . . . as the words of an original, a master, yes, a genius, even if the best was yet to come, praise be to God, the best was always to come. Yes, Slamunster energetically, freely, and unselfconsciously telegraphed the fact that he was a superior being, and that this particular room full of students was being accorded the highest of privileges, that is, the students having enrolled in the course by a number exceeding one hundred were being accorded a rare opportunity to witness his presence. Simply, it was a limited edition. It was a characteristic, if perhaps a learned, manner of being merely indicative of the gulf of reality. No gratuitous insult was intended. It would never have occurred to the correct, right-minded, right-thinking Slamunster to consciously, to deliberately insult the students, the futurama of America.

Slamunster implied that he would be willing to spend most of the classroom hour discussing the novel with the class, that is, somehow the thought was implanted that, yes, he was entirely at their disposal but, commonly, he would ramble for most of the classroom period, leaving only a few minutes for random comments from the uninitiated, the mystified, and the naked, that is, from the students, the clear implication being, intended or not, that a few minutes with the master was more than most of them warranted.

Predictably, however, when AP Slamunster spoke, no matter for how long, his aggressive, intense manner belied any sense of drift. His sounds were invariably clear, high-pitched, and penetrating. His long narrow head, his thick long black hair, shook with emphasis. Long fingers and long arms chopped and carved the air incessantly. Even his long legs appeared involved, swinging one over the other as he paced back and forth in front of the class, ready in reserve, prepared to advance at the notice. He always looked as though he could traverse anything, anyone, anywhere, anytime, up and down, across and over. He thought he could. He was awaiting great triumphs, awaiting, he fervently believed, the conquest of evil, that is, pardon, once he came upon evil, once he discovered evil, and discover evil he would because he knew evil, he would know evil when he saw evil, he would know he was discovering evil, bravely baring his soul, unhesitatingly, to evil's insidious effect. Meanwhile, AP was marching onward with dispassionate dispatch, marching forward.

"On the back cover of the paperback," he began, drawing the students' attention to the third printing of the Bantam Classic edition of *The Idiot* the class was using, "it says that Prince Myshkin was a saintly, good, pure man who was destroyed by a corrupt, venal, grubbing, covetous, slothful, lying, parisitical society."

He paused.

"Well, perhaps it does not say quite as much as that."

The class laughed on cue.

"But, is this true?" he looked around, wide-eyed, as if incredulous. "Is this broadside proposition established?"

Having put the question, he forthwith provided the answer.

"If you believe it, you are yourselves idiots, and not of the saintly variety."

More laughter.

"The society described within *The Idiot* is indeed corrupt. The society is venal. The society is grubbing, covetous, slothful, mendacious, adrift, vicious, menacing, every bit of that. Yes, the society is parisitical," he boomed, his right index finger pointed to the ceiling. "But Myshkin was a saint without defenses. Myshkin destroyed himself," Slamunster concluded. His voice dropped, his right index finger pointed to the floor as if pointing to hell itself.

What great enjoyment there might have been for the students had they only been aware and been able to appreciate the fact that, secretly, AP Slamunster not only saw himself as a Myshkin but, more or better, as encompassing a Myshkin. He was a soul on fire. He had no difficulty believing that he, himself, possessed the soul of a saint, but he also considered himself to be an actor and a sage of the world or an operator of the quotidian, smarter and more capable than the devil. He could master and maneuver anything, he thought. If he acknowledged any problem at all or any uncertainty at this stage of his life, it was merely to ask: what should or could be mastered or manipulated, co-opted or conquered? What was worthy of the effort? And to answer that question it was his ambition to fully comprehend the nature of the world he lived in and his role in it, thereby transforming it, as it were, verily into his own private world. Yes, knowledge was truly power, and truly he must know what his choices were and, more importantly, what his choices were not with the added proviso that he desperately needed to ascertain which choices he wanted to make. At times, the last perplexed him more than anything, at times it infuriated him, at others it depressed him, but always it obsessed him. While Slamunster was quick, even eager, to exhibit passion over whatever interested him, it was necessary first that he find an object of interest, always that, always the unending quest for motivation, for stimulation without which there might be nothing.

In changed circumstances, outside the classroom, Slamunster was nonetheless unchanging in his preoccupation. He would listen, of course, if he were interested, engaged, but it was necessary first to interest him, engage him and, in or out of the classroom, he expected little of others except that for which he was looking, a lot. He expected from them what he demanded, nothing less and much more. When he was disappointed, which was often, he personally seized the day. After all, his basic working assumption was that most of what others had to say was not worth hearing, even if, paradoxically, he found most of what he heard endlessly fascinating, whether because of disbelief, horror, or amusement, or because he, himself, had heard it with his own ears.

The classroom for him was a platform from which he could hear his own ideas, as articulated by himself, aired, reverberate, bounce off others and back to him, kind of like a boomerang. In the classroom he evaluated himself. He was his own compulsive audience. But his relentless self-evaluation continued outside the classroom as well, at any time or moment, in any situation, whether he was at a dinner party or sitting on a bar stool, with the result that wherever he went or whatever he was doing there was always the possibility of encountering himself.

A bus stop was the ideal setting for Slamunster's monologues in the universe. A steady but changing succession of paying passing patrons suited him perfectly. While it was blessedly guaranteed that not a single individual would ever remain for long in attendance, some one individual would always be serendipitously adrift, listening or overhearing, pretending not to be eavesdropping. With some one body always to his left or to his right, Slamunster was bequeathed and enjoyed the unbroken illusion of a rapt audience at stage center. For example, in recent days a passenger would arrive to catch her or his bus, and Slamunster would turn and say to the unsuspecting, nonplussed soul:

"About Myshkin. You have to keep in mind the fact that he is an epileptic, as Dostoevsky, himself, was."

Uncomprehending, the passenger either would look quickly away or offer, "I beg your pardon?"

Or, startled, stare at Slamnunster, involuntarily waiting to hear what he really was talking about or simply what he was about. In effect, Slamnunster would simultaneously ignore the passenger-in-waiting as he looked that very same individual directly in, through, the face, saying,

"You could limit yourself to explaining Myshkin's behavior simply in terms of his physical condition, but, of course, Dostoevsky does not want us to do that, does not do that himself, does he?"

This last would be uttered with the utmost, tantalizing gravity, as he continued:

"Dostoevsky, he of the once mother Russia, wishes to make of it a spiritual, even a mystical state. Or, if you wish, a religious state. All the same it is madness, Dostoevsky's."

On occasion there was sufficient time for the startled soul in passing to begin to comprehend, to nod, uneasily, yes or no, a little knowledge of Dostoevsky being helpful, but not time enough to offer a comment, a comment that Slamunster would not want to hear anyway, for the bus would arrive, the particular listener or passenger would gesture awkwardly, point embarrassedly toward the bus, "Ahhhh . . . ," and with the opening and closing of the door of the bus be whisked away forever, saved.

Whereupon, Slamunster, with little break in his thought, would turn to the next pilgrim and add,

"Of course, Dostoevsky sought to create a duality, a tension between the physical and the spiritual, mystical or religious. Myshkin embodies that tension, so to speak, as some have claimed that Dostoevsky, himself, did, and, yes, he left no doubt which of the two he considered the more powerful, which would triumph over the other or, alas, destroy the other, obliterate."

A second bewildered passenger also would stumble speechless onto a bus and Slamunster, again unhesitatingly, would offer the observation to a third unsuspecting soul that

"A century later the German novelist Thomas Mann attempted the same feat in *The Magic Mountain,* and it is edifying to compare the manner, the style, and the spirit of the two novels and their authors, because both deal with the cultural and spiritual dreck of their time, and both speak to and of the insanity of our own time, perhaps of the coming end of all time."

However, undoubtedly Slamunster's long-time favorite forum was The Purple Union, which he regarded as his very own special creation at the university, a weekly gathering in the evening on the tenth floor of the main building at Washington Square College, where by Slamunster's decree anything could be read or said by faculty or by students or, for that matter, by any of the masses, the latter being loosely identified as among any of those unaffiliated with the university, that is, literally the rest of the world, those from the streets or country, be they fowl or beast, whether they had flown or crawled to the weekly gatherings of The Purple Union, where anything or anyone could be attacked or analyzed, torn asunder or ballyhooed, ridiculed or cheered, ignored or booed or jeered or pilloried or, perhaps, even hung although admittedly it had not yet come to pass.

When Slamunster, himself, spoke, he always sought and expected to annoy and to mystify his audience. What he desired most of all, what he dreamed of was that there be an eruption of sorts, that in the questions that followed, in the discussions of the pages presented, someone, best of all one of Slamunster's faculty colleagues, would start screaming, yelling, falling on his face rolling on the floor. Even the threat of a little violence, just a soupçon, would have been acceptable. However, failing a general uproar, Slamunster prayed at the very least for an element of uncertainty, of wonderment, and the more experimental and mysterious and bizarre the better, for the experimental, the mysterious, the bizarre nature of the process of interaction and development interested him most of all. In the chaos he sought the uncontrollable, he sought the new creation.

Slamunster thought he could always recognize the exact moment when his listeners began to feel uneasy, a sign at the very least of the evening's minimal success, exactly that for which he had hoped. Mostly, squirmers would be students. They would begin by appearing to enjoy what he was reading, insisting upon it, but shortly they would be hesitant, uncertain of what they were hearing. There would be nervous laughter, titters. Some would exchange glances, look quizzically at one another, raise their eyebrows as if to say, "What did you expect from Slamunster?"

Two or three of the few faculty present would express immediate and obvious disapproval on their faces at the first titter, although it was likely that Slamunster's reading would displease them even more. Frequently, they themselves would be induced to squirm, wondering if he was mocking them. In the years he had been on the faculty, they had come to expect the bizarre from Slamunster or, as some of them termed it, the infantile. However, the question forever lingered as to how far he dared to go. Yes, yes, how outrageous could he be? What was possible? Anything?

But what pleased Slamunster most about the gatherings of The Purple Union was the sprinkling in the audience of what he liked to call the "unidentifiables." Most of them he thought came from the city, of course, most likely from Washington Square Park or the Bowery because of their proximity to the university, although it pleased Slamunster to imagine that they came from all over the city, that after panhandling the fare, they came by the under-the-ground subways, not via the over-the-land buses, the innocuous vehicles of the surface, the automobiles and the bicycles and the like. Or perhaps they had started days, even weeks ahead of the scheduled readings and walked from all of the outlying boroughs, from Brooklyn, the Bronx, Queens, Staten Island, or had flown in a hot air balloon across the Hudson from New Jersey, having parachuted from the Palisades, or had been pulled as if by magnets from the great beyond perhaps, stretching, stretching as far away as Long Island, even New England. One and all, bums, reprobates, eccentrics, scoundrels coming to the readings, the people of any and all revolutions who came out of the woodwork for the readings of The Purple Union.

One of Slamunster's favorites was not, strictly speaking, an "unidentifiable," although she, a small woman, certainly played the part. Her sharply pointed nose jutted from underneath one of her large, floppy hats, a hat that usually sprouted an oversize green or purple feather. Her face was wizened and her body probably had the dimensions of a grotesquely large sparrow, probably, because it was impossible to know if she had a body, draped as she always was in a black cloth coat several times too large for her, her "judicial robes," advised Slamunster. But she was not properly an "unidentifiable" because she was intimately, if mysteriously, associated with the university's lore, its milieu; she had at some time or other popped up in almost everyone's literature course. She was famous. "Mother Hubbard" they called her, perhaps because she gave the impression of being a permanent inhabitant within the walls of the university, of literally living within the walls of the main building, and because she might have been a perennial mother to all of the students, mother to generation after generation after generation, but who knew?

In fact, professors had commented that they had never seen her outside the main building, swore to it, in fact, the building where all of the literature courses were held, had never seen her simply on the streets or on the buses or subways, not even in any one of the nearby coffee shops and restaurants and taverns. They wondered if anyone ever had? No one admitted to it. Although it was rumored that Mother Hubbard had been around for years, no one seemed to know precisely who or what she was, and though everyone testified that at some time or other she had been in his or her course, not a single one could remember for certain exactly what course it had been or what grade she had received or whether she had ever even written a paper or taken an exam. No details. It was as if she had fallen from the pages of a book some student had smuggled into the university years before. Slamunster surmised that the secret of Mother Hubbard could be found somewhere in the vast antiquated bureaucratic machinery of the university with which he often warred. By now, perhaps some computer contained the information, waiting for someone to accidentally push the correct button. He hoped no one ever would, that her secret would never be revealed. Actually, he probably need not have worried, for she was more likely contained on a single dusty file card lost in a box in a drawer in a room in the original underground basement of the building. She may well have been a descendant of the original student.

Slamunster cherished Mother Hubbard. While everyone else, he hoped, might be simultaneously disoriented or provoked to silence by his or others' readings, at some moment in the evening she would invariably observe in hushed tones—with the turn that when she became excited her voice had a wide range of squeaks—that she could confirm what he was saying in his "fairy tale," for she called everything a "fairy tale," confirm an idea, a thought, a date, an incident, confirm something, and confirm from her very own life. Had Slamunster read from the telephone directory, Mother Hubbard would have found a parallel to that fairy tale in her existence.

For Slamunster there were never too many of the "unidentifiables." Although they rarely formed a tenth of the audience, what number there were owed their continuing presence to him. One or two of the faculty or student members of The Purple Union would periodically complain about their presence.

"He is only here for the coffee and cookies afterward," was a common complaint.

Or, "All she wants is to escape from the cold."

Or, "Sleep, that's what they all want, a place to sleep. Is this a flophouse or a university?"

"Not so," Slamunster would retort, saying, for example, "You see that character in the brown suit? Yes, I know it is dirty, and who cares if he doesn't have any socks on? But have you ever heard him speak? Yes, I know he rarely speaks when spoken to, but have you ever talked to him and heard his beautiful diction? He was educated properly. Maybe he is an actor, or was, or would you believe a professor? But he is obviously here looking for something lost. Do you begrudge him that? He will listen to what is being read. That is more than most of the remainder of the audience will do. Let them stay. Let them all stay. We can spare the cookies."

As it happened, that was John Darnell Slamunster's introduction to Angus Anguish, if that is what it was, for, in truth, Slamunster had only recently begun to suspect that there were tales to tell about the man he called Angus. For the name of Angus Anguish was Slamunster's own chosen designation. He was fascinated by the fact that Angus Anguish did not always speak the same language, let alone the same words. Angus Anguish did not always wear the same clothes, the same outfits, suits, combinations, colors, mixtures, mixtures of mixtures. It was a kaleidoscope but, strangely, one of somber hues. And for all Slamunster knew Angus Anguish had indeed lived in a flophouse, but he suspected that he had lived on Park Avenue as well, both literally on the street and in an apartment, and Slamunster had the conviction that one day or night he would find out the true identity of Angus Anguish, and he would not believe it. In fact, he had made that his updated, near religious mission, his latest assignment in the world unknown to be known.

Flophouse or not, it would not have mattered to Slamunster, at least that remained his thinking. Nevertheless, on more than one occasion Slamunster had restrained one or two of the unknown souls from walking immediately to the coffee table. When a first-timer entered, appeared to sneak into the room, stood still momentarily looking furtive and anticipating being discovered and thrown out, Slamunster knew the street-traveler was seeking the food. He would go and wrap his long arm around the visitor, explain the rules, and escort her or him to a chair. He did not at all mind the fact that their appetites might have been for the coffee and cookies and not for the images and ideas. Sometimes, at the end of a particular reading, he would take one of them out and buy the wanderer a meal at some nondescript lunch counter or bar that tolerated derelicts. There were a variety of those places in the Village, particularly in the East Village, places that were drab and depressing and never disappeared. Once seated, a single question from Slamunster would ordinarily prompt his guest to talk without interruption. Slamunster believed little of what he heard from anyone, but on these occasions he was ordinarily an attentive listener. Invariably on these occasions he confirmed or broadened his vision of the universe. However, of late there were intimations that his universe had begun to expand and shrink simultaneously.

Aside from the bus stop and The Purple Union, a job selling tickets at a race track or handing out welfare checks at New York State Employment offices throughout the city would also have relieved Slamunster's mind admirably. However, in his role as a professor of English, on this very day and at this particular hour, it had been his intention to seize the class period and set it in isolation for his essay on Myshkin as mystic and Myshkin as earthling. Without a doubt, Slamunster judged Myshkin to be too much the earthling and he intended to convey that, and, what was equally clear, Slamunster intended his "discussion" of *The Idiot* to occupy at least three weeks or fully nine classroom hours, partly because it was an outrageous way to conduct a course, to run amuck with the novel. Again, Slamunster did not always disdain discussing his ideas with others, any others. And at New York University, he had little control over who took his classes; in fact, it was his opinion that he too often had little control over whom he encountered in the waiting city, encountered in life, but at times and with selected individuals he would talk, and sometimes listen. In this respect, at least, the classroom was the great selector, the great lottery.

Presently, he stopped pacing and focused his eyes on the front row of students. He was conditioned to drama. He was particularly anxious on this night to fill the void. What turmoil could he generate this evening, he seemed to be asking? His body appeared to grow larger, as if he were near to bursting with creative energy, and every student seemed to notice it. He paused for emphasis, but before he could strike, a hand was raised. Slamunster often seemed annoyed when students raised their hands. He was too impatient to wait on anything or anyone, sometimes even himself. But, contrary to his better judgment, he was not ungenerous and, regardless of his annoyance, he always recognized the questioner. Still, having just begun, he was particularly irked that someone already had a question. Had they no sense of timing whatsoever, no sense of priorities? Did they not understand that if they had only listened to him for a few minutes more they would not have been left with any questions? Not that he totally disdained questions. On the contrary, questions were proof of interest, stimulation, absorption, all directly attributable to Professor John Darnell Slamunster, himself, of course, and it was perfectly understood that no student would understand everything he said. Still, at the moment, AP John, as he was also affectionately known by the aficionados among his students, did not think he wanted to hear what any student had to say, nor did he have any wish to speculate about what any student would have said.

But the waving hand of the student belonged to a young woman in her mid-twenties, a blonde Swedish woman named Hilde Johnson, direct from her job with a New York magazine, *Night and Day*, or was it *Day and Night*? Slamunster could not keep it straight. He knew her slightly, knew her name her face, a little of her personality, and he desired to know her better. He thought she might be a serviceable individual, although generally he did not have a very high opinion of those who worked in journalism and publishing, of those who, as he put it, processed pulp rather than originally produced visions. Oh, he was willing to concede that an individual of intelligence and worth might become temporarily waylaid by what he regarded to be a parasitical network, lost in a mindless maze, and that was possibly the case with Hilde Johnson. She often asked questions. Paradoxically, when Slamunster was disposed to answer a question, he regarded that as a very positive sign.

"I just want to say that," she began, having first closed her eyes and then with her first words opened them, "that is, what bothers me about these nineteenth-century Russians is that they are so unrelentingly intense, and so gloomy. I mean both the writers—although Dostoevsky is the worst—and their characters. None of the characters behave casually. Normality is that everything is crucial, irrational, life or death. Disaster and ruin are always looming around the corner. And, God knows, they're always turning corners under cover of night . . ."

The class laughed. And Slamunster smiled.

". . . corners that go nowhere. Even their happy moments are so overwrought that, well, you almost wince, you almost don't want them to be happy, because you know that when an individual is happy that is precisely when sudden devastation is imminent and inevitable. Is that the point I am missing?"

More laughter.

"I wonder what . . ."

"Klara Blazek?"

Okay, Slamunster had been sidetracked. And he knew it. But he could wait on some occasions because he not only believed in seizing the moment, the moment often seized him. And whether Klara Blazek's hand was raised or not, Slamunster had always eagerly called upon her whenever he thought he could, when he thought she was of a will to speak, when he could use her, either to intimidate, to provoke discussion, or to pre-empt it or simply because in the past she had unfailingly galvanized him personally. And now, yes, they were a superb team with fresh, unlimited possibilities, he thought excitedly, forgetting himself in his enthusiasm of this immediate moment, not uncharacteristic, although he knew, even if he did not care to acknowledge it, that there were grounds to doubt her intent to serve, as well as questions about whom she would serve, if anyone at all. So, in truth, to speak of their being a team was a bit of wishful thinking on his part, perhaps even risky thinking, particularly in light of recent events.

It had happened one night. She had come to his apartment after class. He did not know how it had happened, even if he had reasons for it to happen. Certainly he did not remember asking her, saying anything. But they had left his classroom and gone straight to his flat, where they had made love quickly, almost without words. Not only had he yet to recover, he had a sense that he would become entangled without remedy. And he had never asked. She had left without speaking.

Although Slamunster had never seen Klara Blazek at The Purple Union, it could be said that she was herself an unidentifiable of her own order. Without a doubt, AP John Darnell Slamunster's most absurd encounter with an unidentifiable had revolved around the mystery of Klara Blazek and, extraordinary as it was, Angus Anguish. The confluence of events had been uncanny. It had begun months ago, on a night at The Purple Union, when he had learned that cookies were not the only bait. When he had learned that mixed within the classrooms and wandering the corridors of New York University were perhaps all kinds of so-called ordinary citizens disguised as down-and-outs who played roles as foreign or government or interplanetary unidentifiables. And why not? Had there not been scandals and outrages before at Washington Square Park such as during the shellhunt for Communists in universities everywhere during the previous decade, the 1950s? Which was precisely to the issue in question, and it was all very confusing.

It had happened at The Purple Union although, again, Klara Blazek herself had not been there. At the time, Slamunster had at first thought that he was approaching Angus Anguish from behind, until he had noticed the white socks the man was wearing, totally unlike anything Angus Anguish had ever worn, and AP John was convinced that Angus Anguish had probably worn almost everything there was to wear. But this man had been in a plain brown suit, and in his plain garb he was, in effect, in no disguise at all, for he had no description. He was truly an unidentifiable, or, as Slamunster had detected on the spot, this man, this Man, was one of the Fabulous Boys of Intrigue, one of the High Priests of Involvement, his occupation being to involve anyone he could. What Slamunster could never have suspected, but should have, was that he himself would become involved.

Slamunster had taken the plain-garbed one to Anybodys, the nearby bar of saliva and scuttlebutt, and once there he had let the not-so-anonymous Fabulous Man spin and twist his tales, let him unspin.

"They are everywhere," the Fabulous Man had said, "and some of them are in the wrong places. We must observe them and keep track of them. We need to know about them. Everything about them. As a true patriot, we knew you would want to help. The Purple Union . . ."

Eventually the Man had said:

"Klara Kovacs. She is from a Communist country," he said, driving the nail. "Hungary. You know her as Klara Blazek."

"Ah," started Slamunster, experiencing speechlessness for just a moment, which for him was true vertigo, "I believe she came to this country when she was a little girl—she once told me that—long before Hungary even went Communist, which I believe was about 1948, was it not?"

The Fabulous One was quick to set events and Slamunster straight.

"Do not be deceived by the fact that the perverted minds of Bela Kun and his dogs in Hungary were exterminated in 1919 when Klara Kovacs was a child. It makes no difference that the Bolsheviks were stopped at the Danube once. Hungary had it in it and always will have it. And the fact that the country went Communist again in 1948 proves it beyond a shadow of a doubt. In contrast, the United States of America will never go Communist. It will not even attempt such a fatal move, not before Armageddon."

"Armageddon, huh?" Slamunster was getting interested. "Then what are you worried about?"

But the Great Anonymous One could not be dissuaded from his journey, because he had no other path in mind.

"Since the Senator died we have had to be especially vigilant. Just because we exterminated most of the vermin from the universities in the 1950s, and from most walks of American life, that does not mean they cannot return. And we do not want them back. The university is a natural breeding ground with its free thinking. And they are crafty tigers. They are natural political schemers. They will not hesitate to use naked force. They are well versed in the skills of deceit and murder. We should have destroyed them all in the 1950s. But they went underground like so many cockroaches. Too many of them."

"Underground?"

"Yes. Many went underground early to cellars."

"Cellars?"

"Yes. They had upper and lower levels."

"Levels?"

"Yes. Above- and underground."

The nail was in place. The Fabulous Boy of Intrigue had gone on and on and Slamunster had become impossibly fascinated. Surprisingly, he had never personally encountered such thoughts before, not in his classroom, not in the entire university, thoughts he had found impenetrable. But he had loved the idea that he might be able to pull the strings of intrigue himself. He had imagined that he could create tales of intrigue at will. And talk about a captive audience. The more he created, the more the Fabulous One would return to listen and record, and probably bring others with him.

Yes, Slamunster had recognized the adsurdity of it all almost immediately, and he had become quickly embroiled. But he had balked, had been truly bothered by having to deal with real names, real people. Like Klara Blazek, although admittedly the thought that she might be a card-carrying member of the American Communist Party, as the condemnation went, only added to her allure for him. And then, what had Fabulous said? Dear old Emeritus Professor Vernon Johnston, and, not so surprisingly, Professor André Cordon?

Well, the stories heard throughout the university about Professor Cordon already bordered on the ridiculous, so what did it matter. The accumulative weight. Had he really fought in the Spanish Civil War? On whose side? Both, according to what Slamunster had heard at different times from different parties, because he might have been the prototype multiple agent. Could he have been in China too, as a correspondent? Well, it was physically possible, but . . . and on and on the stories went, until they implicated dozens in the university, on and on to, well, yes, the fabulous, stretching their tentacles into the land beyond, naturally and directly into Washington Square Park, involving even Angus Anguish, perhaps the ultimate unidentifiable.

But then the Great One-Eyed One had skillfully deflected Slamunster's thinking. He had mentioned Slamunster's father, Henry, The Judge, deceased within the year. Not that AP had not known that his father, the old crusty one, had dabbled in socialism in his youth in the 1930s. What intellectual in New York at the time had not, or so it had seemed? Or even that father Henry himself had been a member of the Party. Somehow Slamunster had always known that, or suspected it, and did not care, because he did not think of himself as political. Besides, he had assumed, not suspected, that his father had left the Party many years before. It certainly made sense if one had boldly and resolutely struck a career in the law and had risen to the highest court in New York State. And Slamunster had not asked.

But what was that? What was Whatever-he-was saying to him now? Why, what he was saying answered the question that Slamunster had been asking himself, which was, why me? His father had been quite helpful, he heard it said. A true American. Very helpful. The good patriot. And, surely, the loyal son would want to carry on the tradition established.

So his father had been an informer. The revelation more than deflected Slamunster's mind. It skewered it. He did not know exactly why, just that he would have to reflect upon it, as he knew he would, daily. And then he had remembered. The boxes and boxes of his father's papers that, following his father's death, he had put off sorting, discarding, filing, whatever he had to do with them. He would look at those, he now thought. That night he would look at them. And he more or less made the decision to do what he was going to do with the Fabulous One. He would play along. That was the thing. Play along.

Besides, Slamunster had told himself, he had confidence that he could invent names and characters to satisfy even the Fabulous One's appetite. And, anyway, Slamunster had liked the notion that he could be the catalyst for yet another fanciful purge of God-knows-what. It was a wonderfully ridiculous idea. Why, ironically, he could be charged with tampering with the minds of the people, which was a wonderful thought.

Despite the fact that Klara Blazek was considerably older than Slamunster, in public he had always called her Klara Blazek. It was a sign of respect and awe, of course, for it seemed that everyone who knew her at the university called her that. Not Klara. Not Blazek. But, Klara Blazek. Not Mrs. or Miss Blazek, and certainly not Professor Blazek, much as she might have deserved the title, but Klara Blazek. Indeed, perhaps for all the ages her name had been commonly spoken out loud, as if the entire university were an arena of law and she were a defendant that everyone daily and publicly accused of murder or treason, or whatever. Klara Blazek. Announced it at dawn. Klara Blazek. Echoed it through the hallways. Klara Blazek. Shouted it before the court of justice. Accused her of something dramatic, something horrible, something sinister. Klara Blazek. Klara Blazek. Klara Blazek.

Certainly most believed Klara Blazek capable of murder. Capable of anything, which, naturally, intrigued them. She both frightened and fascinated them, both repelled and lured them. Most things about her life must be unusual, they thought. Probably always had been. From birth. One wondered how she could have possibly survived to this moment. There was no other conclusion but that she had to know her way through the underground passageways of life. After all, speaking of corners, she was turning the corner of years. She was still beautiful, but, you could see it, she was growing older. Everyone knew it. On certain days when she wore certain clothes, was not there the hint of a paunch? And her hair was so compellingly black—it directed your attention—surely she dyed it. Regularly. Who knows, maybe she had even had her chin lifted, although that would have been out of character, smacking of a concession to a superior force, and she would probably have considered it an affront. But how could she, herself, be so superior, so haughty, so disdainful? How could she behave that way? One also wondered how many lovers she had possessed, and as night followed day in their mental recordings, how many abortions. Those were the caliber of thoughts people had about her. There was that air of intrigue. Yes, there were many within and without the university who were of the conviction with or without evidence that she was brilliant and dangerous, if odd, both in bed and out.

And now, the woman that had captivated Slamunster—he swore to himself that his recent and sudden assignation with her had nothing to do with her alleged Communist background—this woman, Klara Blazek, spoke. Truly, there was an imperious, proud, slightly contemptuous cut to her voice. In fact, everything about her manner coincidentally recalled the words of one of the characters in *The Idiot*, to wit, "'One can't help looking down on people, and they all insist on respect.'" It was Slamunster's favorite quotation from the novel, and he thought it had been coined for Klara Blazek. And she was paradoxical. She railed against the eagles and falcons of her society although she herself possessed all of those qualities. She was elegant, aloof, superior, confident, absolute, towering, killing. Oh, she was nothing if not paradoxical. She demanded responsible behavior of herself and others, expected everyone to perform the duties of good citizens, and yet she was not and did not want to be a member of the community. In fact, she was capable in a flash, unprovoked, of tearing apart the society. A severe outspoken critic, iconoclast, she loathed society, charging that all around were the ignorant, the crass, the irresponsible.

"Dostoevsky wrote with intensity," she began, speaking over the class rather than to it, "because he was a deranged, passionate, disturbed man. That is one of the reasons, just one, that he was a great writer. Everything we hold back distances us a little more. We have to express anger. Even hatred. Dostoevsky knew that. We may lose what we seek if we release our anger, express it, and certainly we risk when we hate. But if we are to touch, we have to touch with truth and fantasy. Anything less and we risk losing life. There is a sense of doom in Dostoevsky's writing, because he realized that doom was imminent, as well as immanent. One only had to wait and be aware. If individuals in this class expect to find in this novel a reflection of their familiar activities, reinforcement for their comforting view of life, as opposed to Dostoevsky's troubled vision, they will be disappointed. One wonders, however, why they should wish to read about their manner of existence, rather than escape from it."

Hilde Johnson appeared pale and uncomfortable, but she was not finished.

"The question," she started, "is whether Dostoevsky touches everything willy-nilly and, indeed, loses everything, loses a sense of discrimination, proportion, I mean, God . . ."

"Thank you," said Slamunster, interrupting her, "but we must move on. Hold your comments until the end, please."

It was not that Slamunster did not want to hear what Hilde Johnson had to say; in fact, he was already devising a plan to elicit more from her later, but he thought he had a pretty good idea where this discussion, this neo-confrontation was headed. Intellectually, the ideas had been registered, the boundaries set. No mystery left there. What was unpredictable and threatening, and thus of possible interest to him, was the clash of personalities. Ordinarily he relished such moments. However, at the moment he did not care to indulge himself. Not after what had happened, not just now. Oh, yes, he loved the mix of these situations, loved to let these delicious little confrontations get out of hand. But he had so many things on his mind, and it seemed to have happened all of a sudden. And, yes, he had to ascertain whether or not it was today or tomorrow that he was going to meet the young man, the . . . what? . . . the Son of the Godhead? And, thus, he could not become distracted any more than he already was. He had to devise plans, plans. And he was, he was going to find out just who God was. There would be fresh tales to tell the Fabulous Boy of Intrigue. And Klara . . .

At the end of the class, what Slamunster could not possibly have realized was that Klara Blazek, who at times saw him for the conceited, supercilious bastard that he in part was, and reluctantly had found herself attracted to him for it, was at that very moment looking directly at him and seeing a tall thin man, totally bald, with thick lenses that appeared to have pulled his eyes from their sockets. She often had visions like these. She knew that rather than the present moment, they spoke of the future or the past, but she never knew of which. That was not given to her to know. She did not know if she was seeing an ancestor or a decendant of Slamunster's or perhaps Slamunster himself, aged, whether the intrusion of the past, or young men old. It was both the power and the enigma of her seeing.

It was not so much that Slamunster was formidable, Klara thought, as he was dangerous, which is perhaps what she saw in her vision. He was dangerous because, ironically, he actually believed in the power of ideas, in the impact and mystery of the imagination. He actually thought he could make a difference. Thus he would act. And she had already seen that he looked to Klara to lead him to what he wanted. But that would come. Later. She turned away quickly and left the classroom. She had responsibilities.

Perhaps it was no coincidence, in turn, that just as Klara Blazek had been disintegrating Professor John Darnell Slamunster with her acidic vision, the Fabulous Man had been approaching Slamunster again like a dark cloud for yet another encounter unidentifiable. Out of the corner of his eye, Slamunster saw Klara Blazek leave. There was that tug, that pull. He knew it was getting stronger by the hour.

3

In Another Country

The bus was down from Montreal. Having crossed a border, it had left one country for another on the way to Boston. Timothy Brown King stepped upon the Vermont Transit bus and took his seat in the vacuum. He was already absent, vanished in another country, unmissed. The interior lights of the bus were switched off and the stark singular brightness of the few outer lights of White River Junction made it even darker within. Three other passengers, sitting apart from each other, were silently looking out the windows, surveying what remained. Timothy had seen all three when he had stepped upon the bus and, strangely, he could picture them vividly now without having to look at them again. They stood out as if on a beach under a bright moon. They ignored each other, each separate and alone, but Timothy had little doubt that each one had stolen a glance at him when he had stepped upon the bus, that each one had observed him when he was not looking, and that each one could picture him perfectly now without having to look again. Together then, they were presently thinking about him, wondering who and what he was, what his intentions were, where he was going. He did not believe they would ask. They did not personally care. There was little chance that they knew. But if they were a threat to him, they would simply act and they would act in concert. Silently, it appeared. Simple and quick. There would be no questions.

Young, he looked younger than he was. It was his blue eyes and fair skin. Not that you could see the color of his eyes in this cave of a bus. And he was thin, very thin. Had he eaten anything today? Not that he would remember, remember, but someone might be able to say, would be able to testify as to whether he was in any danger of wasting away forever, becoming a ghost. Perhaps he looked like a ghost, ethereal, late at night in black and white with Bela Lugosi. Because, what was he doing on a bus at this hour, on a bus bound for Boston, ultimate destination New York City? It was so very late and he felt so very young and lost, unborn. The other passengers could imagine, hope, fear, whatever their dispositions, their needs, their predilections. The possibilities were limitless. It was a free country. But ghosts and vampires are of the past, yet eternal. They do not exist in the present. They are of death and dreams and thwarted desires.

Truly, Timothy was an earthly comrade of the Japanese soldiers, stragglers displaced from World War II, some only now emerging, almost twenty years later, in the 1960s, from the tropical jungles, caves, and islands of the South Pacific, ragged, emaciated, diseased, vaporous and, worst of all, irrelevant having lost a part of the past, never to find a part in the present, forever emerging in the partisan violent future, wandering in front of tourists. Where are you John Wayne? The Japanese soldier was Timothy's comrade. Hello, comrade.

Surely, somebody on the bus would remember, would suddenly unfurl the rippling, waving flag, point a finger at Timothy, and shout for glory, for heroism, for all America to hear, shout "Remember the Commie Baby Cell!" Someone might believe, fervently believe that Timothy was the original suckling of the first native cell, the very firstborn specimen of the Communist baby cell that the Attorney General of New Hampshire had investigated in 1954 just a few miles from Dartmouth in Franklin, New Hampshire, erstwhile environs of Daniel Webster, for heaven's sake. Why, other cells of the baby brotherhood might have spread throughout the New Hampshire woods and across the Connecticut river, leaping the border to Vermont like a wildfire. Why, what was the Attorney General's name? Whyme? Whyman? Whymother? At any rate, Attorney General Whatever had failed in his official capacity by not immediately sending a posse up and down and across the river and into the trees to investigate, loosing a raiding party into the hills and valleys of New Hampshire and Vermont to snuff out the newly born. To have failed to investigate was totally unlike Attorney General Whathaveyou. And now it was probably too late.

In all other respects, old Attorney General Whatsoever had given new meaning to what it meant to be a perfervid Commie Hunter. That great old American boy had known that the U. S. of A. had to defeat Communism and not succumb to the moral laxity of coexistence. You could not be too careful. Why, as early as 1921 another great American, Calvin Coolidge of Vermont, had asked, "Are the Reds stalking Our College Women?" Coexistence was sick, cynical and decadent, a disease of the soul, possibly even effeminate, certainly not made in America.

No, America had to meet the Commies, face the Commies, and destroy them like cockroaches at every turn in life, as well as in the kitchen. It was a challenge that faced us from the classroom to the courtroom to the bathroom and we had to stand ready to risk life itself, not to mention death. Communism was everywhere like a green creeping slimy fungus that coated your teeth and gripped your liver because it was in our drinking water. It came from under the seas and the rugs of our homes, across the surface of the earth and the bridge of the nose, even from outer space like spiders and bodysnatchers. We had to look up and down our coasts and look away, and then look in our towns and temples and five-and-dimes, from our playgrounds and universities and our dumps to our churches and dentists' offices, look everywhere for those cowardly, hidden Commies. We the champions of freedom and breakfast cereal and industrial bowling leagues everywhere stood steadfast, fastforward, and in reverse against the slavery of the mind and the freedom of the body that the Commies practiced day and night. In contrast, and in glorious technicolor and fireworks, we as a Christian nation were unrelenting and uptight in our encouragement of genuine religious freedom, for example, freedom of crucifixion, while as a double bonus at half-price we fostered quality economic freedom with credit cards, down payments, layaways, and cash-ins, a higher and better and returnable standard of living than any other readymade spot on earth and, this above all, we owed the sum of it all to the profit motive, to the almighty consumer, to the great honor and dignity of mankind, whether consuming or consumed.

Except it was too late. By now that newly born suckling would have grown because it was said on the movie reel that time did not stand still, even that it marched onward rapidly, relentlessly. Yes, maybe Timothy was only the only Commie-simp-suckling of the 1950s, the only one that had escaped the predatory, incestuous clutches of the FBI, all grown up now, a big boy Red sneaking out under cover of night to do some mischief to the Grand Republic, having lain in wait for almost a decade, incubating, sleeping like Rip Van Winkle, hoping the rash of anti-Communism, the feverish fervor would dissipate. Hey, how could they already be saying that the 1950s were bland? Why, it was a time when the enrollment of FBI agents in the American Communist Party was at an all time high, without whom there probably would have been no American Communist Party. Glory be to J. Edgar Hoover. Hell, "Remember McCarthyism" would be undoubtedly enshrined one day as one of America's great rallying cries, like "Remember the Maine" or "I have but one life to give," which was the whole point. And what about Little Rock? Federal troops in a U.S. city? How could you beat that? Oh sure, you could argue that Little Rock was a foreign city or, for that matter, that America was a foreign country but, oh, those were the days, the real days.

Yes, remember the Commie baby cell, indeed, whether it was too late to mind or not. It was a rallying cry that had possibilities, never no mind even if the stock-in-trade of Daniel Webster's baby cell had been baseball bubblegum cards, the real thing, say hey a kiddies' baseball card collectors' group. Believe till the end of the day and the beginning of the night that the baseball bubblegum baby cell was probably a Commie front. You bet the Commies knew how to blow a bubble all right, having stolen the secret, probably even knew how to exploit Babe Ruth, by God. A perfect opportunity. What a wonderful perversion. An obvious ruse, a cover. The word also spread that volleyball was big among the Reds, so you did not play volleyball if you did not want to arouse suspicion. And you did not share anything with anybody, because the Commie Simp Pinkoes shared everything, probably including dirty underwear. You could never be too clean or too careful in America.

God and Political Science 101: who was a Commie, what was a Commie, why a Commie, God why? That was the proper declension. What was AMERICA? The question was asked in relation to the anti-Communist fervor of Americans, the glorious historical/hysterical anti-Communist fervor of the United States of Americanism, their brand of patriotism, patriotism in their lifetime, yes, the rallying cry was, indeed, "Patriotism in Our Lifetime," being that the true patriot was against anything that was not American, that is, you're either with me or agin me. Yes, young American boys were reared to fight Communism. That is what it meant to be an All-American, a true fighter for freedom, kill 'em before they get free. America was another chance or opportunity, a new life, a fresh start, a new beginning, all of which imply the illusion of getting away, of escape. From?

The rolling of the bus made Timothy look out the window. He was already in the lonely countryside, beyond all help. The bus had left its stall, passed through the narrow deserted silent streets of White River Junction, slipped into the dark silent winding roads of the Vermont hills. His journey was under way, probably the genesis of a new life, the new manifesto, the promise of forbidden discovery and exposure, and he had missed its beginning. Timing was the answer to everything.

Timothy looked to the outer blackness and saw dots of light across the clear nightsky, here and there in the countryside. Horrors and homes, he thought. If the missiles came tonight, would he see them, crisscrossing, bursting in air, exploding in colors like fireworks, red, white, and blue stars? An ending without a beginning. The first atomic bomb blast had turned the sky white and purple. Otherwise it might never have happened.

He picked up his journal from his lap and began to write what were apparently haphazard, isolated words. His pen wandered as if on a ouija board:

MISSILES RELIGION SEX COMMUNISM

Impotence AntiCommunism Hell Evil
(Any place for Heaven?)
Destruction Victims Scapegoats
God Mortality-Immortality-Morality
Death (Is salvation possible? There are certainly the damned,
but
can
there be the saved?)

"I stopped believing in the existence of God when I was thirteen," Timothy had said to the College psychiatrist, Doctor Herman Spreight. "Or maybe I was twelve. I am not certain, because I did not begin my journal until I was fourteen, so I have no way of checking. I can only remember. Is it treason to remember wrongly? But I think my last official act in the relationship was to pray to God to let me be high scorer in a crosstown, grammar school basketball game, Forest Hills versus Central Streams. Sounds like the deer against the antelope, doesn't it? Maybe I should take the Fifth or is it too late for that? Have I said too much already?

"But for a young, devout, intense, passionate believer, a true believer, to stop believing in God, ohhh, that was momentous, that was to stop believing in existence, to end awareness, consciousness. It was the clean slate, yes, but it was also more than just a blank slate, an empty slate. It was the slate obliterated. Clearly there was nothing, nothing. Everything was extinguished, not merely the Bible, but life, history, the world. You do understand, don't you? Were you a Christian? Some other mythology? Perhaps you were going to return as a dog, a cow, an asparagus. I assume that is past for you, as well. At least for your sake I hope it is past. I wish it were past for humanity. Oh, the loss, the trauma. Is it birth all over again? It is certainly death. Although, I do not know if the death of God is another, entirely separate, distinct death, a second death, despite the fact that it comes before the final death, the last death known to the living, or whether it is death compounded. You know what? Death should be capitalized. Always. I mean all five letters, D . . . E . . . A . . . T . . . H."

He paused in memory to trace the capital letters in the air with his finger.

"But how can we allow this to happen? The effect upon the human species is unimaginable. Have there been any studies? We should be told, you know. We should be told of our fate as soon as possible. Can you possibly know how I felt? Surely you do. Nothing, nothing, try to imagine nothing. And the immediate, desperate question was, could there be something? Something without God? Just that.

"Actually, at first I felt liberated. Mighty. Powerful. Not happy, but excited and in turmoil. Generated, no, driven by the force of a tornado. I could do anything, which is precisely what every human being desires, to be free to do anything. Lord almighty, indeed, I had everything to do. Oh, yes, I was afraid. Not because I was alone, absolutely alone in the universe. A sightless speck. The human being aware, but unseen and unseeing. No mirrors. Yes, that was intolerable, not to mention frightening, but that exhilarated me, too. It challenged me. I loved it. And I felt honest, pure. I was even proud of myself. I believe that was my first genuine experience of pride, my first encounter with hubris, the very first time I was swathed in that froth. I had been confronted, struck by a terrible truth, shocked, and I could stand and face it. Behold, an imagined beginning, solely my own beginning, and I had conceived it. Whoaaaaaah. Day one. It was all up to me. It would all start with me. No more angels, papas and mamas. I had total responsibility for whatever happened from that moment onward. At least as much responsibility as a single human being could claim. No, I do not mean to qualify, to hedge. I mean more. Secretly, I claimed more and I was certain of my claim. I was certain of it I wanted to claim it all, demand everything. I felt superior. I was a superior being. In defiance I had eaten of the tree and become the first of a new, superior species. I would establish my own standards. The tale was no one else's. It was entirely mine. I was the creator, and no one else.

"Those who believed, believed in God, or who believed in any god or supernatural power, they were ignorant and sore afraid, superstitious. Except, listen, I do not know whether people are superstitious because they are ignorant or because they are afraid, or whether it is a combination of both a chain reaction, a terrible moment that every individual faces that alters the horizon of the soul for eternity. Mostly I think it is fear. Fear is a devastating thing. It explodes in our midst and it reduces human beings. In retrospect, if you dare dwell on it, fear humiliates and cripples you. Fear is such an awesome, limiting, intimidating force. It makes people do horrible, ghastly things. I would not want to tell you some of the things I have done. And you will not laugh at me because I am only twenty-one. People recoil from fear. They wish to obliterate it. They do not want to remember. We have so much that we do not want to remember.

"Yes, human beings are ignorant because they are afraid. They cannot bear to face the truth, live with it. I sympathize with that. It is difficult. I understand that because, as I said, I was afraid, too. And, to tell the truth, the primary reason I was afraid was because I, because I, because I knew for the first time, really knew, that I was going to die. It was not God I bemoaned, I mean the loss of God. Actually, as long as it has nothing to do with the subject of death, I am glad there is not a god. Ha, sounds like a contract, doesn't it, setting conditions? But, I really am glad there is not a god. I would not want there to be one, a being, a force, a pressure, a powerful, all-knowing greater-than-me, Yahweh. I want to be God, my own god, to control myself, to tell my tale, do my own diddling. As I said, to be the ultimate creator, doodler. But think what it would be like if we had both God and death. An all-powerful God who let us die. I would fight that revolution—I would be the one to kill the king I should be struck dead for that, correct? Ha. Are you a Christian?

"No, what I ceased to believe in was the theology, the fantasy that promised immortality. *That* song. I bemoaned the loss of immortality or rather, as I said, I bemoaned my new knowledge of death. With death, *it*, my existence, would be over. No it. There would be nothing else. No awareness. Nothingness. So much for being all-powerful, for wanting to be God. Just as it began with me—ah, my great pride—so it would end with me. But think of the pressure that places on the human being, the pressure that places on me, on you. I am not a scientist, but do you think we could devise a formula to measure the pressure by the square inch? This is absolutely all we have, this right now, every moment now, now, now, now. This is all I have. I have to do it this moment or not do it, never again do it, it, it, it. Oh, yes, the sense that anything could happen, that anything is possible, that anything could happen when you turn the next corner, that you could walk directly into . . . what? But, oh, the torture, the paradoxical sense that nothing has happened, that perhaps nothing has ever happened or will ever happen and I must wait for it to happen. Come, come, speak up. This is the first and the last time, this is the original. Every moment is mine, mine to live. I have to do it or lose it, it, it, and I will lose anyway, be gone, gone, gone. It is too late. Oh, Christ."

There had been a lull, a moment of silence, but no tears, no grief. He was too young for that. Only dry, silent agony.

"I still think about death all of the time, which angers me. How puny I am if, the very first thing, I cannot conquer death. No, I have never gotten over that. Nobody does, you know. Everybody is concerned about death, although they do not all admit it or know it. Mostly, they do not talk about it, but death is responsible for many bad moods, bad smells. I know that. People blame it on what? Low levels of blood sugar? Poor hygiene? Hah, what do they know? An Alka Seltzer will not do it."

"But at some point, I do not know or remember when—what song is that, Rodgers and Hammerstein, Lerner and Loewe?—I became depressed about something else. And then lethargic. It was as if I had contacted a fatal disease. Cataracts of the spirit. Warts. I could not shake it. I could not get rid of it. No, they will not write a musical about it, no song there. I still have not conquered it. But for the longest time I did not know why I was depressed, why nothing seemed to matter, why I was so listless, why I simply did not care. And it was crazy: I who loved life, craved new experience, would attempt anything, hungered for everything, my intensity distanced me from others, placed me in a separate sphere where I could not touch or be touched, alone. And that was the point, I guess, because then I knew, now I know. What had not dawned on me was the people thing. I mean, I have come to the realization that all we have is other people. That is all there is. There is nothing for me beyond my earthly relationships with other people. It is the same for everyone, for you, for me. Do you understand that? All you have is me and I you. Do you truly understand? There is nothing transcendent. Odd, isn't it? That is what 'There is no God' really means. And that is what I cannot live with. 'There is no God' means there are only people. Ha, the original super patriots really got it right, didn't they? 'Of the people, by the people, for the people.' Ha, ha, ha, but the laugh is on them because they also really screwed it up originally,—'One nation under God.' The big lie and the big truth. No, that was not Madison Avenue hype. Was it? James Madison? No, they did not do that then. Did they? No, nah."

He had said it less as a statement of fact than as a question from one who was stunned by the realization.

"That is all there is?"

There was a hollow but dull ring, an emptiness, but no echo. It was a question that he had asked no one in particular or anyone at all, a question posed to the gods or spirits present, rather than directly to Dr. Herman Spreight, who, after all, was physically present, and it was then that the psychiatrist, rising from his seat, sighing, had dismissed Timothy with a nod of the head and a shake of the hand, albeit a limp grasp. Having failed to heal, the healer would care for this patient no longer.

Except, as he shook Timothy's hand, the words came thusly:

"You are a credit to yourself and to Dartmouth for having arrived at this position by yourself," Spreight had said, and Timothy was sent on his way.

It was a don quixote. Later, wandering across the campus green in the late afternoon, slightly dazed and disconnected, Timothy recalled that the psychiatrist had seemed tired.

"You cannot start walking if your shoes aren't tied, is that not correct, Grandfather?" he said to himself.

He had thought that all psychiatrists knew that. Was not that lesson one? What's up, Spreight? Yes, all we have is other people, he thought. He laughed.

"And I, Timothy Brown King, I, the Attorney General of New Hampshire, I would like to say, I would like to announce to all good Americans, to all of America, that all we have are people and they are all Commies. Reds. Communism is a disease, right? It leaves our boys impotent, unable to perform as true American patriots; it strikes masturbators everywhere. Yes, the disease of Communism has infected our great land, beloved America, America, the fruited land, is rotten. For the Pinkos, by the Pinkos, of the Pinkos. There are Reds everywhere, it is in our water, the rivers and streams are running Red everywhere. We the people will be dead red in the morning. You got that? Everybody's got it, got it, everybody's doing it, doing it, everybody is threatening, threatened. You understand me, boy? You better respect me, boy. I demand respect, you got that, boy?"

Timothy continued to stare out of the bus into the blackness. He wondered how quickly they were receding from the Canadian border, the border Grandfather Hezekiah had crisscrossed many years ago as the Boy Preacher of the Grand State of Maine, proudly we hail. His granddaddy the Boy Preacher. That was how the Boston newspapers had heralded Hezekiah, as the Boy Preacher of Maine. He was only sixteen, blessed, blessing boy. Yes, those had to have been wild, exciting times for Hezekiah. Hard times, of course, but wild and exciting, too, if for no other reason than that the young, wiry Hezekiah was a wild man, himself, possessed with the thought that all he had to do was march forward with his word of God. God's wild, wiry young man in a wild young wired land, was that it? He wanted to tell the people. In the great democracy, they had a right to know, for sure. But he wanted to be the one to tell them. Be the messenger. Bring the word.

In the process of crossing and recrossing that wild border, and eventually even that must have become tedious, despite all of the dangers, unnameable dangers, Grandfather Hezekiah had discovered his wife among the people, Beatrice, his woman, Timothy's grandmother, perhaps herself the world's most zealous, wild-wired, white-haired Christian. And he, Timothy, had always heard that she, Beatrice, was beautiful, if white-haired, and sexy, too—did they say that then? was a grandmother sexy?—and that she had gotten crazy with her crazy-with-religion man, they had done the religion rag, yeah, yeah, what an electrical connection that must have been. Truth, it was the truth, that is what they said about her, if they said anything at all, that she was Bible-crazed and sexy—they did say that then—and white-haired before her time, glowing like a burning cross for Jesus. That and nothing more which was odd, as well, that and nothing more.

But, was this the very same soft and gentle Grandmother Beatrice? His tiny beloved Grandmother Bea, the one who had looked down upon him from her fluffy white mountain of pillows and sheets? Yes, that one, Grammy Bea, that miniature, shrunken, yes, fluffy white-haired little creature that he had visited as a little boy. He had marched up alongside of her high hospital bed upon which she was perched, the top of which he could barely reach, barely reach her, and from which she could barely reach down to him or to anyone, waiting to be blown away like a feather, he had marched up and with trepidation he had touched her translucent, silky hand. There had been no electric shock.

"Timothyyyyy?"

As if to say, is that you down there, my little boy?

"Timothyyyyy?"

Yes, Grammy Bea had touched him. Her warmth had been incredible. Such a little thing with so much heat, she had sent love through that withered, twiggy little hand, through that miraculous touch. She was nothing more than a puff ball. What was she then, two hundred years old? Maybe seven hundred years of age. Except that at his age, one and one-half years, possibly barely two years old, he did not think in terms of aging, only that Grandmother Beatrice was, always had been, and always would be at least two hundred years old, forever ancient. It was not a process. It was a thing. Immutable. They were forever separate. But they were forever.

Sex-crazed? His beloved Grammy Bea? Well, if that were true, how could she possibly have tolerated her long later dim years? How did anyone? One did not want to die and one did not want to age, one did not want the lights to go out. And did not one want to live? Hideous.

Where, oh, where had Hezekiah found Beatrice, where, oh, where had he found his beloved Beatrice? Somewhere over the rainbow. No, somewhere near the border in the town of . . . what? Calais, Maine? Yes, it was a town near the Canadian border, and it was the hometown of Hezekiah's good friend, little Rabbit Hunter, that is, his short little friend who was indeed a hunter, particularly a rabbit hunter and famous to boot, known to all hunters everywhere far and wide, who was called Rabbit because of how he moved, hunted. For example, when he came to a fallen log in the woods he hopped over it. He did not step over it and he certainly did not walk around it. He hopped over it. That was undisputed. Hippety-hop. It was also the same town whose claim to fame was that once upon a time a farm family had been found in the loft of their barn, cut into small pieces and stuffed into a mattress. A whole family. A mother and a father and a grandmother and a grandfather and seven children. Like cut-outs from a coloring book. Only they were cut-up. The entire extended family. No one ever knew why, how, or what. At least they were not telling. But was that also the town of Calais? It could not have been frigid Norway, Maine, or forbidden China, Maine, or foreboding Poland, Maine. True, they were all well within the borders of The Grand State of Maine, deep within, but they were too far south of the Canadian border.

Except you could not really say that it was the same border now as it was then, not the same border when you reminded yourself of the fact that Grandfather Hezekiah had first crisscrossed, had first danced his silhouette across the horizon when he was sixteen years old, which would have put his original crossings somewhere in the nineteenth century. They would not have made a movie about it. No barnstorming Dan Daily and Betty Grable. There was not even an extant map, was there? Would they have even bothered to survey that territory? For what, religious spirits? Was this before geiger counters?

No, not the same century and not the same border, oh no, absolutely not, not when he was not even a grandfather, just Hezekiah Brown King, HBK, the preaching baby boy. He had no degree. He had a Bible, but he was not ordained. Nothing was in those days. He had preached in settlements that neither knew nor could they afford an ordinary preacher. So you could say that those settlements had gotten their money's worth because Hezekiah was certainly not ordinary. Tall and thin, fair skinned and blue eyes, wavy, curling brown hair, curling around large ears, tufts of hair protruding. A splendid dresser of immense, varied . . . proportions . . . ambitions. Black tails, white shirts frothing at the chest, polished mirrored black shoes, gray striped spats. A broad, playful, victorious smile. A moustache? A beard? A charmer. There were pictures of him by himself, holding the Bible, holding the Word. He looked like Timothy. Or was it the other way around? And there were other stories told, stories about Hezekiah, stories that were at one and the same time Timothy's stories because they were humanity's stories, and then again they were not Timothy's stories just because they were humanity's stories. Timothy was beginning to appreciate that more and more. An understanding, a crucial understanding, an understanding that he was more than but less than those stories.

Because it was as if Hezekiah had just fallen from the sky, come tumbling down. Timothy had thought that before. That that was the very beginning.

Hezekiah and the angels had fallen from the sky and, in a sense, Timothy's world had begun. The emergence of the I. His show had opened. The lights had blinked, the horns had flared, and Hezekiah had introduced the first act. The start-up. Balloons, tinsel, player piano, let it roll. Even God had to do a first draft, Genesis 1:2. Yes, the old one, two.

Hezekiah was Timothy's grandfather, hurray!

Hezekiah was Timothy's grandfather, hurray!

Hezekiah was Timothy's

grandfather, hurrah! hur/is Timothy

coming?

coming out to play?

Honest to God, really and truly, Hezekiah was Timothy's grandfather. Or that is what he became anyway. Why would anyone lie about it? He was headed that way. It was foreordained, was it not? It was in his genes. Or was it the other way around? You could not do it in both directions? For all Timothy knew, no one single person in any of those towns, outposts, had asked Hezekiah to come or had known he was coming. No degree, no background, no word, no telephone, no printed invitation, and no welcoming blaring loudspeaker. The boy preacher had just arrived with his message. No conspiracy there. He had been called by his God, if not by anyone else. Except maybe Beatrice. Come here, boy.

Maybe like me right now, Timothy thought, except, who had called him on the telephone? Not God. He did not want to talk to any god anyway. He wanted to be god. Could he call, call upon himself, call collect, dial direct? Could you do that? Or did you have to go through an intermediary, depend upon others? And, if that, whom could you trust? What were the rules? Whose rules? And what were the consequences if you broke them, violated the spirit? But, of course, he had been called, on the telephone. He knew that. He should not forget that. He had felt that it had been a voice he should have known. The voice had intimated that. He had just had that feeling. But that was ridiculous. Was it a call from the dead? From his ancestors? Why should he think that? A call from spirits, ghosts. Yes, that was it. A conspiracy of spirits. He liked that. A call from the dead meant that there might be a flicker of life. A beautiful paradox. "I am," the voice had said before tailing off, before hanging up.

True, just as Hezekiah was not the end of the story, neither was he the beginning, for Hezekiah had also had a father and a mother. A miracle, the species was a miracle. Keep that line going, oh, keep it going and do not worry about the direction, because, contrary to accepted advice, it is not a question of whether or not you should go backward or forward. You go in any direction you can. Just move. You do not quibble with opportunity. Just keep moving. That is the ultimate value. If you can do it, do it. Move it. Even sideways.

Patrick Brown King, Timothy's great-grandfather. Anne Harmon King, Timothy's great-grandmother. Maybe they had put on a good show as well, give them credit, except that it was difficult to give credit when the details were scanty, if intriguing. What Timothy liked best and what made the "Great One"—as he was known in the family—a hero for him, or the "Great-grand One," as Timothy liked calling Patrick, was that he had deserted in the Civil War, probably gone fishing. A subversive, you might say. The blue-ribbon special was that Patrick had been a crack rifleman, yes, the Great-grand One had been a sharpshooter, decorated on several occasions—they do keep records on those things—but he had said take this skill I do not want it and you cannot have it and he had simply walked away, probably with his fishing pole. Patrick had wandered to some obscure spot, apparently, probably a fishing hole, where he had been found again, presumably, although no one in the extended family seemed to know. What was known was that Hezekiah had come afterward, so Patrick must have been found, unless Hezekiah actually had dropped from the sky. Which made him what? A true spirit? A true hero? A true American? He could fly?

Beyond that, all Timothy had ever heard about Patrick was that he liked to drink too much. Not just that he liked to drink. Or that he drank too much. But that he liked to drink too much. That was what the extended family had reported. And that was the entirety of Great-grandfather Patrick's history as far as Timothy knew. Anne was entirely without history, without a word. According to the extended family. Oh, there was a black-and-white photograph taken in 1871 in Newfoundland of Patrick and Anne together. The two of them were sitting on a wicker settee placed against what must have been a false background, a detail of perhaps great significance, sham because behind them on the left was a large cactus, probably the biggest in Newfoundland, and on the right perched on a hill was a small house with a severely pitched roof. You had to wonder who lived in that house. Curiously, the grass beneath their feet looked real.

The presumption was that it was their wedding day. Actually, Anne, dressed in white, looked like a spirit, herself, a ghost, a spectre. It did not matter that it was her white veil, presumably, that made her features pale, almost indistinguishable. Timothy had looked at that photograph on countless occasions before he had realized that she was wearing a veil, covered with her own shammy. But the first impression remains. He had thought of her as a ghost because she had a pale face. His very own Great-grandmother Paleface. He had always thought of her as having a pale face, but why did he also always think of her as "Annie"? A diminutive? How could a ghost be called Annie? Ghosts were not diminutives, no sir, no ma'am.

Patrick was dressed in black, at least, yes, the black of black and white (and there it was again), and he looked quite real. A chain, probably gold, was attached to his vest. There was a flower in his lapel and a small pin above it. A tall bowler was aslant, tipped back on his head. Beneath the rim of his hat a charming wave of hair was visible. And he looked bemused or disgruntled. That was the problem. One could not be certain which it was, and the answer to that riddle, again, was perhaps crucial. He was almost smirking. Was it amusement or skepticism? Cynicism? Had someone just told him a joke? Did he think the photographer was inept, comical, a regular Charlie Chaplin, maybe even a teetotaler? Or was he thinking to himself, "Oh boy, have I got all the answers," or "Why bother when I already know what's in store?"

At any rate, he looked alive. He was dead, but he looked alive. And he looked like Timothy as well. Or vice versa. People said that, and Timothy liked hearing it. And, actually, there was still more, more known. Or more said. By the extended family. Patrick had been a Catholic, a fact the extended family of Protestant fundamental zealots was reluctant to acknowledge. Better to have been a drunkard, if that was what he was, better a drunkard than a Catholic, as if that were one of life's choices—"Do you solemnly swear to be a drunkard and not a Catholic so long as you may drink?" But the truth was, he had come from Ireland in the first half of the nineteenth century, from a long line of Catholics, presumably, straight to—to where? To Maine and then to Newfoundland? Had he made it by himself to Maine and then gone back to Newfoundland to have his picture taken? Was not that the reverse order of the way it was supposed to be? Unpatriotic even? You were supposed to, sworn to even, go from Newfoundland, from another country, to Maine, like the real thing, like a genuine, patriotic immigrant, not to Maine and then back to Newfoundland. Way to subvert American history, Patrick, baby. Almost like a traitor to your country. You cannot even blame it on the Revolution, although you never could have been a Tory anyway. But then Patrick had come back to Maine again. All by himself. Probably running guns or something, no doubt having received the aid of some secret, foreign agency. Was that a precedent?

Who knew. There was a lot in life that you had to take on faith, take somebody's word for it, the word of some source. In a way, that was all there was to human existence. That was what was meant by human history. You could take it on faith that somebody had been here, but not that they had gone anywhere afterward. That is the way Timothy had thought it was, that you could take the past on faith but not the future. You could know that "Kilroy Was Here," but no one had ever said anything about Kilroy's present or future whereabouts. Until now. And, by the way, there was no liquor bottle visible in the picture of Patrick and Anne, no bottle whatsoever, full or empty, unless it was hidden, aha, stashed behind the cactus. People did things like that. Or perhaps the photographer had asked, maybe insisted that it be removed, the photographer being a good, aha, teetotaler.

But after the fact—after the faith?—there was a son, Hezekiah, as in "and Patrick and Anne begat Hezekiah, and Hezekiah crossed the border," crossed the border in one direction or another, never mind which. And Hezekiah had left the Catholic Church, the one true faith, had left to become the Boy Preacher of Maine, simply formed his own Protestant fundamentalist denomination and called it The Onward Christian Church of the Grand State of Maine. His church, his army, with the possibility that he might have acknowledged that it was also God's church, God's army. God's franchise, perhaps? (It was not recorded if Patrick approved or if he knew about it, or cared, or where he was even, if he was still alive and kicking, or drinking. And a few other details.) Somewhere along the way, Beatrice, not yet a grandmother-in-a-bed, from somewhere in Calais or Poland or China or somewhere else, Beatrice had marched out from her church choir, all ablaze in passion, probably singing

"When first to this polluted earth
The holy Saviour came,
So humble was his place of birth,
Few cared to know his name,"

and marched alongside of Hezekiah, which made for a straighter and narrower journey, and then some. (Was that why Timothy thought of her as Beatrice not Bea, other than the fact that she was certainly not a diminutive? For example, you would not call her cute, cute as a button, say, but neither would/could you have called Grandmother Bea-on-a-bed cute as a button, say.)

Whatever, Hezekiah and Beatrice had marched from outlying posts to campgrounds in the woods to summer prayer meetings by the fresh waters to county revivals in God's country and, as in a fable, or so it seemed to Timothy, a following had grown, swelled to become the army of The Onward Christian Church complete with chorus and band and music sheets until, decades later, Hezekiah had gone on the radio in Portland, Maine, had gone from being the Boy Preacher of northern Maine, leading his Onward Christian soldiers on the march, to become the "King Preacher" in Portland, to being the "first voice of Christ of the Onward Christian Church ON THE AIR."

The radio. Yes, the radio, that connection. But then, in the end, his radio station was raided, of all things, by his own Onward Christian soldiers, his very own followers, breed, horde, kind of an original uprising. A house divided. A doctrinal dispute. Why, what were they, some early breed of revisionists eating, devouring their very own? What kind of species was it that devoured its own? They must have come swarming by night like secret marauding warriors of the Prince of Darkness, chanting,

"He preaches that we are a race of murderers.
When we murdered Christ, he said God ceased to exist for us.
We are condemned to kill ourselves, he said. It is our destiny.
It is the Curse of Hezekiah.
It is the Curse of Hezekiah."

What do you do with a crazy senile old minister who will not stop preaching? And who still has followers? You overthrow him. But what if he is your grandfather?

crazy
radio
sex
crazy on the radio
Jesus keeps getting in the way. Not to mention God. And death.

And that is what happens to you, because for most of his life Hezekiah's craziness had been enthralling, spellbinding, and protective, but then something snapped, the trance, the spell, was broken. The magic lies mostly in your own attitude and somewhat in the eyes of the beholder, but it does not take much to change things. Something slips, some small thing changes and it all changes, it all comes tumbling, falling down. It is the Curse of Hezekiah.

Timothy felt he had missed something. He looked out the window of the bus and saw nothing. There was a heavy fog, a mist, almost like snow, but it was hanging, not falling, it was suspended. Spirit weather. It remained dark within the bus. The air was smoky, close, yet he could feel a draft down his right hip and leg, as if a door had been opened. Why was he pressed against the side of the bus? And then he noticed that the bus was full of people. There must have been many stops along the way that Timothy had missed. On Timothy's left, in the seat beside him, a dark, black-and-white shape slumped, huddled. She was sleeping. The nun was asleep.

This was incredible. Timothy was both excited and alarmed. Although he had barely missed by a century becoming a Catholic, himself, everything about Catholicism had always fascinated him since as a child he had first encountered the black-and-white silhouettes of priests and nuns on the streets. Actually, he had always thought that nuns were much more fascinating than priests. It was true. In fact, as a boy he had often gone out of his way to cross streets or to reverse his direction in order to pass closely by nuns, do not touch, oh, no, pass closely by, even follow them in total anticipatory fear, perhaps in the wonderment of horror, but do not ever touch them. He found that exhilarating, rousing. Nuns excited him. He liked being near them in their black habits and, in reverie, he had imagined them flying everywhere like huge, black birds, having been released from on high in the rafters of Catholic churches.

The first time he had been inside a Catholic church was when he had gone to the funeral of the father of his friend Bobby Bragdon. The father had worked at the sulphur-stinking paper mill in Westbrook, Maine, for forty years, although he was only in his fifties. Timothy had felt obliged to attend, obliged to Bobby. It was at St. Mark's. There had been incense, not sulphur.

There had been chanting, solemn tones and rhythms. His eyes had followed the movement of the black robes and, yes, he had listened closely, although he had understood nothing of the spoken word, nothing of the Latin. It was not exactly the Pledge of Allegiance, but he had listened closely because he had thought it was better. Those simple, distant faces that stared from the walls. The gold and black and purple and silver. When everyone had kneeled, he had kneeled, willingly. Not that he had understood why but, he thought, there should be incense in the air everywhere, twenty-four hours a day, and instead of streetlights and lampposts, bleeding Christs crowned with thorns, silent, serene saints lining the streets. Much better. A madonna in every doorway. Bells ringing. It might not be truth, but it was something to believe. Instead of spies, you had saints.

The nun shifted in her sleep, moved her legs. Her right leg was now pushing against Timothy's left leg. Uncomfortable and uneasy, Timothy tried moving closer against the side of the bus, but he was already tightly against it. There was no escape.

There was another gap somewhere. True, John Brown King, Timothy's father, JBK, the one who had appeared alongside Kennedy, shadowed him, the very same one, who had emerged somewhere along the line, who history had it was definitely a part of that line, who had been begat by Hezekiah and Beatrice, which meant that he was of very interesting, if speculative, stock, John Brown King had considered becoming a preacher, himself, also at age sixteen. (Was that a coincidence or was that a tradition? If it was a tradition, Timothy was not certain if he regretted or was thankful that he had stopped it, or at the very least had interrupted it. It was the end of something, but could he imagine being a man of the cloth? Oh, yes, he could have played the role, like a zealot. He could particularly imagine with relish being a Catholic priest, especially a Jesuit. (Apologies to Hezekiah, but he would have understood the temptation.) But Timothy was damned if he knew why, and probably damned if he did not. Oh, maybe he had an inkling, maybe there was something dark and definitive there, something dressed in black, better scarlet, a belief in spirits, some thrilling adventure of the soul, decisive, foreboding, explosive, oh, Hezekiah.)

That is, the idea—or had he said it was a vision, a visitation?—of becoming a preacher, a man of God, had occurred to John Brown King when he was sixteen. Not that he would literally enter the Onward Christian ministry at that age. Times had changed. Primal urges were processed in the twentieth century. Seminary would have been necessary. Even the Onward Christians had their own seminary by now. But had John Brown King told Timothy Brown King that the idea, the motivating need, had been to find a spiritual father? Was that in the tradition? Was it one of the few things he had ever told Timothy? Had it been a sign of weakness? Fear? Did that mean he was a Christian? Was? Maybe he would have even reached back to Patrick and become a Catholic priest.

perhaps a Jesuit? Had he said that, told Timothy? Who knew? Who could tell the tale?

Because it was true that the Reverend Hezekiah Brown King was frequently on the road traveling throughout Maine, and after a while to Boston, which meant that, at best, Hezekiah, the father, was present for the most part only in spirit, as it were. Even though he had his own Onward Christian Church in Portland, Maine, his own stationary church of the Father, so to speak, the Reverend Hezekiah was constantly on the move, a moving spirit, preaching, while Beatrice remained at home with son John. And there was talk, there were stories told even by distant relatives, stories about how the Reverend King had a traveling secretary who was more to him than a secretary. That was how she was referred to as *the* traveling secretary. After all, Hezekiah was a charming man, it had been said, inferred. Everybody acknowledged it, nodded knowingly if not approvingly, particularly the women; the men winked.

But everybody except Timothy seemed to know everything there was to know about Hezekiah and *the* traveling secretary. They had that air about them. As a child, Timothy remembered wondering when the time would come when he would be able to become one of the initiated, when he would know everything there was to know about what everybody wanted to know about, and who would do that telling. He had known that it was somehow connected with becoming an adult, not with maturity, but with the simple accumulation of years. And later, he had come to recognize that it was connected as well with idealism, or disconnected, that is. That is, as long as you remained idealistic they would not tell you anything, no matter how old you became. Angels, for example, could not be trusted. (From idealism there were offshoots to purity and innocence and saintliness and a few other outposts.) But he did know that Grandfather Hezekiah, like Great-grandfather Patrick, liked to drink too much. Where that left a beautiful and sexy and white-haired Grandmother was not clear. Where had that left his mother, Helen Eaton King? And why the desire to even ask the question?

But just like that, or so it seemed, son John had entered Dartmouth instead of the ministry. He had been an outstanding student at Deering High School in Portland, Maine, and a leader of every school activity you could imagine, with the result that he had come under the influence of the school authorities, who had pointed him in a secular direction. It was also said that he had come under the influence of the most striking, the prettiest, the most determined female force in school and in town. It was rumoured. Whether or not it was true or traditional that she, his English teacher, had also become the most pregnant in town before son John had left for Dartmouth had been a subject for inquiry or rather speculation even in later years, kind of a legend to be determined or denied. Or was it that *the* female force had come to town and carried son John off, kind of in emulation of Hezekiah and Beatrice, only in reverse, she had carried him off perhaps in revenge. Not that generations revenge generations, that is, living generations, but in the world of ghosts knowledge is pervasive, knowledge is just there.

Meanwhile, Hezekiah, at age five hundred and eighty, had gotten his law degree at night at Northeastern University in Boston, just like that, the first degree he had ever received, and he had returned to northern Maine to take up the cause of abandoned mothers and children, that is, those who had been abandoned by fathers. Quite a new crusade, an ironic crusade. In turn, son John had continued as a brilliant student at Dartmouth, had been captain of crew, president of the Dartmouth Forensic Union, Phi Beta Kappa, and had entered Harvard Law School where he had made the *Law Review*. Quite a bright societal star. Glitter. Blinding. A potential American success story. Maybe even a hero. Quite breathless. Mid-century, twentieth-century madness, from sea to shining sea, gathering all of the wheat of the fruited plain on the way except, ironically, it could be said that, like father like son, John, after all, had indeed come full circle, had followed in the steps of Hezekiah. He had become a lawyer. So what if he, John, had practically gotten there first, if Hezekiah had in fact almost followed him. You do what you can. You go in the direction you can go. Have to go. Move it.

And apparently there was a tradition of keeping pace, of following footsteps, and thus a tradition to be threatened. In the short history of Timothy Brown King, Timothy had already glittered at Deering High School, entered Dartmouth, joined crew and the Dartmouth Forensic Union, and looked to a career in law. But without enthusiasm. And in the last few days, just like that, he had totally abandoned that idea, abandoned the tradition or it had abandoned him, and if he had not gone fishing he had certainly gone adrift. Actually, he had abandoned crew during his freshman year and he had stopped attending classes in the middle of his freshman year, managing somehow to appear only for examinations in subsequent years, sometimes only for final examinations, once or twice not even that, having recognized the futility of empty gestures. The phantom student, of near legendary proportions in his own time, a new spirit of the age, having presently abandoned both the Dartmouth Forensic Union and Dartmouth and, willy-nilly, a career in law, he, in effect, had done more than abandon the tradition. He had effaced history. You could say that. Had he abandoned the human race? Could you do that? Was it possible? Short of suicide? And if there was nothing else, if all one possessed was other people and he, Timothy, had abandoned the human race, what then? Not Kilroy was here but, was King here?

NO MYTHOLOGY?
Have to create one
should have
probably
what must have happened

he supposed that
what probably happened . . . Right?
you had to think that . . . did you not?

(no you did not)
(yes you did)
There is/was a mythology—but who can know it?

you look to the Grandfather and maybe even to the Great-grandfather, except that does not work because you have to look through the Father the fffather is a blinding page and therefore is a blank page, one-dimensional,
non-romantic, not really larger than life, no no no matter what you think,
is he not? You cannot just skip it, forget it, because if you do you cannot get there from here . . .

"If I kind of nudge her," Timothy thought, which he considered to be a risk and a bit risqué.

He did, he actually raised himself off his seat, and coughed for emphasis. Sure enough, the sleeping nun moved, but instead of moving away, she pressed closer. The nun's right hand now rested between them, that is, between Herself and himself, half on Timothy's thigh and, from what he could tell, half on Her own. It was time, perhaps, to become bolder, to jostle Her. Timothy raised himself again and with great vigor coughed more loudly. This time nothing happened. Hell, how did you tell a nun to get Her hand off your thigh?

He had last seen Hezekiah more or less in the flesh at The Onward Christian Church Nursing Home. Hezekiah himself had, years before, before the raid, raised the funds for the construction of the Home—had he preached for them?—and he had been taken there for his last living hours. He had lost his radio station but he had also built his own mausoleum. No raids planned and no raids occurred. Timothy's father and mother, John and Helen, had taken Timothy there that day. JBK had just returned home to Portland, having cut short a business trip to some industrial firm in Boston. (Did Timothy remember that it was electronic parts? Submarines? Firing pins? Or was he just imagining it? Was it this spy stuff?)

God. It was not so much the nun's leg that concerned Timothy now as it was the nun's hand. Had it not moved entirely onto Timothy's leg, or was he imagining it, fantasying? Timothy had not felt it move, but at the moment the hand was like a weight on his thigh. Was that his mind, his imagination, or was it really Her hand, his thigh? He would have to wake the nun. The hand was very heavy. Warm. Pressing. He would swear before anybody's god that it were so. But who would believe?

His parents had gotten Timothy out of his class at Deering High School and had taken him directly to the Onward Christian Church Nursing Home. Timothy had never liked the place. It was full of old women and old men, never to leave and left to die, who stared from the wallpaper and the woodwork and, of all things, the red carpeting. Some stood motionless and silent in the hallways like sentinels in hell's halfway house. Most of them were parishioners, long-time recruits, Onward Christian Soldiers at the end of the march, after the battle.

There were two that Timothy remembered especially, Nora Liddon and George Peabody. He remembered Old Lady Liddon in her faded, blue, flower-print dress that clung to her skin like blue moss, fastened at the throat by a brown cameo that Timothy thought had long ago pinned the dress to her skin. Withered skin, crinkled, old and loose. And the bun of hair at the back of her head, screwed tightly as if it knotted her skin to her body. She had a habit of moving just enough to get in Timothy's way, as if she needed to touch him, to pinch his cheek, which hurt—that told him she was alive.

"You should take the Reverend Hezekiah's place," she would say, pinching his cheek. "He needs you to take his place because young Johnny did not. That's a good body."

And again she would pinch his cheek.

It had always struck Timothy as odd to hear his father referred to as "Johnny." Too personal for JBK. And, more than that, his father was not a "Johnny," was he? Or was he? Well?

George Peabody accompanied Nora. Always a few steps in the rear. It was as if George could not quite keep up with Nora, which was a kind of miracle all to itself. George, deaf and bent over, would say nothing. What he did do was nod his head quickly whenever Nora said,

"That's a good body."

If George was deaf, and Timothy had to believe that, what was he nodding at and why always at the same time, why always at "That's a good body"?

Timothy considered that the nodding was a disease, a nervous reaction, a reflex, the last measured flicker of life in the asylum of the insane and the dead.

And then he had noticed Nora clutching George's hand, and he had realized that whenever she had spoken, her words had passed however faintly through the connection of the hands, the words had passed, however weakly they had passed. Praise be to God . . . the fruit of thy womb Jesus . . .

It had bothered him greatly that he had been unable to feel sympathy for those old people. There had been a great deal of guilt. Or was it that he had sympathized too much, that he could not bear the reality of their aging, simply that their bodies were nearing the end of a long process of decay? He knew, of course, that it was a journey that he was on as well, a journey that after all was not so long, and he did not like being around them. There was nothing of the spirit about them. No incense.

God. He was embarrassed. He had an erection and if the hand did not stop moving, it would bump into it, and god, if the nun woke up then how would he explain it to Her, she being a nun? He swore the hand had moved. It was not where it had been before, which could only mean one thing: it had moved. But he could not feel it move. Only afterward. He knew it had moved. And he knew he had an erection. That made him feel responsible.

And the woman of the night who was supposed to meet him on the bus in Boston? He, Timothy, had been asked to come alone. Well . . . she would sit beside him if there was an empty seat. Well . . . no, he was not alone, and the seat was not by any means empty. Which bus? Was this by chance the woman he was supposed to meet, an agent in disguise, in the disguise of a nun, a black-and-white nun? Whose agent, The Onward Christian Church's or the FBI's? How could you tell? No, not, never.

What he hated, what had kicked him in the head was seeing bloody old Grandfather Hezekiah's dead body. No, not the body. It was his face, a face Timothy had loved. Oh, he had loved the body. He had loved the spirit. He had loved the man. And the decision had been made by Timothy's father, John Brown King, to cremate the body of Hezekiah Brown King. Had it been done in anger? Timothy had protested. He had not liked it at all, and he had shouted his protest, but, in truth, he was allowed no say. There was nothing in the by-laws of The Onward Christian Church that forbade the cremation, and apparently Hezekiah had never indicated a preference. But the act bothered Timothy. He was not certain why. A primitive reaction? That you should not destroy the body, burn it, remove it from the face of the earth? That it would be helping death? No, worse. It would be as if Hezekiah had never lived. Not that Timothy liked the idea of being eaten, eaten dead, eaten by worms and maggots. But what about the spirit? What about the idea, the image of the body in the mind yet extant, yet alive? Would you not risk the destruction of that? And should that never be allowed to happen? Was not that a fragile, precious thing? After all, the person had been here on this dear, good earth, blessed Grandfather Hezekiah had been here amongst us, yes. He had been seen and heard, a spirit hero. Never.

Before the cremation, they had witnessed the rigid body one last time on a slab. Timothy had gazed upon Hezekiah's face. Closed eyes, were they yet blue? Prominent ears, yes, arching nose, open mouth that did not speak. Fierce, raging, horrific protest. Timothy had been transfixed. He had not been able to walk away, to stop staring at that face. It was Hezekiah's death mask. Timothy's body had shaken. He had felt compelled to leave before he collapsed, and yet he had not been able to bring himself to leave. He could not leave. At that moment his body had not been his own. Bereft of will, he had no choice but to stand there and look at that face, that death mask, look, stare, simultaneously feeling that he had to leave before he, himself, died of grief and anguish, knowing that he could not say goodby, never say goodby before he collapsed, never. Finally, his father, JBK, his very own father, his father had put his arm around him and led him away. The most intimate moment Timothy and his father had ever shared together, he and JBK. Both of their bodies shaking. Because of Hezekiah's death mask. Must have been.

Talk about no longer believing in God: was that the same thing as talking about D . . . E . . . A . . . T . . . H? Looking at Grandfather's face, looking at death. Why no meaning? Crazy Hezekiah. Not so crazy. Beloved Hezekiah. You pay a huge price if you are different. Or you can. You must not only be strong, but independent, invulnerable. Otherwise, they will crush you. Maybe you need to be immortal. There had been no death masks with his father and mother. Not a chance. Why call upon the dead or why believe the spirits of the dead to have powers? Why believe the spirits of the dead to be evil? Immortality and loss and a perversion of the natural order. Sell the soul for immortality. Sell the soul for immortality. He would do it.

Surely the nun would get off in Boston and surely the woman would be able to sit beside him on the bus bound for New York City. Surely. He had to do something. Timothy knew that. Surely. He opened his eyes, looked out the window, and, in the distance, he could see the shining lights of Boston. Behold Boston, Grandfather. What pretense could there be now, when he felt intense pressure and he was aroused. He had an erection, he could feel the heat, he could feel the warm moisture inside his pants, the beginning seepage. If he did not do something soon, there would be an eruption, an explosion that he would never ever forget. On fire, Timothy reached down and gently removed the nun's hand.

Monday, P.M., October 22, 1962–Tuesday A.M., October 23, 1962

4

The Red Menace

["I have been told that JBK wanted you to have these letters after he was dead, if the occasion never presented itself while he was still alive, or if he became unavailable. I send them to you now for my own reasons. I think you might as well have them now. Be careful."]

Dear Timothy,

My son, I do not know when you will receive this. I do not know if I will be alive. I do not know what the condition of the earth will be when you read what little I am able to say. Human beings are capable of unimaginable atrocities, even of mass suicide. Although you and I are not very far apart in age—less than thirty years—the state of our civilization as I knew it when I was your age may be radically different by the time you do read this. It is odd. There was a time—some would say, long long ago in my youth—when "radically different" would have suggested something very specific to me, something that would have answered my youthful dreams and would have appealed to what was then my fervently idealistic innocence. A new man. A new world.

You see, ironically, I have always secretly detested the idea that I, like others, might be space-bound, culture-bound, that I could not transcend my historical condition, that I could not escape the banality of what has been called, irritatingly, the human condition. It hurts me to say this, admit it, yes, confess, but I know now what an amusing triviality that notion is. I am as limited and, thus, as perverse as everyone else. Oh, but I rage against the idea——

I see that I am overwhelmed by my task. I lose control. No, the truth is, as much as I would like this to be the fullest possible revelation of my deepest dreams and desires, of the outer reaches of my imagination (the latter, I feel, is our only solace) it, alas, can be but a short inadequate letter to you.

I am pressed by a sense of urgency that may be false, but I cannot take the risk. You may hear certain things about me that you will have difficulty understanding. Whatever you learn or think, I want you to know at least a modicum of the truth, if even that is possible. I want you to hear it from me.

So let me get right to it. When I was at Dartmouth in the 1930s I joined the Communist Party. Does that shock you? Ah, how quickly I expose myself. I ask a simple question because I desperately need a simple answer. And yet, what has happened to my life is a mystery to me, how can I expect other than bewilderment from you? No, there are neither simple questions nor simple answers. And you, you are a young man, still fresh to life, but I know that you are complicated beyond your years. How odd it is, how odd! We are primitive creatures possessed by extraordinary fantasies. We know we must die and we forever dream of immortality. How strange. How hellish. We are born with great ambitions and, alas, nothing attainable worthy of our grand visions. We desire total control and we are powerless. Ah, but I shall never lose hope.

I still believe that my becoming a Communist represented an advancement in my personal enlightenment. It was a magnificent moment, you know. Revolution. To actually shape the world. Change it. An opportunity to put a great socialist ideal into action. Not that it was unusual to become a Communist during those years of what you know of as the Great Depression. No, we were everywhere. Although our numbers were not what we dreamed of, they were much greater than they would become, greater then than they are at this very moment, greater than has ever been told.

But Maine, and unless I am mistaken you have already discovered this Maine can be a backwater of the soul, and simply to *become* in that nether region constitutes an heroic act. (I am, of course, talking about indigenous souls, not visiting royalty.) To be born and grow up in Maine can instill in one the sense that the earth is simply there and that to do anything is to commit a revolution. Yes, lethargy is awful.

And yet, we Kings have a history of moving on. You know that, don't you? My grandfather, Patrick—your great-grandfather, of course—he deserted the Union Army. He would not kill for anyone. You knew that? As significant, he left the Catholic Church, as he should have. My father, oh Hezekiah! your grandfather, *he* created his own church from nothing. And that was enough for one man to do. Give him credit. No matter what one might think of mawkish theology, that was a significant achievement. But he did not stop there. He turned away from one life's work and started again. He became a lawyer for social justice. He did not know it, but I was proud of him. Had he kept his health and lived longer I wonder what he would have become? Oh, but what am I saying? That we are immortal? He was almost one hundred years old when he died. It is simply that I remember him during those first few years after he finished his law degree, when he was still vigorous, energetic, commanding. He was something. What a character he was. Before he became ill

Before he ran out of time. It was not alcohol that finished him, no matter what they say. Has anyone ever told you that?

Yes, it is odd. You might think that Hezekiah was my inspiration, that in some way he was responsible for my becoming a Communist. But he was not. No, we lived apart from the beginning. I mean that literally as well as philosophically. When I was a boy he was never at home. I used to think that he had abandoned me. But later I knew he had not. He was just hurrying on, trying to get to the next century. How could I blame him for that? You see, we belonged to different centuries.

No, I went at it alone, by myself. I thought I did. I wanted to transform the world. I thought that was possible. I really did. I wanted to stop the exploitation of man by man. Sound grandiose? Pretentious? It did not then. I did not want to betray my country. My country was betraying humankind and I wanted the world to become my country. My country at peace. Our slogan was "Keep America Out of War by Keeping War Out of the World." The dominant thought on our minds then was peace. That was the issue. That was our goal. Peace. That is what I wanted. I was incredulous that everyone did not feel that way. You see, I am trying to remember how I felt then, how it was. *Peace* was the issue then. We were in a depression. People were out of work. People were starving. Oh, Capitalism! And nations were arming themselves. That should give you insight into human nature. Millions of people were starving and nations were spending millions on armies. Did you know that the Russian people loved Americans then? Anti-communism has been the scourge of Western Civilization. That phobia has distorted our culture. Diseased it. Or maybe that's putting the cart before the horse.

For a young person like yourself to hear someone speak of thirty years ago, well, it must seem like ancient history simply because you were not alive then, which also creates the illusion that one's life span is lengthy. It also makes it seem that we, you and I, are far apart. But I tell you we are not. No, you and I belong to the same century. It is only that we are locked within ourselves. I remember how excited you were in high school when Stevenson gave his atomic test ban speech in 1956, and how surprised and angry you were when the American people did not arise in applause. However, I recognized then in you the existence of a personal ideology that must have come from your genes (I smile when I write that), an ideology that most do not equate with political ideology, although it is very much that. You felt different from those around you, different from your peers, from the neighbors, everybody. Actually, I don't recall that you had many friends. You were a loner. Perhaps, even at that young age, you were already an alien in your society, already revulsed. And, most importantly, you liked that feeling. You wanted to feel that way. You did not want to feel that you belonged to your surroundings, that you could be explained by what had preceded you. You wanted to feel like no one else had ever felt before. You wanted to become a new being.

Do you know why I recognized it? It was because I was the same in my youth. When I became a Communist I thought I had liberated myself from the past. The human past. I thought I was free. I believed that I, an individual, could be a creator, and not simply repeat the history of my wretched species. I had made a great leap to the beginnings of my own life. By joining the American Communist Party I believed that I had obliterated everything known and secure. I had nothing but my future, the world's future, the future of socialism. And there was no going back. There was nothing to do but take the next step. I liked that. Again I, too, felt different. I felt separated, apart, distinct, unique. I was not, like everyone else, merely a creature naturally and inevitably evolving. I had made a free choice to create a new life for mankind. What I did not recognize was that, ironically, given the direction I had chosen, the seeds of my destruction were inherent in that self-awareness. I had become a socialist, yes, but when you join the Party you take orders forevermore and you never question them. There is nothing creative about following orders. You are an automaton for the remainder of your life. Your creative self ceases to exist. Do you realize how many millions of cases of arrested mental development there have been in this century because of Marxism? When something is accepted as given, thinking stops. That grated on me from the beginning, but it was only later that I realized that I was trapped. I realized it too late.

I know that you understand that Marxism was created out of historical circumstances. Nothing new there. But what generally passes in this century for Marxist theology—a witticism, that—that which is pandered as theoretical dogma, ironically does not recognize the human animal. Consider the idea of a classless society. Unfortunately, that is an absurdity. It is impossible. Nor does it make sense to say, as some do, that we cannot really imagine what a classless society will be. That it is a metaphor for the unforeseen, a concept to be interpreted, as has been the case over the centuries with the Bible. The fact is we do not think or act on the basis of what is yet to be imagined. Lamentably that is the reality. Thus, predictably, small minds have sought to impose a brutish order. They will continue to do so. They will continue to attempt to rule, to force, to oppress in the name of their misbegotten plan. I will not dignify it by calling it a vision. And why should that not be the case, given their historical roots? Stalin showed the way. We cannot institute fundamental change without blood. The problem is we become what we do. We talk about being corrupted if we lived before the Revolution, but what if we lived during the Revolution—and after? And what new world is it that we have created? What has changed? In what direction can we turn? Yes, what we have is yet another confrontation of evil orders.

The 1930s? That time, yes. Those years. Thirty years ago. We students had our socialist paper, *The Steeplejack*. The great Orozco was there painting Peace. How do you explain what has happened since? Are we not all human beings? The Jews. The bomb.

Helen, your mother, is worried about me. I can tell, although, as you are aware, she rarely speaks. Do you know that I have never told her explicitly that I am a member of the Communist Party? Yes, incredible. But she knows. And it has probably affected her health. I have never told her for reasons that you can probably guess, including the nature of my work and for her protection. It is for the same reasons that I have been afraid to get too close to you. I tell myself that anyway. Perhaps I have also been afraid that I would not be able to explain to you, explain everything, this, because I cannot or do not want to explain it to myself.

Oh! how well I remember your grammar-school debates. Are you surprised? I was very proud of you. It was a good beginning for you, for my son. You were playing politics rather than, say, baseball, although I know you played that as well. (No, I have not forgotten when I got the free tickets to see the Red Sox in 1948 and did not take you. I could not take you, but you never forgave me, did you?) But it demonstrated your sensitivity, your awareness. You possessed a social consciousness. You cared. You wanted progress. You had dreams. And then, only a few years later, you were so young, you retreated into—what? I cannot really call it cynicism, nihilism. You were too young. You *are* too young. Were you disillusioned? By what? Me? But it has lasted for too long. Has it become depression? Why? Oh, look at me, talking about you as an historical figure when it should be the opposite. And soon I will be just that, probably. Or at least I will be dead.

But I wish I could help you. Perhaps we should speak of disillusionism. Depressionism of the soul. If truth be known, the world's omnipresent, ancient plagues. Talk about disease! We desperately need a cure. Can there possibly be one? I wish I could tell you what direction to go in. I wish it for myself. I would not want to choose for you, even if I had the power to do so. Your life is your own. That is your glory and your burden. That is why I have kept my other life a secret from you. I can say that to you.

But the end for all of us cannot be far. You see, we are moving into the skies (that has been my work). A decade, maybe two, three, four, if we are lucky. Not more, for sure. Not even that. We already have Satan's fireball. It will be delivered. We will do his bidding. The social issues are almost irrelevant now, moot. My work? What a joke. Have I come to your position, state? The father looking back to the son. How odd, when some would say that I am near to assuming meaningful power. But the end may be nearer for me. If you read this it will probably mean that we did not die naturally, Helen and me. She will go with me. My sense of urgency may be false. I shall try to write more.

Your Father, JBK

5

The Cult of Klara

Klara Blazek stood firm in Boston, scowling. She was waiting for the Greyhound bus bound for New York City to pull into its stall. It was thirty minutes late, a fact she had conveyed to the man at the ticket window, "You incompetent idiot," she had branded him. He had reeled off the names of a dozen or more towns in New Hampshire and Massachusetts, stuttering and jabbering at her fury that the bus had to stop at all of them. That was not an explanation, Klara had railed at him. Either the bus ran on a schedule or it did not.

"You fool," she had shouted. "What are you saying, that it is out there freelancing? Stupid American."

The world is coming to an end, she scoffed, but the mediocrities of mankind shall continue to muddle the while. Perfectly delightful, like cockroaches they were indestructible. Klara had left the window cheering the end of the world, raging, "Idiot, idiot," all the way to the bus stall. The man at the ticket window had been left to die, to cope as best he could.

Klara was uncommonly tense awaiting the anonymous bus with its special cargo. She realized that its arrival signified many things, perhaps without limit, without definition, certainly the unexpected, and she felt threatened by the unknown, the coming force. Her great anxiety made her wish to be in the company of Seema, her as yet innocent but strangely marked child, her very own daughter, thirteen years old, to be fourteen in a week. Children were on her mind, especially those we leave, leave behind with our illusions, ideological and spiritual descendants, and at this very moment Klara wanted most of all to get home to Seema whom Klara had designated and had often spoken of to others as the motivating force in her life, as the single extant reason for her to remain alive. Beginning when she herself was a young girl, near Seema's age, Klara's life had been marked by harsh, depressing moments, and perhaps all that sentiment would allow, all that had been distilled was a grim, humorless, relentless determination to do and to perform all for her female child and for her female child alone, to spare Seema the coarse, grim realities of the floating spheres. Or was that not the truth?

It was true that Klara had often left Seema alone, instilling a sense of abandonment and isolation in Seema that would always be a part of her consciousness, a sense that ironically would do more than anything to link daughter to mother, but Klara invariably told herself that Seema would be upset only if Klara did not return at the appointed time, at the promised moment, when without Klara the sudden sense of being alone in an unstructured universe would be too frightening for Seema, would overwhelm the fairy child.

Seema would be especially upset tonight, Klara thought, because Tuffy was at the apartment, brooding and anxious, waiting and forgetful, wondering and worrying. Seema suspected, loathed, and feared Tuffy, and for her to be upset tonight, particularly for her to be disturbed on this night, that would be an intolerable development. On this very night there were many active, knowing forces coming together in the universe for the first time. Klara knew that. As depressing and monotonous as human affairs generally were, she knew that this could be a momentous evening under the stars. Thunder in the heavens. The torch of light. Blinding. For all.

"My little trolls are at work," she thought.

That only happened when she was unavoidably involved, implicated or irrevocably committed, and her "psychic control," as she put it, took over. But the proof was there to be interpreted. Klara had been knocking her elbows all day and night, knocking them against doors, at the apartment, at the university, on the subway, getting on and off the bus, everywhere. It was the most significant of signs. It was undeniable. It augured the unexpected, whether good or bad.

As Klara's daughter, and like Klara a spring soul, Seema also possessed a sixth sense, and if her mother were unduly late Seema would not fail to become suspicious. And Klara wished to prevent those occurrences as much as she could. In this matter, and perhaps in some others, she did not wish her daughter to awaken to her full powers. If Seema were to become suspicious too often, no matter the pretext, she might eventually be led to guess everything, and that Klara did not want. It was unnecessary. No, she forbade it. She wanted secrets to remain secrets. She was too weary to explain. She did not want to end with what would be regarded as a forced confession. It was so very complicated and so very mysterious.

Was Tuffy a secret or had his time come and gone? Because there were tales of Tuffy that no one would care to hear. General Tuffy, Seema called him behind his back, ridiculing what she regarded to be his at times fawning attitude toward Klara. That was the only manner in which Seema had seen Tuffy behave, the only guise she had perceived, so that was the only Tuffy she knew. Typical youthful intolerance and certainty in an untypical and uncertain and profoundly insecure child. To Klara's knowledge, Seema only saw in Tuffy a six-foot-five-inch, two-hundred-and-fifty-pound, gentle, whimpering, cowering bear. Yet, General Tuffy was truly a brave man, a courageous man, a man of heroic acts. Klara knew that. If pressed she might have even acknowledged it. At least, formerly he had been. Once upon a time.

General Tuffy, alias Professor André Cordon, alias what he had chosen to be, what had been impressed upon him, to wit, in recent years holder of the Empire Twentieth-Century Chair in English at New York University's Graduate School of Arts & Sciences, known internationally for his literary criticism and editing and, ironically, both for his Marxist criticism and for his variorum editions of the seventeenth-century English poets Donne, Herrick, and Herbert. It had been said in more than one outrageous book review, convention corridor conversation, dinner-party bubbling that Professor Cordon had imbibed catholic tastes, and had imbibed and imbibed and imbibed. In addition to and behind and beyond the printed page, numerous rumors, allegations, lies, secrets, reports, and speculations also had it that in the previous, lost fifty years he, in not all the same years, not always simultaneously, not always as the same personage, and never forever, had also been a Communist pre-Khrushchev's rumbling and rocking 1956 speech revealing the terrors of the satanic Stalin; had been married three times; allegedly, had killed only once, but had been near death himself on a dozen occasions in a variety of complex circumstances; had lived with two men; had attempted suicide, as a young romantic in the eighteenth-century tradition of Goethe, of course; had become an arachnologist, that is, a spider specialist; had once earned one million three hundred thousand pounds in a day, in an era when the sun had yet to set on the British Empire; had saved a life (a woman drowning); had seduced two fifteen-year-olds (this simultaneously); had served during World War II with the British secret service, Section D of M.I.6, sabotage and propaganda; had fallen drunk out of a second-floor hotel room in Toronto and broken his nose; had written, under pseudonyms, four cookbooks, French, Thai, Spanish, and Hungarian cuisine; three novels, philosophical, historical, political; and numerous short stories, detective, erotic, fantasy, all this beyond the realms of academia.

For the Professor, eating, fornicating, spying, teaching, and telling apparently all went together. And more. Indeed, he was a man who created prospects, changed arrangements, offered possibilities, titillated fancies. Life was invention, certainly intrigue, cabals and calculations, excitement, never the void, never that, pray no. In fact, if there was a secret to his personal magic, it was or had been his ability to skirt the void. While others plunged helplessly headlong, Professor André Cordon danced around the edge, laughing and inventing. Or so it had been, so it had been said, so it had seemed. Many people had tales to tell, were eager to talk and swap, to contribute to the myth of André Cordon. He was a culture treasured.

But Klara was not eager on this occasion to see André Cordon or Tuffy, depending upon his current mental and physical condition, not until she absolutely could not avoid it, regardless of his personal involvement, be it material, spiritual, political, or sexual, regardless of how profoundly he might be implicated, menially or mortally. No, not immediately, not tonight. For years she had suffered his aberrant orders, his dramatic outbursts, and his arbitrary entrances and exits, and she wanted his bags of groceries, his dollars, and whatever else he either was anxious to lay at her feet or she could extricate from him or, increasingly of late, intimidate him into giving her—"You'll never see this bed again"—during the elaborate games they played on his weekly visits to the apartment, the only remaining circumstance in which they openly acknowledged their peculiar, ripened brand of intimacy, but she did not want his thick, strong fingers on her body tonight. No, not tonight. God, not this night. She had told him that, shot it at him.

Nevertheless, she was convinced that he was at this very moment still at the apartment, lingering. Hulking. Who would have guessed that he was a distinguished professor of seventeenth-century English literature or in whatever guise he was presenting himself professionally or clandestinely these weeks, this day even? He was a Red dog sniffing with his tongue hanging out. Had he not heard her? Did he dare not believe her? What he wanted was an advance report, of course, and most of all a lead on her presentiments, but he was not going to get either. No. Not tonight. Absolutely not. Not this night at all. She would share nothing. He could work it out for himself, depending upon whatever particular fanciful turn his consciousness took on this occasion. He had created his own maze, lost, invented, and reinvented his very own way. He could find his own devious path this time, all by himself. In fact, he had better be gone when she returned. He would be gone. Klara demanded it. There were loud voices in her head.

Actually, on most of General Tuffy's, that is, André Cordon's, visits, Klara could detach herself, feel nothing, play her roles. Play distant music, play tunes of the past. Klara Blazek could make believe with the Professor, make time stand still, return to fantasies, embrace the future. But not every week, not always. There were odd times, unpredictable times when she could be bruised, when she felt more than vulnerable. Almost helpless. When memory rose. When she was but a child of the universe once again, beyond anger and within reach. When it was like starting life all over again. Oh, God, she did not understand that. And she did not want it. Her chronic plague. To return again and begin again. And Cordon was there, eager to teach, instruct, beckon, whisper, arouse, and sooth.

Ordinarily in recent times she had used Tuffy well, she thought. She had let him come to her apartment once a week instead of meeting elsewhere, as in the past, at different locations such as at the Chelsea Hotel on 23rd Street or the Taft on 50th. He appeared usually on Friday evenings with his money and moods, with his ideologies and his tales and his memories, particularly when he had been drinking, and with his groceries from Balducci's in the Village, and he often came with a surprise, something she had not asked for, a nice fish or a new bread, a particularly good bottle of wine, for he could be very charming, he could raise your spirits on the spot, but she did not always let him touch her. On occasion he came simply with a bit of news, with information, perhaps with a new outlook, for he had been capable of inventing at will on the very spot of existence.

One rainy night he had come late without money or groceries, that apparently being his surprise, and she had not let him in the door of her apartment. The voices in her head had been insistent.

"Where are the groceries?" she had demanded, looking at him with astonishment as if she had asked, "Where are your clothes?"

And he had responded as if he had been found naked, and was shamed, guilty. The Professor had been General Tuffy.

"Klara, please, I . . . I . . . I had matters to take care of. There was not time enough. Please, let me in, it is pouring out. I am all wet."

"It will cost you a hundred," she had said without hesitation.

"Be reasonable, Klara, I am soaked. Look, I am sorry, I have less than thirty dollars on me. I bought some books in the Village. At the Strand. I . . . uh . . . including a first edition I especially wanted. It was late in the afternoon and . . . well, I simply could not pass it up. It was too late to go to the bank. I had to have it. Look, let me show you. It is a first edition of Paul Bowles's *The Sheltering Sky*. In mint condition. You know I have been looking for it. A very good price, too. Uh, actually, it was not that much, only seven dollars. I mean . . . uh," he stammered.

"Go home and read it."

And with that Klara had shut the door in Tuffy's face. That had been her surprise. It had been a revelation. She had invented a new chapter in their lives because it was the first time she had ever dared to do such a thing in all of the years in which they, André Cordon and Klara Blazek, had been together in various ways, in all that they had been exposed to together, meant to each other, forgotten. She had dared to risk being her true self with him, dared to reveal her true feelings toward him, her anger and her growing contempt. He was a man, was he not? And Tuffy had made what was, for him, the fatal decision for his vested future. Instead of threatening to end the relationship with unhappy consequences for Klara if she did not perform as he bid, he simply had resolved not to make the same mistake again. Above all, he had thought, do not disappoint her, do not bring her bad tidings, do not make her angry. For he no longer wanted to clash with her, or with anyone.

Yes, she had learned how to condition him perfectly. She had taken possession of him. Rather than her master, he had become almost entirely her pawn. He had learned that to provoke her was a grave risk. And on those rare occasions when he dared to demur at the prospect that Klara would not let him into her bed, that did not gain him access. Frustrated and humiliated, he protested, raged only when he lost control, and then only briefly. Increasingly in Klara's presence, André Cordon's once dominating figure, his towering two hundred and fifty pounds, became General Tuffy, became a huge mass of quivering flesh waiting to be beckoned. Perhaps the single, most significant alteration was that where in the past neither had needed the other, André Cordon now needed Klara Blazek.

Klara had learned when she was young, and not so young, what it meant to be the victim of a man. In later years, by her own tightly wound perspective, she had more often been the victor. General Tuffy was not the first male to fall before her. Had she the power, Klara would have reduced most of the male population of the world to the same condition. She settled for those whom she personally encountered. She thought her latest project would probably be Professor John Darnell Slamunster, the outrageous inquisitive inquisitor.

The Greyhound finally arrived, forty-five minutes late. Apparently the driver was unaware of the importance of his mission. But the bus would now be an express from Boston to . . . to the Post Authority Bus Terminal in New York City. Klara was glad of it. No more detours for destiny. She had been waiting and waiting and waiting for this extravaganza to begin, waiting for the curtains to open, anticipating it to the point of demanding it. Let there finally be the glare of light. She was overwrought to the degree that she had become tired. Maybe even a little sick, nauseous. For an individual of her strength, ferocity, it was extraordinary that she was on the edge of enervation. Dressed in black, as she often was, she stood rigid, still scowling, as if prepared to destroy the bus on the spot.

And yet, she thought to herself, all she urgently desired was to step upon the bus and get this initial scene of the final act over with, finish it, let her body drain. Collapse and sleep. Except that she had no idea when sleep would come. She had a vision of being with him at an endless dawn.

But now, anxious, she had to find her seat, the right seat. Beside him. The bus could not be too crowded. She would not allow it. Why was she certain he would be there? She was certain. How could he not come? It was time. She felt certain of that at least. The thought flashed through her mind that she would not recognize him. Imagine that. Not recognize him? She rejected that as well. That was impossible, no matter how many years had passed, no matter the past, lives lost and never lived. For once, the years did not matter. If for some reason memory had dimmed the image of the slight, quiet, intense boy with curly brown hair, off by himself reading in some corner of a dimly lighted room, she had only to think of the father as a young man. Imagine. The son of the father in the flesh. His flesh. As he had been. She stood in reverie.

Finally, she got on and looked for him. Perhaps she had boarded before him and would have to wait. But, no, he was there. She spotted him immediately, as if a light had guided the way, as if he were entirely different from anyone else on earth, let alone on the bus, a separate species unto himself, having reappeared in her universe. Inside seat, aisle seat open. He was looking out the window now, passive, serene. He was absolutely still. It was as if he were posing for a painting. Why did she possess the conviction that the painting was already famous? Or perhaps he was in a contemplative mood, a trance even. That would be appropriate, inaccessible at a crucial time, fitting for the moment and for the future, as it had been for the past. His chin was resting in his right hand. A characteristic pose of the family. She had a photograph. Black turtleneck, shirt unbuttoned halfway, he was still wearing a raincoat. Yes, curly brown hair. His hair. The King hair, it was said. It was the King hair, it was. Did he have blue eyes? He had to have blue eyes. Why would that be altered? Those eyes.

She hesitated and stood there briefly, staring, remembering. He was a deer. He had been like a deer, beautiful and elusive. But also a terrible, wild, dark side she had never fully understood, did not understand. That was baffling. Despite everything, she had not really known him. Enigmatic soul. She had never really felt that she had understood him. He brooded and did not speak, she thought. They had battled. The father, the son. Klara knew it was him. The son of the father. She took a deep breath and sat in the seat beside him. It had to be him. She would make it so again.

Timothy spoke immediately.

"Have you heard any more about the missiles? Has Kennedy said anything more? Of course, what could he say? 'A polite exchange is being arranged with my pals, Nikita and Fidel'?"

But there was no laughter. Despite the seeming supercilious comment there was not even a smirk. Instead, without looking at her and without hesitating, he gestured as if he were mute until she understood that he had written something on a large, legal-sized pad of paper. He indicated by half turning it toward her that he wanted her to read it:

Sexually we have been linked through the ages:
THE GREAT EROTIC CHAIN OF BEING.

Day 1 DaY Day 3 Day DAy
(get it up on some bulletin board, do it)
A Highlight of Infinity [vs] American history
|
| missile crisis
| [is it sexual?]
(Second Death) i think this
missile crisis is a horny thing

Flushed, Klara turned away and then quickly looked back at him, looked at the face of the young man who continued to look away from her. What did she see? Where and when was she looking? She scattered her thoughts. Was it something she could yet put into words, sounds, rhythms? Without a doubt it was youthful innocence and earnest concern in his face. She saw it. It was there. Clearly evident on the surface. Was that possible? Well, yes, but his words did not say so. His face said it. His words did not. Playfulness? She smiled. He certainly did not seem nervous. Intense, perhaps. But not nervous, not apprehensive. And he had immediately elicited a smile from her. Incredible. From her. Just like that. Just like the father once had. Klara looked around as if to see if the father were there on the bus. A charmer. The son, too. Then how much did he understand? She realized questions could be expected. He might even have the presumption to demand explanations. Or was it innocence? The blind arrogance of youth. What happened to my childhood? To my father? Civilization? And more. After all, if he knew enough he might think that he had been set aside, displaced. But that happened to individuals. To people. It might happen to the world. Imminently. Did he not understand that? It was always a possibility, present, lurking, something that could happen to anyone. It had happened to whole peoples. Had he never heard of expatriates, refugees, of the murdered sons and daughters of Zion? She had tales to tell him. Tales he should hear. All of the parts of human civilization were never to be in everlasting order, in final, resting, peaceful place until they were no more. Did he not know that? And until the end the order could be changed. Ruptured. At any moment. Willy-nilly. When one least expected it. Or wanted it. Like now.

Oh, god. The King arrogance. Gall. Daring. It had been instilled in him. If you possessed nothing that you valued then you were simply not afraid of losing everything, perhaps your life, which meant that, in turn, you asked for more than was possible, asked for more than life. Apparently that was always to be the approach. No rest. No letup. Risk everything. No matter the times. No, no, throw away everything with not the slightest promise of replacement. It was in the genes. Ancestral. Had to be. But did he have to be so abrupt about it? In the face of eternity, could he not wait for a few minutes to pass? Did he not know what was appropriate, what the limitations were? Yes, of course he knew. Well, yes, she thought again, like father like son. He was impatient and quick to change. Why wait? Sensitive, yes, but paradoxically so eager as to be inconsiderate, impertinent, even callous. Was he reliable? Stupid question. Look at the father. Reliable to whom, to what? The universe? An invented life? God, was he even twenty-one yet? Was that possible? Hmmm. It had not been so long ago really. That was not the way it worked. It only seemed long ago. And then again it did not. Long ago and far away was only in fairy tales. And reality seemed always out of reach, beyond touch. Her mind flew.

Only seconds had passed when she spoke.

"They have probably destroyed half the world by now," she felt prompted to say, which was not something she could envision, not half the world. Her response was unlike her.

"Yes," he said. "Maybe they have finally found the way to destroy the entire world."

"No, on the contrary, I believe that they will find a way to bungle it," she said in measured pace, an observation that again was unlike her, for she thought that they were quite capable of achieving total extinction, believed that they desired it.

She looked from the corner of her eye.

"Or would you rather they did not?" she added. "Bungle it, I mean."

Was this concern or cynicism on her part? Who was speaking? Except for Seema, she knew she did not care. She could no longer allow herself to care.

"No, I am not worried. I just hope we get to New York in time to see it."

"You think that is where it will happen?"

This was curious, different. What did he know? Was he of a determinate, recognizable age?

"No, but they will have it on television."

"Ah, yes. Of course. On all three networks."

"And I need to get another newspaper. A later edition."

"For what, the television listings?"

Why was she being so flippant? This was ridiculous. It was out of character for her, out of age. It should stop. Surely it was not because of him? What did he suspect? Expect? Did he know of the world in which he lived? And if he did not, what expectations could there be?

But he stopped her with his answer.

"No. The Chinese have attacked the Indians and the Indians are fighting back."

"What?"

"Millions of people have become soldiers. Or is it billions? Armies of billions and billions . . ."

He must be joking, she thought. Despite all of the years that had passed since she had first come to the United States, there were still recesses of the American psyche that she did not understand. And, apparently, he was thoroughly American. Just like the father. But what else?

"Norwegian coastal liner has sunk off the coast of Norway . . . two-thirds of ninety have drowned," he announced, as if broadcasting on radio, as if play-acting.

But then like a child he became quizzical.

"What is a coastal liner? Is that why it has sunk off the coast rather than deep at sea?"

And the sage.

"Can these things be explained?"

And then she understood, at least on the simplest level. He had unfolded a copy of the *New York Times*, taken it from his lap and begun to . . . to what? Embroider? Interpolate? Speak in code? Whatever it was, it was as if he had become a verbal runaway, as if he had been captured by extraneous thoughts, the thoughts of unknown, random others from space who had stolen his mind over the airwaves.

"Soviet Ambassador to Brazil and a junior member of the embassy staff drowned in the Rio surf. It does not say why they were swimming together. Why both drowned. It does not say whether one was a male and one was a female or anything at all about that. What happened? Was one attempting to rescue the other? Was it a suicide pact between lovers? Murder? . . . 86,000 Japanese—they are described as being 'leftist intellectuals'—protesting U.S. military bases in Japan. Imagine that? 86,000. Not 87,000 or 85,000. But 86,000 precisely."

He paused for just a second and once again glanced at her quizzically.

"It does not explain how was it determined that every one of them is an intellectual, apart from other considerations. Strange, but I never dreamed that there were that many leftist intellectuals in the entire world, let alone in Japan. You know, I could never have imagined it. Do they wear badges? What if they are in disguise?"

Was he trying to tell her something? She was not prepared for that. It was as if he was attempting to report on their world. Or perhaps he was attempting to describe it for himself. There was that question. There was the feel of an insistent question about his whole being. And she would have to answer for it.

". . . train killed a seven-year-old Long Island boy while he was riding upon his bicycle. How many pounds did the seven-year-old weigh? How much does the train weigh? Was there any impact? Is that a joke or a riddle? No worry, though. You can buy cigars with 'It's a Boy' imprinted upon each one of them. All of this I have learned in the first edition for Monday, October 22, 1962, of the *New York Times* where all the news that is printed is fitted. Oh, yes, half a million Jewish refugees are flowing into France. A more intense rate than at the end of the Second World War. How strange. Where are they going? Why into France? Were they invited? Why now? You would know about that. And the poet Yevtushenko says that Stalin only pretends to be dead. They are going to triple the guard at his grave to prevent his spirit from rising. I am wondering if there has been a further report. Would you know anything about that? Does the Russian God live? The missiles will kill him. They will kill all of us. I must get the next edition when we get to New York City to see if it has been reported."

He paused for a moment as if expecting her to respond, but then he quickly added a last bit of information perhaps by way of explanation.

"I am a debater, you know. Do you know that? Debaters must do research.

Therefore, I am researching the universe. I must know everything and anything there is to know even if I know nothing about it at all."

It was as if he had attacked Klara Blazek all at once from all sides with an entire army, shock troops, a blitzkrieg, flares, bugles blowing, horses and donkeys and camels scrambling. She would know about that? About what? Russian god? Was that in the newspaper or did he make that up? No ceremonies. Maybe there was charm, too, but there was something in addition. Yes, he was a summer person, she thought. Early summer. Born in early July. Not that his birth date was crucial. The shift and bend of the universe was the key. The spheres. But his intensity. Integrity. Hard and pure. Nothing theatrical about it. Incredible, but he meant it. For better or worse, he meant it. Well, that was all right. Early summer. She respected that. No theatrics. No pretense. Hard and pure. He meant it.

The bus pulled away. All right, she had been wrong. There were no blank pages, simply new pages. How strangely but how easily it had begun. She had been surprised, startled, which was rare for her, but it had been quick and easy. No matter that she felt a bit breathless. In spite of herself, she was full of anticipation and, although she would never openly acknowledge it, excitement and interest and mystification. But why? Something had changed. Who would have expected that one could create on the spot a new order. Yes, the son of the father.

To retreat for the moment, she leaned back and closed her eyes. She still wanted time to gather herself, to . . . well . . . prepare for whatever had to happen. What would happen? Something was happening. Something had to happen. Nothing stayed the same, and would not between the two of them either. That had become evident immediately. The quickness of the nuclear age. Basic processes were bypassed and things would be different.

Timothy was staring intently at her as she appeared to meditate. She was not what he had expected. That is, he had not anticipated someone who would have an immediate effect upon him. One never anticipated that. Actually, he had not anticipated anyone, any type. She had said little, but he knew already that he had never before met anyone like her. Or had he? What was it about her? There was such, well, stark presence, as if she had appeared on a screen in a dark theater, as if he had suddenly seen her. That aura. They had been together before. He involuntarily smiled to himself, shuddered. Another ghost. Bela Lugosi again.

He had this strange sense that he could tell her everything and that he wanted to tell her everything. And that she would listen to him even if she knew it all. That would not matter. Nothing would be too trivial. He could put himself in her hands—her arms?—and she would tell stories, describe the world, make assurances, draw pictures. She would understand. He liked her face. The lines were strong, her nose and her chin prominent and balanced, her cheekbones high, her forehead broad. There must be only one person like her in the world. Were her eyes black? Her lips were full, her lower lip, he thought he would never forget her full lower lip. Her face had the appearance of a mask, imperious, but he sensed that she was not unapproachable. Her filmy, shining, white skin looked as if it would tear easily, tear like silk. Tear away the face, tear away the mask. Her hair was black and straight and came to her shoulders. It had a subdued metallic sheen. Impregnable? The white collar of her blouse shone over the neck of her black suitjacket. Her legs were crossed and her skirt came to just above her knees. Timothy thought her beautiful. Hers was a beauty to remember, to recall, in the lights and shadows of the bus, traveling, images of her, ebony and ivory, ebony and ivory.

It now occurred to him that he should not have been the first to speak. Perhaps he should have played dumb. He might be prejudicing the matter, tipping the balance in unexpected directions. He knew he would think of the reasons why later.

"Regarding the letters from your father," the strange, agitated voice had said over the telephone, "if you are interested take the 11 P.M. bus Tuesday for Boston and . . . the bus for New York City."

The letters had arrived on his desk in his room that day. His mind kept coming back to that as if it were a crucial matter, the explanation for everything. His door had been unlocked both when he had left and when he had returned. He knew that, he had arranged it, and yet he always locked his door. And Ham had already left for Washington. Also, Timothy had only been gone for a half hour or so, at least as far as he could remember. That must have been when the letters had come. Very convenient. Precise timing. They had simply arrived. Like arrows. And yet he might have locked the door. And then what? Okay, so it was no big deal. There were people who could pick locks in a second. That is what he presumed anyway. Fly through the air like a speeding bullet. Jump buildings at a single bound. Only kryptonite could stop them. So what was the big deal about getting into a room? Somehow perhaps he had known he would receive the letters and subsequently a telephone call. But did he therefore possess all of the answers? Maybe he only thought he had deliberately unlocked his door.

Otherwise it went back to his first thought. The first ghostly presence. Odd, he thought. Not really funny, just odd.

He had instructions, did he not? Limited information. Food and lodging awaited in New York. The opportunity of a lifetime, presumably. A new lifetime. A destiny. All expenses paid. Lucky him. Lucky Tim.

". . . Everything you will need for a few days, I presume. If there is anything to be done, I will take care of it. It was probably time to contact you anyway."

It was? There had been no opportunity to ask what was going on, to ask why he should do this, or to say that he would not do that, which was exactly what he more often than not said to anyone. To ask, why now? Why in the fall of 1962 when the missiles are coming, the missiles are coming?

But he sort of liked that. Destiny. No control. Wildly buffeted, propelled in one direction or another. The headline would read,

"Mighty, unknown forces to contend with for no known reason."

Bullets. An explosion. Smoke. Fire. That was the universe. Fog and bogs. If nothing else, he was excited because he was just a little bit frightened. Maybe a lot. He felt alive. There was a purpose. He did not know the nature of the purpose, but he felt a purpose. The momentum of an original purpose. It was wonderful. Rushing onward. He would take it, even if it was not his to take. Someone else's purpose. He would steal it. And, besides, there were other obvious reasons why he had to do it, why he had done it. Done what? Speak in shadows to this mysterious woman of the end of all life? Did she really care? Did any of them? Who were they anyway? Were they listening at this very moment to his and her words? Eavesdropping? A bugged bus. Yes, the Commies. Threatening the American way, the family, mom and dad, all relatives and friends, and things, toads, brothers, girl friends, uncles. The Commies. Them again. The phantom Commies. The evil spirits of America. The devils. An ear on the universe. While missiles whirled overhead in the nightsky, he was about to meet the boogie man on his hands and knees. Or, what was better, meet the boogie woman. On a Greyhound bus. In fact, he had already met her.

The parable was that the philosophical overview was always there

WHAT HAPPENED or
SOMETHING HAPPENED or
HAS SOMETHING HAPPENED?
or IS SOMETHING GOING TO
HAPPEN? and what does
it MEAN TO
!?AMERICA?!

Close to each other, at times touching thighs with the roll of the bus, rolling around curves as they left Boston, the illusion was that Timothy and Klara had chosen to be together. The forced separation of the seats, in front and in back, fed the illusion. The small enclosure, the intimacy of the darkness, was it true that they could not be observed? Heard? True, if they spoke, they would be compelled to speak to each other. But if they spoke, they would speak only in low, soft tones, undetectable, in the shadows, speak of the past, of time and lives.

"Not so many years ago I was in Maine," said Timothy, still looking at Klara. She was beautiful. Mysterious. Did he know her? He must know her.

"Yes," she said quietly, as if to beckon to him.

Perhaps this was a beginning, she thought. To go back in time. But did she want that so soon? Did she want it at all? She had to have made the contact, she felt, but why she had felt compelled to do so had not as yet been truly revealed to her. She had simply imagined the worst. She had not asked.

"In my bed in my upstairs room."

"Yes," again quietly, softly, seeking perhaps to calm Timothy, soothe him.

Odd, but she sensed that there were reasons to be both perplexed and apprehensive. What could that mean? There were plenty of signs, but why could she not interpret them? Was she the one being impatient? She had always instructed Seema never to be impatient. To wait.

"I had never before been this far. Not back then."

"Hmmm."

She did not think that could be true. But neither did she believe that he was deliberately lying. Perhaps she did not understand his vision, his own imagery. Precisely what did he mean by not having been this far? Of what and when did he speak? Did he always speak in oracles or were these simple terms? What did he think he was doing anyway, was he a human being apprenticing to be a god?

"Oh, I was thinking all the time about going," he grinned, looking in her direction, not even aware of her closed eyes. It did not matter.

"Long before this moment."

Klara said nothing, breathing evenly, deeply. Musing.

"The trouble was that I did not want to leave my room. I hated to go out. Even to school. I had no reason to go anywhere. I wanted to talk, but . . . not to just anyone. You know what?" grinning again.

"No."

"I hated to go out so much that I . . . I did not even want to leave my room at night to go to the bathroom. . . . I . . . I used Pepsi bottles."

Klara opened her eyes. He had pried them open. She looked at his youthful, dark outline. And then she involuntarily spoke what she was thinking.

"Odd, but that is just like Seema's father. He would have said something like that."

"Seema's father? Who is Seema?"

She bit her lip. Oh, God.

"What? Oh, Seema."

She had said it without realizing it. She had not merely thought it. But it did not seem like the time to go into it, although she had this strange feeling that she already had. No, it was premature. Maybe she would never have to explain. At least not everything. Wait a minute: why should she explain anything? That was not the attitude for her to take, regardless of what was contemplated. Do not be personal. They could not know what was going to transpire.

"Seema is my daughter."

Why had she even told him that? She would not tell him more. Not at this time. At the moment she could not bear to say anything more. And most people did not know everything about their world. Nor did they have to know everything.

"Oh. How old is she?"

"Fourteen."

"Are they waiting for you? I mean, your husband and your daughter?"

She looked at him again and then moved in her seat. This was maddening. How could she have lost control like this?

"Look, we should not be talking. . . . I . . . I do not know why we are talking about this. I am not married . . . now. I mean . . . I am separated."

She had reached for that, grappled, for what did one say?

"I am sorry. I mean, that you are separated. I did not mean to pry."

"It is all right. Perhaps you shall meet Seema. I think you would like her."

She had been sufficiently vague. But so hadn't he, to say the least. They must be playing with each other, she thought, for their various reasons, for unfathomable reasons.

"Well, it is true. I filled up a lot of Pepsi bottles . . ."

He would rush on. There he went again.

". . . I hated to go downstairs, particularly late at night when everybody was sleeping, because they would hear me. The floor creaked—it is awful to make a noise when you do not want to—and then I would have to flush the toilet, another noise, and go back up the stairs again, they would creak, and probably have to come back down again in half an hour because I was drinking so much Pepsi."

She was still looking at him.

"Oh, I mean real Pepsi. I had to empty the bottles before I filled them, didn't I?"

"Who paid for the Pepsi? Not that I mean to pry."

She was beginning to develop a sense of not knowing where she was.

"What?"

Klara smiled and closed her eyes. And then she opened them again. This was another unexpected direction. Might as well pursue the meaning. Go all the way, far afield. She was beginning to sense a force, a pull. Coming apart. There was no reason to oppose it, no sense for that matter.

"So you have spent all of your life in an upstairs room drinking Pepsi and not wanting to make noises and . . . whatever?"

"Probably."

"Probably?"

"Maybe I have. It seems like all I have done for the last two years at Dartmouth is to stay in my room. Except when I would come out occasionally to debate about nuclear weapons or God. It seems as though I have been doing that forever."

Klara nodded. She did not allow her face to change expressions. You never knew how the connection would be made. Momentarily, she had forgotten that. Everything was connected. Dartmouth and the missiles. And God. He was clever or prescient. The genes. The life.

"Why then, life has been a room-to-room existence while waiting for the missiles, is that it? Something like waiting for Godot?"

She was not backing off, which was probably unwise.

"As a matter of fact, you know what?"

"I cannot imagine."

"Well, this may sound strange to you, but it makes me think of my first memory."

"Your what?"

"My first memory. I must have been a baby, because I was helpless."

"You were helpless," she repeated, and then without pause she broke into distant tones, as if beginning to chant, startling him: "'I remember the womb. Sound, sound, sound.' It is from a poem. That is all I can think of at just this moment. No, there is more. 'Sound, silent, sound. I can remember being in the womb with you.' I have never told anyone that. I do not believe I have ever told anyone that. I have known it, but I have never articulated it."

"That is incredible," he said. "I believe you."

But what was incredible, she thought, was how his mind roamed and she could understand without explaining it. Was it youth? Or maybe it was something else yet to be identified. He was not trying to trap her, was he? Why had she told him of her memory of the womb? He made connections. He made too many for his youth. And he made connections for them seemingly effortlessly. She worried about connections that could be made. She had avoided many, now and throughout her life. But she had been trapped by many, destroyed, she thought. It was in the nature of things. She had always envied those who could live in the present, discover it.

He went on.

"I was in a bed. A crib, maybe. A room, it must have been, was dark, though there was light nearby . . . out there. A pool of it, soft and spreading, or about to. Probably from underneath a door—and then somebody opened the door and said, 'A rat, yes, it's a rat. Shhh . . . get it before it gets near the baby.' I don't remember that anyone was afraid. Not that they saw rats every day. I think the rat was probably a mouse, and the room in the house was not in our home but in someone else's, because I think we were going somewhere, traveling. . . . It was not in Maine, but . . . I do not know if I am supposed to remember because . . . you see . . . I was born in Maine."

He paused, as if uncertain of himself, uncertain of the way, uncertain of what he was saying.

"I do not know how I got all of this information, this story."

She had an inkling. "I would think that it came to you. You were without choice. That is the nature of knowledge for us."

"I mean, a baby. How could a baby know?"

"Yes . . . but . . . I wonder, how do you know that it is your first memory?"

But just like that Timothy stopped talking and looked out the window and she knew he would remain silent for a while.

For Klara it should have been a welcome silence, the return of silence, except that again it was a silence that seemed unnatural, as if there were something wrong, that there should be no more silences. But, at first, when he had been talking, it had seemed unnatural as well, as if there were something wrong even then. For a while she had wondered if he would ever stop talking or where he was headed or if he was going to become hysterical and, if so, what she would do about it, what she would finally say, explain. She thought she would feel the need to do something. It could become unnecessarily complicated. Messy, even. And yet, she still did not think that he appeared nervous. Strange, but not nervous. Other-worldly. Manic? She was certain that sooner or later there would be a last bridge established between the two of them and one or both of them would be forced to decide whether or not to finally cross over. They did not have to cross over. Ever. No matter who might want it. They did not even have to approach one another. They were worlds apart, were they not? It had been so. Or maybe they were simply at different points of the same journey, returning, passing, never to meet again, because there would not be time to turn around. She could leave him in New York, simply walk away again, forever.

She remembered hearing once from his father that he had difficulty as a child playing the game Hide and Seek. Or perhaps difficulty was not the precise word. But after all of the children had run away to hide and the person who was *it* counted with hand over closed eyes and then announced here I come ready or not, all but Timothy began to make their way back to the telephone pole or the tree or the grate in the street, hoping to make it back unseen, all but Timothy, for even if he did begin to make his way back to the telephone pole or the tree or the grate in the street, no one ever knew if he did, no one ever knew about it, and he was never caught, for he never appeared again and no one could ever yell, "Allie allie in free." Yes, Timothy always went to hide and never came back.

But why was this happening now? Why was she wondering about him, about what he was up to, what was happening to him? About what to do? Why should she, they, care anymore? What could possibly be changed now? It was too late. Why had she even agreed to make the contact? She was not supposed to care. She had made that decision long ago. And she would not care now. Never. That was his concern. But it happened at times, things like this happened in life. Even in incidental moments you became curious, perhaps interested. And then, if you were not careful, you became involved. But not her. She had long ago learned how to avoid these situations. Had she not? What was there she should avoid anyway? Intimacy? Surely there would never be a danger of that again. Who was in control here anyway?

But then, looking at the dark outline of the back of his head, she thought again that he was like a child. Whom was she trying to fool? Of course she cared. She had never thought this day would come. Oh my God she cared. And the bridge was already there, had been there at the outset. They had arrived to find it. It had already been crossed once before. Together they had built it. She knew that even if he did not.

Timothy had not turned to look at Klara again. Had he at that moment, she would have looked away herself, afraid that he might look into her soul. This male youth, yes, for her he was simply a male youth, because in the floating spheres that is all he was, he gave her pause not simply because of who he was, but because she saw in this young man something that she must of necessity regard as false, something that she had refused to believe forevermore. But she saw it, she saw purity. The truth. It was like a mirage, a reflection, a dream, that which had the power to return. Yes, she knew that long ago she had come to feel a certain contempt for most men, young and old, and she knew that she had frequently sought to manipulate them, just as they had always sought to manipulate her. Slamunster was attempting to do just that, and she was being forced to consider her options. But this young mind, this young body, he was intense, vital, erotic, in mind and body, a purity, challenging, promising, and uncorrupted, burnished. Fascinating. Never to be explained. And it would not last. It would not last forevermore.

Ironically, in that sense she worshipped youth, as if separate from life, and sacred. Separate and sacred. An icon. That which was sacred was separate from life. Yes, that was the cruelty. But she scorned the temporality of youth, its incapacity to fulfill its promise, its mere suggestion, its insignificance because it was inconsequential. Its illusion. It angered her. Youth was simply a disconnected entity. Misunderstood by most, unappreciated and unworshipped for its true value, with no meaning beyond its immediate glow, for it could have none, and it needed none. Worthy of worship simply because of its design and ardor, its brilliant moment. But there were qualities of youth she scorned as well, the happiness, the gaiety of youth, the frivolity. Again, they were unearned, undeserved, irrelevant. The young had paid no price, met no demands, achieved nothing, lost nothing. Klara had said that to her daughter, Seema, often. Especially when she was angry with Seema. For the most part, young people generally made her angry for no apparent reason, or for too many reasons. A great many things made Klara angry. She had many memories.

Klara closed her eyes. She had been exhausted many times in her life, but she had rarely allowed it to show in the presence of others, particularly men, even young men. Her first memory of being tired to the point of nausea was in 1927, when at nine years old she had arrived in New York from Hungary with her mother and stepfather and they had taken a room in Harlem. One night her mother had sent her out for bread.

Klara opened her eyes again and looked at Timothy.

"I have a first memory, too."

"You do?" said Timothy, looking back at her as if astonished.

"Yes, I do. And it is not altogether unlike yours. I was a little girl in Hungary . . ."

"Hungary? You were a little girl in Hungary?"

He reacted as if she were telling him a bedtime story, and he looked quickly out the window, as if magically they were in Hungary at that very moment. He still felt as if he were in a foreign country. He had felt that way ever since he had gotten on the bus. It was a feeling he liked, a feeling of being away, floating, disconnected, of being unknown, mysterious, never to be defined, never to be found out, never discovered, never recognized. He looked at the scattered lights, at the faint lines of the land they were traversing. The bus was still in Massachusetts, or perhaps it was in Connecticut, the bus itself a foreign substance. What were the people out there doing? He looked back at Klara. She seemed mysterious, enigmatic, exotic. Was that because she was Hungarian? Was he certain that he had never met anyone like her before? From now on he had met her and her alone.

She was looking away from him, as if she were peering into the interior of the bus, looking into her crystal ball.

"I had been left alone in our house in the country. I could not have been more than four years of age. There was a storm. It was light outside or there was a light outside. Perhaps it was in the day but it was dark. I kept hearing a noise, maybe a voice, as if someone was trying to get inside the house. And I was afraid that they were after me. But each time I looked out the window I could not see any one or any thing. Which was strange but not strange, because I, the house, was in the steppe-land."

"The steppe-land."

"Yes. A vast, flat, open plain. A beautiful wasteland. It spreads east and west of a large river. I am from west of that river. The Danube."

"But you could not see anything."

"No. In that open land I could not see any thing and there was no thing to hide behind. That is the memory. I do not remember any thing else."

"So we both have a dream."

"Mine is not a dream," she quickly corrected him. "It is a memory. Did you not say that yours was a memory?"

Perhaps she should not have told him. After all, she was telling him more than he realized. And it was all there in the memory.

"Maybe I did dream it," he went on. "How can I know? Why should it matter? At least I do not worry about making noises anymore. Noises that people will hear."

Ah, yes, he was a strange young man, Klara thought, which pleased her. She was fascinated by the fact of his being in her presence, of the contact having been made again, even if he might prove difficult for her. Maybe impossible, fatal. And what could he know of life anyway? At his age, nothing. That was simply a fact of existence. Certainly nothing of the past, of the struggle. He did not even know about his father and his mother. Astonishing, but true. Did that put him at a disadvantage? Or was it an advantage, an advantage not to know from whence you came, because that meant that you did not fear where you were going? Which meant that you could be dangerous to others, to other things, that you could be powerful. Of course it was an advantage. Like father, like son. You would go where no one had gone before.

He looked so healthy. Thin, yes, but healthy. He was not frail, like Seema. At his age he probably did not have a healthy, daily diet, but he nevertheless looked imperious. He was well-bred. He had been well-stocked. That could not be achieved in a single lifetime. He could live off the ease, the frivolity and fat of his American and Hungarian forebears. Privilege. She knew something about that, just as she knew about frailty and loss. She had withstood both. Both were in her past. He might disagree, but she knew that he had never known severe material deprivation. Had never done without. In that sense he was completely out of touch with his true heritage. Took too much for granted. Her father had been a mayor in Hungary, the leading citizen of the town. And then nothing. That is what it was like to be a Jew. She had come to America with her mother and stepfather, but she had come with nothing. He had never experienced anything like that. No matter what had happened. She would not hear of it. For he assumed he would have power, control, affluence, forever and always. American heritage. Protected. Placed in a groove that negated questions. He had made this trip, but that did not necessarily mean anything. He could still withdraw. She could arrange that. As long as there was no knowledge, there was ample time for withdrawal. At his age and in his position he could take risks, experiment, have dreams while he still had the strength, the energy, and, most importantly, while he was still ignorant enough to possess the desire to dream. At this stage of his life there were few significant consequences and unimaginable possibilities. What did he know of fear? He had been neither humiliated nor crushed. He would not anguish about what could be lost. He could dream about what might be gained. She had known men in situations like that before, young men, and they were always men.

Of course, she had to admit there were exceptions, as much as she did not like to admit any such thing. Exceptions. Yes, she flushed, like father like son. True, this son, this young man, this Timothy, he did seem sensitive, even gentle. She had sensed that already. It was easy to detect. That pleased her. So rare. Was she, then, wrong in her judgment? What judgment? Had she made one? Surely she had not forgotten it?

But there was something else. She resisted the idea, but he seemed to be grieving. Was that it? No, that was not quite it. Was it a kind of agony? Was he in agony? She did not like to think it, because of his advantages. Money and everything. She was certain that went with it. The reason she resisted it. And she did not like to think it, the sort-of-agony, because she was drawn to that. Her reserve was lessened. It diluted her anger. No, not really that. What could he know of life? Nothing. Nothing. Nothing.

Forty-four. Odd, but hers was a beauty that would last until her death no matter how many years later that moment might arrive, or it would surprise and suddenly disappear, disintegrate. There would be no gradual, graceful transformation. It was in the women of her family. She remembered that. Her black hair accentuated her pearl-white skin. She knew that. It was why she kept her hair totally black. Her body was delicate but strong and shapely. She was scornful of a display of sensuality in women, unable to hide her own. A dancer's body. Having danced in her teens and twenties, she had powerful legs, full thighs, trim ankles. She had stopped dancing professionally at twenty-five, when she had begun studying for her doctorate in English, but she had continued with strenuous exercising. Now, in her middle years, she had only a slight paunch. She was strong in both mind and body, as strong as one could be at her age, and with her past. Mostly that.

He began again.

"If the bomb comes down now, why should I care? I mean, if you think about it, we really do not exist anyway. As we talk, our words are gone. A slip of the universe and we are gone. There will be no memory, individually or collectively. So how can I take all of this so seriously? It is ridiculous. How can they take themselves seriously?"

She looked him steadily in the eye. She wanted to take him in her arms, but, she said back to her voices, she had absolutely nothing to do with him. Silence. Not with what he had become, whatever that might be. So what is he to me, she suddenly asked herself, and realized that she had not consciously asked herself that question before. She had not acknowledged it. But the question had been there almost from the beginning, triggered by the thought that she was getting old and it was awful. She remembered him when he was a very little boy, not much more than a baby. His hair had been blond, blond in a blue navy suit, of course. She knew the picture well. A blond and blue baby. Quiet and sweet and probably even then a loner, independent.

He turned his head away from her, pretending to look out the window. She knew he had blushed. And then she herself blushed, realizing that he, the son of the father, had elicited her emotions, and that she had responded, she had shown her own desire. She did not like revealing it, nor did she like to admit it to herself, to know it, have it motivate her again. There were those memories, those spectres. She never had liked that, and she liked it even less now that she was forty-four. One thing was certain with her: in no way had the level of intensity decreased. Oh, the illusion of youth, the misleading beginning of life. Our whole life was in our youth. She remembered the feeling of uncertainty and discomfort which one felt at the beginning of anything, certainly at the beginning of life, and the driven need to plunge onward at each moment. There were the young and the rest of us were the walking dead.

She remembered sleeping with him the night before he disappeared . . . died. She had had a presentiment of it, that he was supposed to perhaps die. She had known it or thought it. The knowledge had made it different. He had clearly wanted her passionately, but she had made it so that it had not yet been possible for him to be passionate or powerful. First the initiation, the preparation. Then it would happen. It would be time. The burst. But he would be the gentle lover at first. She had guided him. The premoment when she had mouthed his penis, the premoment, the premoment when he had reached to caress her alabaster buttocks, the head of his penis looking distant, far-off, detached from him, a glistening shining ball, globe, the primordial universe. When she had moved to kiss him on the lips he had gently turned her on her back to tongue her as if for the first time. It had been a rare moment in their love-making; she had sensed that it would never happen again. She had been so agitated that she had felt that her entire body was liquid. Excruciating, pleasure. She had never experienced it before nor afterward. When he had entered her it was like being shot. She had thought it must be so. Shot with desire. Shot with exquisite passion. Yes, making love with a god. He had said afterward that if he had ever doubted that she was a strange sort, a mystic, he doubted no longer. Mystic she was.

And then she remembered, as if incongruously, she remembered that she had thought, recognized with horror,

"What if he has made me pregnant again?"

And as if on cue, reality had returned, he had said,

"I have not made you pregnant, have I?"

He had possessed total confidence that she knew. He had long before seen her that way, come to know her that way. He had looked at her with alarm, with horror in his face.

She saw his face. She remembered it. She remembered those words as if they had been her last.

"That is how we propagate the species," she had said, acidly. "You have known that for a while now, my little boy."

Timothy talked occasionally, broke the silence, and Klara listened, apparently because she had forgotten something. Her eyes were closed again. Occasionally her tongue moistened her lower lip. She was thinking how curious it was that he had to die, how all sons and daughters must die, all children, youth.

Tuesday, early morning hours, October 23, 1962

6

Angel Baby

Seema awoke suddenly. Her eyelids lifted, snapped open like a doll's. She looked the length of her simple bed to the twisted and gnarled branches of the tree framed by her bedroom window eight floors above the city cement. At first she did not know where she was. The branches, touched by frost and aglow from street lamps, looked like strips of a neon sign. Seema attempted to read the sign and she was frightened when she could not. Signs were important to read. Klara had taught her that. All wisdom was in the reading of signs.

"Why can't I read it?" she wondered.

She was growing more and more fearful and apprehensive in the crescendo of her youthful awakening from her powerful sleep. The sign was twisted, distorted, burning brightly. It was an evil sign.

"I've got to tell Myshkin what the sign says," she thought with alarm.

Myshkin was Dostoevsky's idiot and in her dream, still partially with her, Seema had not altogether approved of him. She approved totally of Natashya. Natashya was beautiful, mysterious, unpredictable, commanding, volatile and Russian. It was a good thing to be a Russian. That is what Seema's mother had said many times, although it was Seema's understanding that Klara believed that it was good to be anything other than American, with the possible exception of specified Hungarians. Klara said that Americans were adolescent, superficial, venal, and gross, as well as pampered and indulged. And spoiled. As for the Hungarians, a number of those who had escaped their country during the 1956 uprising and had fled to the United States were fascist murderers. So said Klara.

Of course, for Klara most of humanity came up wanting. She judged them absolutely and devastatingly. In her panorama the skies spread before a swarm of beggars and locusts, parasites and vipers, and other malevolent earth wonders destined upon wanton destruction, not to mention perversion.

Altogether, Seema knew her mother to be a person of singular views. For example, according to Klara most men of the world, not merely American males, were either woman-beaters or open, secret, or latent homosexuals, or both, which to Klara meant that most men hated women, were afraid of women, and behaved vindictively and cruelly toward women at every opportunity under the sun and stars, particularly under the stars. To make it harder for women, men had all of the power, which mainly meant that men had all of the money, and all men were constantly exploiting or attempting to exploit women, usually with great success and often with public show, the latter a late-summer behavioral characteristic that Klara often commented upon, although if pressed she would admit that not all men were born in late July and in August, just as it was probable that not all men were either woman-beaters or homosexuals or both. But that did not matter, the literal facts did not matter. There were explanations. The concentration of the spheres, the daily, even the moment to moment concentrated and distributed pressures of the universe determined all.

The predominant form of man's exploitation of woman was sexual, one perversion intertwined with another, with another, with another, an ancient and complex interlace with many indecipherable, untraceable, forgotten strands. Unfortunately, most women were malleable in men's hands because they eagerly, sometimes passively and helplessly, and always mindlessly, allowed themselves to be manipulated and cultivated into becoming exactly what men wanted them to be, servants to men's needs, caterers to male desires, liars before the grotesque masculine ego. Women readily encouraged this perversion. They wanted it. Simply, women were the flesh of the hearth and the queen manikins of the fashion parade. And, actually, it was no secret that women relished using their bodies to get what they desired. Over centuries of conditioning, females had become body junkies. That was absolutely undeniable.

Thus was Mother Emphatic Klara as translated by Daughter Precocious Seema. Seema's was a developing, thrashing intellect, a mental sharpness that threatened to duplicate her mother's, and yet she was delicate and timid and a vulnerable, ethereal spirit, as her mother had been long ago and far away.

The hallmark of Klara's philosophy-in-translation was that practically everyone, male or female, was anti-Semitic. If you were a Jew you never forgot that.

"I am one-fourth Jewish," thought Seema. "My grandfather was a Jew, but my grandmother was not, so that makes me one-fourth. Mother is one-half. One-half Jewish woman. I am sure of it."

Of course, Seema was referring exclusively to her maternal grandparents. The ones from Hungary. The Mayor and the Grandmother. The obscure, mysterious paternal side was never discussed and rarely alluded to and even then mostly inadvertently, by misdirection. It was the great mystery of Seema's young life, and thus the first subject. She had been told nothing directly of her father and, regarding that body of lore, she had never been encouraged to ask questions. Based upon what she knew, she had a cut-and-dry case to have been born of no father at all. And yet, for as long as she could remember in her young life, she had always cherished the dream, harbored the conviction that her father had been a very special personage whom she would some day or year or century recognize in the universe. This despite the fact that Klara had never discussed the subject with her, nor did Seema have a sense that Klara would discuss it anytime soon, perhaps not in this world. In fact, Seema did not even think of her . . . father or whatever he was or was not as either dead or alive. He was simply a presence in her consciousness, an image of her vision. And he was open to endless interpretation and wonderment, a kaleidoscope for her mind, a chameleon to her whims.

Seema rubbed her eyes and yawned. With the growing dominance of dawn, the natural neon was not as bright now, and it no longer seemed important that she could not read it. It was not menacing anymore, because it was not glowing as much, and simultaneously with the ebbing of the light the radar of the dream was fading. Like Sleeping Beauty, she might yet awaken.

What Seema did not like in Dostoevsky's novel was the fact that Natashya spent so much time with Rogoshin. Rogoshin was frightening. He was an animal and not a very nice one. Why did Natashya run away with him? And abandon poor Myshkin? How could she leave Myshkin? Poor Myshkin. It must be awful for him to feel abandoned, she thought. Secretly, Seema really liked Myshkin, but she would never tell Klara that, because Klara liked Myshkin as well, no matter what she might say. How Seema had come to be so certain of that she did not know, but she knew, apart from the fact that she read everything her mother read, every book her mother was reading for her classes and more, more and other books her mother had read in the past, the past before Seema. Thus she was reading Dostoevsky's *The Idiot*.

Myshkin was young and sensitive and . . . pure like a saint. And beautiful like Natashya. Natashya and Myshkin belonged together. Seema thought that she and Myshkin belonged together as well, which, however, occasioned as yet little or no jealousy toward the ravishing Natashya. In one respect, Seema did not know with certainty how she felt toward Natashya. She did not know if she linked Natashya more with herself or with Klara. And she did not choose to dwell upon it.

The only problem with Myshkin was that he was sometimes . . . he seemed weak. If she were granted the power, Seema thought, she would slap Myshkin when he was weak. Kick him. Or make him take his clothes off and stand outside for a half hour in the middle of the winter in Russia, preferably in February, although she would have to check up on that in the library, maybe look it up in the Farmer's Almanac, see whether or not February was the coldest month of the year in Russia. But she imagined that in Russia, regardless of the month, it would be much colder than it was in New Jersey and New York, as yet the only temporal boundaries of the world personally known to

Seema. Seema assumed that everything about the Russians was of a more extreme nature than for the Americans, even Americans beyond New Jersey and New York.

Like the Emporer Napoleon, General Tuffy would never survive a Russian winter, so maybe Seema would not make him stand in the snow, especially if he agreed to go away. Curiously, she thought that Klara would make General Tuffy remain in the cold and snow and ice and the howling wind of the night for longer than a half hour. Seema was certain of that as well. There would not be a hint of mercy. It was a fact that Seema had difficulty understanding, because if General Tuffy froze to death he would not bring them any more groceries. Their lives would change dramatically. As much as it pleased her to think of Tuffy gone forever, she could not imagine life without his presence. Actually, perhaps Klara would only make him stay downstairs in the bar.

A door had shut. Yes, that is what it was. And Seema did not have to worry about the sign anymore. She looked to her bedroom door. Closed, of course. Closed because General Tuffy was out there. Or had been. That is what had awakened her, General Tuffy closing the outside door at the end of the hallway. Had he left? Gone to the bar? Probably. Maybe not. If he had left, that meant he knew Klara was not coming back tonight. Otherwise he never would have left. Seema did not know why he had come tonight, anyway. Was it not Tuesday? Wednesday? He usually came on Friday. She had begun to pay attention to things like that. Clearly, on this day, perhaps during the coming days, something out of the ordinary was happening, something mysterious, something having to do with Mother Klara's stars.

More and more, Seema was learning that older people did not want you to know what they were doing or why they did what they did, especially if they did not know themselves. So they lied to you, or to themselves. Or they just did not tell you anything. All you could do was watch them and wait to see what happened. Klara had said that she was going to Boston to see a Hungarian poet. Something about translating his poems. But Seema had not believed her. True, she knew her mother had translated poetry for a number of Hungarian poets, especially since 1956. She knew her mother did a lot of things for a lot of people, mostly literary. But this time she had not believed Klara. She did not know why she had not believed her, but she had not. Perhaps it was because Klara had seemed to insist upon the version of her journey that she related. And perhaps it was because Klara frequently did not tell Seema anything. But Seema knew that on this particular occasion Klara was telling a tale, not the truth. Seema knew that.

Klara also would insist later that she had told Seema at what time she would be back, but she had not. Whenever Klara arrived she would insist that that was the precise time she had given. She was never wrong, she was never late. At least now Seema knew Klara was not coming back tonight. Unless General Tuffy had tired of waiting. No, he never tired of waiting for Klara.

Perhaps he was anxious, which was not unusual, and he could not wait for her to come to him. Perhaps he was going to meet her. Or he had gone to the bar to drink until her return. That was not unusual, either. Of course, he might have made a mistake. Seema thought that he was quite capable of that. He might have decided that Klara was not coming back tonight when, in fact, she was. Older people were mysterious, but they were not infallible. Seema had learned that recently as well. For a long time Seema had thought that adults were both mysterious and infallible. She had believed the two went together. She had believed it was a law of the universe.

But what fun she could have now. Terrible Tuffy was gone. The General had retreated and Klara had not come home from seeing the Hungarian poet, or whatever it was that she was doing. It was time for a celebration and, indeed, Seema had something to celebrate. Tomorrow was her fourteenth birthday. Today, actually. Not that she and Klara would celebrate it. Klara did not believe in birthdays.

"Of course she doesn't," said Seema out loud as she lay in her bed.

She raised herself to her elbows, lowered her chin to her chest, and, growling and scowling in imitation of her mother, said:

"'How ludicrous of poor, pathetic human beings to think there is anything special about the fact that they were born, that they exist.'"

Seema laughed hysterically. Her mother was so fierce and foreboding, and frightening. But not now. She was not here now. Now, Seema could celebrate. She rose, turned on the light, and went to her mirror and dresser, a large, chipped, gold-trimmed oval mirror on top of a stack of wooden fruit crates painted black. First she would dress for the occasion. She sat down, and then hesitated. Should she wash before she did anything else? If General Tuffy was out there, she would not be able to wash. Or would not want to. The bathroom was out there as well, down the hallway. She would never walk by General Tuffy in a nightgown. Actually, she would never walk by anybody in her nightgown, except her mother, and she would never walk by anybody in the nude, including her mother. So, she would make believe that General Tuffy was out there. She would dress without washing. Or, rather, she would adorn herself first and cleanse herself later.

The mascara. Thick, black on her eyelids. Long, chestnut hair with just a tint of red, smoothed and stroked with her long-handled silver brush, her hair falling to the small of her back, to just above her small buttocks. At the end of each stroke, Seema thought of the hard bristles of her hairbrush striking her buttocks. More makeup. Under and over her green eyes, green eyeliner. Lots of red, rose rouge. And lipstick. Deep crimson, almost black. And then, for a final touch, she smoothed, brushed her hair straight down her forehead, pressed it against her flesh.

Seema smiled, having thought of one more thing. She looked down at the front of her sheer, blue nightgown. It was piled in delicate layers around her. It had once been Klara's. That Klara could not deny. What she had tried to deny and what Seema had elicited from her in an unguarded, uncharacteristically open mood was that Klara had worn the blue nightgown in her youth, in the days when she had traveled the country dancing in nightclubs and bars and hotels, days that must have been wonderful and exciting, Seema believed, romantic, lovely days in a blue nightgown. No matter what Klara said Klara had been a teenager then. Not much older than Seema was now. Klara had been precocious about everything. Advanced. But, Klara always emphasized advanced in relation to things of the mind. Things of the mind. So she never ceased to remind Seema.

Seema parted the nightgown, and hesitated.

"I wonder if Greta Garbo would do it?" she thought.

She had been told many times that she looked like Greta Garbo, so many times that she had come to insist upon it herself.

"No one knows if Greta Garbo did it and no one will ever know if I did it either," she decided.

She parted the nightgown and dabbed the nipples of her small breasts with the lipstick. She closed the nightgown over her secret.

So what should she do now? She could go to her house above the ocean, high above the waves, the white surf, the black rocks, white water, black rocks, surrounded by gray-black clouds. Seema lived alone in her house of a hundred rooms and four floors. Maybe five floors. She had never been to the top of her house. Alone except for a large, sometimes larger, black, sometimes red, dog. She also had a horse she rode mostly in the afternoons. She rode it now while she sat at her dresser. She also went for a walk on the beach with her dog. Neither the dog nor the horse had names, because she never spoke to them.

Suddenly Seema got up and started dancing around her room, throwing her arms up and out one way, up and out the other. This was doubly delicious, not only because Klara was not there, but because Klara would not approve. Just as suddenly Seema stopped dancing, realizing that she had not made certain that General Tuffy had left. On her toes she went slowly and quietly to the door. She remembered the first time she had opened the door of her room with General Tuffy here in the apartment. The first thing that had appeared was General Tuffy's huge buttocks thrust into the air. She had closed the door quickly, uncertain of and frightened by what she had seen. And then, overwhelmed with laughter, she had buried her face in her pillow. Until that moment it had never occurred to Seema that General Tuffy was a big man.

Presently, she opened the door slowly, and looked. Klara's bed, small and empty. The small table Klara and Seema used for meals, and where Klara studied, wrote, and prepared her literary work. Two bookcases, filled. Klara had made them. Boards and bricks filled with Paul Valéry, Henry Miller, Virginia Woolf, Henri Bergson, Anais Nin, Henry James, Charles Baudelaire, and others. No room for anyone else, except maybe a child. And Tony, the stray, mongrel dog Klara had saved from the pound. He was probably lying down in the kitchen. How many cats? It varied. None presently, but ordinarily there was at least one. As many as four at a single time. Cats Klara saved from starvation, from the cold, and, she said, from other human beings. She nursed them, brought them to health, fed them, fed them with a nose dropper. Weak, sickly animals. And usually found homes for them. Sometimes they ran away, disappeared. Sometimes, if sick, they did not recover.

There was no room for anyone else. Klara's apartment. It was sparse, ascetic, angular. It was not barren. Anyone else was an intruder. And, at times, there were intruders, mostly men who came and disappeared, men brought and sent away, dismissed, by Klara. A new man recently, tall, thin, kind of a nervous man. Seema knew better than to ask names. He had been appearing more and more lately. All of a sudden. That was not a good sign, Seema was certain of it. But what could be done? And General Tuffy was a constant intruder, a constant presence in the apartment. Or so it seemed to Seema's imagination. Which made Seema, looking silently through her partly opened door, feel he might still be there. There was no sound. There was no General Tuffy. No Klara. No Hungarian poet.

And then Tony suddenly came into the hallway from the kitchen, stood there and looked at her, his ears raised. Friendly Tony, the black mongrel dog. Presently Seema and Tony lived in the apartment by themselves, in the apartment high above the bar, high above the waves of sound.

"You silly, dumb dog," laughed Seema, and she whirled into Klara's room, pirouetting.

The freedom was wonderful. The entire apartment, hers, overwhelmed by her house above the ocean. She ran to the beginning of the short hallway and, taking one long step, a half jump, she landed on a small rug, and, as if on a magic carpet, slid by the bathroom and kitchen doors all the way to the outside door of the apartment, bumping slightly against it as she rode above the waves. Tony jumped back into the kitchen, barely getting out of Seema's way as she slid by. As soon as she passed him, he ran out and leapt up on her. Giggling and slightly out of breath, Seema stroked Tony's head, ruffled his black fur.

"Oh, yes, Tony, I do love you, you dumb dog, even if you are Klara's dog. Some day I'll let you meet my dog and then we'll have such fun. But only if you don't tell Klara. You mustn't, you know, my Tony. Come now, let's dance."

The girl and the dog went back into Klara's room. Seema took Tony by his front paws and danced with him in a circle, laughing, while he barked in excitement. They became entangled in the blue nightgown and, quickly, Seema shed the gown and they resumed dancing around it. Around and around they danced, the slight, nude girl with painted nipples, painted face, her brown chestnut hair tossed in the air, the black dog, awkward on his hind legs, falling out of her grasp and quickly jumping up again.

And then Seema stopped and stood still, because she was certain that Klara was standing there, standing in the doorway, staring at her, scowling. Was she alone or with a man? Seema stood motionless, silent, her arms hanging at her side, her head down. She was embarrassed by her nudity, frightened that Klara would see the makeup. Tony circled her, wiggling his body and shaking his tail, stopping and looking up at her, and then wiggling and shaking again, confused.

"I have sacrificed everything for you," Seema thought her mother might be saying, "and you are an ungrateful creature."

For although Klara appeared to be mightily pleased at any single thing that benefited her daughter, and despite the fact that she would apparently do anything to advance her daughter's cause and allow nothing and no one to deter her, it was also true that her fierce propensity for moralizing was frequently soldered to harsh and unrelenting criticism of her daughter as irresponsible, selfish, willful and inconsiderate.

"Seema!"

Slowly, Seema looked up and, at first, she saw Klara, indeed, standing there, angry, dressed in black, scowling. And, like a shadow, someone was with her, someone Seema did not recognize, someone she sensed she should know. But Klara was not there, not even alone. Despite this, Seema continued to feel Klara's presence for several minutes, continued to feel that something had happened. Slightly chilled and weary, she bent over and picked up the nightgown and went back into her room and shut her door. She had better go back to bed, she thought. After all she did have to go to school this morning. And then there was afterward. There would always be afterward. Tomorrow.

Tuesday morning, October 23, 1962
or Wednesday or precisely . . .

7

Sentimental Journey

Associate Professor John Darnell Slamunster finally realized that Hilde Johnson stood before him alone. It was after 10 P.M. Everyone else had left the classroom. She was talking. She had been talking. What had he heard? He was hearing things and not hearing more and more these days.

". . . embarrassed the other night. I know what I said probably sounded stupid. It came out the wrong way. I did not really say what I meant to say, although what was I saying?"

Hilde waited as if to see whether or not the Professor, Professor Slamunster would hear her, recognize her. It would be mortification if he did not.

She laughed nervously. And then she had no choice but to continue talking. He had pressured her into it simply by not responding.

"I mean, I did not mean that I disliked the brooding, dark Russian soul, just that I wonder why they were like that, why they write like that. Why doesn't anyone talk about that?"

"You can find out from me. I have a Russian soul. I think that we all have Russian souls, including you."

He was either attempting a wayward witticism or he was commenting compulsively. But she did not appear to have heard him. Their wired nerves fenced them off from one another.

"Oh well," she said, feeling more and more awkward, "I thought it was worth talking about. There are just too many shadows over there."

She wondered if she should just walk away. But she did not think that she could or she did not know how to, not at the moment, not with him in this situation. If she walked away he would notice her and then she would be embarrassed again. But why should she feel that way? Was she not attempting to get his attention?

"Not just over there."

At last, she realized, he had spoken. At least she thought he had spoken. But to her?

"I think it must be the way Russia's buildings and roads are constructed. And a few other things."

"I'm sorry?" she asked, bewildered.

"I am not really joking," he said, conceding defeat. "The shadows? Oh well, it is just that I am too tired to go into what I have not thought out. I agree with you. It is quite confusing, and mysterious."

They looked at each other for an instant, he with wonder at the thoughts he was having, she with wonderment at what he must be thinking. And then he took her by the arm.

"You must come with me. I have to show you something. I must show somebody."

He had made the decision that very moment. For Slamunster, life was both frequent and, sometimes, instantaneous change. This was pure impulse. He was troubled. He was wondering exactly where Klara Blazek was at the moment. Where was she? He was not yet desperate, but more and more troubled and perhaps this would help to provide some answers. It might lead to something. Who knew? He had to return. He would take her with him.

"But . . . it is late."

"Exactly. A perfect time."

"I don't understand."

"At this point you should not understand, because I don't understand and that is why I want you to come with me. I have to show somebody something, something you must see for yourself. I can't explain it. If I attempted to . . . you would think I was . . ."

"But . . . I . . ."

"Come. Don't talk. Now. Just come. I want you to see what an extraordinary world you and I live in. As I said, there are some things that I do not understand, and perhaps you can help me. At the very least you can not understand along with me."

He laughed nervously.

She was both flattered and bewildered. He seemed very much out of sorts. Like a creature she could not identify.

They left the classroom together without another word and without looking at each other. As they walked down the four flights with a sense of urgency, they could hear the building emptying, emptying at levels into the Village, into the city, the footsteps passing to quiet, elevators descending, street sounds nearby, with doors open, sounds coming to the classrooms, the offices, the hallways.

Outside, they walked briskly, Slamunster still holding her arm as they crossed streets, taking her, long strides, passed blocks, crosstown and then headed uptown, walking quickly along up Sixth Avenue until they arrived at 14th Street, where they got on a crosstown bus in the opposite direction, heading east for the journey into carnival land, the lower city rapidly changing the further east they moved, a journey that was long although physically they did not travel far, a journey into the cheap, gaudy, cardboard sidespace of the city that was always going out of business, shops of nobody's clothing, pawned upon goods, neoning signs, foodpastes, the city gone tomorrow, maintaining a shabby, fragile state of permanency in a breeding ground.

Weary and feeling strangely vulnerable, Hilde Johnson had lapsed with the jostling of the bus into musing about her childhood, her body lolling about in her seat. She was of slight build, but she was wiry, limber, athletic. Her spirit had evaporated, easily.

When Slamunster pulled her sleeve, she returned. She glanced up quickly, frightened, remembered her place, having yet to fathom it. He nodded, indicated it was time to get off the bus.

"Why here?" she asked, as if pleading. "What can you want to show me here?"

"You will see soon. Come on now. We must get off. Just remember that it is nothing personal. I have nothing to do with it. Nobody does, I think."

And they were on the street, the bus forgotten as quickly as the classroom had been, walking by the shady, jazzed nightpeople, the jingles and the smells, exhaust fumes and fried food, olived, straight along until they stopped at a building, a deterioration with a neon marquee harping:

Marie's Delights—Adults Only

"Here? We are actually going in here?"

Without responding, Slamunster bought tickets and entered, as if he could not wait, and she felt compelled to follow, having rejected instantaneously the only other choice, of remaining on the street by herself. Then, too, it was probable that she was committed at this time, this late evening, under this spell, to follow him anywhere, regardless of the consequences. At this moment, he had complete power over her. At any rate, she followed him without a word, and Slamunster said nothing, moved toward a flight of stairs indicating a balcony. At the top of the stairs they passed through a curtain into the darkness.

Slamunster stumbled now, fumbling for the way. There had been a fundamental change. They groped for seats and sat down. They had stepped into the space of darkness, sensed their elevation, although they could see nothing, except the bodies on the screen. Rather, two breasts, each twenty feet in diameter, rose beyond and above. Two massive hands squeezed.

Hilde Johnson was shocked, muscles tight, constricted, her personal siren on high, shrieking in silence. She stared at the screen, the people, a man and a woman on a bed. It was in color. She was warm, awkward. It was the most extraordinary sensation, because she believed that she was being watched as she watched the screen, embarrassed. Her head felt as if it were being squeezed, as if it were in a cloud of pressure, felt like putty. She had protested their coming, certainly—had she not?—and she would have continued to do so had Professor Slamunster only asked her as he should have asked her—he had not said a word since they had entered the balcony of the make-believe theater. Not that she could call this a theater. She was aware that these movie-houses were scattered around the city, concentrated on 42nd Street, she had thought, knew that they were a familiar sight, their marquees of enticement, the still photos of nude women which she had considered revolting, degrading. She had never entered one until now. Never.

Loooking, she had first seen the exposed breasts, comprehending that they were breasssts, the man and woman embracing, intercourse, simulating simulating. She was shocked and electrified, breathing with difficulty, she was captivated looking at and disgusted with the bodies, beginning to anticipate, her head swelling. She had imagined before what was to be seen, almost anything, not believing, but she had never specified to herself what almost anything could and would be.

By now she could see others in the audience in front of her, to her left and to her right. Not wanting to be seen, she looked, surprised that after black blindness she could see so well, curious to see who would come to such a place. Why? How could they? But, of course, she was there herself. There must be unimaginable reasons.

She noticed that the balcony had sides, sides that extended, dipping to a slightly lower level like a moderate roller coaster, less in sight the further away they were, more and more in shadows to pitch black. Could one learn to see there as well? Actually, why would anyone dare to go there? She certainly would not.

"That is what I brought you to see," Slamunster whispered, having seen the line of her gaze. "Let's go down there."

"What do you mean?"

They rose from their seats. Standing, having elevated themselves, they could now see for the first time the floor below, see it as if it had suddenly appeared, had appeared because they were looking, could see that the audience was sparse and widely scattered, scattered and looking abandoned in sprawled repose. They descended to the left, along the sides of the balcony, stepped carefully and slowly down a short flight of invisible stairs to the next plateau, to the next lower level where the side balcony extended all the way to the front of the theater, to the left of and beyond the screen, ending without a doubt in absolute darkness, behind the lighted screen.

Slamunster stopped and whispered in her ear again. He had a story to tell by way of a mystery.

"The first time I came here, ah, I'll tell you why later, perhaps, but I began to notice while I was sitting in the back balcony that a number of people, but one by one, would go down the side passageways, down here, down there. A constant flow. They would come back, one by one, but only after a passage of time, a duration. Naturally I became curious to see what was there. It was a diversion. I thought it took my mind off what I had come here for in the first place. I followed somebody here."

He paused. She said nothing. And he began again to whisper.

"When we get to the end we will stop and lean against the wall. It will not take long. Just watch. If someone approaches you, do not worry. Just avoid looking into their eyes. Otherwise they will think that you are interested. One of them. Then it could happen to you too."

As if in a trance—Hilde Johnson did not ask why they were doing this, what they were doing or where they were going—they walked slowly further along the side balcony, toward the front and to the left of the screen on which the man and woman had yet to finish their embrace. She continued to watch while Slamunster had apparently turned his gaze elsewhere, taken his interest elsewhere. The further along they went, the closer to the end of the balcony they got, if end it did, the blacker it got as they passed gradually and nearly out of the path of light emanating from the screen.

Suddenly, two bodies brushed by them going in the opposite direction, two bodies that must have touched both of them, which confused her. He had said one by one, but this was two, and this two was also a man and a woman. The pale light from the silver screen revealed a black man and a white woman. She sensed that they had come from the screen itself. She felt them look at her and Slamunster, felt their pause, but nothing was said and they moved away.

Slamunster grasped her arm.

"Whew, unh, unh, unh, that was close. They thought we were competition, I think. At first, well, well, well."

But now they were near the end. The whisper again.

"The wall is here. We can lean against it. Watch, but I won't say enjoy."

She wondered what he could mean because she had already been watching —how could one be immersed in total darkness and not look toward the light?—and for a few minutes Hilde Johnson continued to watch the screen, now at an angle, a half-screen, barely in view to the right. The man and the woman were still having intercourse, which was beginning to bother her in new ways. How long would it last? A few more steps and the screen would have been blocked out by a short wall projecting straight out from the back or, as it were, the front of the make-believe theater. Coitus interruptus.

After a while, slowly, stiffly, she moved her head, turned it ever so slightly, as if a hand were pushing her unwilling face to the left. From the light of the half-screeeeen to the blackness, she was blinded. She saw and then she was blinded, back and forth, until she stopped looking backward to the screen. A few feet away, cut off from the lighted screen by the projecting wall, and in darkness, she could barely see two or three figures standing, leaning against a back wall. To the left she could see another stairwell dropping off, descending still further, probably to the depths of the make-believe theater, beyond the screen.

At short intervals, single people passed, coming from the back stairs or from the side balcony. Some kept moving, slowly, never stopping, as if in a procession, pacing in step, descending the back, last stairway, disappearing, or returning to where Hilde Johnson and Professor Slamunster had been.

And then one shrouded figure stopped next to another leaning against the wall. She thought it was a male, and it was as if he had stopped to converse with the other, another male she thought, as close as they were, although no words could be heard, she could not hear them speak. They were facing each other; they were very close. Were they speaking? Why did they not speak? Was it not time?

Hilde Johnson looked back to the screen where two men were now groping, stroking, lying with the single woman of the exposed breasts, two exposed penises.

She sensed that it had already begun before she looked again, that the man whose face she could not see had already reached for the young male, or perhaps she had looked just as the man reached . . . for the young male. He . . . had reached and taken the young male's penis in his hand. She could tell by the motion. She could see that. So it must have begun before, he must have unzipped the young male's pants before she had looked, started fondling when she looked back as if on cue. The young male, slight of figure, was still leaning, except now he had straightened, stood straight as the other, the other faceless man, bent down, crouched and—Hilde tried to swallow, except that her mouth and throat were dry—took the young male's penis in his mouth. And then another, the other who had been leaning beside the young male, moved closer, leaned and kissed the young male on his neck. The kneeling figure continued mouthing the penis, only he was now pulling down the pants of the young male, and the other was pulling, had already pulled, tugged the coat off, was unbuttoning the shirt, exposed his chest, was stroking, caressing his chest.

Hilde had not realized it before, but there were now five or six more figures standing around in a semi-circle, as if directed there by the projector of the theater, all of them reaching, touching, apparently caressing the young male's body. Hilde imagined that, assumed that, because she could no longer see. The young male was surrounded, out of view, covered from sight by bodies, touched and covered by hands.

Hilde could hear him, someone, groaning. She turned her gaze back to the right, back to the screen and beyond to where, over the heads of the abandoned bodies below, she could see another side balcony, to where she could see single figures, one by one, moving into and out of another darkness, another darkness to the right of the screen. And then she moved her head, rotated it back to the left, swept her gaze back across the screen again to the left toward the groaning.

As if Slamunster knew that he had gone far enough, too far perhaps, that perhaps he had lost control, lost his way, which in part was precisely what he had wanted to discuss, he took Hilde out of the make-believe theater quickly, but not before they passed down the last dark passageway, passed again at the bottom of the last stairwell the black man and the white woman, except that the black man simply stood there impassive and motionless as a white man had intercourse with the white woman. Must have been. From off the screen. Simulating.

But what had startled Slamunster the most before he had left the theater with Hilde Johnson was that moment when he looked into the eyes of the man he knew, one of his colleagues, and saw someone he did not recognize. They had stared at each other for only an instant but it had seemed forever before the two of them had passed on. Slamunster had not deliberately sought the encounter. He had not wanted to be seen. Not now. Maybe never. Who could foretell? He had known of its possiblity, but he had not been prepared for it. There was never preparation.

Professor André Cordon was amused at what he took to be Slamunster's stunned reaction, and after watching him and his female companion disappear around a dark corner, Cordon climbed the dark stairwells until he had arrived at the scene of the young man and his attendants and forthwith intruded himself, pulled the young man's shirt and pants completely off and observed the completed performance.

Lights, camera, action.

Slamunster and Hilde Johnson left by a side exit, framed for a second by the light from the red neon exit sign over their heads, left quickly. They did not speak or look at each other. They left and walked to a corner. Without asking, without agreeing, they continued walking, walked uptown, up the east side avenue. They walked for half an hour until they stopped by the river, the East River, stopped on a walkway, a platform, and stood silently looking out at the tossing river waves, rough waves, unpatterned, cool evening, quiet black waters.

Slamunster spoke first.

"Tell me if it is none of my business, but . . ."

He stopped, and not just to pause. He had stopped. And she said nothing. Ordinarily he would have asked his question without hesitation. He would have begun with a peremptory preface that cut off any objections the person might make, simply stole them from the individual, spoken in a tone that suggested that he, of course, assumed that the person whom he was addressing would give a complete, thorough answer to his question, to any of his questions, no matter how probing, no matter how personal the answer required might be. He ordinarily assumed that no one would refuse him, and ordinarily they did not. Had the individual not answered his question Slamunster probably would have been reduced to silence, like now, except that in this instance he had not asked his question. Rather, he resorted to what for him constituted a confession.

He did not begin with questions. Images of Klara Blazek had been interfering, flashing, shuttering on and off in his brain.

"I wondered how you would react. You could not possibly think that is the way it is. But, of course, it is because we saw what we saw."

"Yes. I . . . was not prepared for it. I was there and it was happening."

"I ask myself why we were even there, why I continue to go there, I mean. Were you frightened? Not that you should have been if you were not."

"Yes, I guess I was. I don't know. Were you? I mean, I felt awkward."

"Because you were shocked or because you were aroused or both?"

"I guess . . . I kept looking at the screen and back at . . . what they were doing. I don't know. It was unbelievable . . . awful. There was a woman on the screen. And then there were all men. And then there was another woman. Do you think anyone in the theater could see them?"

"We could. Perhaps everyone was involved, implicated. Perhaps everyone kept changing places, roles. Except for us, of course."

"Do you think that other people know that, that, there is a place where people do these things?"

"Yes. Maybe they do other things that these people do not do. Ha. They do, indeed. I am beginning to think . . ."

"The woman was on the screen, but I seemed to sort of dissolve as, well, me. I did not feel or think like I was Hilde Johnson."

Neither spoke for a moment. She asked the next question.

"Why do you go there, that is, I assume you have been before, I mean, we went straight there . . . so you knew . . ."

Her question had been lost.

"I am not the only professor who frequents that establishment," he rejoined, smiling in a knowing way, and then not smiling.

He did not think he was justifiying himself. But what could he say? What could he explain?

She recognized his answer for the non sequitur it was, saw the disturbance on his face, and then, unbelievably, he darted in yet another, completely different direction.

"I am certain they go there for discussions of foreign policy and to swap secrets."

"I don't . . ."

He laughed nervously.

"Not that they neglect domestic policy." He laughed nervously again.

"Although they should probably call it world policy. They are all secret agents of all of the governments of the world. Yes, I have been showing you something of the nature of the world tonight. Something of our society. It reaches everywhere. America. The skin flick. Of course, we all know that it is a Commie stronghold. The theater. What else? They are all Commies in there, crawling all over like rodents. This is what G-men must combat, which is why they are in there as well. You understand me, of course?"

He laughed again.

"Absolutely not."

"I tell you, this is underground sexual energy and more. I . . . wonder what will happen . . . I mean, it is smoldering in here, I mean there, all closed up, closed off. And maybe some day it will explode and spread from here to . . . everywhere, eternity. What would that do? It could connect everything. Like radiation. Forget nuclear missiles. They are superfluous. This has transformed my thinking."

Professor Slamunster had been leaning out over the railing, leaning further out as the intensity of his words increased, leaning as if he would stretch clear across the river, staring out at the river. Suddenly he turned to face the city. The traffic continued on FDR Drive. They started walking again.

"Do you know what I think of?"

"No."

"Have you ever seen Brueghel's 'The Triumph of Death?'"

"Yes. Pictures of it. Yes, yes," she said, as if impatient.

"I saw it in Madrid. At the Prado. Horrifying. And fascinating. What we saw tonight could be regarded as simply a preliminary sketch for that painting. Not even that. A pale suggestion, a touch. And 'The Triumph of Death' was done in the 1500s. It is a grotesque, chaotic moment that has been forever. Death is an army. An overwhelming army of skeletons destroying people. The dead destroying the living."

He shook his head.

"But . . ." he began, after silence, as if he were quoting someone, "art should divert hearts and minds from the observation and the representation of death . . ."

"It should? All art? Who said that? A religious figure? No, that could not be."

"And perhaps that does it, or it glorifies it. Frightening. It is like a dream when something horrible is happening that you cannot stop. But it is happening. It is the joke of life. Life, the cruel joke, the fear of something you cannot prevent. But if you can fear it, there is the worse illusion that you can stop it, that you must, but, God! You cannot. An army of skeleton footsoldiers, a wagonload of them like vermin ready to be let loose, led by a white, gaunt horse with another skeleton on its back. The people are thrashing, pathetic.

Using spears, if you can believe it. Attempting to stop death with a spear. You see how defenseless we are? A single man stands there as if ready to draw his sword, but, as in his own nightmare, he cannot, not so much because he is fearstruck, although he is that, but just because he cannot. Like a dream, a nightmare, he cannot stop it. There are thousands of heads, coming, heads of skeletons. They are here. There is no more waiting. You feel that. Now, they are here. There is a sense, though, that the human beings, the live ones, had begun destroying themselves before the skeletons—death—arrived, attacked; that the skeletons were just finishing the process. I am not certain, but there are caskets around either filled with the newly dead—funny to say that, the 'newly dead,' or it is just another way of a dead footsoldier arriving. Maybe it is just that the dead are always around us, death is waiting in abundant forms, new forms, or always arising like fumes to claim us. There is a boatload, too—probably on the River Styx. I do not know if that is correct."

And then, having remembered something, he added,

"But if God was not dead in 1500, perhaps he is now after all. We shall see. That is quite amusing."

But he was not laughing.

They were once again approaching Washington Square Park and Professor Slamunster began looking over his shoulder, looking around.

"But that is what I feel in that theater, if that is what it is. What I felt. I wanted someone to see it. I did not know this until recently, but, because I do have other work, ha, I had other work, but that is what others must feel their work to be, as if they are fighting against death. Like those people in Brueghel's painting, as if it is a fight they might lose, which is a horrifying, a horrifying thought. How else explain the terrible distortions of life? But the real pressure, when I am working or thinking about it, is that what is most intense is the driving feeling that one has to resist. And when it is best, it is as if one will not die as long as one resists. Like the dream. You know it is inevitable, but if you can only wake up . . . maybe you will not die."

"What are you talking about?"

She had no doubt that he spoke in earnest, even if she did not quite understand him. She was frightened. Chilled. But she felt enveloped in pressure and liked it.

She began to wonder what they were doing as she noticed, realized that they were retracing their steps around the perimeter of Washington Square Park.

"I also wanted you to see this theater," he said, having abruptly stopped.

"Theater? Where?"

"I came here because of him," he continued, ignoring her. "I think he is crazy."

"Who is crazy?"

"He is," he repeated with emphasis, pointing down the street, "except I am not certain that I have ever before encountered such insanity. I think I know who he is."

She looked, at first seeing nothing, and then, continuing to look, she saw a heavy-set figure on the top rung of stairs leading into a townhouse. The figure had stopped and appeared to be looking back over his shoulder at . . . at them, perhaps, except that he was not quite looking totally back, back over his shoulder, he had not turned his head quite far enough to see them, instead pretending to look into a mailbox, except he indeed appeared to be pretending. She felt a sense of guilt, as if she had been caught in the act of following him, spying upon him, as if she was participating in some silly charade.

"He is ponderous. He sometimes talks in French, he is so heavy, like a dust collector," said Slamunster, agitated, seemingly annoyed, "But his pretense is always so obvious except—can you understand this?—I don't think he knows it. He lives in the boarding house and his great performance, his . . . I don't know, his dramatic outburst occurs when somebody is coming behind him on the sidewalk, at which point he either walks past the steps or fumbles at his mailbox, obviously faking it, then he goes up, I don't know how to say it, heavily up the stairs to his corner room. Complete with beret, dirty, mumbling, sometimes raving about revolution, labor, tonight, City Hall. If you get close enough to him he garbles something about assassination."

"What? Assassination?"

"Yes. I think he says something about Mayor Wagner, except you cannot be certain."

"Oh my God, Mayor Wagner? Do you think he is dangerous? How can you know he would not do such a thing?"

"Ah, I think he has killed everybody in his mind. All of western civilization. He killed Aristotle. That was the birth of tragedy."

He was pointing at the townhouse in front of them as he spoke, as if he were directing a tour.

She was confused again.

"What is it? A historic building?"

"Oh, yes, it probably should be. And not because I moved here this year," he laughed.

"Oh, you live here?"

"Yes. I have concluded that it is a boarding house for retired, anonymous, former, finished spies. Actually, it is a complement of apartments. No, cells. Isn't that funny?"

"Retired spies? I did not know there was such a thing."

"They didn't either, but they're finished. Every one of them. Some have gone to seed. Some are mad. Some are displaced. There are new recruits always. Quite bizarre. Maybe it is this instead of death because they are the ones who were not murdered or imprisoned or executed or whatever."

"Who pays for them?"

"Well might you ask because, actually, it is quite an elegant house for former spies."

The building was a contradiction. It appeared an ordinary building on a street of old, elegant townhouses. As if overlooked, it had survived destruction. Only in America.

John Slamunster and Hilde Johnson entered the inner sanctum. In the darkened building, walking up a flight of stairs, down the darkened hallway, Slamunster stopped.

"Did you hear that?"

"Did I hear what?"

"They are all crazy. That was her again. She is always spying on me. She once saw me walk to the shower in the nude."

He shook his head.

"I'll explain later."

And then he used three keys to unlock a door.

Slamunster pushed aside a police lock and they stepped into a world apart. There were only two rooms but they were both large. The floors were carpeted, deep black wool, black shadings of oblongs, parabolas, streaks, curves, thick lines.

Hilde was dazed.

"In case you were going to ask, I call it 'post-revolutionary.' I arranged it myself. My father was rather affluent. A judge."

Black leather chairs, two leather sofas, a king-sized bed. Prints, lithographs, etchings, three oil paintings, contemporary mostly. There was also a series of wooden cabinets, some floor-to-ceiling, some on the walls, filled not only with books, but with wineglasses and goblets of many shapes and designs. Plants hung from the ceilings and walls. The kitchen, a tiny nook off one room, the bedroom in a corner of the other. Both corners papered differently.

Slamunster made a fire in a slate, stone fireplace and without asking made two martinis.

"It is a good building to inhabit," he said, handing her the martini, "my boarding house for spies. There has been murder, fire, rape, robbery, drugs. It is a building that is full of non-persons. I now know where they come from for The Purple Union. And who would have thought it? Not just spies, I mean. Winos, prostitutes, hustlers. Most of them are middle-aged or older, much older. I rarely see them. Yes, there are a lot of crazy people living here. I came here because of Angus."

"Angus?"

"Yes, Angus. He's the guardian of Washington Square Park. The gatekeeper. The gaoler. I do not know who he is, really, although I know something about him and I intend to find out more. Everything if I can. I just observe him. And he knows I am observing him, in his own crazed way. Sometimes I think he wants me to find out. But I do not know if I feed off him or he feeds off me. He would provide answers."

"He is here?"

"Yes, this is where he came. From where I am not totally certain, although I have some leads. Maybe from here actually. This place may actually have spawned him. I have gained a great deal of experience following people. And spying on them. There is much that is obvious, more than you could imagine. But there is much I do not know. All I do know is that what I do not know is grimmer than what I do know. As soon as I think I know the worst, I discover something beyond it."

"Yes, it has become quite clear to me, and to the class, that you have a bright view of life. You and the Russians."

"What is its promise?"

"The promise of what?"

"Life."

"It is what we make of it."

"Surely. Have you spent much time in, say, the Bronx? It is San Francisco after the hundred-year War of the Roses. It is the used-car lot of the world. It is the kingdom of hell's angels. It is the seagull's smorgasbord. And need I add, it is all of the survivors and the descendants of the concentration camps and nobody wants to care."

He paused, and she said nothing.

"No, perhaps you are correct. I have been following certain people, all doing certain things . . . and I may have lost my way. This is supposed to be about hopes, ideals, visions, all of it altruistic, pure, and yet you would think that the reality is New York City crime. Something is different in my life. I do know that it is stalled, close, that it is going to explode. It has to. There has been too much of an accumulation of, well, gases, fumes, smoke, fog. I don't know. I rarely see any of the people living here, although at night, they can be heard. They are definitely there, here, on the other sides of these walls. A murder a night, I think. During the first few weeks I often awoke in a sweat convinced that someone was being axed or flailed alive. Shrieks and shouts and groans were commonplace. The terrible noises always seemed to come from the same directions, from behind the same doors, from the ceiling, through the left wall. I wondered how many times the same person could be beaten and survive or, for that matter, murdered and come back from the dead. And why and what for. After a couple of months I stopped hearing. No, that is not true. I have never stopped wondering what was behind the walls and doors. Often I would stop in front of an apartment door on one of the first three landings, but I rarely heard anything. During the day there are practically no sounds at all. At night I sometimes hear scattered, muffled voices, shuffling feet. The sound of squirrels or mice. Or rats. The more threatening noises seem to wait till late at night, and always when I am behind my locked door. And I wonder if they are all pretending, every single one of them, and the pretense has become their life."

"I wonder if perhaps you have been in the city for too long a time."

"How can I have been in this city for too long when you cannot get out of this city. It intensifies our beings and transforms them. Or destroys them. I could not conceive of living elsewhere. But you must know that."

She seemed startled.

"How would I know that?"

"As an agent how could you not know?"

He reached for her. He touched her on the shoulder as if to pull her toward him, but she was already sliding off the couch ahead of him onto the ragged rug. It was as if they had deliberately conquered each other by frightening themselves, by overwhelming themselves with fear before he reached for her and she maneuvered him into her arms. He was on top of her as quickly as she slid under him.

"That makes us both recruits," she managed to say, with no response from him, as if the living breath had been squeezed out of their beings.

He was thinking of Klara Blazek and wondering if she was with the son of God and he could not stand his image.

PART TWO

8

Huddled Masses

Perhaps they were being watched until the Greyhound bus disappeared into New York City's darkness, darkness although Timothy Brown King, the innocent, the morning promise of America, saw spilled light exposed in their pathway everywhere, pockmarks and splotches, dimples and sparkles, depending upon the mood of the investigation. Darkness with a faint glimmer of light, ebbing light from struggling, worthless, dying human beings, pathetic, moribund, nearly extinct. Darkness with gorgeous, gay, intoxicating nightflames, set gloriously ablaze by vivacious, delirious, enchanted, triumphant, immortal human beings. Dawn could not be far away in the city, but it was nighttime, a time of ecstasy and evil and evolutions and eternity, a time to entertain the limitless, the intrigue of possibility, the lust and the pain of desire and want, the beginning of time, a time of finality. Dawn might never arrive in the city.

Down from the silent north country, pursued and in pursuit, in peril always, at the beginning of dreaming, at the end of an endless dream, endless nightmare, Timothy, mind arun, wondered if the multitudinous dots of light were a heaven of starlight, if perhaps it was only a moment, an instant before the balls of fire were to erupt and to explode into full bursting holiness, a moment until the heavens would blind, blind and expose them. Or maybe all had once been incandescent, maybe they were arriving after the fall, after light and life, and the darkness was encroaching, spreading, engulfing like fog. Maybe it was only a moment, an instant before the darkness covered, a time before the eternal night, before the last pops of divine light sputtered and went out, leaving them unseen. That could happen. The loss of humanity.

"'When there is light,'" the words seeped into Timothy's consciousness as he sat hunched down in his seat, knees raised, "'we must work and be virtuous because we may be seen. At night, we sin with vengeance because we are invisible.'"

So had said the erstwhile Boy Preacher Hezekiah Brown King in his last days of preaching. And this was night.

Timothy had been in Manhattan only a month before, albeit in his previous life, with the budding-honorable if not venerable Charles Hamilton Jackson III, Ham, his Southern, good old boy Dartmouth roommate, who at this very moment was probably wondering where in the universe he was, when they had debated against a team from Columbia University in a private pristine performance before five most illustrious justices of the New York State Supreme Court in the Broadway law offices of Henny Kingsley, lawyer of the stars. The topic which was being debated throughout the land for the entire year by eighteen- to twenty-two-year-olds from America's institutions of higher learning was, perversely, "Resolved: That the further development of nuclear weapons should be banned by international agreement," which Timothy had translated to mean, "Is there a future for nuclear weapons?" It was an irreverent, if innocent, rhetorical question to have voiced before these courtly bastions of order and pretense, but, ironically, for a brief shining moment young Timothy had been able and willing to indulge himself glory and pride when all five justices had voted him and Ham the winners of the debate. Afterward, Him and Ham along with their fellow word warriors from Columbia had been toasted with sherry by the justices, Ham a shining light unto himself, a glowing beacon to humanity, Him burning up within, a human torch in the desert, Him and Ham on the hot circuit, deciding the fate of Western Civilization. All five justices had remembered Timothy's father, JBK. Amazingly, one had even claimed personal acquaintance.

Timothy Brown King and Charles Hamilton Jackson III had been dutifully studying the question of nuclear weapons for a year, although in reality there was no question. Timothy knew all about military might, many explosions, mighty blips. Theoretically you could rearrange at will, for the will had always been there for the big bang. He knew all of the weapons, all of the strategies, all of the perspectives, all of the histories, all of the rationalizations, or he thought he did. The only ritual he thought he had not observed was to play war games with Ham and his fellow debaters in the nightly enclaves of the Dartmouth Forensic Union deep in the New Hampshire woods, play with the boys into the early misty mornings, supplied with heaping ashtrays of cigarette butts, boiling pots of rancid coffee, heightened rhetoric, and rising passions. He had not been interested, and he had wondered about the deadly difference, about why the others had become embroiled and he had not. Certainly the threat to the celestial spheres was real. Part of the problem for Timothy was that he did not hold "our leaders" in reverence, owing to the neutered nature of his social nurture. Had "our leaders" similarly played too many war games in their youths? Whom and where were our leaders leading and who and what was leading them?

When Timothy was but a little kid in Maine he had thought, however briefly, that there was a planned order to the whole incredible thing. He had grown up thinking, for example, that Presidential elections were carefully controlled, significant events involving highly important people, that they were about mighty ideas, loftly ideals, about how society should be nurtured, structured and organized, about what human beings should be, represent, strive for, profess, that they were all about constructing and sustaining values. He had learned to take one and all so seriously, including himself. When miraculously and not by design he had reached high-school age, he had even written a political column for his hometown weekly newspaper, the *Portland American*, complete with prurient political analysis in the best journalistic tradition and with his own popular telephone polling system fueled by America's people opinionating. But, he had soon discovered, people running for President, running everywhere, running around, were, alas, intellectual cyphers. More, that people running governments were meddlesome mediocrities at best, more likely incurable incompetents, their heads bobbing as they ran, with no solid fuel sense of society, certainly not of the world as a whole, one people, no vision, all up for the universe. Some possessed a picture postcard of history, but they went mercifully blank on the future. They did not even suspect what *vision* was, or they regarded such a concept with suspicion, as an effete affectation. They did not understand. And all it amounted to, the real thing, was a banal grubbing for control, for power. With such primitive beings involved there was to be inevitably stupidity, crudity, and finally violence. In the perspective of the mythical rational person crazy things were bound to happen. Senseless things. Frightening. Terror. The Prospect? A disaster waiting to be realized. To be produced and presented by an elected official, by "our leaders."

Imagine President John Fitzgerald Kennedy, or any President, thinking to himself, "What do I want to accomplish during my administration? What do I want to be remembered for? What projects shall I construct for the nation and for the world?" Which was appalling. To think that the world should be anybody's personal playground, and the implements of the most powerful government on earth, toys for the playpen. Plainly, our leaders had grown up playing with their erector sets and shooting their model airplanes, playing with their prides and blissfullingly shooting their airplane glue. What was more, oh, democracy, the people skipped along with it, in blissful ignorance, sauced with the utmost solemnity and pretense. It was the accepted ritual of the day, the manner of the conduct of human affairs. Any idiot idol could sit high on the throne and the world would follow below. It was a Broadway play, a commercial success, a musical. Great! Prestigious! Triumphant! Why, it was nothing but a collection of banalities, absurdities. Yes, more leadership of this ilk and, guaranteed, there would be no further questions, no, none. The theater of the absurd encounters the cold war.

Yeah, he had been taught that society or government, that is, organized social and civil relations, social structure, was necessary to avoid human chaos, to either control or to keep the reins on negative human impulses. But whatever order existed was tenuous. It was a joke. Chaotic. Dangerous. There was nothing guaranteed about what was going on out there. The crushing joke was that what had been organized in the world into the power of the states were those very negative impulses. The signature of the twentieth century. Somebody had said, "States fight wars because that is what they are organized to do."

To wit, Herman Kahn, resident comic of the Rand Corporation, he of the thinking-in-the-tank-fame, had written, ". . . War is horrible, there is no question about it, but so is peace, and it is proper with the kind of calculations we are making today to compare the horror of war and the horror of peace, and see how much worse it is." Subterranean translation: peacetime equals planning time for wartime. Apart from such brave new thoughts, it was proper to ask, what were we doing with such toys anyway? Clearly a new, twentieth-century form of degeneracy. What could you expect from any one or any thing, any species, who or what had done some thing as idiotic, as crazy?

But if mass suicide was our destiny, apparently by special delivery, so be it. Cut the cards and pass the ammunition. Wherefore, whyfore, whyman worry about nuclear war? It was inevitable that night would follow day in technicolor once again. And so, and so we were going to die any way. The species? There was no question, we were not to be.

Actually, Timothy had firmly believed since high school that in nuclear weapons we now had the sufficiently nurtured means to extinguish, *e^vapporate^* the species and, lo and behold, he had written a paper in his American history class on the certainty of nuclear war within the next twenty years. Blue and pink and purple clouds were in the forecast. It was something you could rely upon, kind of a new faith, he had suggested, with the promised land in sight if you looked quickly over the horizon to New Mexico. His teacher, a woman who had formerly been a journalist, whose tall person daily distilled upon their small heads the sacred nectar of freedom of the press, who wore her hair in a black bun, she an erstwhile favorite of his and he of hers, her little darling, his big mama doll, had refused to accept his paper. Write something else, she had said, for, yes, there was absolutely no question that she would not accept such dire dribble, might not any longer accept the little darling himself in her classroom. Rewrite, redo, rerun, or be gone, little darling doomsayer, be gone, said the mad mama doll.

"I will die before it happens."
    or
                                                                                    "If I should
die before I wake," indeed.
                                            "I cannot imagine it happening. Life will go
on as it always has . . .   "
"You were young. Naive." [I was young. Naive. I was.]

And now, several years later, sure enough, here they were at this climactic moment with so much at stake, and Timothy mused that there should be an entourage of official greeters in top hat to mark the occasion of their Greyhound's arrival in the city, that at least here in madding, mid-century Manhattan there should be a squadron of flashing police cars, perhaps a sprinkling of blue knights on horseback, along with shrieking red fire trucks and, of course, wailing white ambulances, for surely there would be extravagant Yankee carnage in Gotham with or without play bombs, although in this American Century, long since known as such, pomp and circumstance did not go with a beheading, did they? Or was it a bleeding, a butchery, a bebop bludgeoning? Did it matter? Was there choice? Would this take long, be delayed, or would it be over at any moment in an instant, like a shot?

What Timothy did not know was whether this woman by his side slept, this woman of visions, of his memories, whether she too had dreamt, had nightmares, whether she were in peace, or if her eyes were also merely closed in polite pose, plotting. However, perhaps it were best and proper that there be no sirens, whistles, horns, shrieks, for until their moments of inevitable disclosure, of ultimate revelation, secrets were not for public occasions, and presently he had the feeling of being hidden alone on the bus, of being separated, drifting like a satellite far from her, of entering the city secretly by himself, by remote control, untracked by radar, cloaked, in disguise

For his part he had been dreaming about grandfathers and holy men, yes, dreams about grandfathers, greatgreatgreat Hezekiahs and greater Patricks, Kings one and all . . . great-grandfaaaaaathers, distance equals greatness, the faaaaaarther away the greater, the closer the smaller unto disappearance, until nobody is there, until he would not be there. Drama enough, his own, but whose secret was it really, whose knowledge, whose would it be at the denouement? Or, for that matter, whose drama? Would he even be present? Was he to discover or be discovered? Play a role or be a spectator? Or perhaps a combination of the two, that is, be a victim. Let the interrogations begin, he thought. Oh, hurry, do not delay. To delay was the worst sin. And, besides, the teacher, he would not be able to bear it much longer.

"Have you ever been, boasted of being, wanted to deny being, protested, spit at, kissed, lost or found, bought and sold, played baseball or canasta with, attended church or left synagogue with or without, and sung the praises or shouted everlasting condemnation of, a carnivorous Communist?"

In anticipation of sudden revelations, he was alternately exhilarated—a voice would speak, a face would appear—and apprehensive that he might be plummeting like a stone into a black hole, cast there by this beautiful, mysterious woman, this, to him, unknown nameless female Hungarian of whom he, paradoxically, felt certain he possessed profound knowledge and she of him, who after quick embrace would look harshly and laugh piercingly waving her black shroud after him as he fell away into the mist.

Manhattan, a phantasmagoria, the seat of the frivolously frantically fabulous, was the perfect plain, a delightfully darkly dramatic setting for wonders and catastrophes. But what if, on cue, no one was watching? What if all of them were to be overlooked? He thought that might happen. The ultimate embarrassment, to be extinguished by accident, erroneous effacement. Someone might forget to turn on and off the lights. Deliberately. Purposeful, perverse bastards, with malice aforethought, because of jealousy, envy, spite, maliciousness. One could not possibly allow that to happen. If any tiny little thing at all was cherished in this great country, any thing at all, surely if one had a sacred task it lay in the American individual's primary duty not only to prevent disappearance but to promote recognition, surely. Not to be, but to be noticed, that was the answer. For that endeavor there should be a rare alliance of sworn citizens, a confederation of the people whose motto forever would be, 'Anything Goes Under God.' And perhaps there was and it did.

The bus bounced as if in tune with his sudden thought.

"You know what?"

It was time, no, it was categorically necessary to once again rout the silence and, as if in play, without fear, Timothy still felt like testing, although he did not know why, except that without question he was being tested himself. Certainly he felt the anonymous, omnipotent pressure of heaven and hell.

"What?"

Klara had wondered how long his silence would last this time. Clearly, and not surprisingly, he was a young man of extremes, and she did not know if she preferred his eternal silence or to be diverted by his antics, his puppetry, his mental machinations, his . . . what was it . . . struggle for enlightenment or for simple sight? Klara herself had been musing about the skies, the stars, the planets. It was her wont. No yoga. No mystery novels. And no regrets. Rather, the spacing and the space of the zones. And why not? The zones determined all. And little could be done about it, except that one could have premonitions, foreknowledge, be prescient, move effortlessly with the flow of the forward march, the unabated continuation of the tragedies. Or, yes, one could be a prophet. He had said that in his sleep, of that she was certain. He had fallen asleep and, yes, without a doubt, he had spoken. It was uncanny, but she was certain that he had been asleep while she had been awake.

"When the spirit is upon you that makes you a prophet," he had whispered, softly but distinctly.

And then:

"'If there be a prophet among you, I the Lord will make myself known unto him in a vision, and will speak unto him in a dream,' so saith Hezekiah."

So he was dreaming, softly dreaming, but why was he not more fearful?

Why no trepidation? Surely there was apprehension? With such an imagination, with such genes, it could not be avoided, there would be perceived danger always, his mind racing, out of control or madly creative or both, certain to invent delight or disaster. Or perhaps there was indeed fear, perhaps his animation was precisely that. Why think otherwise? She knew it took many forms. The glitter of the age, ragged nerves. True, they were not of the same generation, she and he, but they still killed Communists nowadays, one way or another.

"Everyone should place bets on what is going to happen."

He had said it almost immediately, spit it forth like a machine gun. He was sitting up now. Only seconds had passed, rat-a-tat-tat.

"They should be forced to bet with their lives," he continued spraying. "There should be odds posted with at least one long shot on the miraculous, on a new age, on immortality."

"How can you bet with what you do not have, which is the opportunity? How can you bet on what you call a long shot when it is precisely the long shot that has been taken off the board?" she asked.

"I know," he said, matter-of-factly.

It was not an answer, but a dismissal. She was not in the correct sphere.

"Perhaps there should be more long shots than anything else," she tried again, having had further thoughts. "Or only long shots," she added. "That way everybody will lose."

That was a thought she did not think he possessed, although she was not certain. She had yet to satisfactorily interpret him anew for herself, which both annoyed and fascinated her, drew her closer despite her best efforts to maintain the impassable gulf. That was her wont as well, to spin a tighter web around herself against her will, to spin a web and invite him in. He should be corralled, she was thinking, and he would be, eventually, fatally. Everyone was, not just him. But not by her. She would not do it, not to him. She had begun to feel that she could not do it, that she did not want to do anyone's bidding. For him she thought his prospects sad. And it was not because of the planned, imminent ending. Everyone had an ending. All tales ended. Even fantasies.

"You mean long shots on the bizarre, on the fantastic, place bets on the incredible, the marvelous?"

He did have the uncanny ability to elicit her anger, to arouse her. She must be the father and mother in one.

"No, that is the idle, frivolous yearning of pampered youth. It is what happens when one is too often left to speculate rather than compelled to act. You must learn not to beg the issue. You will learn respect for small things in life. Humility. It will be forced upon you, I assure you. I mean a long shot on anything at all happening. A long shot on the continuance of life. Another day. That is all we can hope for, and perhaps we should not even hope for that. Hope is ignorance. We should not cling to pathetic hopes as if we were dogs drooling for biscuits. There should be a modicum of dignity. It is a trifle anyway. We are a trifle. Life is harsh. Life is tedium. You need to do more homework."

Timothy did not like Klara's answer, if answer it was, for it was a pronouncement as well. Was he being asked to force things? But was that possible? It certainly did not seem appropriate. And what could that mean? Did it all depend upon him? Was he to be the creator of the world? Finally? Well, if so, he would change everything. There would be no hesitation, absolutely none. If given the opportunity, he was convinced he could come up with, no, not the answers, but the statements. Make them up. No matter what. He would act in his own fashion, no matter what she said. If that was all there was, how could one fail to do it? But perhaps he was also to be the catalyst for the end. Give him a chance. Yet, he had begun to sense as well that she had the capacity to make him profoundly sad. Melancholia.

At that precise moment he looked through the window and was astonished to see an all black, blackmasked, chorus, chanting, raging, gesticulating. Was this the beginning, the sudden beginning? Yes, the new act. He felt an urge to wave, to acknowledge their presence. Surely it was demanded. But instead of waving, he tensed. All blacks, blackmasks, on the streets, all whites, whitefaces, on the bus. Perhaps he and the other whites, whitefaces, on the bus were lost, perhaps they were intruding. Was an attack imminent and, if so, who would attack whom? Or perhaps he was imagining things, and who was there to tell him which it was?

Klara saw the look on his face. She smiled in apparent condescension.

"Is this your first trip outside of America?" she asked, her eyes closing once again, wishing to forget for the moment who he was, wandering her zones, sliding spheres.

Despite everything, she thought, just another young American who did not know his own country. That might be the single, sole characteristic all Americans held in common. Ignorance of one another, not to speak of the world. Ignorance of themselves. Know thyself, said Emerson, the great American know-nothing, know-everything transcendentalist, transcending knowledge. And why not? Except for a few of his occasions of insight, his random eyeballing, she was not a great admirer of Emerson's, but she did grant that, ironically, he knew his countrymen. He knew precisely what the nature of the national failing was, what was lacking. He personified it as well, the forefather. Yes, it was the American way, it was endemic, spiced with lots of pretense and bravado, and yet it was not an act. An immense, un-self-conscious, ironic power pressing itself upon the world. USA karma.

Sensing that he had left her momentarily, that he was the one on this occasion that had retreated within, Klara herself looked out the window as if to find her own special answer. Her eyes darted, attempting yet again to see for the first time, instinctively, uninstructed, unable to stay with any single sight understanding and disbelieving. She saw blacks, blackmasks, strewn, knocked into the gutter creases, into and down the drains, swept away to the sewers They were wrapped around telephone poles, smeared on stop signs, tangled in electric lines, lost in swirling dirt. Bodies flew by. Debris. On a corner, a group of ten disappeared in a cloud of soot.

And then, abruptly, the big, wounded bus moved, Klara and Timothy both snapped to, jerked down one of the tunnels, Fifth Avenue. The swollen hulk of a bus, broken, stuffy and creaking, belching and smoking, rumbled, groaned through the multitude of blacks, blackmasks, at the beginning of the big, big city, fingertall buildings with tunnels of everything everywhere beneath the upward, rising gases gasping into the sky. The bus, misshapen as if it had been pummeled but, nevertheless, indomitable, shook and plunged onward like a bear. Much of the black sky, most of the universal whitestars had been long lost to sight.

The bus stopped uneasily, stopped for a red light. Outside in the street, it appeared to Timothy that hundreds had rushed to surround the creature of the bus, to capture it, to liberate it, to seize it for their rescue, their salvation, to impound fate. He felt it was a certainty that the bus would never move again, never go anywhere, while round about them in the city, a battle, pandemonium, boom-boom-boom, drums boomed, wailing and flashing, piercing, whaaah-whaaah-whaaah, hidden fingers pushed, horns arose, whaaah, whaaah. It was an intense, desperate struggle, the people swarmed, waved their arms; lips moved, eyes squinted and glazed; they cursed and jumped, laughing, shrieking.

Timothy watched a man standing on the corner holding a book in his extended left hand, his right hand twirling in circles, probably saying in and to the tumult that he was the messiah. It looked as if the man was offering the book to the people around him, and the people looked to be ignoring him, cursing and laughing, talking one and all, shouting to themselves. At intervals the man raised his eyes upward, imploring perhaps, perhaps talking to someone on top of one of the tall, tall buildings or maybe, unheard, in whispers, he was rehearsing a part in the play, because it appeared that he was talking to no one person around him. Maybe the people were unseen by him, maybe they were not there, not there for him at all, or maybe he was praying mercifully for the heavens to deliver the missiles at once, end his vigil.

The light turned green and the bus parted the crowd, like a miracle it broke through, and it shook, lurched nearly out of control, and wheeled around the corner, as if it were about to disintegrate, crash and explode out of sight like a loosed bomb. The tall buildings teetered inward, sealing off the sky. There would be no witnesses after all.

But the bus lurched apace once again and Timothy and Klara were jostled, his left thigh mashed against her right thigh, Timothy squeezed between Klara and the side of the bus, his cheek rubbing, pressed against the slightly steamed, begrimed window. Déja vu.

They moved deeper into the dark city, the bus pushed further within, waded through the blacks as if crossing a river, until a few whites, whitefaces, began to appear.

"Heads are so small, small as eyes," Timothy mumbled.

There must have been millions bobbing between the buildings, which had grown to unseen heights, grown and grown forever. The bus stopped for another red light, although it continued to shake, rumbled as it waited, as if incubating, agitated. Outside the people hovered again, swarmed around the bus, climbed over and crashed into it, crossing in front at the corner, disappearing behind, climbing under. By now most of them had turned white, whitefaced, a magic act, alchemy.

"Look at them stare," said Timothy. "Maybe they believe I am the new messiah, the leader of the band."

"They will stare at you or not at you," said Klara, irritated, "but they are not looking for anything especially, particularly, including you, and so they will not hear you or see you or anything. And not hearing or seeing you or anything, they will not follow you, for they will not know that you are there. There is nothing to be done for it. I know."

She spoke with certainty and her eyes remained closed. But he continued.

"Actually, I have given some thought to starting a new religion. It is in my genes, you know. My grandfather started a new denomination. A wacky hodgepodge of ideas to help you cope, is that it? We cannot be asked to endure all of this? When you cannot stand it any more you start a new religion? It is either that or suicide. But, is that the same thing as joining a religion? Like my father? He joined one rather than another or joined one and left another, didn't he? You know about that. But it is really hard to know what to do, isn't it? The problem is, you see, who knows what evil lurks in the hearts of men? Or wouldn't you say so? But believing in a religion is a creative act, or at least you have to make it that, don't you think? Make it up. That is the trick. You have to do make-believe. Is that the same as doing voodoo? Hey, if I was the new messiah, that would make me the son of God, wouldn't it? However, perhaps it is too late."

With effort, Klara kept her eyes closed. Was what he said an incredible accident, a fortuitous strike? She did not know, but she would let him run on and on. She thought she should do that. She hoped she could do that. Run on and on and on and forget where you came from, my young man. She realized that she was now in a constant state of agitation. He, something, had done this. But it would pass. She would will it so. The voices would speak. What she had thought she had suddenly had a vision of would not happen.

The bus rocked and teetered and Timothy and Klara bumped and pressed again. The bus moved as if it were trying to disguise its intended destination, trying in pathetic fashion to shake its tail.

Timothy felt heated. He also felt self-conscious without knowing why. He did not understand the feeling. Irritation and frustration were beginning to surface. He was disoriented. There was an itch between his shoulder blades, a beginning fungus, a rash.

"Where are we going?" asked Timothy impatiently, as if skeptical that the bus was going anywhere, could possibly have anywhere to go.

"Do not worry, we will get there," Klara said in a low voice. "Worry afterwards."

Corner after corner, turning and stopping, the thought was that they had been on this street, this crossway, before. It looked like it. Except it was the first time. Always, after the bulky bus stopped, it would start abruptly, as though suddenly it were actually, decisively, finally going somewhere, although there was nowhere to go. The noise, the lurching, the strain. Or was it that in reality the bus was out of control, a runaway? With no one to care. Each block of the passing city was shrouded in glossy glowing light, vapors, alluring, blurred. Now, the bus rumbled downhill, as though the driver had given up, admitted to no destination, asked the furies to take control.

And then, suddenly, the bus tipped and shot upward, as if a giant had reached out, grabbed it in the palm of his hand, and swept it away. Timothy's and Klara's backs pushed against their seats. The bus swerved round about, the city was gone. The bus rolled onward, around and around, up an incline, and then leveled, glided smoothly and, just as suddenly, jerked to a halt in the cavernous Post Authority bus station. They had arrived and there was very little light, if simple light it was.

Timothy, his teeth grinding, looked out the window and saw the drab, faded uniforms. Cymbals crashed. Trumpets blared. Drums thumped. Incredibly, there was a welcoming after all, there was a sustained singing of loud, toneless voices. Hosanna?

"They have come to greet me," he thought, "to take me away, to take me back. I will never escape them. It has come to pass, just as Grandfather said it would. 'He that loveth his life shall lose it.'"

In truth, Timothy had seen stragglers of the Salvation Army many times. For him they had always been the ambassadors of the living dead. He had thought of them as having an endless tune but with no place to play. Propelled in tune, they were the natural allies of the Onward Christian soldiers, the latter having sprung up like scarecrows on the wintry ridges and rocks of Maine, itinerants, mongrels of Christianity, a horde whose banners were "Jesus Saves" signs stuck in country churchyards, whose word ran in neon in milltowns where nobody cared to read. He had thought of them as having no names, no relatives, and, above all, no memories. Poor and listless and barren. Unadorned truth. Anonymous. Oh Hezekiah. Oh humanity.

For a moment, he also felt slightly nauseous, vertigo. And then he realized that this Salvation Army of secret agents was performing for the soulless in the bus in front of them, a bus with darkened, impenetrable windows, a bus that now moved forward, leaving its abandoned space invisible in fumes. The noise-music ceased and the platoon of uniforms filtered away.

Timothy saw their faces briefly, saw them in the one moment as they had looked over their shoulders, as if they had looked back at what had been denied them, at missed opportunities. He was beginning to feel better. His courage was returning, for no apparent reason. He imagined that the departed bus was full of open caskets, warm bodies, grotesque, hideous, floating faces, alive. Left behind, the soldiers' noses were draining and, true warriors, these great secret army agents, they were going off to conquer and occupy. There was, after all, security in secrecy.

How wonderful if the soldiers of the Salvation Army could be the Pinkoes in a passion play, the Commies in costume, crisscrossing America, so to speak, the faaaded reds, say, with few to notice, secret sentinels standing on the corner singing their song in the traffic. But, Pinkoes or Fascisti, how did you decide which one you were? Did you get to choose or was it like being one of the elect? Were the Onward Christian Soldiers pinkoes in disguise, too? A rivulet of pink, a subsidiary in pastel. Despite all of the good the Salvation Army had purportedly done, and Timothy had little reason, certainly no factual knowledge to deny that they had fed and sheltered the poor and the hungry, the dispossessed, despite that, he thought that he would have no difficulty in believing that they actually were the emissaries of Satan, the vanguard of the force of evil. Why he felt that way he did not know, he only knew that he liked feeling that way. Perhaps it was a trifle, a mere question of style.

"May the curse of Hezekiah be upon them," Timothy happened to say out loud.

Klara's eyes widened.

Hezekiah, again.

Timothy laughed. But then, with the army gone, the dim cemented interior intruded again, grimmer than troops from hell.

What could they be doing here? What was it? A dungeon, a torture chamber?

Or perhaps it was the hiding place of the soulless.

Crude, closed, cement.

"Do not get off the bus," Klara whispered. Hezekiah? That was a name she would never forget. Ancient history.

The walls, after all, were not those of a cave. There were no pictures, no writings, no colors. Drab, lifeless, smooth, the first layer of cement waiting forever to be covered. Never history. What sinners were relegated here? Were they all dead? Insane? What was the meaning of their punishment? Were there to be no messages? How did one know what to do, where to go, and why? No traces? Had anybody been here before, anybody at all?

Klara started to rise, and then she hesitated. She looked at Timothy. The thought occurred again that she could leave him right here, end the history. In his state he would never get out. And who would ever find him? Who would look? She imagined that it would effectively deal with everything, that he would never, ever emerge. Her and a lot of other peoples' will would be done. Like father, like son, done with. Except it would leave something unfinished, something she wanted, wanted done, had to have. She would not ask why.

"Come with me," she said, as if she were a guide to a pilgrim in a strange land, taking him to he would not know where.

But the aisle was already full with passengers, and they had little choice but to wait for the line to pass, unless they wanted to be aggressive and push their way into the flow, fight for their territorial rights. They waited and they stared at the passing people who stared back, expressionless, as if they had come from funerals.

They did not think Timothy was the messiah. They did not know what it was to look and, therefore, they did not see.

Then what was the question and what was the answer? Were they being followed? Would they be intercepted? Who was spying upon them and why? The big bellies and the weary faces, the bright eyes, the bespectacled and the babies, all had now left the bus. Who among them was the informer?

"All off, you two. This is New York. You ain't goin' no further."

The bus driver had a voice.

Klara tugged Timothy's sleeve and began to lead him down the aisle, as if they had no choice in the matter.

"This is better, isn't it?" whispered Timothy, agitated. "It is better to be the last ones off the bus, correct? Did you see who got off before us? Friends or foes?"

They were indeed the last to leave, and now they moved past the bus driver as if guilty, condemned, past the bus driver who did not even look at them despite his urgent command, did not even show Klara and Timothy a welcoming face, showed a clipped moustache, neatly trimmed.

"Should we ask him if he knows why we are here?" asked Timothy.

They stepped down from the bus, not exactly on soil.

"He looks like a friendly soul," continued Timothy, looking back over his shoulder at the bus driver, who had looked away. "At least he does not look unfriendly."

They remained airborne, above the ground in the labyrinth of cement. Obviously, thousands more were in there with them, the unseen as well as the unseeing, preselected victims, renegades, sinners, refugees. Despite the modern drab leveling, the interior after all apparently had been designed with the purpose of recalling ancient structures, unless accidents that repeated themselves. Passageways, stairs, little tunnels, no clear continuous line of sight, not an oversight, not unintended, no exit.

Timothy looked around as if to find the way, as if to find the sign that was not there. He spotted the last of the bus people, somebody, descending as if a trap door had been sprung on them because they were the basest of the base, disappearing, running away from Timothy and Klara, as if afraid of the association, allergic to notoriety, impervious to knowledge, although it was quite possible that these were messengers simply moving on, running ahead to pass the word that they had arrived, that they were coming.

"What happens now?" asked Timothy. "Immigration? Customs? Be frisked, strip, and all fall down? Or straight to the dungeon? Is this like crossing the border? Could we be arrested at any moment?"

"Come on," said Klara, agitated again. "There is nothing for you here. Nobody is paying any attention to you or wants to bother with you."

He was twirling like a top, although she was not certain who was out of control.

"Hey, buddy! Hey!"

Somebody was yelling at him.

"Do not be so certain," said Timothy. "It isn't allowed."

It was he of the moustache, the bus driver. He was yelling at Timothy as if he had discovered something that did not please him, that annoyed him.

"Maybe he's a counteragent," Timothy said, bowing to Klara, beseeching her to wait.

He walked quickly back to the bus. He and Klara had already drifted fifty feet away.

"That yours, sonny?"

The bus driver pointed to Timothy's suitcase. He stood looking down at it, annoyed, staring at it as if it were the latest evidence of Timothy's sins.

"Oh, yes, it is. Thank you."

As Timothy bent over for the suitcase, the bus driver suddenly grabbed his wrist.

"You sure that's yours? You got a ticket? No ticket?"

Timothy began fumbling for a ticket, although he could not remember being given one. What he did suddenly remember, recall in a picture flashing in his mind, off and on, off and on, was old Falstaff with the numbers on his forearm, placing Timothy's suitcase in the trunk of the taxi, Falstaff saying goodbye.

"There is," Timothy began speaking, mumbling to no one in particular, "a paper on Fyodor Dostoevsky's *The Idiot* in that suitcase. Would that help?"

He thought Falstaff would like that. And then he realized that this might lead to unimaginable difficulties.

"Ah, take it," said the bus driver, rescuing the impetuous youth. "If you don't, someone else will. Do me a favor."

Timothy took his suitcase and went back to Klara. Nothing had happened, but his heart was pounding. Klara walked quickly away. Timothy followed a few feet behind. He did not know that he really needed a suitcase. Destiny was uncertain.

"Where are we going? I do not even know your name."

"You know my daughter's name," said Klara, immediately regretting it, annoyed with herself.

"But not your husband's."

And maybe he knew her name as well, thought Klara. Maybe he had heard it spoken in a time before. It was something she wished she knew. It annoyed her greatly that he, this child, might be toying with her. But, of course, that was impossible. He knew her name, just as she knew his. Their names were in the recesses of their minds.

When she hit the downward-moving stairway, Timothy, just behind, almost toppled over headfirst. Not because Klara had stopped to let the escalator carry her, for she had not. She had kept walking right on down the stairs as if to disdain the aid, refuse all help as she descended under her own fury. But Timothy had been unprepared for the sudden descent as well, unprepared for the trap door that indeed had been sprung on them, unprepared for the change in levels. Almost before he had regained his balance, they had reached another level where, at once, they were immersed in a crowd that moved in several directions, alien forces in chaos all around them, menacing forces threatening to pull them apart. It was the perfect time for an escape, perhaps the last time.

Timothy sensed a change, something was happening. What was it? A bomb had been dropped in their midst? A new, divine purpose? Another being? A different species? Nothing gradual. Nothing was happening gradually. Suddenly this, suddenly that. To the right, people were going up, to the left, down. Obviously, a shifting hierarchy of morality.

"NO LOITERING," a sign read.

"The motto of the modern age," Timothy said, daring to raise his voice, his voice, throwing it breathlessly after Klara's voice.

But Klara was able to cut easily through the crowd, shooting forward at just the right moment. She had lost expectation, anticipation, hope, which helped immensely. She was untethered. She demanded, she took, without doubt, occasionally in anger, decisively. Timothy went as if pushed, pulled. He was not yet desperate, but neither was he in control. He wished she would stop and at least tell him where they were going, because he was feeling increasingly disoriented, not that he thought he would understand, or even desired to understand. More and more he thought that understanding was overrated.

"Hey," Timothy called after her as they passed a newsstand, "shouldn't we at least buy a *New York Times* and see if we are still here? I should get the latest update on reality. Are we in heaven or hell?"

She stopped and turned. She had yet to correctly gauge him, she thought. This was not simply a flippant mood. There was still an edge, an edge she could not grasp.

He laughed, a knowing, broken, sad laugh. It was as if he knew what he was looking for, knew that the newsstand would have it all: purity; innocence; idealism; virtue; freedom; opportunity; immortality; the Good Guys and the Bad Guys; Ours; Mine; Us. The answers were to be found in the daily ponderous, pomposity of newspapers, buried under tons of newsprint, beneath an avalanche of posturing. Perhaps he was saying, imagine that we regard each other so. Regard the human being.

"You would think we would know the difference, wouldn't you? I mean between heaven and hell?"

Klara, saying nothing, stood there and waited while he called out the names of magazines on the newsstand as if to ask her which was the precise one he should purchase, which would tell the tale. But he had thought it necessary to invent every one.

"*Pretensions*?" he asked. "*Bold*? *Jock*? *Dismal*? *Mobile Home and Surburbanazia*? *Bed and Castle*? *Competitive Display*? *Profit*? Hey, listen to this cover story in *Night and Day*—or is it *Day and Night*?—What's the story? you ask. Listen, on the cover it says, 'War or Peace—Which is best?' On the inside it says, 'The world's longest experiment,' and it claims, 'All the latest polls. Results were thorough and extensive, although no conclusions can be reached until the last war,' they say."

She let him continue. Perhaps he would stop.

"Or this issue of *Timeless*. It will spin your head. 'Is God Dead?' is the cover story. They have interviewed '139 bishops, 72 priests, 97 ministers, 101 nuns, 47 choir boys.' Maybe they should call it 'Who Killed God?' Wouldn't that be better? How does that link up with the subject of death?" he asked, turning quickly to look at her.

Death was a fundamental matter. But was it ironic that he should be obsessed with death and yet act so frivolously? Of course not, absolutely not. That was entirely appropriate, precisely the point. A don quixote, JBK would have said. It was a don quixote. The contrast, the contrast, the contrast———

But she had been forewarned.

He shifted gears, pretending to read an advertisement for a magazine that he saw in the newspaper.

"' . . . magazine that gives all, saves all, catalogues all, indexes all, and files all the news. All the news will always be there. Are you anal retentive? Read this magazine.' Hey, this has to be the one. It has to be in here, doesn't it? I mean, everything is here. All the . . ."

He paused for a moment, whether to catch his breath or because he needed to read more.

"But God is dead," he went on, shifting back. "Godless Communism, right? Hey, didn't I read somewhere that there are more FBI agents in the American Communist Party than there are Communists? Where did I hear that? It couldn't have come from J. Edgar Hoover, America's foremost comic, could it?"

He was ranting.

And now he became engulfed in a sudden crush at the newsstand, a squall of people. Crisscrossed hands extended and withdrawn. No one asked for anything. It were better to give and receive in silence. People came and went and Timothy filtered back to Klara. He had bought a *New York Times* and a *New York Mirror*.

"The *Mirror*?" Klara asked with obvious surprise. "I do not know why you bought that fascist rag. But you probably do not know either," and with that she started walking again.

He called after, a guttural sound squeezed from his throat. He was not finished.

"Hey, don't you want to hear the latest headlines? If there is even a hint of the story, the *Mirror* would probably do it first, wouldn't it? This is their kind of stuff, correct? Or the *Daily News*?"

"If there is a story," she said over her shoulder.

"Well, is there or isn't there?"

For the first time he sounded exasperated. There was an accumulation, perhaps a crack.

"Oh, I don't know what I'm looking for or why."

She stopped, paused, stood there and stared while he turned the pages and pretended to scan the columns as if he were actually looking for something, as if there was something to find, a signal, a message, an explanation.

His brain was all a jumble, racing in desperation to pull it all together. Castro said Kennedy was a liar, but Kennedy said the Russians lied. Showdown on the high seas. The armed forces had been directed to prepare for any eventuality.

"I wonder if that includes mutiny?" Timothy blurted out without explanation.

And then, having apparently found what he was really looking for or not looking for in the *Mirror*, he began to read in an increasingly louder, sing-song voice, both building and impeding his crescendo for, yes, he had become "the eyes and ears of the world," the paramount news of life, the minister of news for the world.

"Husband kills . . . Santa shot . . . by him . . . See without glasses . . . will be a free burial policy . . . at which olive oil will be put in your hair . . . and his severed human arm will be reattached . . . to the real Cary Grant . . . whose beer is Rheingold . . . the dry bear."

He was smiling, although he did not look happy, but she did not respond and after a while she began moving again, this time more slowly, perhaps to coax him along, keeping an eye on him. As she measured her steps, he remained close behind her while he continued to read.

And then his voice rose:

"Hey, wait, I've got it. 'U.S. SENATOR COMMUNIST SPY!'"

She stopped and turned again. This time she was frowning. Her face was whiter than her own white.

Timothy laughed again, apparently pleased with himself, privately pleased, alone with his comprehension.

"Or better yet, the President of the United States? No one would suspect, because they could not imagine it. But, think, we have just slipped through the lines of millions in a Greyhound bus. Can you imagine slipping through, surreptitiously, like guerrillas in a bus? You never know what to expect these days, I guess. Maybe J. Edgar is funny. But no one pays attention anyway, isn't that what you said? But, look, they used to prosecute Communists, execute them, didn't they? And they still follow 'em when they can find 'em, right? Somewhere, there is a threat to the American way. Is that where it is, the American way, is that where we are going?"

He paused, looking into the *Mirror* again.

"Here it is, and this time it is the truth. An English navy aide has been discovered to be a Red spy. Vassal's his name and he is a clergyman's son. What do you think of that? Is that irony or coincidence? Or both?"

This was a dimension of youth she could do without. She liked its aggressiveness, its insistence, its uncontrolled imagination, but not its irreverence, its insolence. Disrespect. It was mostly that, its failure to show respect, that angered her. But, no, that was not true. That was a subjective judgment to which she did not really subscribe. She was falling into a mental trough along with greater humanity. Was she growing senile? It was not so much a lack of respect for tradition, for the achievements of elders. It was the lack of recognition. The refusal. That was the purity of youth, the irreverence. It was warranted. And then she had a sudden thought. She wondered if he had been drinking. But that was absurd. She had been with him. She had smelled nothing. Drugs, then? He had looked unwieldy. Was that the explanation? What kind of drugs? No. She ruled that out as well. A drugged soul, perhaps. But, again, she realized that there was something different here, something . . . else. Previously, he had been . . . well . . . zany. . . . Was that it? And this was direct, a strike to the core. At least you could see it that way. My god, now he had her feeling as if she needed to be careful for his sake. He might break apart. There would be fragments. Slivers. Who would be his next of kin?

"Why are you a member of the Party?" he struck again.

"I am not a member of the Party."

He had not taken her by surprise, because she had expected the subject to be raised. The only surprise was that he had waited for so long.

"What do you mean you are not? Aren't you a Communist, so help you God? "His laugh was forced.

"No."

"No? What are you doing here, then? Oh, you know what I am saying. Why did you meet me? Why did they send you?"

"There are some things we do in life which are not political and for which we do not get paid. Who is 'they'? We are not all Communists. You may think we are. Americans think everyone is a Communist except themselves, which is exactly what the Party likes them to think. Fear and loathing. The end is near. Americans fear everything. I do not ask questions. I do not know the nature of the apparatus or even if it exists."

"How old were you when you joined the Party?"

"I told you I am not a member of the Party. My class in Hungary was wrong. I am a Jew. All of that complicates things."

She paused and then she spoke again.

"I am a poet and a teacher. My name is Klara."

"Communists are not poets. It says that in the Book of America. Klara?" He knew the name, she was certain he knew the name.

"I have been a dancer and a model. Klara. I have posed in the nude for . . . for an artist. Klara."

She did not know why she had revealed that. It seemed pointless, unnecessary, no matter what she eventually told him.

"Americans do not do that either," he insisted. "Americans only take their clothes off to make love and to wash them and wash them and wash them. I knew that you were not an American. Klara."

She moved closer to him. They were engulfed again by crowds and she was forced to speak loud enough for him to hear. She had to cast her thunderbolts among the swirling numbers. But, surrounded, they could not have been safer, more anonymous, or more intimate. It was a free moment. A moment for the brave to cross bridges.

"Look, you may have questions, but that does not mean that there will be answers. At least I do not have them all and I doubt if anyone else does. Look, I think I should take you home. I want to take you home. You know that, do you not?"

"Take me home?" he half laughed.

And she was thinking, he was a perfect stranger to her, which was odd, he was, he was, but she felt the need to take him over, to bring him home as she had brought home stray dogs and stray cats. Did she make love to strays? She would resist.

And at the same time, oddly, she was making him feel stranger and stranger all the time. He could not resist the urge to smile, which began to irritate her again.

"For heaven's sake," she burst out, "what is so funny? This is serious."

"But you make it sound like I am a child—'I am supposed to take you home'—are you my mother? Hey, that's okay, but shouldn't I know? Wouldn't we both enjoy it more?"

She looked angry and pale.

"You could be my mother."

"What a foolish thing to say. Although it is true that I am old enough—is that what you mean to imply?—it is not the case. It is not the reality. Do you know what reality is?"

"You could have given birth to me."

"I did not."

"You could have. You really could have and I would not have known the difference."

"What does that mean? Was your real mother a sit-in at birth?"

"How would I know? How would I know anything? I neglected to take pictures at my birth."

"Are you always so flip? If you do not watch it you will flip yourself right out of your life."

"What about you? What about your anger?"

That last had burst from nowhere.

"What on earth are you rambling on about? I do not have time to waste on you. Come on."

"Yes, mother and child."

They were standing each other off at this stage, face peering into face, their bodies nearly touching, together in their own separate vacuum while the remainder raged about them.

"Okay. Home. Is that where the food is?"

"That depends upon you."

"Oh, I get it. First, you want to know what I know. You want my confession. No confession, no food?"

"Wrong again. First, it is not my concern to know what you know. Second, I am not interested in confessions. Besides, what could you possibly have to confess at your age?"

"Unlike you?"

He winced. His brutality surprised him. It had just snapped forth. And he could tell that it had found its mark. He was immediately sorry. But did she not have something to do with it?

And then he attempted to make up for it.

"I am ob . . . sesssssssed with death."

But she chose to ignore him.

"Third, your witticisms, your attitude, will change nothing, as sad as that is for you. What has happened, has happened, and neither your life nor any subsequent life will change that, as terrible as that may be. I know. The first fundamental question this morning is, are you hungry? You do know it is morning, do you not?"

"I do not know what I know. What is it to know? Is this what I know . . . Can't you really imagine a U.S. Senator as a spy? What a coup for the Russians. That is hilarious. It is so funny I cannot stand it."

At that, neither spoke for a bit, both looking away in different directions into the crowds.

And then it began, gushed forth, left him naturally.

"But why didn't he tell me? I would have loved it. I really would have. Why didn't he understand that? Most people are so limited in what they do with life. They have no vision, no imagination. Look, don't you know we start with nothing, which means we can do anything. Look, we are going to die so the sky is the limit, if you get my meaning, just as I guess it was for him. But not only do we lack vision, most of us . . . well, some may have the vision, but we also lack the strength and the courage to sustain the creation. That's what's so bad. We cannot stand out there alone and take it. Do it. What he did. . . . What did he do? I want to know."

"What if it finally came to be more than he could manage? What if it was not his fault?" she whispered. "He was just a man and he tried to do too much. He broke the bounds."

But he did not seem to hear her. He was shaking. His face was suddenly wet with tears. A sudden soaking. He could not stop because it was not his to control.

Resolved: . . . oh, no, it could not be . . .
Resolved:
Issue of being stunned that your father was carrying on a . . . *career* (you know, he was doing things, doing unmentionables) that you did not know anything about, except in nightmares and fairy tales, in lies and propaganda, in my country tears of thee.

Issue that you did not really 'know' him, that you were not close, intimate, in truly heroic All-American embraceable me fashion, that he was distant or could not show emotion, did not show emotion, maybe that he was self-centered or ego-centric, whatever that means, meaning the center of his life, the center of your life that is cold and indifferent to you.

Issue that you find out—the letters you get from him from someone else, the telephone call—is it about him?—can it be about him?—that he was, what, deeply idealistic, humanitarian, a man of vision, peace, of cosmic perspective, philosophical, politically engaged—what? Bullshit.

"I never did understand him," he started lowly, slowly, as if resigned. "I never had a sharp sense of what he was. I always attributed that to the fact that I never saw him much. But, even so, something did not click. I mean, supposedly what he did was make money. That was it, as far as I could figure. That was all. And even that did not set right with me. I think from the beginning I have always hated business. Businessmen. Great capitalist, huh? I am probably what you would call prejudiced. I came, I saw, I made money. That is a life? A total life? That is devotion? Dedication to a higher cause? Can that be the sum of your existence? He knew how I felt. But then, every so often we would have a conversation, a talk. About 'world affairs' or the nature of society or something like that. One of those forced things, stilted, artificial, between fathers and mothers and kids and dogs and cats. And we always seemed to agree. I could not figure it out. I would ask him: why do you do what you do? How can you do what you do? What do you do? And he would give me some vague, equivocating answer. That made me angry. He was extremely . . . uncomfortable. I felt frustrated. We would part on negative terms. I could not figure out his anguish. His anguish? My anguish. Did I hate business or did I hate my father? And he seemed so at ease with the world. He was of the world."

"No," she interrupted. She finally spoke. "He was not a man made for this world. And yet he became very much a part of it. It was painfully difficult for him. Someone once said that about him."

"I . . . were you his mistress?"

"That does not even begin to say everything. You cannot know. And we cannot talk about it. That is not for me to tell you about. It would be too intimate, too sad. I could not bear it. He . . . he was not himself. I don't think any of us are."

It began to ebb.

"I did not know him," he said. "Not at all. I did not. My god. Oh, god. I hate it. Just like Grandfather. He was something to me then. I mean . . . my father. My biological father. Oh, well. I was going to commit suicide for America. It all just seemed so awful."

"Suicide for America?"

"I had not figured it all out."

"And how does it all seem now?" she asked softly.

He did not really hear her question. He was not giving an answer.

"So you have chosen to live, after all?" she repeated carefully, prompting him.

"I do not think it is a question of choice. I do not think there is choice. I am interested enough to stay alive. I know that. I am interested. I am interested. I can be led onward."

He would at some stage, he guessed, make a choice. But he doubted if he would ever feel that he could not have made another choice. Ah, that was funny. Was there, after all, a heaven and a hell? Maybe that was it, that he did not think he would ever feel compelled to choose . . . anything. Unless, of course, he would be compelled not to make a choice. There was so much interference.

But he had nothing more to say. Nothing more for now. If his father had been a Communist then he, Timothy, had no background. He did not exist. He had not really been a part of it. How could you be real if you had no background? That was the felling: no background. And he did not think it had anything to do with the fact that his mother was dead—she was his mother and she was dead, was she not?—and his grandfather was senile. Or was it that his father was saintly? Satanic? His grandfather was dead and his mother was sexy. Senile? How could he begin life if he had no father? Could you have a mother without a father? Could you without either? If God was dead, did he have a beginning? How did one continue without having begun?

He had grown quiet and still in the crowd. Stunned by the revelation of the revolution. It was so weird. All of these things were going on. Was that possible? Was God dead or not? What did they want from him and who were they? Anything was possible, or was it? The contingency of death. He would do anything. If he only knew how. What choice did he have? Could you escape? What could he have done to change this situation? Nothing. This woman knew what she was saying. He was involved and yet what had happened had nothing to do with him. He did nothing. Of course, it was also that he now began in a vacuum. He had no connections. He might not be able to do anything. Ever.

But how could he possibly have been expected—and lord knows they were making demands, they were—to fit himself to their schedule, their world, their existing social historical community of human beings? Life for the individual had to be discovery, for heaven sakes, creation, in seven days, of course, otherwise you ran out of time. Plus, the 'schedule' was so arbitrary. Thus the 'decision' to disappear into nothingness, which threatened him anyway. Or was that the 'decision'? And did he have the power and the glory, the choice, to make that 'decision' anyway? Did he know yet?

He looked out over the bus station, above the thronging. Somehow they had come to another level and he did not remember when or how. But like an epiphany, he suddenly had the very clear understanding that after a night without sleep, early in the morning before the day for most people in the city had begun, you might have an unusual sense of your own destiny. Eight million people sleeping. Or whatever the number was. Would not that generate some kind of city mood, some kind of subterranean force? Except that the *New York Mirror* had reported in three separate editions that "the city was on edge." The city that was sleeping was on edge. He had bought all three editions, one in Hanover, New Hampshire, one in Boston, Massachusetts, and one in New York, New York, and he had read three times that "the city was on edge." The edge had lasted throughout the night.

She stood looking at him.

He turned to look at her.

"I am Timothy, Timothy Brown King," he said.

"Yes, and I am Klara. Klara Blazek."

"I know," he said.

She was not exactly seeing him at the moment. She was remembering. They would make love again, she thought, because we remember and it is not enough, not nearly. She had decided.

Tuesday, early morning hours, October 23, 1962

9

The Last Letter

Dear Timothy,

I must write while there is time. I just think you should know everything, know it all, if there is time. I have not been a very good father to you, so perhaps I need not worry about disillusioning my son. Is he already that? Perhaps I need to talk to you and to tell you what I know—or think that I know, although I am not sure—in the hope that you will understand and forgive and benefit, if that is at all possible at this time. Oh I wish I could talk to you personally, in the flesh, that we could be together, but that is not possible, it just is not possible anymore. You see, apparently there is slightly more time than I thought. Presumably there was more time than I thought. Perhaps. That is strange. Peculiar. I mean that there should be more time, not less. Although, how can one speak of how much time remains? Does not Einstein say that time is not an absolute? But it is yet critical for me.

There is much I want to tell you, if I can, about my life, and therefore something about your life, and I hope you will listen. But are there some things that cannot be explained? Oh that is true. Ah, a stray thought. Do you remember when you found out accidentally—I think, Helen, your mother, must have said something—that you were not a planned child, that your arrival was a surprise, sort of? It appeared to depress you, and I do remember that, as if you understood a fundamental truth. You apparently made something mysterious of it, and well you might have. You did not say anything about it, so I did not know. But you actually disappeared for a couple of days. We were frightened and worried sick. The police were involved. I had thought that you were in the woods, that you had gone back to the woods, which you often did as a child when you were disturbed. But I finally found you in that Catholic church in Portland and I never knew what made me go there to find you. Remember? You did not want to leave. Was it St. Mark's? I think you were twelve. Perhaps younger. Maybe you were eight. Is that possible? Heavens, it is as if I am talking of the stuff of myth. Well, there is something more, something additional that you should perhaps know. I wonder what you will make of it.

But first, yes, I want to tell you about committing yourself, whether it is performing a single act, committing yourself to a course of action, or committing yourself to another human being. I want to tell you, you, because to do so is to make a choice for life, something that is irrevocable, although in the beginning one is not aware of that, one cannot be. To commit oneself. A single act of commitment. The simplest, most uncomplicated act becomes an absolute act. And it is forever. Every time it is forever and unrecoverable. And it means, every time, that life has changed and that life is over, something special about life is over. You will never again be the same. I feel that most of all now. It can be dreadful. It is crushing. So much is made of identity. And yet identity can be both fleeting, frivolous, and it can be fatal. Arbitrary. Artificial. Forever. Any and all. It is important to grasp.

I wrote previously that blood, death, whatever, could not be avoided, I found out, if you were going to transform the social organism. Radically transform. Originally I did not think that, as a youth I mean, and I wonder what has gone wrong since. Every encounter, every convert, I believed then, was another ounce of strength, no matter the cost, one more chance to tip the balance, one more effort to change the mood of the world, one more advantage that would be counted at the day of the grandest encounter of all. One had to be patient, persistent, and have faith. Oh, Hezekiah.

But, yes, that is youth. Sometimes motivation is nothing more than energy. The energy is the motivation, the motivation is nothing else, and it carries one. And that is youth. That is sad. People do not gain wisdom, they lose energy. Do you understand? You must. It is important to me that you do. How else will you possibly understand what I have to tell you about my life—and yours?

What did I write about blood? I won't be able to reread this. I cannot do that these days. Let me tell you, human beings are better promoters than doers. The promotion succeeds because people want to believe. They can do that. The preliminary. They dream. They are dreamers. But the doing, the action is mostly terrible. It is tragic. We do not produce. We have not learned how to accomplish, and perhaps progress is an impossible task for our species. Perhaps it is not in the nature of things. And I did not know that then and I wonder if you know it. I lost myself in a movement, a cause, a vision, maybe an idea. To work for the future, for socialism, is to be at the center of things. You do not worry about who will cook your eggs. The apparatus controlled my life; it supported me; organized me; stimulated me; spiritualized me; defined me; *gave me meaning*. The Party did everything for me. I did not exist without it. I stopped asking questions. Real questions. Perhaps I even forgot what the questions were.

But eventually there is a breaking of the bond, usually because of an isolated experience, an individual response, and the self is freed. Hah, freed. Loose in space. But that is when it gets tough. Oh, Hezekiah. You realize that it is entirely up to you. You wander. You are left naked, stripped of all pretense. The void is overwhelming. But you are no longer a youth. There is no longer a life to be had. You cannot afford to wait any longer for something to develop, and yet there is absolutely nothing to do. What do these principles mean? Anything? No. I was working for something that could never happen. I now attempt to maintain what can be had, the best of what can be had, and it hurts, it does not excite me. People. Not what we think, idealize. I think that people are basically all the same. If you put those on the bottom on the top or vice versa, nothing would change. That is why the structure of society is crucial. We do not control ourselves, we do not know ourselves. We do not know each other. We dignify our actions by naming them. Revolution. Hah. We grab. We have urges. Those that have less strength, less energy, that do not see, they do not have. Oh, arrangements and institutions do protect. If you are weak but born into it, the arrangement, you may be protected.

I—we—joined the Party because of ultimate disgust with the behavior and morality, or lack of it, of human beings. But what is morality, nothing more than a symbol of the need-desire-thirst to be other than what we are. That is a form of recognition. We cannot bear the reality of our selves. A standard of something 'better' or other than what we are, that is morality. OR, at the very best, the need-desire-urge to *become*, a kind of expression, and as we *express* (during the process of becoming), morality equals a running commentary, description, or evaluation of what is happening. I—we—wanted a system that human beings would be forced to adapt to, not the opposite. That was our only hope. I—we—knew that the only possibility for change lay in radical measures. If change was even possible, nothing less would do. Unfortunately, I—we—learned that it meant doing away with subtleties and fine distinctions. Only an unbending, massive, relentless, crude, merciless force would do. The proverbial heads had to fall. Bloodletting was inevitable. And yet it is easier to talk of blood when you are young. It means less because it is simply an idea. Ironic, is it not, that such should accompany the idealism of youth? Bloodletting. The betrayal of human beings.

But when you get older death becomes palpable, never mind what you thought before about death, intellectually, even if you have been obsessed by it. I tell you it becomes palpable. When one is living, death seems impossible, it is unknowable. It is as if to die, then, becomes a supremely moral punishment. One pays for being passionate about life, for being extreme in the ultimate. If there were not some outside force punishing us—the punishment being death & thus aging, growing old, etc.—we would live forever in eternal youth. That is what we have lost and what we need to regain. I believe that. And I will never lose that. I wonder what Hezekiah would think of me now. For most of my life I have not wondered at all.

I think I was at one time a heroic figure. Oh, I would like to think I once was, but how can I take that figure seriously twenty, thirty years later knowing what I know now and what I did not know then? It is tiresome. Oh, what a torture. What a fool. I should not be writing to you this way, but I would give anything to be able even to regard myself as simply a tragic figure, and that too is an impossibility. You see, the concept of the modern world, of *modernity*, represents an attempt to escape from the horror of our personal selves. It is in our art most clearly. The more obscure it is, the clearer it is. But to abstract the world is to invite explosions. There must be ways to divert the pressure.

You are aware that I was in intelligence during the war. You know that I was based in London. Ah, yes, land of loyalties, divided loyalties, split loyalties, perspectives, views, sophistries. What you do not know is what I did in the name of intelligence. Yes, I intend that. And think that I, too, had my loyalties, my perspectives, my interpretations. You will learn that one can play any role, be that role, believe it, and play the opposite, purely, absolutely, genuinely for a period of time. But one cannot be one thing consistently, steadily, forever. And there is the great loss. There is a great capacity or non-capacity possessed by human beings for committing acts, for doing things that leave absolutely no impression. One forgets, represses, or, again, no impression is made, thus there is nothing to forget, nothing to repress. If our desires are strong enough or if it is convenient we can justify any act, feel no guilt, go on from there. Guilt is imposed and thus it is a question of force, strength, will. This is the way it is. Or we can act now and feel remorse later. The remorse is ineffectual. In many respects, Freud was full of his own fantasies and falsehoods and therein lies one of the unexamined stories of the twentieth century. Therein is an explanation, an understanding if you will, of the horrors of our time. No, of my time. It is difficult to tell.

You know that I met my wife, Helen—your mother—at a gathering at Smith College. She was quite beautiful. You have heard that story more than once, that I went to Northhampton in 1934 with other Dartmouth students to attend an anti-war convention with students from other colleges and universities from throughout New England, although there were no more than 100 of us altogether I think. And there I met your mother. (Joseph Wood Krutch guessed correctly in the 1930s when he said of undergraduates that "not many are red.") Of course, your mother was a student at Mount Holyoke. I had already joined the Party. Your mother was not a Communist, she had not joined the Party, although we were both members of the American League Against War and Fascism. For American society that was more than enough or, rather, that was much too radical. We were both young and idealistic and passionate. About ideas, that is, not about people. We actually believed in ideas. We thought ideas had an independent existence. I think we even believed that we could explore ideas to the exclusion of people. Ah, dear, dear youth. But you know all of this—not until now that I was in the Party, alas—

but that Helen and I met at the convention, is what I mean to say. I remember it was called the Connecticut Valley Student Congress Against War or something like that. Somehow that sounds both funny and lyrical to me today: a valley rising against the war. Believe me, it will take something of that nature. A Biblical ending after all. Oh Hezekiah, indeed.

Do you know what also strikes me as not funny, but odd? A name came into my head yesterday. Damnedest thing. It was Perley R. Bugbee. Quite a name don't you think? At first I did not know who Mr. Perley R. Bugbee was and why, for heaven's sake, I should think of such a name although, in the order of Ichabod Crane, it is, indeed, a name not to forget and not to conjure up in a vacuum. And then it came to me: that he was president of the local bank. In Hanover, I mean, when I was a student in the 1930s. I think it was called the Dartmouth Bank or Dartmouth National Bank even then. But still, that did not explain either why I should be familiar with such a name or why it should come back to me. It is extremely doubtful that he was any friend of mine or even an acquaintance despite the fact that life is full of oddities. But as I began to think of, remember, other associated things, things of the time, the period, the circumstance, I thought that it was perhaps because he must have been the local symbol of capitalism. One of them, anyway. Undoubtedly I encountered him in those days. Perhaps, for some reason, I was thinking back to the beginnings. Perhaps as a student I simply had a checking account in the bank. Interesting, is it not, that many have their first checking accounts when they go to the university, the seat of learning and culture. As innocent as that. But I think it must have been something more. Oh, Perley R. Bugbee. Could such a man have been so formidable? It does not seem likely, and yet I am certain there were those workers who found him exactly that, and probably not a friend to them, although they gave him what little money they had because they had no other choice. That has the appearance of a frivolous matter, my son, which makes for a dangerous thing. There are fundamental matters in life that can be skirted, and there are frivolous matters that can steal your life away. That is what I like to call a don quixote. I remember Perley R. Bugbee, you see, and yet I forget the name of my friend of the same era who committed suicide. There was one, you know? He jumped from Baker Tower. He was Jewish and he was depressed about Hitler. And I do remember his name. Tony Greenstein. I had talked with him the day before, the day before the end of his life. It is a true story. Anyway, we exposed our enemies at the convention, of course. The D.A.R. and the American Legion, who glorified the soldier, the armament manufacturers, who profited from war, and the Babbitts of our society, who glorified capitalism, among others. Oh, yes, I knew Perley R. Bugbee's wife.

But that is not what I have to tell you or retell. I digress. I met another woman at that very same convention as well. She was brilliant, and so young. Precocious. What promise she had. But she was a tragic woman. I could see that immediately. I loved her. I hope you can understand this. I had to love her. I had to give something to her. It was not a predictable thing or something I could control. You will learn at some moment in your life that a kind of love can be a dangerous thing. It is like an unexpected storm that can destroy you and there is no way to prepare for it, there are no rational decisions to be made, not for God, country, or Party. I say this because I think it has not happened to you as yet, but I suspect that it will. Perhaps I should wish for your sake that it does not. I think you are more sensitive than I am, more impressionable. Anyway, so the two women I loved I met at that convention. That is truly possible, you know. I can testify to that. But that is for later. You will have to understand and you will have to forgive me, if forgiveness is necessary. But no matter what you may think, Timothy, your mother did not know. I spared her that. Despite the depressions, the melancholia your mother has suffered from throughout her life, she did not know. She was spared this. You must believe that. I know that she did not suspect, and yet it has bothered me all of these years.

I met someone else at that convention. A professor. A professor of English who was about 10–15 years older than me. He was quite a striking figure and he was to remain so for me. Convinced. Articulate. Confident. Persuasive. Worldly. And stylish. Oh, yes, was he stylish—which admittedly planted a doubt in me from the beginning, because in some respects it was quite beyond me. But quite the figure, so easy to admire if you were young and had dreams and ambitions. And he was a solitary figure. He had been a member of the Party since the 1920s, almost from the beginning. He could make you proud to be a human being. The grand illusion. You know, another individual can be the motivational force for almost any act. One person can have a great impact upon another or others. In a vacuum where there are no compelling values or goals or there is no system or ordering or there are no beliefs or directions, one can be motivated to do something, to perform, simply to please another, simply because another expects the individual to perform in a certain manner. He was that kind of individual. He galvanized others. He gave people values, structure, direction. He was a great man. Or so people thought.

But now that I think of it, he was other things as well; now that I remember, he manipulated others even then. He was forced to, even then. He was quite good at that; he was clever. It hurts me to have to say this to you. And now, almost thirty years later, I believe I have heard his anthem. He said to me recently—yes, we have known each other all of these years and, it so happens, he had known of me before I knew of him—that he had been for radical change in this world practically his entire life. He had not sought material advantage or comfort for himself. He had dared and sacrificed for principle, for an idea. He had dared many things. But, he said, in later years he had come to understand the profound truth that people are moved more by a sense of their own destiny than by any ideology or, for example, by questions of national security. The dangers of a passion for national security, yes, but it is more a question of personal security. The ideology is a protection or at least people cling to it as one, as a shield. Drop that shield, that meaning, and they face alone the awful truth of meaninglessness. Nothingness.

"And look at me now," I remember he repeated, over and over. He kept saying, "And look at me now."

He said he felt shaky and insecure generally. About everything. Despite all that he had dared. For example, he said his automobile was falling apart, a 1949 Studebaker, and he could not really afford a new one, he did not really want a new one, another. Over the years he had allowed himself, no, he had become fond of that car and he had some fond memories, but he would find himself thinking of its rust spots, of a motor that would stop at any moment, and he would shudder. He felt weak and vulnerable. And he knew that if someone gave him a new car or somehow all of a sudden he had a new car, it would constitute a rebirth for him and that that fact would constitute a turning against the past. Life an ice cream cone on a hot summer day. He would feel wonderful. Strong, secure, confident. At least for a while. Until the next rust spot.

"Is that not disgusting?" I remember him saying. "Me, the revolutionary," he said. "This is all that man is."

He said that he had indeed succumbed, that he had accepted his badge, his mark as stamped, his identification, his limitations. Getting a driver's license, registering a car, accepting a social security number, these were only the beginning.

"But can you imagine?" he said. "These are traumatic moments for me!"

He had accepted them so thoroughly that he felt that if something went wrong, if his license was lost in the mail, if he could not pay for it, if some bureaucrat said that he did not exist or if somebody found out about a transgression of ten years ago or, if anything, if he did not receive a check and pay his bills on time, the telephone bill, the electric bill, refuse, he would have no identity. Surely there would be no social security number. He would not exist. And once he reached that state it would be final. He would be unable to recover existence. And then he said, "Wait a minute, did I say security?" He laughed. "'No social security without national security against aggression.' Or, 'maintaining national security through increased secrecy & security—secret from one another, secure from one another. Security in secrecy.' Oh what a lovely poem."

And he laughed again. Did I like that, he asked? And he laughed. And laughed.

He thought that was hysterical. He could string words together. He could go off on tangents and lose himself. Not living your own life, he said, a borrowed life, can make you or allow you to be preternaturally carefree, facetious, satirical, loose. The illusion of a free shot. One leaves the Party and becomes a secret agent, he said, to further the life of a nation or a cause, yes, an idea, and secret agency becomes the life; sex as a tool to further the goals of said secret agent—sex manipulation becomes the life.

He did not know what reason was any longer, what the term signified. What it supposedly stood for—he put little value into it. He found it had very little to do with what we are anyway. He did not know what imagination or creativity was either, he said. However, what it stood for seemed to be the best of one's life, of man's, the best hope. Even irrationality. He said that some of the best moments of his life had been the so-called irrational ones. (I would add, some of the most fearful as well.) Perhaps sex was fear, he thought, because sex and fear rules us more than anything. In his most fearful moments, he said, he had felt it in his loins.

He had believed in giving voice to the 'dignity of man,' he said, although he no longer knew if individual human beings possessed dignity. His work in intelligence had involved degrading individuals, finding them, degrading everywhere—often by their own hand and through their own choice, which ended with his realizing his own degradation.

"'Dignity of man'?" he scoffed. "We all become securitycrats."

That is what he called himself, a "securitycrat." I do not know why.

"We become angels of death, agents of Satan," he said, "and it has nothing at all to do with the fact that we are Communist agents in a capitalist country. We are all born spies. Everyone."

He used sex to get information in his intelligence activities during the war—what a misnomer, he said. Sex had ruled him quickly. He had enjoyed it. Revelled in it. With both sexes. Made it, at times, the absolute goal, value, guideline of his life. Sex continued to rule him, even when he did without it, could not have it. Could not perform is what he meant.

"And who and what are we really spying for?" he asked. "Principle, morality, power, just another way to organize one's time for the period called life. No real meaning. Who are we really spying on? Ourselves."

There was a time, years ago, another odd thing that I remember, when he said to me something to the effect that, it is great to sit down and watch a football game, say, Notre Dame against Army at Yankee Stadium. Lots of excitement. The roar of a crowd of thousands that engulfs you. But then the game ends and you are all alone. It is over. You have to get up and go home and go to the bathroom and brush your teeth and no one is there. And then he laughed, and I will never forget what he said.

He said, "That is what happens when you live for an ideal—your teeth go bad."

My sense of it. We certainly are not born with dignity, we are not granted it—even so we must profess it, force ourselves to become dignified. Perhaps we lose that battle. We must profess values, create them—force ourselves to sustain them because there are none independent of us. There is no other choice. Oh, I have spent a lifetime attempting to rule my life, losing everywhere, professing to others that they can rule theirs, knowing, in fact, that we are ruled. I know I will never stop struggling.

You know, the town characters have always rustled my sensibilities, but never so much as now. Particularly the ones in the cities walking down the street talking to themselves, looking over their shoulders. There is the fine line to cross. It is always in our way, in our path. Originally, I thought that the problem for me was in trying to separate my relationship with my father—some would say my lack of a relationship, but that is only because they would not see it as what they would consider a normal relationship, but I had a relationship and it was to a man in the distance, in the mountains, not in the clouds—from my perspective on life or from what I judged the nature of life to be. That is, that my relationship with my father influenced, even determined, my view on life. But I do not think so now. I think that my perception of life is valid, and it is my own. This is what is. Actually, maybe if I had had a so-called normal relationship with my father, that would have prevented me from understanding life as it really is. 'Family' for many, I think, is a veil of tears and emotions and laments that obscures.

There is a family story about Hezekiah that he got loose once in his old age, that he ran about in his long johns in Deering Oaks Park in Portland. Sometimes the story has him running around naked. On a Sunday. I have always thought of his doing that—I believed it—as wonderful and hilarious. Alas, I was not there. But that tale has helped me in innumerable situations. I cannot think of Hezekiah as a broken, disillusioned man. As senile. And here I am. I cannot forget him. I need him. My, oh my, where would I be without him, without his example before me. As a child, I thought of every Sunday as another death. The gray of Sunday. The Onward Christian Church determined it. What irony there! Life was squeezed out of the house like air out of a seat cushion. Thus, how wonderful was the running of the naked ghost. The story was supposed to be a tragedy, a disgrace to the family, but it was not for me. Naked running thru the park—"He was crazy," they used to say, but I do not believe he was crazy. You must believe that he was not, Timothy. Do not think that of your elders. Think of them as impassioned. They once were.

And that man I have been telling you about, perhaps you have already guessed. He came to our house in Maine on a number of occasions. You knew him and you liked him. And he liked you. Remember Tuffy? André Cordon. We called him Tuffy. Affectionately. He inspired me. No matter what he says, he has remained the most important figure of my life.

There was a woman who came with him on one occasion. You were quite young so I do not know if you would remember her. She came to that house in Maine only once or twice. I did see her at other times in New York. What I am struggling to tell you is that she is the woman I loved. And with whom I had a child. But even though I want you to know everything—I wrote that, I know I did—you cannot ask. Because we will never know what happened anyway—

or why. That is not given to us. That is the nature of things. Even if someone presumed to be able to tell you, you would not believe what you heard. You must believe that. All you can do is perform now and wonder as little as possible about what you have done. I know that for myself. But I do not know if I will send this to you, Timothy, I really do not know. I do not know if I can send you this letter when I am basically talking about myself as much as about anything. I do think that I am threatened. I think we all are. I am not certain I should do this to you. There is more to tell.

I love you as my son. Believe that.

Your Father, JBK

10

Oh Holy Night of Passion Play

Okay, the Grand Event, okay, in defiance they were going to make love. It could not be avoided. Was it not all of it obvious? The Grand Gesture. It had to be done. America demanded the outrageous act. Everything compelled it. History, providence, nature. In the absence of the father, the mother would love the son. It would be a lustful grab for immortality. It would be a love that had withstood death. They had stood there alone among millions and she had seen that he needed to be rescued, caressed, embraced. As a mother, she knew it, having conceived the need. She would boldly take the son to her bed, the son of the father, and she would love him as her very own. Yes, in defiance She would be his spiritual and sensual angel of mercy. She would save him although as the son was he not supposed to be the savior? If that was an alteration, she approved. But she had the sense that having encountered each other again they would linger this time. She thought one could say that. Something had happened to the two of them, something had happened to them together, bound them, seared and fastened their souls. He would stay no matter what occurred, and she would not ask him to leave no matter what was said or thought. For a while she would stir his mind and soul and link generations. They would make love because they had no choice. It would be the final perversion of life. Somewhere I have been before, she thought. Somewhere a nun was flying above the holocaust.

The night before, it had seemed like the night before, actually early that very morning or early one morning, because time had disappeared, Klara Blazek, Timothy Brown King's woman of the night, the shroud, the bat, the nightkite, the harpy, the siren of dark mystery, Klara Kovacs Blazek had dispatched Timothy Brown King from the Post Authority Bus Terminal to the netherworld of the Hotel Sun, not the home she had promised, she had never promised, merely a way station of ritual, where Timothy had spent the day, the night, days, maybe, presumably, waiting. Only to both of them it had seemed like the night extended. Film noire. He had spent days, the extended day turned night, black and white, without her at the Hotel Sun, where she had perhaps abandoned him forever again, where the light never appeared, that is, where natural light never appeared in the Hotel Sun, where she might never reappear. After all, she had naturally disappeared into the ground, into the subway from which it had seemed she would never ever emerge from herself, unless, rising from the depths to make love, they were elevated together, turning time forever. There was that promise of a profane miracle to defy all gods.

Dining for two had been the prologue. Or at least some food. At Nedicks, in the caverns of the Post Authority terminal. Courtesy of the Communist Party, apparently. A Nedick's hot dog paid for by the Commies. How about that, Mel Allen would say. Actually, they had ordered tea and muffins. It was not what Timothy had wanted. He had thought of having a coke, a hot dog with mustard and sauerkraut, a Nedick's special, and a potato knish. More like what had naturally appealed to him. But when Klara had said, "Let us have tea and a muffin," he had not felt as though he could say no, even if he did not like tea, certainly not with milk in it, which she had promptly added without asking him, assumed he had wanted mother's milk rather than bitter lemon. He would have preferred the tartness of lemon. She had not really asked him, and she had eschewed both milk and lemon for herself. She was in apparent control, under orders and giving them all around, controlling the skies. As Klara had eaten her muffin, she had skillfully kept her fingers and the corners of her mouth free of crumbs and butter with a paper napkin, the proper role model, although she had not been obtrusive about it. She had not been overbearing. She had not been dainty. But had she been giving signals to secret agents as well? Would a mother do such a thing?

What was certain, what Timothy could not doubt, was that they had been sitting at a Nedick's counter in the middle of the Post Authority Bus Terminal having tea and muffins while hundreds of people milled around them, thousands unto millions if you considered that they were in the middle of New York City, their own little circle within circles and circles of people emanating outwardly, an explosion of centrifugal force that could only be found in Manhattan. An arrogant way to be a spy. Daring. This was obviously the world of espionage. Safety in numbers applied here, although at the same time Timothy was convinced that they were being watched, and they were being watched, there could be no doubt about that, it could not be avoided. But the Communists meeting over tea and muffins at Nedick's to plot the overthrow of the free world was not what Timothy had anticipated. That is, if that was what they were doing, and why should he have presumed otherwise, what should he have imagined?

Certainly, by anyone's definition, American Communists were freaks. You could look it up. That was the fundamental lesson learned in graded grammar school. Yes, Communists were spooky spirits; they were spirits and spooks who were lurking everywhere in all of America. There was no question, few could be found who doubted it, doubt that they were vampires, ghosts, boogiemen, monsters, evil marauding phantoms who were yet threatening to pounce upon all patriots, to take over the country, a spreading mystical mold, a force constituting a grand attempt to create, albeit interesting, exciting, fearful drama on the world scene. But, meeting at Nedick's? After all, Timothy did not think that this was what the founding fathers of Nedick's had in mind. Unless, of course, Nedick's had metamorphosed into a Commie front. Perhaps a new revision of rotating America was, after all, in order.

Yes, yes, that is what it was, history said so. It was just what Earl, the would-be Bear Browder, the erstwhile General Secretary of the American Communist Party, had called it in the 1930s when JBK had joined the ranks: Twentieth-Century Americanism, that Communism was twentieth-century Americanism. No, not Twentieth-Century Fox, but Twentieth-Century Americanism. First Nedick's and, heavens, then what? Woolworth's? Mickey Mouse and Donald Duck? Did this mean that Communism was actually the inner lining of crazy-quilt capitalism, capitalism, the fifth column, the reverse of the coin, the grandest popular front of all? The last loudest extravaganza?

And then, Klara Blazek had hustled Timothy Brown King through the streets of Manhattan as if they were attempting to shake a tail, beat the morning rush. So it had seemed. She was anxious, driving herself to her urgent task, scurrying, looking over her shoulders, looking around, looking everywhere at everything. Stepping off a curb, Timothy had nearly been hit by a green Cadillac that had not honked once before whipping by, its fins waving, sashaying menacingly. The driver had not even bothered to look solicitously back. Obviously a hustling capitalist in pursuit of profit, quite probably driving the Green Hornet.

A woman standing in a doorway had stared at them, vacantly, her yellow dress pulled tightly around a protruding belly that looked borrowed, the belly suspended high above her knees, her thick legs. Her hair was red, her rouge was blue, but Timothy did not think she was a pregnant American spy and Klara did not appear to notice, which did not confirm anything. Self-conscious, Timothy walked on, awkwardly, wondering if the red, yellow, and blue woman was watching him, wondering why it was difficult for him to put one foot in front of the other as he had finally learned not so many years ago.

Suddenly, Klara and Timothy were forced to step back into the street in order to maneuver around a hovering of people picking at a vegetable and fruit stand, both people and fruit in abundance, overflowing the sidewalk, and although Timothy had been hungry moments before, the sight of eager, aggressive hands pawing fruit made him nauseous, ripe fruit, prime, withered, he was not certain he liked its smell, not hungry, he did not like the smell of frying and fried food, forever greeeasy, emanating from a grill in an open window, open to the world. He had not seen that before. What were they frying, orange squares, long black things, dead or alive? Why and how were they eating what, were they eating whom, were they devouring themselves?

In those brief moments when Timothy had dared to take his eyes off Klara, who like destiny would not wait, he had felt compelled again to look upward to the supposed end of tall buildings, buildings that seemed again to be tilting toward him, leaning over to press him, thumb him in particular, into the asphalt. Spinning, like a boy from Maine bedazzled in the big city, he had become dizzy and stopped bending backward. True, as he had gazed heavenward he had imagined the bombs falling in slow motion from the heavens, the cheering throngs leaning out of the windows of the skyscrapers, the fluttering confetti. He had been possessed by the vision. At last, a grand American hero's welcome to New York City.

Meanwhile, Klara had rushed on and he had kept pace with her, but he had not felt as though they had been moving in any particular planetary sphere. Where had home gone? Had he truly lost his way on the range?

He had looked up at the Man smoking a Camel above Times Square, blowing a shroud over the City

———streets of Manhattan

Man ddddddDrinking over Times Square

a place everyone had walked through, you felt, Times Square, that everyone had walked through your mouth, everyone had been there at the very same moment, everybody had been there, every night, all night, standing there, loitering, not lifting their feet, shuffling, everyone here right now, where one was supposed to be, where everything had happened, would happen, waiting for Kilroy

The Guy Drinking
      and
The Guy Smoking
The Big Guy
like a god,
Huge, large,
gigantic
(a King-sized smoker)
as big as you can get
gl^{it}zy

The biggest mouth ever seen, a giant blowing smoke rings the size of Hollywood swimming pools, huge lips, huge cigarette, huge eyes, Timothy stared, transfixed at the biggest mouth ever seen drinking forever, drinking from the bottomless glass filled forever with Canadian Club.

Suddenly they had stopped.

"That is it," Klara had said, reluctant now, ambivalent, wavering, wondering if this could be forever. Goodbye father and son.

Home?

"The Hotel Sun. Over there, across the street. I have stayed there before. I have memories of JBK. Even before you were born. Many have stayed there over many years."

She paused, as if waiting for another thought, a different thought, before continuing again.

"Including your father. I want you to stay there. They will give you a room."

And maybe take you off my hands, she had thought. Perhaps now just as he had appeared so would he disappear in reverse, sucked back into the void. Perhaps she would never ever see him again, leave him, appropriately, on the doorstep at the Hotel Sun like an abandoned bouncing baby boy, forget him over and over again, goodbye, JBK. Murder and mayhem at the Hotel Sun.

Klara had given Timothy a paper napkin, fresh from Nedick's, on which she had written in pencil, in precise, intricate, small print, exactly the room to request and where and when they would meet again, at which rendezvous and sphere, she had promised, she would take him to a bar named Anybodys, she promised, where everybody had known his father, where his father had drunk, and drunk, and drunk. Downtown, she had said, in the Village, like father, like son. Meet me in Manhattan and we two will go to Anybodys on the morrow, downtown, just like your father. No, tonight or was it a fortnight? By the stars, one could not tell, but by the clock, the new day had begun. And with that she had left, gone. She had just left him. Sort of. You cannot get there from here without me, she had said, but I will take you. Sort of. No further explanation. A new day, but Timothy was still to be kept in the night.

It had occurred to him to ask her if he should chew and swallow the napkin, but he had not done so. And he had wanted to ask her if anybody would be at the bar, but she had not waited to listen anymore to his manic, rambling, provoking chatter. And, and she had just left him, it had seemed. Meet me at Anybodys, she had said, but you cannot get there by yourself from here, which was a promise, sort of. We will go backwards and forwards from the bus station, retracing our steps, everybody's steps, including your father's, to the Hotel Sun to the bus station to New Jersey to the subway to Anybodys, USA, we two will go home again to where you were born and it will be as if it had never happened. But first you must go in to go downtown or it will never come to pass for us in this last hour of our holy need.

It was undoubtedly a riddle for the common man. A riddle about reality. A Communist riddle, or Hungarian at least, obviously foreign, set to a mystifying tune about Timothy's father. Go in. To where? Over there, over there, go over to the other side. Across the street to the HOTEL SUN, where she had been before, she said, and he had as well. He had? Had she said that? Over there, over there, go over to the other side, over there. An ancient neon sign sticking straight out from the side of the building. It looked awkward, it was incongruous, embarrassing even, a symbol of human incompetence, and yet it looked ancient, looked as if it had once meant something to someone, looked as if someone had discarded it long ago by tacking it onto the plain flat facade like a message never retrieved. A modern gargoyle. That was the secret. Not ancient. Ageless and obsolescent and menacing and abandoned. As a hotel, it was well disguised. Perhaps the sign had been put up first and someone had supposedly forgotten per instructions to build the hotel, the HOTEL SUN. Or maybe it was a planned place where someone forgot to stay, under orders, not a picture-postcard hotel, not a wish-you-were-here kind of place. Not a place of remembrance, a place to forget, to be forgotten, not a monument. But the sign said "Hotel," a universal sign. Another sign on the great glittering Times Square, where he was to be a guest of the Communist Party.

Obviously, the giant, the Boss, had chosen thousands of square yards, had taken an empty, great, unfruited plain, filled it with the world and the Hotel Sun and called it Times Square. Times what? Times Squared. So what was he to do? There should have been a doorknob to hell or the step of a stairway to heaven, some way to begin. Perhaps he should have put a dime in a telephone slot and called ahead. Then he could have paused, delayed while he had a cup of coffee in the morning and a beer and a cigarette at night before he lay me down to sleep. It was the Broadway blues baby bebop shuffle.

The door was a glass door that he could not see through, of course, could not see before him into his own future. He had pushed it open and then he had let it shut while he stepped back and looked around. Nothing. There had been no voice of welcome and no other visible entrance, no other choice, no lights and no ghosts of the past.

Yes, he had been nervous, nervous with jazz, not blues, but he had again pushed open the door and stepped inside from where he could not look back through the glass door, and started up a stairway immediately in front of him. He had actually dared to go halfway up, only to come halfway back down. And then again he had begun to halfway climb the stairway, and this time he had kept on going, his legs had kept on moving, pumping. He had lifted his feet, climbing, anticipating, looking heavenward, not looking backward and downward. Dark stairs, musty odor, urinating, was that it? Memory. It was familiar. He had not heard anything, but was somebody up there waiting for him with an explanation? Oh, courage. Or were they sneaking up behind him once again to take him unawares, to take him away on the bus? Did that always happen, was that the nature of existence? Were the walls closing in on him? A huge, wide, wooden stairway, so huge one could get lost, twisted around, never get off, particularly if it kept on moving, if he never got off the roller coaster.

To the top of the stairway, hurriedly to the end, get it over with, and quickly through another glass door without stopping, no turning back. He had stopped when the second door shut, frightened that he had been so bold, thinking, fearing it was too late, convinced that the door had shut for eternity, that he had mistakenly retraced somebody else's steps and would never find his way back to himself.

The hallway, he thought it was a hallway, was dimly lighted and he could barely see. But then the walls, shadowed, he began to see the shadows on the walls as if in a tunnel, and the walls had looked to be covered with millions of large . . . bugs. Of course. Absolutely. At least, there had been something moving. The wallpaper was impure with ancient black bugs or the wallpaper was abugs. No, it was in the ascending hotel corridor where he saw the breasts and thighs and monstrous penises and vaginas, it was the design of the wallpaper, yes, how amazing, although the obscenity laws of the State of New York would not apply, but what could be expected in the biggest garden of evil, the fruit of knowledge? And then the shapes had begun to assume the visages of people's faces that he could not quite recognize.

Why, he had been afraid that he was about to collide with someone, that people were walking all around him, creatures hovering, floating. He could not see. And then someone had actually brushed past him, nudged him. No apology. He had resisted the desire to press himself against the wall, he could not see anything, and he felt embarrassed that he wanted to do such a thing, thinking that he should drop to his hands and knees.

And then his eyes had adjusted. There was a hallway. And what? A desk at the end. He had thought of crawling toward it, but instead he had walked upright, maturely, waiting for the bugs to fall, jump upon him, inevitably, looking up and down and to the sides, looking lost and bereft and foolish, but you had to, it was necessary.

Was there a man there, sitting at the desk? A blackmasked man sleeping. He was asleep. He was a hotel clerk. And what was to be done? They were expecting him. Must be. He would not ask for a room because they would not give him one. He was in the Hotel Sun, where he would not ask to be put up, ask for lodging. Where he would not be asked if he wanted a room for a day or a week or a month. Where he would not register or pay or be fingerprinted by the FBI. A guest in the HOTEL SUN on TIMES SQUARE, courtesy of the Communist Party. Red Square, USA. Lost and found. For this was the way the boogieman did it, bug off.

The hotel clerk had spoken so few words they were words to be forgotten, Timothy had forgotten, had almost forgotten his very own name. The hotel clerk had taken Timothy to his room without fanfare, without a sound, without an exchange, without waiting after he had opened the door, for the seventeen dollars had been paid in advance for a lifetime.

There had been no mirrors or windows in Timothy's small room, no opportunity to look out at the world, to look ahead, more a cell than a room, probably a Communist cell, maybe a prison, where a strange, never-seen-before rash on his skin had told him that it was more than likely that he had been closely observed as the walls closed in, which seemed bizarre, because, he questioned the darkness, from where were they looking at him? and who was looking at him? and what was there to be seen looking at him? and would they see everything from where they were looking at him? Unless, of course, they were practicing subliminal torture on him and he had already confessed unknowingly, a blank page, turned himself inside out to the authorities or gone over and out to the enemy.

He had spent the hours in noiseless space, spreadeagled on his back, lying on top of a torn, worn, faded white bedspread, so thin, with a single light bulb hanging straight down from a yellowed, paint-peeled ceiling, pointing straight down at his belly-button like a hanging umbilical cord. In the words of Hezekiah, he should have been "sore afraid."

But it had seemed so silly. And, he wondered, was this his first exposure to socialist realism? Silly, as blackmasked human beings walked by his door in an unlighted hallway, he had heard them, he had imagined, he had assumed that they were all black, blackmasked like the hotel clerk, the only person he had seen, assumed he, Timothy, was the only whitemasked human being in a black dark world of socialist revolution, because was not that the way it worked? Outside, the sun had been shining. He had been convinced of it. Inside the Hotel Sun he had been in purgatory or a movie reel.

Shocking, somebody might have said. After all, Klara had said she was going to take him home, and Timothy had instantly talked about mothering. Instead, home to the Commies must have been a code word for going underground to the grave, for stashing him away out of sight, even for kidnapping. Brainwashing? What a perversion. How un-American could you get? The Commies would stoop to anything on the vulnerable prairie.

Meanwhile, mother had gone underground to the subway.

Just as she had done countless times in other worlds, Klara had walked through the spotted, soiled crowds unseeing, as if in walking down the long wide passageways she were absolutely alone with her voices as she directed. Up stairways, up one, two, down three levels, around corners, turning left twice, right once, walking into rooms within rooms, moving further to inner rooms, fewer and few people, until she was in fact alone without pursuit. The light dimmed, the shadows increased. Finally she had reached the electric roads within, passageways big enough for her thoughts, white actually gray dingy, no, colorless clouds of walls enclosing. To an empty bench, she would sit on a wooden bench and collapse, shrivel. Convinced she was alone. Exhausted. And, remembering, try not to remember, the details, the broad strokes, isolated moments of pasts.

Nothing more than a rumpled, folded black coat, her black-stockinged legs protruding as sticks, she might just as well have been going back for her weekly encounter with the old man, Tuffy, as she once called him affectionately, called him André Cordon in moments of scorn which were moments of anger. He would be there waiting for her while she would have kept him waiting forever, if that were possible.

Seema, by now fourteen years old, would have let him in and retreated to her secret castle, while he would be waiting, waiting impatiently, circling and stalking, expectant, anxious for her arrival, although he would not speak of his impatience when she arrived, would pretend calmness even though his anxiety would be evident to her. Just the way she preferred him. She would treat him scornfully, harshly, unkindly, as she had done before. He would want to touch her as he had done before as soon as she came through the door, but he would not dare to do such a thing, certainly not, and she would take her time, have tea and a muffin, talk of how tired she was, act totally unconcerned, indifferent to him.

Finally, with Seema in bed in the back room with the door closed, she would take off her silk blouse, her black skirt, fold them, and lie down on her bed in the dark middle room, off the kitchen and the hallway, both lighted. She always kept her black bra and black garter belt on. Tuffy would take off all of his clothes, he would insist, lie on the bed beside her and press against her his big graying chest of hair, his still-large, muscular legs, his powerful arms Even in his state, at his age, sagging but still powerful. His money would already be on the table, a bag of groceries in the kitchen, his books. Let the games begin. A dismal prospect.

And yet, presently, she was exhilarated against her will. Subway trains whizzed and whooshed because this could change it all, it was a new spell, she felt the newness, the aura, although it was impossible to acquiesce.

Black pocketbook, newly purchased black bread and cheese. Three or four books, a manila folder with papers, poetry, readings. All at her feet on the cement floor. She would lower her head again, chin on her chest, and close her eyes. Her secular temple, constructed now for her, she would not think, her passion and anger and hatred dissolved in the barren cavern waiting for the undergrounded subway, grieving for him, for both of them, for all of them together, let us pray, as if in a gigantic tomb, sounds distant and muffled by the earth.

Her life, staccato, segmented, fragmented, whirlpooled, had always been insecure, without guarantees, with short periods of illusory stability, demanding, torturous, brutalizing. Men were weak and cowardly, she thought, particularly older men, but if this were so why was she the one deprived, drained, dunned? She admitted to herself that, occasionally, she had slept with older men out of choice. If she had desired any man, old or young, she had slept with him. She always had, always chosen. It had been her freedom, her choices. After the first, that is, dancing, when she had been sixteen, dancing, afterward she had done the choosing, she thought, after the dancing. However, with older men she had experienced, recognized in herself, a secret, guilty desire. When they had slept with her they were corrupting her again, like the first time, the recurrent nightmare, always corrupting her pure, virginal, young body, and she had received intense pleasure from that, revenge, she had been in control finally. Always virginal and young, she had stayed young forever, preternaturally virginal with young men like Slamunster. Afterwards, guilt, anguish, remorse, hatred.

No, that was not true. André and JBK. She had met André at the artist's colony in Saratoga in 1940. She was there to write her poetry, he had said he was there to write and to paint, although he did not seem to belong there. But painting was a skill among skills he would use, be asked to use, and yet it was what he loved most, more than the writing. He was an artist used, abused, he was everything, remarkable, he was. There was the danger which he ignored, just as he ignored many things. His neutrality was not declared, his indifference, if that is what it had been, was. Whether what one had done was contrary to the interests of the world, the universe, let alone the artificial equation called one's country, was forever debatable. She had slept with him for that very reason at the colony in Saratoga Springs. There would be no involvement, no commitment, no emotion, no memory, she had thought. A pure physical aesthetic act, balletic. He had been in his small sparse room painting his nudes and she had joined him and they had made love as if he had never stopped painting. She had gone back several times. His money came from an inheritance, he said. Thousands, maybe millions or maybe only hundreds, it was difficult to tell. From his unnamed, mysterious mother, not from his paintings. He had sold them, but not many and not for much, and he had never cared whether he sold them. She had never told him that she was afraid of his paintings. And he did not know that she was afraid. His paintings, those snakes he called nudes. She hated the fact that she was afraid of them, as if to be afraid of his paintings was to be afraid of him. She had been afraid of his paintings from the very beginning in Saratoga. When she had induced him and then let him make love to her. Which is exactly the way it had been. She had been in control. No, that was not the case. He had been an overpowering man, but gentle, even then. At the time, she already knew JBK, knew him from before, from further back. She had gone to him again later. He had taken care of it. He had saved her. She thought he had saved her. The voices pounded her temples. He had never told her that they were brothers.

She had known, knew that there could be no future, no future with JBK, the younger, just as there would be no future now with Timothy, merely the everlasting present with André, the older, the many presents. She knew what to expect, and she knew what happened to young lovers and she would tell him, tell Timothy, even if she had not raised him. She would tell him that she had finally agreed to pose in the nude for André Cordon, yes, that it was André for whom she had posed, not JBK.

And they, she and André, had been lucky, if that was what one called it. Somehow his eminence, if that was what one called that, had saved him from exposure. Until now. This could not be avoided. And how funny it was, how hysterical, that she had probably been saved because she was a woman. What was one to expect from a woman? From a mother? She had been overlooked because she was a woman and a mother. How else explain it? She had not been asked to explain.

Information. Give them enough information. Just enough. Just as she had done. Had she killed JBK? She would never, ever know. But she could not believe that he had disappeared of his own volition. They had probably killed him to save him. Dead, he could remain the upstanding, the outstanding, the All-American. Alive, he would be disgraced. Possibly jailed. They would find a charge to save themselves.

But all is well that ends well because they were going to make love as if this was what they had to do, of course, as if to cheat reality. He was a perfect stranger to her, he was, he was, but she was taking him over, yes, she would bring him home like she had brought home her stray animals. Did she make love to strays, the tired, the poor? She could not leave him in that hotel, not again. She could not wait to go back and retrieve him. The forces governed her voices. Her trolls were at work.

She left the subway platform quickly, knocking her elbows on the railing as she ran up the stairs. She had decided that she must go to get him, save him, bring him to the apartment and hide him.

She would probably say, and said, under the sign of the Hotel Sun, having lured him from his bed in the netherworld, having returned to rescue him slipping down dark corridors:

"Why do not you come with me downtown in order that we may go upstairs to the apartment? Seema will be asleep."

She would say it and not say it. The words had rushed together into the vortex.

It was another riddle, another ruse.

And Timothy would nod and follow her. Back to the bus because, first things first, she had to show him, show him the past. The bus for New Jersey, because Communists did not really belong in Manhattan, it was not their town, they had met in Weehawken, New Jersey. But it had been the necessary, obvious diversion: go through the tunnel—leave the frozen city, see Manhattan frozen like outsiders from Weehawken, New Jersey, and then return. Just like that. No, it would not be that way. But how would it happen for them now? How would they presently manage it? The moustachioed bus driver would be waiting for them, that is what, would drive the bus back down the cement roadway backwaaards, down and around and out into the same city from whence they had come. In eight minutes they would reach Lincoln Tunnel and disappear into and under the Hudson river, leaving New York and the FBI behind.

As if on a tour Timothy saw the large, red-brick apartment building on Potter Place in Weehawken, New Jersey, where JBK, his father, had visited her, a plain eight-story walkup, where they had walked in and up and out again, where they had waited, two blocks away from where they got off the bus, from where they had seen Manhattan together for the first time across the water frozen in the night of another country, silver and gold lights, looming pointed lighted black towers of the kingdom. A drab building, away from magic, not an easy spotcheck for the FBI. And then they had reversed their steps because you could not get there from here, could not get there from Weehawken, New Jersey, could get there only from Manhattan.

After crossing rivers and worlds and climbing stairs, after unlocking the door to her apartment above Anybodys in Greenwich Village, she turned and held her finger to her lips.

"Seema will be asleep. Do you remember Seema? My daughter. You will probably meet her in the morning."

Which was extraordinary, that she thought him in a daze? deranged? totally out of touch with the present? That he had learned her name, knew her daughter's name. Was this the way it was supposed to be? that you could know the children, start the new chapter, but not know the parents, not know the old chapters? But he did know her name, and she his. He knew her name was Klara under investigation.

They walked quietly into the short hallway and turned left into the kitchen, where a single light was burning. She took his coat, told him to sit at the kitchen table, and, holding her finger to her lips once again, she disappeared into the hallway, became invisible, turned toward the impenetrable darkness that he had sensed when entering the apartment.

The kitchen was sparse. A table with three wooden chairs. Three? A few cupboards, a bare counter, no dishes or pots in sight. Salt and pepper. No sugar bowl. A medium refrigerator and stove, small and old. On the floor in a corner two bowls, one with water, the other food. An animal. (Get it before it gets the baby.)

Light bulbs, naked light bulbs.

Remembering, or failing to remember, isolated segments, different moments disconnected, separated wholes, there had been no sense of progression, no sense of what would happen next, no knowledge of a future, because the past and knowledge of the present were too overwhelming. Rather, completeness, constant pacific fulfillment. He sat at the kitchen table alone, perfectly content, having been within himself and at ease every step of the way. Or was that not true? Stay, remain, do not move.

Timothy knew that they were going to make love. He, the innocent, the inexperienced, had certain future knowledge of this powerful experience of sin with his father's mistress. Yes, there was a Biblical quality to it: something sacred, a great transgression. A violation. He could feel it.

He was not certain if he should confess to her that, with her, he yet felt as if they were virginal. This would be his first love, her first love. Perfect. And this, too: all of his other precious moments of worldly passion, in fact, had been other-worldly, bizarre, preternatural, profane, damnable, not of this earth. Not a one ordinary. Not even his birth, and he wondered why on this earth he remembered that, knew that. She had said that she remembered being in the womb, the womb, that was all that she had said. And he knew that he carried within him great guilt. It ran in the family, did it not? The blonde pregnant working-class Betty Grable nineteen-year-old who had slept with him in hopes of tricking him into thinking she carried his child and he would be compelled to marry her. His child. But he knew she was pregnant before the fact, knew that she was tricking him. Or did, had he? All he had to do was trust her and it would have been happily ever after.

Perhaps this was all in restrospect, a natural, human, perverse, carnal bent to weave twisted, complicated threads of invented tales together, a craving, gnawing need to do that, a kind of unmanageable, unbearable creativity, native to the species. Like father, like son. Actually, she had been his first. All very innocent. The Abenaki woman from Boston. She had been eager, but drunk. She had passed out in his arms. In bliss? He had not stopped. Had he therefore made love to a corpse? Oh, come on. Had she really passed out, fainted? To what lengths would he go to reinvent the past before there was a present, desperate as he was to invent a damaged life, to create a dark legacy? The older woman with tuberculosis. Exploiting vulnerability. In the slums. His second. And his third. Innocence retained? Was that conceivable?

The moments in the bus had amounted to one long idyll of foreplay for the gathering of the storm.

And now. He was repeating something. The pregnant girl. The Abenaki Indian. The TB unmarried older slum woman. The manic-depressive Irish poet girl. God, he had let her down. Lyrical. She had needed him and if only he had known then that he needed her for his life. He missed her. Even now. He had dreamed her. Was she the most alluring of all? That look in her eyes. That crooked look. Wonderful promise, wonderful mystery, wonderful bizarre beauty. Wonderful nose, mouth, chin. Save me.

And now? This woman, a Communist, he presumed, had to be, no other explanation, no matter what she said, she would deny everything, naturally, a foreigner, she said that herself, all Communists were foreigners, of course, cannot be an American and be a Communist or a Communist and be an American and tell the truth as well, absolutely not, a Hungarian from the Danube, the mother of a fourteen-year-old girl, this woman twice his age who had been the mistress of his once upon a time missing father, he was certain of that, this mystery woman of past destiny, of once more, of never before. Timothy sensed that she was a concrete link to the past, this woman who was old enough to be his mother, who could have been his father's wife, the most intense human being he had ever met, magnified many times because she was about to become his lover, no, that in the fact of becoming his lover, he her lover, the full mystery of life would be revealed, he would go where none had gone. She would be his true and only love, full circle, full fusion. Although it was true that nobody had promised love. Had he slipped into unreality again? It ran in the family, did it not? A concrete link to the past, but a free love because no one would ever care to know, would ever dare to know, would ever know. He wanted the whole world to know.

He went on. As the war rages, he thought, we are going to make love, for this is the way the world goes round. Truly this would be the Grand Passion, the Grand Affair, the Great Romance, the Ultimate Sin. What was it that Hemingway's Maria had said in *For Whom the Bell Tolls*? The earth moved. But there would be no need of metaphors on this occasion. Steinbeck would approve. And for that Steinbeck had that very day won the Nobel Prize for Literature, or the day before or after, he had won the Nobel Prize and they would shortly fire the missiles in his honor if they had not done so already. Realism on the rampage.

How would they manage it? They would not manage anything. It would happen. Human beings were incapable of managing their lives. Human beings were managed by their lives. That much was certain. There was no choice.

That changed. He did not exactly remember her coming back, although she had, had he remembered her leaving and being aroused, sorely tempted? Had he desired to follow her into the darkness? No. It was just that they were standing together beside the kitchen table, conscious of a single hanging light bulb burning hotly, the only sound the murmur of the refrigerator, another source of energy, warmth, power, beginnings.

She said something, a few words. About what? Again about Bergson? She had spoken of Bergson on the subway, under the ground. *Creative Evolution.* Her daughter, Seema. Perhaps the dog, that there was a dog, maybe he had asked if there were animals, but that the dog would not bark and he should not be frightened of the naked dog, barking on the horizon.

Except that she must have said that afterwards, not as a prelude, but after they had kissed. No knowledge that he had kissed her first or she him, but they were kissing, he was kissing her on her neck, her cheek, her lips, as if he were trying to consume her instantly, they were kissing. Full of warmth, tingling, he was kissing her passionately. He had never felt such a fierce desire before. He became more and more aware that he had grasped her buttocks, that he was the aggressor, that he was pressing her against his body, she was both resisting and pressing against him, wonderful aggressive buttocks in the gathering fury of their lovemaking.

Their faces were wet and pins had fallen from her hair as if in shock, her suddenly long black hair that he had undone, surprised himself with his boldness, she had been surprised, he was surprised at the length of her hair, her hair surprised, she had been taken aback by his fury.

Maybe the bomb was more than just a phallic symbol. Maybe it would be unnatural to stop nuclear testing, nuclear proliferation, the big bang, let it go baby, Adlai was a wimp, wimping in the U.N. at Fidel and Nikita. Maybe we had to live unnaturally in order to survive and that would be the true perversion. Yes, we had to strike against the true nature of our species, a strike more powerful than a locomotive, more devastating than a nuclear bomb. Suicide month in Rhodesia, it had said in the *New York Times*. But what did they know? Did they have fallout shelters in Rhodesia? We should all go hide in shame in our fallout shelters. Rocky and his fallout shelters. Dens of iniquity.

And maybe her hair, undone so fluidly, had come undone itself, like magic, fallen because of her and his, their near violent movements. She had taken his hand

"Come with me," she said softly, conquered, in a trance "and we must be quiet," it was done.

and led him into the hallway, a hallway for their passage, then into the impenetrable darkness where at first he could not see or be seen.

And then

"Are you not going to take your clothes off? The bed is here," as if to say well, if we are going to, this is where it will be.

He had started to, had fumbled, but then, surprisingly, surprising to him, his eyes adjusted to the darkness, the light from the kitchen had reached, bended all the way to . . . to this room, their room, and he saw her as JBK the father had seen her.

She had already taken off most of her clothes. She had not removed her brassiere, black, but he was able to see, he was free to imagine her full breasts, and her white thighs, her heavy white thighs, and her full rounded buttocks, partially covered by her garter belt, black, too. The heaviness and fullness of her flesh, although she was not heavy, she was full, the sensuality. She turned and he saw her thick dark bush, the thick glistening hair of her loins, framed by the lushness of her deep belly, by the thin black strips of her garter belt flat around her waist, striking downward black against her white thighs.

Though she had turned to face him, she was not aware that he was looking so intently at her, that he had paused in undressing. She removed her garter belt. He began again to undress.

No longer moving, she stood in the semi-darkness of black and white beside her single bed which was up against a wall, and watched him undress. He was so young. And she imagined that to sleep with your son would be like a rare configuration of the stars. Who could possibly judge it? Might the harm, the sin, not be biological at all, but forbidden because of the knowledge, and forbidden because of the pure, intense, exotic taste? It is only for the gods. We must not disrupt the order. They would have been perfect.

And yet, they would make love, she dreamed. And why not? Why should she not dream? He and she were as good as gone. She only had a past defiled. He, with neither past nor future, he, in effect, did not exist. He was her fantasy. She had made it so in defiance of the gods. She could not be his mother then and she could not be so now. But they could be doomed lovers.

He removed his shirt and she saw that he had little hair on his chest. She adored that. Pristine, pure, smooth white skin. He was not muscular, but lean, not flabby, his arms undulating slightly from his shoulders to his wrists, though his forearms were fairly thick, a hint of force to come. She saw in his upper body, felt, health and wholeness, not power, not crunching, dominating power. Except his shoulders were surprisingly broad. He was young, so young. She wished that he be a virgin. She wanted to hold him as a baby, naked mother, naked baby.

When he bent over to remove his pants and shorts she moved her head slightly, but she did not look away. When he straightened and she saw his lower body, there was a slight twinge in her abdomen, a tightening. Not because his penis was fully erected. But, she was . . . confused, she was mesmerized by his body. For a moment she could not comprehend, she could not absorb the fact that his thighs were so huge, so thick, powerful, she remembered powerful thighs. More, that there was so much hair, his legs, his legs were hairy, his penis erected, so much hair, she remembered. He stood there without moving, not self-consciously, but as if he were in a slight trance, a ghost, as if she were dreaming him, imagining his presence, posing him, posing for him again. The muscles loosened, relaxed in her abdomen and she felt warmth, a warm liquid, a warmth in her loins. She reached for his hand and pulled slightly, guided him to the bed, slowly, smoothly.

They lay beside each other, at first touching. And then she held him in her arms. She would tell him everything, tell him afterward of her dreams. She and JBK. The way it should have been. About the father and the son. About what could not have been.

She spoke softly:

"Your body . . . you are two people . . . you are a boy and a man. You have the body of two beings. It is . . . very different. I wonder who is in you? My father and son, one and not the other."

Yes, she had seen it, it was as if preternaturally he was a combination of both of them, the genes of both, for the first time, the linkage complete.

She turned her head to face him, faltering.

"I want to see him again, then," she thought, looking in the darkness. "This is my opportunity. It is my right."

Both of them would make love to her, she dreamed, and she would have her revenge.

"I want to see him again," she said with intensity.

First the initiation, the preparation. Then it would happen. It would be time. The burst.

and, afterward, poor Klara, beautiful Klara, Hungarian Klara would be ashamed, shy; she a forty-four-year-old woman of much experience was like a child again

Klara would make love to Timothy as if he were JBK, the father, her father. Her thoughts, moaning, she did not realize she was speaking out loud, the smothering, swarming, enveloping, sensual soft voluptuous and warm, yes, passion.

"Oh, to have it again . . . it is again . . . never again . . ."

He ruminated on nonexistence, as if there were nothing, they were nothing spinning. Maybe this was the answer. The joy of nonbeing. What was being anyway? Perhaps he had never known it.

Hers were the original breasts, he thought. He had known her thighs before. He wallowed in her sensuality, aggressive, passionate, close to brutal, violent, burning.

It would be this as they made love, Timothy's words, Timothy said it. She was the mother, the USA. His mother in name, Helen Eaton King, had lived a fairy-land fantasy for as long as she could, looking for the white knight; life was romance. It had seemed as if her life had been shattered.

It is what happens, he thought, when she is virginal, unexplored, undeveloped, and unnatural.

That is, without roots. Who the hell was she, anyway? How could she have ever been a mother?

God, was that what he had to spend his life doing, wondering who the hell she was? What if she was nothing, had yet to become anything? Never had a chance . . . she thought every woman but her was sophisticated and sexy, educated, cultured; she loved but she did not think she could handle love. She could not.

"Oh my son," Klara moaned in passion for it was an undisguised thrill to sleep with the son.

And Timothy knew that the idea of sleeping with his mother was the power to be, it was his realization. Would his father kill him for it?

"'To sleep with thy father's wife is to uncover thy father's nakedness,' so quoted Hezekiah."

To do wrong to someone was to uncover their nakedness. Would a death, a murder result from it? Was that his conscious goal? Like father, like son? Why? Revenge? A duplicate existence. Was it a form of immortality or was it that by duplication you obliterated, effaced the father's existence? Was it patricide? Perhaps he was getting his revenge—you efface my existence, I will redo yours.

He thought a door had closed in another world.

She was delirious. What was she imagining?

"I want him again," she sang to herself, to her soul. "Oh why does it have to be this way? If he was going to die, did it matter?"

What was it about her? A presence. The aura. They had been together before? Having met her, he lingered. You could say that. Something had happened. He would stay no matter what, and she would not ask him to leave. For a while.

They measured the precise enactments of their own gesturings. She reached out and put her hand on his face. She reflected upon the sense that she had just slept with her own son, for he was her son forever. Nothing could ever change that. Nothing. Not ever. Not even a nuclear holocaust.

She stopped him and looked him in the eyes.

"I was blonde. I was a blonde then. Do you remember?"

She held him in her arms, held him, and told him. She told him what he already knew, what it was possible for him to know, she told him what he asked. He was consumed.

When she told him who he was, he knew that he was unidentified forever, that he was totally dependent upon her for his existence, that he was rendered helpless by her existence.

"A revolutionary does not have a child, I thought, her own personal private possession. It was grotesque. That is what I thought," she laughed.

"About me."

"You could not . . . you exist. That is why I could give you up. Except I never did give you up. That was impossible. I gave you to him because . . . because I could not have you."

"I was . . . what? Father? But what about her?"

"I wanted you to be with him even if I could not. But I lost you both in the beginning . . . before . . . everything."

"I thought you said you were not a Communist, but you both were, weren't you?"

"When you became an agent for the Soviet Union, you left the Party, you did not join the Party, you were not a member of the Party. Do you understand? And we could not be together."

"So there were not many Communists, but everyone was a spy, right? There was not even a Party, but everyone was spying?"

She stared at him. She looked right through him.

"Did you know that I was a blonde when you were born? I was a blonde when I gave you to JBK," she seemed to insist.

She was gone forever. He tried to reach her but she was absolutely untouchable.

"We traveled on a bus, didn't we?"

"Well, yes. From New Jersey through Lincoln Tunnel."

"To Maine."

"Yes, eventually, you did."

"We stayed . . . somewhere . . ."

"Yes. And he came and got you at the Hotel Sun. That is why I wanted you to stay there. I thought you would know, that you would remember, just as I remembered . . . that you were once born there."

"But you remembered being in the womb."

"It is all very complicated and strange," she said. "There can be no answers. I wanted our child, JBK's and mine. But it could not be because I, because I could not be a mother, so be it. Life changes everything. Death is supposed to be the great evil, but that is not so. The horrors of life conquer even death. Individual, unnameable horrors. With the holocaust, simply, there was the universal effacement of death, in this century anyway. So why be concerned with death? Death was rendered meaningless, do you not know that? Who can care? Haven't you discovered that? Death becomes superfluous. We finish ourselves off. We do not need death. For a species that can do such things there is no sacred death. Or there is death without life. Once you die you cannot die again. There is no immortality. We do not live to die a second time There is no death for those who are stillborn. There are no tears. You lost ancestors."

She was harboring a terrible secret, he thought, a terrible distortion. She was going to tell him.

Having already done alone what she intended with him, he listened again, for she had triggered it, as she told him of the ancestral obsession with death, his quest. He was asking her to command. At first she was dismissive or, for her with her wit, less than scornful.

"You need to learn the art of distraction," she said, looking away. She might have been training him, prepping him, qualifying him.

But then she told him what she knew, what she had seen, for what did it matter? She began and she would not stop.

"Understanding does not begin to come until death approaches, because until then one is not willing to face reality, one is not willing to understand. One thinks differently when one thinks death is distant compared to when it is near or one thinks it is near. There is a definite alteration. The brain cells change. And then the threat of death makes us incomprehensible. Crazy. Unreliable. You are obsessed with the idea of death, and yet you are still young enough that death is probably a long way off. It is not a reality. It has not begun to impinge itself upon you. Physically, existentially, you think you are immortal. You will always be young. You with your intellectual obsession. You infuriate me. You are a young fool. You know you will die, but you know nothing about the physical fact of death or even aging. You have realized nothing yet. Wait until you lose your energy. No, you have not seen your flesh become flabby, your hair thin, seen your strength dissipate, your eyes dim. And nobody cares."

She paused. She talked through madness generated by pain and horror, talked in riddles.

"How old are you?" she asked from the impenetrable darkness, glowering, knowing the answer.

"Twenty-one."

"You do not know a thing about death. You may not realize it but you think that you are going to live forever. The trouble with you is that you have abandoned your youth. No, you have skirted it. You have not experienced youth. You are supposed to act and feel and think as if you are going to live forever. And here you are at twenty-one, already depressed because you are not immortal. It is a given that youth cannot bear the thought of what is going to happen in half a century. The flesh rejects it. But wait until your teeth deteriorate, your eyes fade, you have back problems, your skin ages, your hair loses color and falls out. Then, and only then, you will begin, begin, to know something about death. Yes, the fact of death is brutal. Without some kind of mystification it is horrible. But aging is, too. If we were real lovers in a real world, in ten years, probably sooner, my aging would eat away like maggots at your love for me. Assuming your love lasted that long, did not decay before. Our difference in age would not be our ally."

He looked at her. She looked straight ahead.

"There are some things worse than death. Living can be one of them. I was dead before I could live. One can be touched in certain ways and never after be able to feel joy or happiness. I desired death. Everything was over for me when the first man, my father, had sex with me. He could have been your grandfather. He died in the ovens. All of us died in the ovens."

Her eyes glistened. She ignored his shock. For him believing or disbelieving seemed irrelevant.

"All little girls are molested," she said tonelessly. "By fathers, stepfathers uncles, brothers, strangers. Sons. It is a matter of degree. That is my obsession It is not intellectual."

He looked at her and knew that nuns were the symbol for him of sinned women and why he was drawn to women who had been sinned against, why he loved their crossed eyes, crossed souls. He knew that he carried within him great guilt for which he had no choice. What he could not understand was why it aroused him.

She looked at him, but she looked through him. Her scowl was full, full of rage, remembering old transgressions, untouchable.

"You should not. Do not. You should not have touched me, with your mouth. My latest devil, the current evil man in my life, uses a substance, some kind of stimulant on himself to help himself get an erection which, alas, does not last long. I once posed for him."

"What? Who?"

He did not know if she was speaking to him or to someone else somewhere else sometime else. He sensed that she was talking about different pasts and alluding to the present, but he did not know, did not know, did not know which or when, what room they were in, what house. What she said seemed strangely incongruous. It was as if she could change realities at will.

"I do not know what. Don't," she commanded, and he did not think that she was looking at him.

"Do you, do you sleep with . . . him?"

He was reluctant.

"Do you think that he gives to us money and groceries for my conversation?"

"Money and groceries? I don't understand."

"I have to spend some time with the poor man . . . poor man . . . has to get something for his money . . . lonely and just wants companionship. No, no no, he does not literally sleep with me anymore. How could he? He is not capable of it. He doesn't even attempt it, never, never, never. But what if he does? Who can care? Yes, he likes to sleep with me but, pathetic old man, he does not dare insist upon it. There was a time when he did not have to insist upon anything at all."

Klara's words blasted him. So perverse. Why was she saying this? So unreasonable. Stop it. Stop it. It was as if she had totally left him, absented herself for another time, another realm, ran on in her own private language, but what was left of his veneer of innocence was scorched. He wanted to probe, probe, probe Klara about her lovers, past lovers because therein lay the secrets of his life. In an instant he had crossed centuries, he had become maddeningly jealous, angry, frustrated to paralysis, as if his legs, his arms, were tangled, tightly wound, tied and looped around his body. He tried stretching, kicking, striking free, and he failed, tripped over his thoughts, becoming more and more angry and frustrated. He thrashed wildly and his soul became permanently progressively entangled. There was a pounding in his head, voices, her angry voices.

She looked and saw how she could hurt him further, hurt him terribly and possess him forever.

"Sometimes my devil performs, he is so big," she said with lowered voice as if in awe, like a little girl. "And sometimes he cannot," she quickly added with scorn. "I do not know why not. I try to help him."

She remembered his tonguing her. The first time had been wonderful and she had not stopped him. It had happened naturally, instinctively, in the flow of their loving. Afterward, after the first time, she had said, broken her words with an air of sternness, hiding perhaps what he had thought to be her feelings of guilt and embarrassment, she had told him that he should never do it again and he had not understood, understood that it had been done before for the first time.

And now the son was stunned, shocked. Nausea rose, dizziness.

It was her bitterness, having been drained spiritually. She would be unrelenting. And then a kind of explosion, and she turned on him. In the darkness she found him with her words.

"Ironic, is it not, that there has never been a true, romantic love affair, and yet you can lose everything in love. I was seduced by my father in my youth and used. I was abandoned by your father. You will do well never to attach yourself to one person."

She was angry, hard, nihilistic, pure as black slate. The ashes of years.

She spoke harshly.

Rasping.

"The genes have forgotten. Anything can be changed. You are not my son."

And then he stumbled forward, groping.

"You translated the Hungarian poets because . . . because you were spying on them, weren't you?"

"You can always find someone who wants the information," she said enigmatically, her face a sneer, not really answering his question, perhaps because she knew it was not really a question. She was practiced.

"But why would you do such a thing? They . . ."

"They were all fascists, all of them who came out in '56. I hated them. Don't waste your sympathy, honey. Besides, I was doing the bidding of men . . . and I needed the money. Information. Everybody wants information and everybody pays."

"But they are going to ask you, aren't they? Don't you know? Will you tell them everything?"

"I told him . . . whatever he wanted to hear."

He did not want to hear her when she said lowly and mysteriously,

"If you want to know about your father, there is someone you must see. You must go see him. You have to go see him. You have no choice. It is the last thing you have to do. Go and see him while there is still time."

He did not understand her. He had no idea what she was talking about. He heard nothing but a beginning roar, which he welcomed.

Enraged, they held each other again, defying the gods. And then he reached for her again and again and again.

As if after the bombs had fallen, as if shelled, he fell asleep dissolved in shadows. He awoke once in the night and saw her in the distance, black and white on the floor. He saw her slip and slide and contract the muscles of her thighs, her calves. White gleaming flesh on the floor and her hair black rinsed hanging down. And he began to remember.

In the darkness. What? Bodily functions? Blithely unaware, like a child, that the body functioned?

" . . . realize how much time we spend feeding the baby . . . "

" . . . you been to the bathroom lately?"

"So what do you expect, that it can be redone, that we will tell him brand-new bedtime stories?"

"He is who he is."

11

The American Dream

Freedom dreams, dreaming, freedom.

Dutifully he returned to the Post Authority of all returns because you got there from here, gone back, gone back to the indecisiveness, the going the coming the anxiety, the freedom, better than certainty. Not to just any bus station with icy glistening chandeliers bigger than a living room, sweeping majestic arches spanning like bridges, spanning continents, where kings crooks and christs meet, pass, leave their sweat, dirt, think lewd, think, he had dreamt it, free dreams on the single bed of the first woman, but there was no sense there. No sense of what he should do, no movement or pressure that was controlling, nothing telling him, anyone, what to do, no god, no. No, everything was decisive in the uncertainty, no choices in the chaos. The bodies and some faces, fleeting, rushed upon him, went through, over, past. He knew that the people, knew the people, the hordes, would probably tear him to pieces in the socialist revolution. He dreamt they were dreaming because they had things to tell him that he did not want to hear so they were dreaming and he was escaping.

Yet, they were toying with him, but at any moment, a heel in his face, another in his groin, grinding, someone rushed by, grabbed his left arm, and left it by the Eighth Avenue exit, while his right arm exited on Ninth Avenue to be sold at the nearest pawn shop. An old man with a walking cast, waiting indignantly for years, claimed his legs, righteous and triumphant, and beat him over the head with the cast before he took the subway, before a tall, elegantly dressed woman reached into Timothy's back pocket and, after caressing him, took out his wallet and extracted his money, his airline money, and walked away.

"I need money for a taxi," she called back over her shoulder, laughing, loving her triumph.

Timothy smiled weakly, grateful for the caress, and then, laughing himself, because she did not know that it was airline money not taxi money, you cannot get there from here with airline money.

A rolling, twisting, revolving disk, a Nedick's lunch counter swept Timothy off his feet, deposited him on a wobbly, spinning stool where almost immediately after a long delay a stubby, smelly waitress leaned over, her red rouged face within inches of Timothy's.

"I figure if you're going to order, order, or get out."

"I . . . "

"You want ten cheeseburgers and ten milkshakes, right? Right. Bastard."

She blurted the order, presumably. Blurted something.

The cook, fat and soiled, sneered at Timothy, the cook's big belly and his fat ass alternately drooping, sliding along his grill, the seat of his pants a patchwork of his American flags. With a flick of his double chin, he covered the grill with dozens of hamburger fat patties that slid greasily on easily. Untouched, mixers whirled and rang, tossed and gurgled milk and ice scream.

Having not said a word, Timothy dared not say a word, dared not look around him, he did not want to establish a Supreme Court precedent, god no god. He knew there were thousands of free Americans crowding the counter shaking, impatiently waiting for their orders, all hungry, and now, furious at having to wait for Timothy's cheeseburgers and shakes. A thousand eyes peered over his shoulders and he knew that if he turned around even for an instant the Communists would devour him.

"I told you not to get off the bus."

Warm, soft tones.

At first Timothy did not budge, frightened she would not be his mother. But when she put her hand on his arm, he turned and looked into the face of the woman from the bus. She was not his mother his lover.

"I'm going to have tea and a muffin. You would like the same, darling?"

Timothy nodded and she ordered for both of them, calmly, ordered for mother and son, gave the request to the patiently waiting, blonde, smiling waitress. The waitress was blonde and she was his mother and she was not saying anything, no, she was eternally silent. The waitress wrote the order on her pad, tore off the sheet of paper, and gave the order to the grateful cook. The cook parted the muffins, plopped them into the toaster of a hundred slots, and scooped up all of the hamburgers, put them between buns and delivered them to the patiently waiting, sitting, happy, joyful people, the workers of the world united in Hungary, Maine.

The muffins and the tea came. Timothy and the woman who refused to be his mother ate their muffins and drank their tea.

Finished, the strange woman turned to Timothy.

"Did you know what you are doing forever and ever?"

She had turned toward him on her stool and Timothy saw that his mother had unbuttoned most of her clothing. He noticed her breasts immediately.

"She isn't so old," he thought. "She couldn't be a mother."

"You must save your father," she said. "You are both in danger."

He felt the change in tone, her words having entered another chamber, rolling, blowing in his ear, echoing in his brain. He felt the insistence, the lips, the presence, and he felt paralyzed, although his toes tingled. He wanted desperately to move, to do something before it was too late, but he was paralyzed, he was too far away, and his toes tingled because of her lips.

"Come with me," she said to Timothy Brown King, her voice fading again, "you are going home again."

Timothy followed. Slightly behind her, he noticed her rounded, undulating buttocks, full thighs, which hypnotized him as he watched, only, only, as Timothy followed, she disappeared. Simply disappeared.

Timothy barely made it to Eighth Avenue.

where he was intercepted and the man said:

"Are you Timothy Brown King?"

Startled.

"Yes, I was. Absolutely. But I wasn't doing anything, I swear. Scout's honor, except I wasn't a Scout, I never was, I swear."

"There is a telephone call for you. I do not know why I answered except I am from Maine, except I am from Maine," the man said, handing him the telephone.

"I am in the bus station," the voice inside the telephone said. *"I cannot say more. I am, but I cannot say more. Be certain to look for me up."*

Timothy looked out from the telephone booth into the crowd and he could not believe his eyes, he could not see JBK whole at all times as he walked through and behind the people as if he were walking through and behind trees. He had to make certain that it was not JBK because that was the answer.

But the waiting lines for the telephone would wait no longer, and he was yanked, thrown from the booth. Kicked, scratched, and punched, Timothy crawled on his hands and knees, dragged his suitcase by a rope, and somehow made it to the waiting outside gutter. A little boy's blond head in a gutter was an unlikely sight even in midtown Manhattan, although passers-by may have thought it half of a grapefruit. Why, oh why was his hair blonde so that everyone would notice and tell the truth? The people in the bus station laughed, pointing and screaming, their heads protruding from every lower and upper window, their arms stretched for one more pinch, their feet dangling and kicking, still seeking Timothy's head, his groin. Every door whirled, revolved, groaned at missing the chance of snapping off that youthful head to tell the truth.

Remarkably, Timothy still had the plane ticket in his picketpocket, or was it in his pocketpicket? However, this much he knew, that he had lost his *New York Daily Mirror*, had it removed, and he realized the profound truth that somehow he had left the lunch counter without paying in America, had left with I scream on his face his mouth stuffed with bread and hamburg and Thanksgiving turkey with the Indians, he had chewed and chewed, convinced he would never finish, refused permission to leave the table, his raised hand in vain. Perhaps the stool had whirled suddenly, caught him unawares, flipped him toward the revolving exit door, tossed him out on Eighth Avenue, where he had landed, full, and feeling immense guilt at not having paid his airline fare. He dared not return, dared not look back, even if he did have to go to the bathroom in the eighth grade.

He was confused. Lying on his back with his head on the curb and his suitcase on his chest, he saw millions of legs cutting like millions of scythes Gaudy, morose, fierce, perky bodies, souls, moved by him, quickly, slowly, the racing and the movement both dominant, both there, oh yes, he would swear to it. He was exhausted and exhilarated after his rolling, bumping by night drive. How they were moving. Rushing by him and yet threatening to descend upon him, a gelatin of colors spilling, spreading, hordes, evil crowds. They pushed by, moving up the block, up the avenue and down, everywhere. Getting to his feet, Timothy dared step in their midst, and for a moment was jostled violently, then flung, pressed against the outside wall of the huge bus station. There was nowhere to go and there were no opportunities for questions.

He felt tired.

The bodies dispersed, and ran together, knifed in all directions, patterned, jerked by and jolted, snapped at right angles across the avenues taking over. Red light, green light, the automobiles went right on through, the hanging street lights signaled their triumph, they raced from left and from forever and went racing from the right to forever, converging as was inevitable.

Have to sleep, he had thought.

Or he was asleep and he would awaken to the present society like Rip Van Winkle. Or was it that Rip Van Winkle had gone back to sleep again under orders from Khrushchev? No, no, no, he had been awake for twenty years and then fallen asleep, having forgotten JBK. The heavy falling mist, softly falling, the hanging night, the impenetrable stagnant haze of Manhattan was like memory was like sleep.

Had to sleep, sleep this beginning morning, get a room with his airplane ticket, except the woman had taken a cab. Exhilarated, Maine boy, sleepy, he made a decision to freely move away from the wall of the building into the crowd as if he were stepping away from a motionless boat into a rushing roaring river. The crowd carried him.

"Rollin'," he mumbled again, grinning to himself, "rollin'."

He was deposited on a side street. Little sense that he had got there on his own, although there was a stirring in him, a notion that a room in America would be cheaper on a side street, that he should get off at the first opportunity at the Hotel Sun.

where he could have stayed forever on the single solitary bed, dreaming, where nothing more would have happened, dreaming, which is always preferable, because if nothing happened he would not die, which is probably why he had finally left, overwhelmed with the sense that nothing was going to happen and he would live forever, dreaming, that history would stop on that bed, come to an absolute stop deadend. There would be no relentless forward march for him forward any more. The missiles would fly overhead from Cuba and he would be prone on the bed under the sun. Which is why it had been decided that he should leave the Hotel Sun for Anybodys, his appointed destination. If he had but one life to give, he would give it in the company of others. Live alone, die together.

She appeared again but she kept receding from him, that woman in the mist. Had she lured him here only to abandon him? They would now swoop down upon him like vultures, the phantoms of the night, Commies, pinkos, reeeeeeeeds!

He awoke in a sweat to a different day. Something woke him up. Timothy woke up and saw that she was staring at him. Seema. He knew it was her. There had been a dream and now there was Seema. Was she a fantasy of the dream? She would be able to tell him.

Seema wanted to tell him because there he was in her mother's bed and they would have many things to talk about.

"You are Seema," he said. "I know about you because your mother told me."

"Yes, I am Seema. Are you the Hungarian poet?"

She had been waiting for him to awaken.

"I am not so certain I know," he wavered, "even though she told me about me too. I mean, I think I am still sleeping. I had a nightmare. I don't feel Hungarian."

He rubbed his eyes.

"What is your name? Maybe that will tell you who you are."

She seemed solicitous. She seemed to care.

"Timothy Brown King, I guess. How did I get here?"

She paused. Reflective.

"Maybe you are lost. Which would mean that my mother must have found you and brought you home. She brings things home that are lost, like cats and dogs, and sometimes people. Not that everybody is lost, I mean everybody my mother brings home."

"Your mother? Where am I then, am I home at last?"

"In my mother's bed."

"Oh."

Yes, he remembered. And he felt the guilt. He had been in her mother's bed. Or his mother's bed. It could not be both. It was confusing, because he did not think that it was possible that they could be brother and sister already. Which meant that they could not have the same mother.

What Seema did not like about the fact that he was in her mother's bed was that it meant that her mother knew of his existence even if he was not the Hungarian poet, at least that seemed probable.

"You are only fourteen?" he thought to ask, as if that were the first thing that had to be established.

"You are already twenty-one?" she responded.

They both giggled.

"How did you know that I was twenty-one?"

"Because that is what I want to be and I know you are not fourteen, like me, unless you look older than you are, which I do not think is true."

They laughed together again. He liked her deduction. She liked her sense of things.

"Did you just get out of the sanitarium?" she asked spontaneously.

Seema laughed, self-conscious this time, and turned her head.

Timothy sat straight up, because she had stung him. He had been facing her, looking at her, leaning on his elbows.

"Why did you ask that?"

"I don't really know. It was silly. I thought it. I thought that you could be Myshkin. I do not know why I thought that. How did you know I was fourteen? Did my mother tell you or did you want to be fourteen again?"

He reflected for a moment, looking at her, and then he answered.

"If I could be like you I might want to be fourteen again because you do not seem fourteen, especially if you know about Myshkin. But I feel a bit like Myshkin."

She liked that, that he could feel like Myshkin.

But it was also true that Timothy could not believe Seema's age. Only fourteen? No. Impossible. She was seven years younger than him? How could she be? She appeared much closer to him than seven years, or seven years was a shorter period of time than he had ever imagined. That was a terrible thought. Or that he had gone awry in those seven years. But if she was truly fourteen, fourteen as he had always known fourteen, as he had never been, then he thought he might be evil because he found her to be very beautiful, an angel from the forest, and he was very much attracted to her, which did not seem the proper thing. Or was that a lingering effect from the night before, the interplay for Timothy between Seema and Klara, like electrical charges, between young and old all around, like depth charges, the flash of light and the intimidation of darkness. She had been his mother. Mother and daughter. She had to be his sister, he her brother. Could they become lovers? Could everyone love? The thoughts seemed to be someone else's thoughts, as if some other order had been prearranged and superimposed.

Suddenly from her silence, Seema blurted out again:

"You have to get a job, you know. Life is not a free ride. Now that you are out of the sanitarium you cannot stay in bed all day long."

Timothy thought that was wonderful.

"That is your mother talking, isn't it?"

"Yes," she giggled, and skipped away down the hallway.

When Timothy was certain that she had gone for the moment, yet not so certain that she had been there at all, he got quickly out of bed, put his pants on, and went in search of her.

He found her in the kitchen. She was petting a black dog that had been asleep, yawning.

"Is that your dog?"

"Oh no, that's Tony. Tony is my mother's dog. She found him. Or Anybodys dog. Tony goes down there a lot. That's a bar downstairs. My dog is running on the cliffs."

That was strange, but it seemed to be right. Timothy knelt down and silently helped Seema stroke the friendly, lethargic Tony.

"So what are you going to do when you grow up, sell hot dogs?" he said suddenly.

She liked that and giggled again, getting up.

"I'm only fourteen."

"I know, you just want to eat hot dogs," he said, rising himself.

They both giggled, circling each other in the nearly bare kitchen.

"Don't you like hot dogs?" he asked. "They are as American as apple pie. Probably more so. They look so bright and shiny . . . and artificial. And nobody knows what goes into them. They should be called 'mystery dogs,' don't you think?"

"No, I do not like hot dogs, because I am a vegetarian. Ooooh, hot dogs are awful, I don't like them at all. And did you know that it is not a good thing to be an American?"

"But aren't you an American yourself? Weren't you born in this country? Ah, I don't mean that you have to be born in this country, I mean, in order to be an American, but . . . oh yes, I guess you must be Hungarian, too, or perhaps you think you are. But you can be both, you know, both a Hungarian and an American. And I used to think that that was what was best about America and that everybody else thought the same thing . . . "

"I am not anything," she interrupted, standing still, looking down and away. "My mother thinks I'm a Jehovah's Witness, but I'm not. I just tell her that is where I go as often as I can. But I am not really a Jehovah's Witness. I dance."

"Why do you tell her you are a Jehovah's Witness if you are not?"

"Because I know someone at school who is a Jehovah's Witness and is a strange person, and when I tell my mother I have to go to meetings and do my duties it is the only time I get to go off by myself and do what I want to do, like dancing, and she would not understand that and she would not like it either, because she says that I have chores at home and that I am not old enough to go off by myself, although I seem to be old enough for almost anything else. And she does not want me to dance because she did, although she says that she does not want me to repeat her mistakes. But I am really Jewish. At least one-quarter. And I do not want to be like her."

As if by signal they left the kitchen together and went back to the middle room.

Seema knew already that there was something special between her and Timothy. She did not analyze it. She did not have to. She liked being around him. It was exciting. Fun. And mysterious. She chose to believe that he had come to the apartment especially to see her. Secretly, of course. She would not disclose that sentiment to anyone. It would be her secret, unspoken and, most of all, to be kept from Klara. It was Seema's secret, although she would let it be Timothy's secret as well, even though they had not acknowledged it. But she knew. She knew what was important, what the delicate balance was. She was vaguely aware that they had needed Klara originally to bring them together, but only in the sense that they were using Klara. Exploiting her, exploiting Klara. That was what they were doing. Everything would be all right now. She wondered what had happened to her mother.

And then Seema knew that Timothy had come from Boston. Klara had not gone to see a poet, she had gone for Timothy. Unless Timothy was a poet, too. But Seema did not choose to believe that for now, because that would mean that Klara translated his poetry and that he was Hungarian, and she wanted Timothy as her own, and not to be Hungarian, although she had not yet decided what he would be or if he would be an American. She only knew that she had discovered him for herself, even if he had been in her mother's bed, which she did not think she had to talk about. She was certain that he was something special for her, that she might be something special for him. And if he was not a poet now, he might become one some day, somewhere. She knew that as well, and she thought she might have to tell him that. He did remind her of Prince Myshkin. Truly, he would be her Prince Mystic, she thought.

"Have you ever been left alone as a child?" she suddenly asked him, realizing that it was important now that she know.

"Yes, I have. Why do you ask? Have you?"

"Yes, we have that in common. I just knew we did."

As if by agreement they both sat down on the floor at the same time, at the foot of the bed.

Timothy was more and more certain that Seema knew a great deal, much that he would want to know, or not want to know, that for some mysterious reason she had become a youthful fount of secret knowledge.

"What else do you think we have in common?" he asked her. "What do you like to do? Where do you like to go?"

"I like to go to the theater. We went to a play last week."

"Oh? What play did you go to?"

"*Who's Afraid of Virginia Woolf?*" she answered immediately, instantly eager and excited.

She quickly got to her feet and started walking around, turning in different directions, stopping and then starting again, almost dancing, she could have been dancing. Timothy watched her, fascinated with her, as she surrounded him with her very own motion.

"It was a strange play," she said, continuing to move. "I don't know why they called it *Who's Afraid of Virginia Woolf?* except that maybe they wanted us to think about it. I think they kept talking about a child that was not there but that existed. Or that did not exist but was there. Or they were talking about something that was neither there nor existed. But they talked about it. And they cared about it. They must have. It made the mother and father very angry at each other, although if there was not a child then I guess they were not mother and father, but they were husband and wife, of that I am positive. Afterwards I felt as though they had been talking about me even if they did not know that I existed. I felt as though the play was about me, that I was the child that nobody wanted and was not real or that was wanted but could not be."

"Is that the way you feel, that nobody wants you and you cannot be real?"

"Sometimes. Although mostly I like not being real. But once when my mother was angry at me she said, 'Whoever heard of a revolutionary having a child anyway?' And then she started laughing as if she could not stop. It was frightening. And then she started crying. I had never seen her that way before and I have never forgotten. It was very strange to see her cry. It was the first time. My mother does not cry. She said that we should never speak of that again."

Seema was silent for a moment and she stood still, looking at the floor, fiddling with her fingers.

"I am not sure I understood the play anyway. Maybe I am not old enough, although I think I am. But maybe they did not write it for me, because I am not an adult yet, or maybe some plays are not written for everybody, I mean that some plays are only for some people, except that they don't tell you."

They were both silent for a while.

Timothy was the first to speak again.

"I think we are not supposed to understand."

"What do you mean? Not anything?"

"I am not sure that there is anything to understand."

"About anything?"

"About anything."

"That doesn't sound like much fun, does it? And no one else says that. I do not think I would like that, although maybe it would be strange."

"So you like the theater?" he said quickly, wanting to change the subject.

"Yes," she brightened, and started pacing again. "And we went to see another play before."

"Oh? What play was that?"

"*A Man For All Seasons*. I think it was about a man who believes in principle first no matter what the cause. But I am not sure what the principle was."

"I have heard of the play but I have not seen it. Do you think the 'Man for all Seasons' knows what the principle is?"

"I am not certain. Maybe he did once long ago, but then he forgot it. Even so, he still died for it. Except maybe he had no choice but to die, because I felt for a long time in the play that he was going to die no matter what he did. I do not like things like that. I do not like the feeling that no matter what you do something is going to happen, like in a nightmare."

And then Timothy remembered again that he had been with her mother. At least he thought he had, or maybe he had dreamed it, because it seemed so far away, and he wondered if Seema had seen him with Klara, spied on them, if she thought that they were lovers, that they had done more than embrace in a dream. What could she think, that he was looking for his mother? Were they lovers? Perhaps, but he did not think that Seema had spied.

After considering it, he decided to ask her:

"Do you think I am looking for my mother?"

"Why would you want to do that? Is she lost?"

"No, she is supposed to be dead."

"Then where would you go to look for her if she is supposed to be dead?"

"I don't know. If she were a Communist, I'm not sure I know the answer to that."

He looked at Seema, but she revealed nothing.

"I don't know where they bury Communists," it occurred to him to say, "or if they even bury them at all in this country. I wonder if they have funerals."

Hezekiah flashed in his mind.

And then Seema asked:

"Is, I mean, was your mother a Russian?"

"I did not use to think so, but why do you ask that?"

"Because if she is a Russian, most of the Russians are Communists, I think, and you said she was a Communist, didn't you?"

"Did I? If my mother was a Russian and therefore a Communist or a Communist and therefore a Russian, that would make her evil like Satan, wouldn't it?"

"Why would that make her evil like Satan?"

"Didn't you know that in America Russians and Communists are evil? That is how most Americans think, you know. Evil. The Russians are the force of evil and their nuclear weapons are the instruments of Satan. I think that would have to follow."

"Really? That's pretty scary. But if the Russians are the force of evil and their nuclear weapons belong to Satan, then who do our nuclear weapons belong to? God? Or do our nuclear weapons belong to the Russians, too, only we have borrowed them? Except that could not be, because how come we have their nuclear weapons if they want to drop them on us?"

"Yes and no. The nuclear weapons we have belong to us, and we made them, but unlike the Russians' weapons, yes, ours are the instruments of God. Or, no, the weapons belong totally to God, and he has just loaned them to us, so we couldn't have made them. But most Americans I know do not think this is a joking matter, you know. They think it is unpatriotic to jest about such a thing. You could probably even get arrested for doing it if you tried hard enough, on a street corner, say, although nobody thinks that happens here. The Russians are out to destroy us, they would say. This is not something to laugh about. Why, they even teach us that in school. Haven't you been taught that in school? And church as well, of course."

"In the first place, I do not like most people, do you?"

"No, I don't either, so why do we care what they think, is that what you are going to say? If so, I agree with you. I don't care, either. And I don't think I ever will."

"Yes, and I do not want to be patriotic either. And I was not making fun really. My mother says that patriotism is mind control. She says that if we had been born at a different time we would worship totem poles. And why would the Russians want to destroy us anyway? What would that get them if we were all dead? Even if I am part Hungarian?"

"Aha, I caught you. You show your ignorance and naivete. You are a child even if you are very intelligent. Why would the Russians want to destroy us? Silly question. Just because we are not Russians. And they are not human beings. They are not even people. They are godless. They are another species. They live in Russia. Most of all they are not us. And they are not free, which is a sign that something is wrong with them, so they need to be killed, exterminated."

"Why do they need to be killed? Why can't they just be freed? I don't want to kill anybody."

"Because. Because they are not free, they are not us. And we are probably afraid that if they were freed they would come after us, and they are already doing that anyway."

"They are not us? Who are they then?"

"The ones who are not free. The dictators. The Communists. They enslave their people."

"So the Communists are not their people?"

"They are the Soviet rulers, actually, the Party. The Communists."

"Then who are the Russians?"

"They are."

"But they are not the people? So the people are not the Russians either?"

She paused for a moment, as if reflecting.

"How did they get separated from the people," she began again, counting on her fingers, "how did Russians get not to be people, who are the people and who are not the people, who gets to be who they are, and where do Party leaders come from?"

They burst into laughter, and then she suddenly began laughing out of control and ran from the room, leaving him sitting on the floor. But she returned quickly with another question, as he knew she would.

"Would you like to run off together and hide? We could go to my castle."

"Where nobody could ever find us and live together by ourselves?"

"Yes. I think you would like my castle. I have never before taken anybody to it. It is surrounded by the ocean on the bottom and by clouds at the top."

"I think I would like your castle, too. I know I would."

"We could go there by train through a Russian forest. That way they would never find us. And if someone accidentally found the castle, although I think that is impossible, we could go and hide on the top floor, where I have never been."

He paused, as if he were listening to a distant voice.

"'I feel as though I had seen you somewhere too. . . . I feel as though I had seen your eyes somewhere . . . but that's impossible. That's nonsense . . . I've never been here before. Perhaps in a dream . . .'"

"Oh, yes," she said, her voice rising in excitement. "I know that, I know that. That is from *The Idiot*. The idiot says that, except he is not an idiot, he is holy. But I don't like to think of him that way. I wouldn't want you to be holy either, because then you would go away."

She twirled around the room while he watched her.

"Did you know," he asked, continuing to follow her with his eyes, "that some say that *The Idiot* is a story of an idiot in passion, in mad love?"

"No, but I would not want you to be an idiot like that either. At least I don't think so. I think it is too early for us. I will have to think about it."

And then she blushed, her face quite pink. First turning away from Timothy, she turned quickly back to him.

"Oh, I know, let's take Mrs. Tilly and Mr. Svevo with us to the castle."

"Mrs. Tilly? Mr. who?"

"Yes, Mrs. Tilly, who lives down the hall, and Mr. Svevo, who lives downstairs. They are both crazy, I think. And I like them both. You will, too."

And then she began gesturing, making faces, pantomiming, bending this way and that.

"Whenever I say good morning to Mr. Svevo in the hallway, he always says, 'Whaaat?' But I don't think he understands anything, which is quite nice. His glasses are so thick I don't know how he can see through them. I guess he doesn't see, either. He is so funny. He is built like a fireplug and he looks immovable. And I'm sure he must be directed by radar, because he always walks exactly down the middle of the hallway, so that you have to go around him to pass him. Everyone walks around him and either swears or laughs. I don't do either. I just say, 'Good morning, Mr. Svevo' and he says, 'Whaaat?' and each of us just keeps on going. Now, Mrs. Tilly is twice Mr. Svevo's size, and she is so fierce and angry-looking that I never say a thing to her, because I wouldn't dare, and I try to avoid looking at her. But I still like her. She is the biggest woman I have ever seen. She has big hands and big feet. She stomps in and out of the building all day in large black shoes. I think if she knew that General Tuffy sometimes sleeps here she would yell out in the hallway, 'Mr. Svevo! Mr. Svevo!' and he'd say, 'What?', and she'd yell, 'He's been here again. Throw 'em all out.' 'What?' 'He's been here again. Throw 'em all out.' 'What?' And Mrs. Tilly would get angry at Mr. Svevo and would forget all about General Tuffy and would kick Mr. Svevo all the way down the stairs—'Whhhaaat???' All the way to the bottom and Mrs. Tilly wouldn't even notice."

And then Seema stopped for a moment as if to catch her breath, or to contemplate, perhaps to wonder if she had spoken correctly or if she wanted to change anything in her story.

Timothy continued to stare at her spellbound. He sensed that they belonged together. He had understood fully her reference to General Tuffy, and he wondered how much she understood of what she was saying, but he did not ask about General Tuffy because he did not want to ask, he did not think that he wanted to hear any more answers.

And then Seema asked the question he knew she would eventually ask. She asked looking directly at him with an expression of intense longing. She had been building to it and building to it. He knew that. This he understood.

"How long have you been my brother?"

"Forever, I think," he said.

It had seemed perfectly natural for her to ask, and he had answered naturally. He was glad that she had finally asked and he was glad that she knew and he did not have to tell her.

"We have been brother and sister forever," he went on, "but I haven't known it forever."

"Then do you know who my father is?" she asked. "Although," she added quickly, "if you do know, I am not sure I want to know right now. I think I would prefer to think about us being brother and sister first. And maybe I do not want to ever know. But you could tell me just that you know."

"It's funny that you should ask that, although of course you would, I mean, I know, I think I know who your father is, because he is or was my father, but I'm not certain anymore I really do know who my father was. I don't think I really did know him, if you understand what I am saying. Hey, maybe we should write a play. Maybe this is a play. We could call it, 'Who's Afraid of a Father For All Seasons?'"

They laughed and she fell down on her knees beside him and they hugged each other, their tears on each other's cheeks.

"I have not known for fourteen years now about my father, and I guess that is forever for me, but it is no longer forever that I have not known that I had a brother," she said in his arms.

"I thought I had known about my father for twenty-one years," he said, "and I thought I did know him, but now that you have asked, well, it seems strange, I wonder why you should ask, I mean, it seems right that you should, because I just found out about my mother, our mother, and I just found out about you. My own sister, Seema, Seema, my own sister Seema."

He paused and they were quiet for a bit before he spoke again.

"I should tell you about Grandfather Hezekiah, because I know everything about him, at least I always felt that I did, even though he died when I was young and he was old and I thought that it was always that way. You would have loved him and he would have loved you very much. May I tell you about Grandfather Hezekiah?"

But then Seema stiffened slightly in his arms, as if something had happened that was unexpected, as if something had entered the room and they were no longer alone together. She did not dare to look up.

"Why is our mother lying in bed?" she asked in a voice that sounded distant, petrified. "Why is she not moving?"

Minutes passed in silence.

"She is dead, isn't she?" Seema finally said more than she asked, still hanging on to Timothy, her face on his shoulder.

Timothy paused for the longest time, and then he said:

"Yes, I believe you are right. She is."

"Did you kill her?"

"But, of course, I must have. Don't you think I should have?"

"But that is just what Rogoshin did to Natashya, beautiful Natashya. The idiot didn't do it. Myshkin didn't do it. You shouldn't have done it."

"I know. I must have killed her while we were lovers, to keep the world from knowing. I was making love to my mother, which is the last thing on this earth I am supposed to do."

"She is dead then."

"Yes. I think we can say that, don't you?"

Seema was silent, staring now over Timothy's shoulder. She stared away at nothing, saying nothing. She stared away for a full minute before she spoke again.

"Did you kill her because . . . "

"Because I think she would have changed everything, and I could not live with that. I would not want to exist in that manner. I did it so that you and I could be free as we wanted. Although we are not totally free as yet. At least I am not."

“Shall we do it then?”

“Yes.”

They both rose and walked to the bed, one on each side, and pulled the covers up to complete their ritual of death.

“Oh, I almost forgot,” Seema said listlessly. “Here is a note from my mother. I guess she must have written it before she was dead.”

“Yes, she must have,” said Timothy after he had read Klara's words. “Let's go off to your castle now, while there is still time.”

12

The Old and New Testaments

In his previous visits to the big city, Timothy had never refused a request from any strange soul to fund a cup of coffee or a bowl of soup, even a drink. Whoever asked, received in reality. Fleeting philanthropy from a fortunate son. And now in his life hereafter, with New York City developing, changing in character before his changing eyes, with significance attached to disappearing small buildings, appearing large, the moral debris of the streets, the human variations encountered announced initial emergence for him, except that all of it had appeared before him, before Timothy had looked hoping to find himself as well, before he had entered the kingdom of nowhere.

And this was a run of humanity. He had been sitting on a bench in Washington Square Park for three hours on what every one of New York's dailies announced as Saturday, October 27, fundamentally untouched, dazed in the park, having drifted, drifting, occasionally watching the fantasy of Seema float and flit and flounder through the gathered, wondering whose fate was at stake while more than a dozen of Greenwich Village's finest had approached him. He had wanted to say yes; he had not learned the meaning of no.

And he understood that he and Seema had no more validity than the others possessed, for they, too, were newly invented. Now, hovering, Seema reinvented herself for Timothy's eyes every moment after moment.

Whenever Seema approached, sylphlike, approached within voice, Timothy sought her advice and she would sometimes say,

"Give, give, Timothy, it is always best to give, Timothy, give to yourself if you would give to them," and she would run away laughing, loose and lithe.

But then, on another orbit, when she would return to this sweet earth, return dancing like a ballerina to Timothy, she would say, pirouetting around him,

"Only those who have can give, Timothy, only those who give can receive, only those who have given are received, catch me if you can," like mother, like daughter, speaking in riddles, running away, laughing again to speak and dance again.

And thus on this day did the mother's daughter inadvertently become the ultimate judge of each beggar's fate. Fortunately for Timothy, no one individual had asked for more than money, that is, for more than he could give, or, surprisingly, for more than a quarter at a time and only one for that, that is, for more money than he possessed. To the minute, his many brief involvements had cost him little more than $2.75. Airline money. He was flying on his own.

Perhaps because of his concentrated focus upon Seema, the floating fairy princess, he was apparently immune to distractions as well, for he and Seema had joined together in their land of fantasy, having left Klara Blazek behind in her barricaded reality that had stopped still. The city was truly their daily home now, the park their nightmare, moonlit bed. A cage had been broken open and two wild creatures, Timothy and Seema, had been let loose to roam the forest, connected to the force of life, wandering the day and night, sometimes sleeping.

To the moment, Timothy's thinking was relatively uncommitted, unstuck and loosely bounded, in suspension, which also meant that it was without measure and direction, what had been the true grain of his life forever. Except he wondered why he should give money to any of these creatures when, simply, he was one of them, he was as disbanded as they. To give to them, would that not be a style of dishonor among thieves? He wondered how they could possibly fail to recognize him for one of them, for he felt more acclimated in Washington Square Park than he ever had anywhere on the face of the earth, more at home in the natural center of Greenwich Village, one of the creatures of this fantastic frightening forest of the city. Did they pass money among the initiated, the intensely invalidated, or simply take from the intruders, the catatonic onlookers? But perhaps he was mistaken, perhaps he, himself, was being prepared, set up, measured, perhaps the predators were awaiting his morsel. That then was the question, whether he was an intruder or a predator, whether or not he had the option, and if he did, whether he had already exercised it and whether he would exercise it again.

Timothy and Seema had entered Washington Square Park together, holding hands, a fast bond, benighted children of the earth forever. Seema had spotted the black man playing chess, and she had run immediately to say hello, hello, she wanted to say hello. He was her favorite of the park, she said, and she was clearly a favorite of his. She made him smile, and nothing else seemed to accomplish that or even led him to look up from his chess encounters. For others as well, Seema was a magical child, especially in the park, and she disappeared in a whirl down the paths and through the trees, anxious to see her friends.

Timothy did not seek to stop her, knowing that every time she ran away they might never see each other again. They had both existed for their entire, albeit short, lives without knowing of each other, although Seema, in some realm, had probably known of him, imagined him, and he had probably dreamt of her. They had imagined, dreamed, that they had shared the same blood, the same heritage without meaning, without knowing, the meaning was in the knowing.

What was this? FamilyAxedBySon. The *New York Daily News* wanted you to know. Action-packed for sure. But what did it mean? What was the exacting date of this *Daily News* that Timothy had nervously picked out of the trash basket, worried that he might have missed many daily lives? Precisely when had the murder taken place was it? Had the funeral been held tomorrow? It was murder, had it not? It could not possibly have been in self-defense, had it taken place? And how many death masks were there for the seeing, oh Hezekiah?

Tune in Sunday, October 28, to the *New York Journal–American* and learn where to go and what to do if nuclear war comes to New York City. Kind of like an advance theater guide in advance of the theater. A full page of timely and practical advice to help you best avoid complete annihilation whether you are at home, at school, at work, or on the subway. Admission free. A public-service feature.

SonAttackedByFamilyAxesThem. The Knicksloseinovertime. A curious word, overtime. Postmodern drift, perhaps. The new American patriotic cry: give me immortality, or give me overtime. And that from yesterday's newspaper. The Secretary General of the United Nations, U Thant of Burma, was speaking of the modalities for negotiations between the United States and the Soviet Union. A lovely word modality. How would Patrick Brown King have pronounced modality? And how many modalities make a life? Was a modality the same in Burma as in these United States? Or had the learned U Thant discovered that modalities were indigenous to Burma? If so, what happened to modalities found in America? Were they confiscated by Customs? Meanwhile, in Cuba, Castro was restraining himself from arresting the usual suspects on a mass scale, while at the Uniting Nations the agitated Stevenson was nevertheless preparing on October 26 to wait for his answers from the Soviet Union until the freezing of hell. In the meantime, the *New York Daily Times* had reported that fares for horse-drawn cabs seen daily splicing and intersecting and heard clippety-cloppeting lovers through the pathways of Central Park were due to increase to $5.50 per hour, and who, oh, who could afford that: oh, what, oh, what hardship of love was thereupon imposed upon whom, oh, upon whom? Speaking of travel, the *Daily Times* had also reported that the Soviet Union had challenged the right of the United States to blockade Cuba, that, yes, the risk had been of nuclear war, yes, Timothy could still remember that. The blockade had long begun, effective 10 A.M., EDT, 10/24/62, and perhaps the nuclear holocaust had boomeranged the real world in this lifetime. Beneath the heavens, it had been underway at sea perhaps forever, forever after A.D. They had all been blown away.

What? What was this? The Hungarian revolt that had broken out in October/November 1956 in Budapest had appeared to be successful until Soviet troops had crushed it? So what was the relevance to him? That it was a revolt from outside the Party, in this case outside the Hungarian Communist Party. That it was a previous East/West competition of note. Mano-a-mano. Another championship season. Yes, but, no, that was not the connection for him. Mano-a-womano. Yes, the woman. The woman on the bus. She had been Hungarian. Klara. Now the mother of his bed and daydreams. His former mother, that is. You could say that his world view was moving in a different tack and direction. He, an American, now had a relationship with Hungary in bed. A personal relationship. The horizon was limitless. Sleeping and Hungary while history was being rewritten. His history. Would it make a difference?Not mother, God, and country, but Mother Hungary. And was the Fatherland next? Fatherwhat, fatherwhom, fatherwhere.

With a great sigh, a man sat down beside Timothy on the bench with the bearing of one who had been expected, as if he had kept Timothy waiting and was happy to exercise the power. Another presumptuous aggressor of the Washington Square Parkland of America, who on the spur of this moment in American history had decided to choose Timothy to wait upon him. Another bold compatriot who had readily assumed Timothy's complicity. Timothy was there, so he must be there for him, there to serve his needs. There were countless, urgent, unplanned appointments ongoing everywhere in all directions in Washington Square Park, and this man, fully prepared, had a sheaf of papers in his long fingers, perhaps his personal history, that he was anxiously shuffling through, apparently looking for something he had forgotten about himself, not looking up at Timothy, not prepared to speak or to be spoken to—Timothy would wait and Timothy was waiting—until he had found exactly that for which he was searching in his life. His thick long black hair jiggled around his long narrow head and his long legs appeared involved appeared involved as well, twisted, intertwined as if themselves involved.

"I've got your file here, sonny," the man said suddenly, without looking at Timothy. "The file of McMichaels."

Timothy hesitated for only a moment because he knew that this man, willy-nilly, was speaking to him, would insist upon it, name or no. Yes, these were his people, all separated from one another, separated from him, insisting upon it, separated from themselves. It was their usual desire, their wont, to talk of the necessities of the day, foregoing the pasts of everyone, the obliterated obliterating pasts. Timothy was only slightly surprised to be accosted in an impatient, aggressive, familiar manner by this total stranger. Time was surely precious for one and all for all time now and Timothy sensed that they had things to say to each other before the big bang. It was perhaps a prearranged and a necessary appointment.

"That is not my file," Timothy thought to say, decided to aggressively engage at all cost, unconcerned with danger, seeking to interfere with destiny. "My name is King," he said innocently, boldly, thinking to doubt it as soon as he had said it.

"Of course it is your file, it must be."

"But can it be my file if McMichaels is not my name? I am King. And anyway, how could you have a file on me already? I have just arrived. I have never existed until now and I was not in this park before. You must know that. You probably have it in your records. Therefore, how could you have compiled this file upon me without having spoken with me? Of course you do not have to answer that, not at all, and I understand that you will not answer it."

"Of course it is your file, it has to be your file. What nonsense if it is not, of that I am certain," said John Darnell Slamunster, excited, although he needed a shave, looking withered and worn but wired, the result of either a studied disguise or discipline gone asunder with passionate resolve and without sleep.

"We keep files," he continued in haughty tones, "on everyone of every description and significance, on everything in detail, including bathroom habits. On all of my students and colleagues. And if it is your file, McMichaels must be your name. If McMichaels is your name, it must be your file. Besides, it is not what it seems that makes it what it is. This above all I now realize."

"All right, if you insist. But who do you represent? What is your affiliation, your hierarchy? You could not possibly be a subsidiary of the Fabulous Bureau of Involvement in America, could you?"

"In heavens name, no, we are multi-national. Cosmopolitan. Universal. We do not discriminate against individuals, particularly individual countries. By the way, about your name?"

"Yes, I am most grateful that you have reconsidered, that you have asked."

"Or, actually, about you . . . perhaps . . . although it will necessitate becoming personal."

"Ah, yes, that is perhaps all right, too, but you should decide."

"McMichaels is, what, Irish? Scotch or not?"

"Well . . . ahhh . . . yes, it could be, ah, Irish. And, well, Scotch. I guess. Maybe English. Perhaps Irish and Scotch and English."

"You do not know?"

"Ahhh, no. Not for certain. Do I have to know? I have never known before."

"There is probably some English there? Can you be certain of that?"

"Oh, no doubt, I cannot be certain. What with the possibility of both Irish and Scotch, what with their both being, you know, living over there, part of the British Isles, being so close together, what with the currents, I mean, if that is the correct drift, if it is, I mean, if that is an acceptable way of putting it."

"I should think so, certainly. Quite so. Evidently. But you should be careful to whom you say that. You cannot know to whom you are talking. We know more than you think. It could betray you now and forever."

"Yes. Definitely."

"But the 'Michaels'—isn't that Jewish? It is quite possible that you are a Jew."

"Oh, yes, I think so. Jewish. Yes. That. A definite possibility. Most assuredly. In this century I have become a Jew. I understand that now."

"Well, what? Dammit."

"Well what do you mean?"

"Jesus. Look, is the 'Mc' Irish or Scotch and did the 'Mc' latch on to the Michaels or vice versa? You see what I mean? On the other hand, I think you must be Jewish even if you are not a Jew. Unless you are being evasive."

"Ah. I see what you're driving at. Ah, that's a tough one. Mc . . . Michaels. Michaels . . . Mc. Oh, good. Right. Ohhhhhh. That must be where 'Mick' came from. But how could that be, I thought it was O'Michaels?"

"You slippery little bastard, I refuse to trust you."

"Yes. Well you might. But if you have a file on me, can you get me a job in the universe?"

"I have several possibilities. Oh, I didn't mean that. Just an old habit. That used to be my cover. Employment agencies for the unwashed. Ah, those were the days. Ah, I remember it well, I well remember our logo."

And then Slamunster waved his hand, and began shouting and talking like a combination of separated, displaced characteristics, each of which were free floating as if lost from their personal moorings, mostly unrelated persons representing various eras of life but perhaps linked by a strain of person, strained. They were persons that did not seem to need counterpoint or contact with another or others with which to interact in order to function, functioning arrogantly on their own, obviously in their own oblivious fashion, demanding and ruthless and strangely dependent upon free interpretation free of thought, if interpretation there was to be at al, al al, at all had lost control:

"'The Employment Agency
that Employs the World,'" he said with a flourish, "owned, of course, by Karl Marx, Esquire. Isn't that lovely?

"Or:

'A
WORLD EMPLOYED IS A
WORLD SAVED,'

becoming excited. "Now doesn't that have a nice Christian ring to it?

"Or:

'THE GREAT EMPLOYMENT AGENCY IN THE SKY:
WE EMPLOY FOR ETERNITY.
COME FLY WITH US.'

"Or:

'WE'LL EMPLOY ANYBODY, ANYTHING, ANYWHERE
blacks, jews, mcs, wasps, toads

(but NO COMMIES*)*

TRULY ALL-AMERICAN.'

"Wait. Did you say that?"

Slamunster had suddenly stopped.

"Did I say what?" asked Timothy.

"All-American. That is a code word. How did you know that?"

"I did not know it."

"You said it."

"I deny saying it. Why would I say that?"

"That is for you to know. Do not ask me why. You said it. By the way, have you seen the grafitti in the '**MEN'S ROOM**'? You should, you know. I did not erase it, because I thought you might be interested. It is fit for the son of god, or for the son of a king, if you will."

"Ah . . . a men's room in the park. What will they think of next?"

"Yes, fascinating, isn't it, the entire park is a men's room and the grafitti is in the air. It is quite fine. As I said, it is fit for the son of god. It says:

'DOWN WITH CAPITALISM!'

^^

' But we can't do away with capitalism. Without capitalism there wouldn't be any unemployment. Even God knows we've got to have unemployment, for Christ's sake.'"

"I agree, that is quite brilliant."

"Yes, all about is bright and clearly understood. That is a song, I think. For what is the essence of capitalism? It is competition, of course," said Slamunster, "directly leading to a war of worlds, as in all roads lead to Rome."

He was apparently intent on answering his own questions if at all possible, for it was obvious that he desperately wanted to regain the control he had apparently lost.

"I have written a novel on the subject," he continued. "It is twenty-five pages long and it is going to make me rich. Somebody wins and somebody loses, naturally. And the U.S. of A. is a winner! I have certainly learned that of late. There are those who whine about our exploiting the world, exploiting other people, other cultures—you are damn right we exploit them, and any politician with balls would admit it. If they are exploited, hell, all that means is that we are winning, we have beaten the hell out of them. And you know who them is. Whatever consequences they suffer, they suffer because they lost, because they are losers, man. Look, it is a free world. And if they were free like us, they could compete just as well as we can, man. If they lose, man, it is their own damn fault, because they are not free. And you had better believe it, man, they are going to lose. They do not have a chance, man. It is all explained in my novel."

Timothy looked away to see that Seema was quickly approaching, lightly, delicately, floating like an angel, curious to see what new animated acquaintance Timothy had made, until she recognized Slamunster and then veered quickly away, thinking that she would return later to take Timothy to her castle.

Timothy followed her movement for as long as he could, wondering why she had suddenly changed directions as if to change the world.

"Just remember that they are all a bunch of informers," Slamunster seemed to be whispering. "Everyone will inform on you and me and themselves if they get the chance. If your name is King you should remember that. What you must understand are the possibilities of life. We are all recruits. Everyone in this park is. That is the great irony of our lives: the Fabulous Bureau of Intrigue & Involvement has overtaken Washington Square Park. We are all recruits to spy upon ourselves. Our task is to report to each other everything we do. That way nothing will get by us. That is why I sent you the letters. And now, of course, it is time for you to go see him. There is no reason not to go. But you should know that I have bedded her, I have, goddamned her."

As if coming out of a haze, Timothy looked back. Slamunster was gone, running away through the park. And for the first time Timothy knew that it had not been a chance encounter. He knew vertigo. Nausea.

What was the time? Seema had disappeared—had she decided not to take Timothy to her castle? If she did not, there would be no place for him to go—and it was, indeed, near the time for Timothy's meeting. His . . . appointment? An appointment. How innocuous that was. And yet it could be menacing. For somebody. For him. His direction was east, correct? Yes, he was leaving the park and moving east. That struck him as funny. Except that this was not a moment for hilarity. An historic appointment. History was not humorous.

Was it raining or misting? Cloud drifts. Darkening. And then Timothy realized that he had not yet left the park, was not leaving it, that he was following a man, deeper into, around and through, the clouds, had been, had he not? It was a feeling he had, as if it were an assignment, his assignment, a mission he had to accomplish before he could do anything else, go anywhere else, be anything at all. Was that the same as being followed? Was one's life not one's own as long as one was being followed? Was one's future always something being stolen, forever running out of time?

Klara had not understood. It was a matter of recognition. Would his father kill him for it (a door had closed, someone had been, was following him through the streets)? The beast crawls the land.

Hezekiah ran in the wilderness, JBK disappeared. What was Timothy's quest?

But Timothy would not take this seriously, would he? A don quixote. Yes, he was curious to hear about his father, assuming that was the tale to be told. But even in that respect he was not certain what he would do with the . . .

information. What possibly could be the connection to him? Particularly since he thought that he might have been detached from the family the day they cut the umbilical cord and he had drifted away from God into space. Hezekiah excepted. That was the meaning. And he could not now think in terms of family even if he had just slept with a mother—mythology to the contrary, mothers did not count in America—nor for that matter could, would he think in terms of patriotism, of country, of politics, of social movements, even of society as he had come to understand it. And he had run off with the daughter, allegedly his sister, run off with her, and she had run off. Obviously, at the very least society was for him, well, extraneous, superfluous. Quite often society was clearly ridiculous. Everyone must know that. If they did not, it was his duty to inform them. Bring them the word just as Hezekiah had done. Explain everything. The truth of it was that we were an abandoned, random species, a form of life with such a short existence as to not have lived at all. Who had time for involvement? (But what if you had slept with a mother?) We are a speck in space, so small that even that has to be taken on faith. (And what if you had desired your sister?) Or you could leave it, which was probably the wiser course, leave faith in space. (And what if you wanted to kill your missing father after your mother, even if you could not identify, know the father?)

Yes, he had come upon himself following a man, but he had kept his distance. This was a huge, a big man . . . dusty, dusty and shady. Why was the man . . . no, who was he? And where was Seema? But why was he following this man? Had he chosen the man to follow or had the man chosen to be followed? The man kept looking over his shoulder as if he were dead, as if to see if Timothy would follow.

Except he now had a new father as well as a new mother, did he not? His father might be a missing father but he was a new father. And his mother, recently new, was now dead, as he and Seema had agreed. How about that, Mel Allen. What did that mean? How would that collide, Herman Kahn, how would that collide with the bodies in heaven? New fun and games. Oh, whom was he trying to fool? Yes, he wanted to know the true identity of his father. And JBK had already given him a clue. He had hinted.

Timothy had kept his distance, but he had attempted to not so much catch the man's eye as to look into it. He had wanted to get a direct look, to look directly into his mind, try to, fascinating, oh my, because just by looking at the man, physically, what past was imaginable when the present was unimaginable? What could be tolerated? What could be seen? Could you look into the soul of another? For that matter, could you look into yourself or must you look away?

Okay, in relation to others Timothy had a disease. He did not know what it was called, but he knew that he had it. Was it the moral equivalent of a venereal disease? It had made life difficult for him, and he suspected that it would continue to do so, for he feared that there was no cure. It had been given unto him, he had been chosen, and among the many symptoms was the fact that it had made it impossible for him to relate to day-to-day today, the quotidian. On the one hand, the day's reality, today, as in I am walking down the street and I step into a dog turd, yes, but to speak of the . . . of a single day in eternity, what was that, how was that possible? Could the *Daily News* report on eternity? And if you could not read about it in the morning newspaper, how could you know? As for the disease itself, he felt like laughing again, because he thought he knew the precise moment when he had caught it: it was when Grandfather Hezekiah had attempted to save Timothy by tying his shoes with both of them squat on their behinds on the floor. Yes, old Hezekiah had probably suffered from it, and he had probably given it to Timothy and Hezekiah knew it, and he had desperately tried to save Timothy, knowing that it was impossible to save him without tying his shoes, but acting that it was not so. Yes, it had to be contagious. Grandfather Hezekiah had done all that he could do, he had tied Timothy's shoes together.

And yet Timothy questioned whether it was genetic. He did not think that it was the gift of the ages, that it could be handed down. He did not think that it had possessed his father. Correction. He had not formerly thought that JBK had been possessed. But what did he, Timothy, really know, because who was JBK, the father? Just a man that had disappeared. The truth was in the commitment. It said so in the Bible.

Curious about the father. God the father, in the Bible. Grandfather Hezekiah had talked about that. God was the Father. I am the Lord your God, He claimed or had claimed or had been allowed to claim. Was it a question of respect? The *Lord* was known by that name in the Bible even by nonbelievers. You could look it up. His Gloriness. Or was it a question of intimidation, fear, because it could not be denied that, *Bibliographically* speaking, God does well by them who fear Him. And yet the mortal Moses was constantly trying to calm and advise and restrain the Lord our God, our Father, as if He, Himself, was nothing but an unruly child. Now Lord, Moses had said, be a good boy and don't lose your temper.

And fathers were a heavy burden, a punitive force even, because there seemed to be no getting away from fathers, because, unlike mothers, they were not close enough, no personal freedom, live your own life, be your own being, not the least because the iniquity of fathers was visited upon the children and there was no getting away from those past sins that, after all, one had not committed, you were held accountable, because unlike sons, children, it was said that, "God is not a man that he should lie, nor the son of man that he should repent," so the children had to do the apologizing. No, there was no freedom, for that matter, there was no quarter for religious or political freedom in the Bible, and certainly none for personal hijinks. The Big Boppa said do it my way or else there will be a Big Bang. And so it had come to pass. And now that Timothy had slept with his mother he was presumably cured of all diseases, for there could not be life after sleeping with your dead mother no matter what you did together in bed.

The man was big, burly, and Timothy could sense his violent, primitive nature, or was Timothy making that up, imagining it? Would this be the type of man who was Klara's sugar daddy? That was what it was, what he would call it. What Klara had was a sugar daddy and his name was General Tuffy. And they would be like two stars colliding in the heavens. Thus, it was a question of affairs of the heart. Yes, he absolutely knew it. Clearly this was the . . . the man, except he was clearly a beast, the beast that Klara was passionately sexually embroiled with, you could see that, sense it, thusly, sitting in park, observing, passing in the distance, thinking, feeling, sensing, yes, he was horrified that there could be such a relationship. And then he looked up and he was gone, and there was little doubt that he had gone, the beast had gone to meet Klara. Yes, Klara had previously admitted that she was going to see him and no matter that she had insisted that she was no longer sleeping with him.

"I have to spend some time with the poor man," she had said. "He has to get something for his money. He is lonely and just wants companionship," she had said. "Surely he would like to sleep with me but, pathetic old man, he does not dare insist upon it."

Pathetic old man? This raving beast in the park? What kind of fool did she take him for? But then it did not actually matter, because Seema had said that Klara was dead.

"I tolyouantolyouan," the beastly man was saying, overheard saying, "kill-Wagnerhavetobastard."

At the sound of the tone in zones Timothy had the paradoxical sense that the world had finished with itself, the bombs might be falling, although nothing had happened or was happening—morbidity, lethargy, paralysis—but that with his head spinning anything could happen, the bombs could fall, the world could begin, yes, anything was possible now, it was definitely happening, and that anything could happen with the next human being he encountered, who could be anyone and probably would be, the next corner he turned, although there were no corners to turn unless he left, went to the outer boundaries of . . . of the park.

He saw Ichabod Craning his neck riding through the paaark chased by Paul reverenced while all of the lemmings followed. That was your heritage as an American. You earned it in grammar schooool, paid for it.

A spinning sense that you could walk directly into involvement which seemed simultaneously primitive and quaint, that one could walk into meaning, just like a walk in the park, he was in the park, the compulsion, the pull to do that, do it and create fantasy. Where was the meaning? They promised meaning. Was it waiting for delivery?

No, instead walking around the corner to discovery.

Timothy looked up and the man was gone, had disappeared again into the park. Timothy would forever think that he had known that man. Did he want to? He would return? The man was gone, and if he died he would never return, he would never rise again.

Life or death. Who died and who did not and did it make any difference at all when one died or who it was that died and why should it, that was the question, those questions.

He suddenly felt exhilarated. It was so strange. Absurd. This swing of emotion, this trance, this brave moment. This might be an event that would change everything, sever all previous connections, such as they were. He might be cut totally loose, freed. But he might not be able to turn back. That was frightening, was it not? Never to be able to return again. It was a plunge into . . . what? The unknown, certainly. But that was what exhilarated him. And why not? The best that life could offer was endless wonderment and anticipation, exploration and creation, was it not? Or instant extinction just a hop and a skip around the corner. It would be all over. Nothing. He felt a knot in his abdomen and suddenly he was taking deep breaths. He could be walking quickly into a determined past forever.

the Big Bang beginning of creation

The parts and pieces are
all there
you just have to find
merely
the right order
connect
[The past in your language
your history in your language]

just like the big boys,
the players,
the god and the devil

By imagining, envisioning enough aspects he could make it real, happen present

he could move past toward the present in the future

when he gets to the present the future will have happened, the future will be the past

Awareness sense memory that it had already happened and all he had to do was remember. But he had not yet remembered so that the past was in the future.

13

The Revelatory Revisions of AC

It was when the bells rang and Seema disappeared that Timothy remembered that he had been here before, that he had been in this intellectual fort, the main living center of New York University, which occupied an entire square block of Greenwich Village. An intellectual mass. Block solid. Under seige. Fantasy retreat. Mind massage. Bats in the belfry.

Timothy and Seema walked through the first-floor door and immediately became a part of the internal movement of the hallways. Seema went to and fro, a waterbug here, zipping and darting, a hummingbird there, hovering and then flying away again naturally. Timothy was engulfed and expelled, became a part of the clusters and the strings of bodies rubbing and bopping and bumping together and apart. No choice there, and no memory, nothing remembered, except that crowds had always made him feel that he was at the beginning of something, something primeval, at beginnings rather, at creation, a time to lean, to press against a wall and feel the forces, feel the crush. Why did not the mass of human beings fly apart in all directions, separate? Maybe they do, that is, maybe they will, eventually. Maybe they will this week. Today. This moment. Maybe they are always in the process of precisely that, in imminent danger of flying apart slowly, suddenly it will happen, all fall down. Seema would know before, an instant before, and she would lead the way to freedom from the past.

But then the bells had rung and Seema had disappeared, and he had remembered. His once and blessed father on earth, JBK, had taken him to . . . to what, to here, had taken him to the bathroom here in this very building. Yes. He suddenly knew that. He was certain of it. It had actually happened. Here at 32 Waverly Place, Washington Square Park, New York, New York, USA. But how old had he been? Not old enough to find the bathroom by himself. Was that the time he had missed the urinal? It astonished him to have a memory like that. Made him quiver. Maybe not a memory, more a sense, knowledge he knew he possessed the instant the bells had rung. Perhaps he could even find the exact precise urinal. A momentous discovery. There at the beginning of something. At first he thought that was all, that he could remember nothing else, that he could be certain of nothing else, neither before nor after. The conscious life of a child began, and ended, and began. Just that. Just beginnings that were endings. He had gone to sleep and woken up fifteen years later. Or was it that he had gone to sleep and forgotten fifteen years? Timothy had woken and found Seema beside him. Klara had somehow left him, having never actually been with him. Seema was Klara's daughter. Who did that make the father? Who what when why, the questions.

And then the ringing bells altered the balance once again. Up and down from one floor to another, elevators jerking and lifting and falling, creaking and moaning, stairways climbed and pounded, doors sliding and swinging, open and shut. He had stood there and watched the people, students and faculty and hangerson, peekerboos, sleepyeyes, and smokers, people of all ages and types, stood there and watched them pass through the doors and hallways, mostly without talking, mostly without seeing known faces. He had been here before. He knew something of what had happened. What had happened? Should he tell? He watched them all like ghosts, shadows, walk into the building. Seema? Timothy?

When Professor André Cordon entered the large classroom he, Cordon, did not notice the intruder slumped in his seat in the distant last row. Had he, he might have remembered the little kid, Timothy, now twenty-one years of age. Only years had passed since they had last seen each other in Maine. Shorter periods and one other longer period before back to the beginning of time, back to babydom. Only yesterday, only a thought. You are eating what? Cordon had asked Timothy that question that summer on the back porch. A peanut butter and mayonnaise sandwich? Peanut butter and mayonnaise. Oh dread and horror, it had sounded nauseating, fit for the ants. Cordon had had a hangover on that day in Maine just as he did on this day in New York, a ghastly hangover. Only in America, he had said to Timothy, the young boy, only in America, my boy. Have you tried peanut butter and pickles, he had asked him?

Helen King had laughed. A striking woman, Cordon remembered. A real strength, he had thought. Tall. Forceful. A waste as a mere housewife, JBK's handmaiden. Not that she had been just that, either. Merely for appearances. She had become a mother, or nearly. That was what she desperately wanted and could not have, could not even pretend, had tried and tried and tried, but she could not even be herself. And she should have been that much more, much more, much more her own visible self. Extraordinary waste. And she had known it. Living secrets. When you go into darkness, you forget about the light. Her depressions. Razor-sharp wit and jet black hair, long black black hair, that was what André Cordon remembered. When JBK had disappeared around the bend, she had slit her wrists with a razor. Deep flowing, dark red blood. Cordon had never slept with her.

The professor also might have seen himself in the little kid, and remembered JBK, the student at twenty-one, the bright shining star at twenty-one or yes. At Dartmouth in the thirties. How many years did that cover? Thirty? Was it that Marxist student study group that Cordon had given his talk to? What was it called, oh yes, oh what was it called, oh he almost had it, yes, yes, yes The Junto, that is what it was for sure, and he remembered, for no apparent reason, that he was supposed to have attended The Junto's testimonial dinner for the Mexican muralist Orozco. But when The Junto had brought the British socialist John Strachey to campus for a lecture, Cordon had encountered JBK in the audience, encountered him for the first time. It was quite an extraordinary meeting, of course, considering everything, considering what Cordon had known and JBK had not. Or had they first met in the crowd at Smith College? At the conference in Northampton, the peace conference, the gathering of antifascists? It was both, of course. It was the time. Yes, that was it. Still a thought, just a thought. They had crossed paths like meteors in the heavens. He had taught at Dartmouth for only a few years in the thirties. And that is where he had recruited JBK, the youth of brilliant promise, and the connection had grown, the strands had tied tightly in unbelievable, unforeseen, uncontrollable ways, and JBK had not known until the very end, had not guessed much of anything, guessed how their paths might have crossed before time.

But Professor Cordon had been absorbed with other thoughts on this day in October 1962, this evening when, prepared to offer himself once again in whatever guise as a focal point for a segment of time, he had made his entrance into the classroom. He had emerged from along the hallway, appeared before the parcel of bodies, prepared to speak in fear or perhaps in boredom, to speak in commanding, bursting fashion, either to grieve or to exult in community, perhaps to plead or to rhapsodize, to defend, or to disseminate. For today the decision should have already been made for him. And more. For example, he had been thinking today that he was ambivalent about the fact that a decade before he had not testified before HUAC, the House Un-American Activities Committee. It had not been his duty. His task. He had not been ordered to speak. Had he, of course, his academic career might have been destroyed, because he would not have been able to tell them the most crucial facts of all, that is, about himself, his own situation, and his usefulness would have ended, his usefulness to anyone. And yet, by not testifying, without providing the necessary details, had he lost his place in history, his one chance for a place in history? Now, he wished that he had that opportunity again. It would have been a proper way not only to end it, to wrap it up, but to begin it. But maybe he still did have that opportunity. In a different way. Perhaps there was potential here. It would be very difficult, of course, to get all of the facts straight now, but if he attempted to remember . . . what could he reconstruct? And what then would happen?

Except . . . except that he had a sense of not knowing what was happening presently. In the past that had indicated danger and he had always known to exit quickly. Pronto. Retreat and reconnoiter. Tout de suite. But if he did that now, he might find out nothing, remember nothing. And he thought he was beyond danger now anyway, beyond its consequences.

Today he was in the classroom, perhaps to read from the seventeenth-century religious poetry of George Herbert, a special favorite, and to be annoyed with classroom sounds, rustlings. Ah, the poetry of George Herbert and nuclear warheads. What arcane conceits were possible in that precious coupling? Answer the question and control the future of the world, control nothing. Or perhaps it was better to read from the metaphysical, erotic poetry of John Donne and to secretly enjoy the imperative of shouting down, in a booming voice, the classroom titters of young, nubile females and males, having knowingly chosen the very poems guaranteed to elicit the smothered squeals and heavy breaths of pleasurable embarrassment. Anxious, urgent sex and war. Tried and true. Of course, with Donne there was an added touch of darker morbidity. A special varietal strain.

Still, very little was known about The Professor, André Cordon. A lot of trivia. He had worked hard on that, had he not? It had been crucial. The question of identity was eternal and trivial. Outside the classroom he could be kind and pensive and absentminded, filling and lighting and smoking and relighting his pipe, that was easy certainly. And involved, seemingly, with the affairs of all of his students, with an ocean of lives through which he drifted aimlessly, sloppily, listening with passing interest, engaged at irregular intervals, missing appointments, always that, always bordering but never really touching the times, schedules, equilibriums of others. Outside the classroom, it was not that he appeared capable of doing almost anything as that he had the appearance, cultured, ripened, the appearance of having done everything, and why not? And now he was merely waiting, making very little effort at holding himself together, because there was nothing remaining to hold on to. Only habit was operative, if that. Perhaps there was nothing left to do and nowhere to go. The horrible possibility existed that he had lost his powers of invention, which if true meant for him that he had lost everything. Having begun with nothing, he knew that stagnation meant death.

"Oh Klara," he moaned to himself in despair.

She was his last passion. He could not know what that meant particularly, because she went back to forever. And it seemed to be his passion alone.

A large man, he moved his bulk into the room, hulking body teetering on spindly legs. Surely if he fell he would break into a thousand pieces, and there would be no one to gather them, gather him. No one would know how he had been put together, and only he knew that he had never been put together. He puffed on an unlit pipe, unlit although he looked to be constantly lighting it, leaving his trademark burnt matches everywhere. He laid books and papers to rest on the large desk. Late, again, not knowing, never having known that he had been late always, never apologizing, he was late again. He would never ever catch up with his life, which was perhaps a fortunate thing. In the classroom, a mystery, an unknown edge he maintained, a face, appearing always to be dressed smartly, grey tweed suit, silk painted tie, blue trim shirt, shined black shoes. Neat, soft, but intense. And shaved, clean, a sparkle in his eyes, his blackened smooth combed hair greying to the white of his sideburns. To look at him at this moment was to be reassured. Even if he did have a hangover. From the perspective of his classroom audience, he imagined that he was an overwhelming force. Unfathomable.

But Timothy had seen Professor André Cordon. He had already been surprised and not surprised, and he had already begun to remember and recreate.

"You ask me here?" he had thought. "You just let me come and see you here after all of these years?"

Yes, Timothy had remembered the Professor's face, this face. The face of the man JBK had come to see, that face. The man Timothy had first met in this building, first seen here, but afterward only in Maine, many times in Maine as he had grown up, so that he had associated him always afterward only with Maine, only with Maine, no harm there, with all of the borders and countries of Maine, except that there had been no Russia, Maine, not even a Hungary, Maine, so how could he have guessed, how could he have crossed that border?

Yes, indeed, why had André Cordon come to Maine on all of those occasions? It was a question Timothy had never before asked himself. On a secret mission, secret missions, which would have meant that he, Timothy, had been involved in this extravaganza, in this world-wide conspiracy from the outset, at birth, at his christening. The eyes of the world, Paramount News, especially, again, the big eyeball on the stork when it had dropped him from the sky as a baby Commie. Because the destiny of the world was at stake, was it not or was it not? What had been the cover used by this immense figure, or did you not need one when you were dealing with a blond baby boy? Maybe old Attorney General Whymeaning had known the truth after all about bubble gum and babies across the river and into the trees from Dartmouth, except that he had not looked into all of the right states of mind. Look closely around and unto thyself.

Timothy had forgotten he had ever met Professor Cordon in this very building. Was it possible, to have it happen, what he was beginning to think, no, feel had happened, and forget that it had happened? Had it happened? What was he thinking? Was the Professor a part of this? Had he been a part of this? A part of what? Timothy's memory would not allow it, would reject it. When was the first time in Maine? When was he born in Maine? For Maine was his birthplace, the birthplace of his grandfathers. Had the Professor appeared on the same day that they had been to see Grandfather Hezekiah on his death slab? Would he have dared such a thing, dared to have been so bold and brazen? Hezekiah had said that the Lord was called the Lord even by heathens. Would that have been sacrilegious?

Yes, and no, it was years before, when Timothy and his very own reputed father and mother, JBK and Helen, oh, fatherhood! oh, motherhood! had just returned from a Fourth of July fireworks display in Deering Oaks Park in Portland, Maine. Oh, patriotism! Oh, Hezekiah! Earlier, it had been a hot day, and his blessed father and his blessed mother had let Timothy, a little boy, run around without any clothes on. Not that Timothy remembered that, either. It was just that he had been there in the park years later on the day that Grandfather Hezekiah in his declining days had taken off all of his clothes and wandered through the park naked. Or had someone told Timothy of that as well? Like grandfather, like grandson, he had been told, told of his own grand lark in freedom. They had tried to make light of it. Why did Timothy remember that the Red Sox had won a doubleheader on that particular Independence Day? Against the Cleveland Indians at Fenway Park. A hot, humid day. Doubleheaders. Baseball forever. What year had that been? Indeed, you could look it up, Casey Stengel would say. Hezekiah without clothes was historical. And hysterical. Hezekiah had been hysterical. In hysteria.

"You just let me come and see you again after all these years?"

Timothy Brown King was talking to Professor André Cordon. It seemed an unlikely situation. To Timothy. Impossible that one of them was not in a faded newsreel, the other watching in a smoke-filled theater, one real and the other . . . had, then, his role in life been preplanned? Was this the stunning revelation? The missing key? Life was not chaos after all? There was indeed a God, only God was/is a Communist, I am what I am, the Bible said.

"How are you, Timothy? Are you all right, young man?"

Cordon was studying Timothy, recognizing that he was in other rooms. He decided, wanted to bring him closer, bring them closer.

"I think it is best that we are going to have this talk. Why should we not? To discuss things. There are a few things I might tell you, after all of these years, one or two little things, fillips that you might find rare, curious, and interesting, for your scrapbook, of course."

Timothy thought he detected a faint smile. Was it a cynical smile, a wry smile, an I-know-everything-and-I-am-going-to-toy-with-you smile, or was it simply the smile of experience, of worldliness, of having been there, a smile that he, Cordon, could no longer prevent? Because those were not the first words Timothy had expected from the Professor, another man who appeared weary, slumped behind a huge desk that was swamped by a pile of papers, perhaps a manuscript in chaos, although it was a pile that simultaneously looked to be carefully arranged. Or was it that the pages had begun to intermingle of their own accord, establish their own arrangement, threatened to absorb the Professor? Was that the manner in which it happened? He was an eminent professor, world renown. In fact, ironically, Timothy had been assigned one of Cordon's anthologies of seventeenth-century English poetry at Dartmouth that very year. All very innocent. And, my god, as full and cluttered as Cordon's life had been, he had even managed to lead secret lives, had he not? There were those suggestions that he had lived a long time, at other times, long ago and far away times. He had done so much. He had such a fascinating history, histories. How did one get that way, get to be . . . that? He was the created man, admirable for that, fascinating, with a wonderful, complicated history. It meant something. Was that not the truth? It was an achievement. But in the end it was evident that something else had happened. It was detectable.

"It has been a long while now, Timothy, since JBK's disappearance, I mean. How are you? Again, welcome to New York," he said, and he must have been smiling.

"Are you all right?" he repeated, probably planning and replanning in his own mind, his mind's eye, the history that he would tell and could not tell, that which he would not tell, would invent.

Nor were those the initial words Timothy desired, perhaps because he himself had not immediately said what was uppermost in his own mind. He had not spoken his own mind. Actually he was not certain if he, Timothy, had said anything at all, or if a short or long period of time had passed. What he did know was that he suddenly had this overpowering urge to say . . . the word. Yes, he had wanted to say the word. He did not know why. It was as if it had been instilled in him long ago for declaration at precisely this moment. His friends in the park would understand his feelings. They had been there, too. They knew all about it. Yes, he wanted to say it now, yell it out even. Except that he did not want to be the first to say it. He wanted to hear it, just hear it like a voice from the depths, and maybe absorb it. JBK should have been the first one to say it. It was his proper place. But if he, the father, could not, someone had to say it and, yes, Timothy felt the desire to have him, the Professor, say it, yell it as if from hell, for had he not made a bargain with JBK?

How dare he not? How dare he, the Professor, permit even a minute to pass without shouting it out, break the thunderous silence, how dare he sit there and stare? Mother Klara had not so much as whispered it in his ear, like a serpent, the mother whose daughter's name was Seema—Seema his own sister? No, he did not feel as if he, Timothy, could be the first to say it. He would not be. Not that it had any power over him intellectually. None whatsoever. He rejected that. Absolutely. All right, some of Marxist thought he agreed with. Not all of it. Mainly he regarded it as too narrow. Too restrictive.

Dull. Boring. The real dismal science. Nothing imaginative, no horror, nothing scary about it, no great mystery to be fathomed, simply ponderous and plodding and tedious and relentless material godless truths.

But, then, why that other word, and why this world of difference? It still had an effect on him that he would probably always and forever experience. Emotionally there was both revulsion and fascination, automatically, as if it were instinctual, genetic, an indigenous, authentic American trauma. Fear and excitement, like a shot in his veins. No doubt to varying degrees you could say that about every red, blue, and white-blooded American child. A word on the frontlines of freedom, not like background music, not muzak in the elevator, more like rock and roll on the ferris wheel. But, paradoxically, also like Wheaties or Cream of Wheat in the morning. He had grown up on it. Like a birthright. Had not every bloody, babied, blessed American? He had been nurtured by it as much as, well, by ice cream, Saturday afternoon at the movies with popcorn, and Tarzan, Gene Autrey, Bugs Bunny, and the Perils of Pauline. Was not the War of Independence fought against those guys? Was not that who the British really were, anyway, had been all along? Did not they wear REDcoats? The original men disguised in RED? Reds. How dare the Professor not say it?

"Did you know that Jefferson wanted to annex Cuba?" Timothy blurted, as if he were the professor of American history and Cordon the failing student, fast failing.

Timothy even pointed his finger at Cordon. But he felt disappointed the moment the question, not really a question, was out of his mouth. He regretted it because the diversion had momentarily blunted his sense of outrage. Why could you not have it both ways? All ways? Anyway, he demanded the full blast of outrage back. He insisted upon refueling it. Definitely. He would not allow the moment to be diffused. He did not want to be cool, calm, and collected, he . . . would . . . break . . . the . . . vise . . . ahhh . . .

"Communist!" he hissed passionately, with the love and the hate of the universe. It was as if the first bomb had exploded within him.

From the moment Timothy first walked into André Cordon's office, Cordon had wondered how much Timothy knew, wondered, of course, what stories he knew and if he knew more than he, Cordon, knew something else that Cordon should know. But that was impossible. He, Cordon, had always made it the rule of his life to know the most, to know it first, to know everything. No, it was not impossible. As soon as Timothy had walked in, Cordon had felt his right eye twitch. He knew from experience, from having long ago as a young man checked it out in a mirror, in mirrors, that no one could see the twitch, no one. It was invisible. Cordon felt it, but nobody saw it, no one would ever know. Still, had he, Cordon, forgotten a telephone call? A message by courier? A letter, perhaps? God, this drinking had to stop. It was eating away the last of his brain cells. This was not early senility, not at all. Just the drinking, which he would cut down. One drink at a time. How many drinks was that?

In a private, stolen moment of detachment he tried to laugh at himself, and he quoted to himself silently as if in his own private chapel or confessional:

"'To say the truth, in a court of Justice drunkenness must not be an excuse, yet in a court of conscience it is greatly so.'"

The truth was that he drank to calm his nerves. Without liquor they raged. And yet he was subject to the most awful inertia, lethargy, apathy. How was that accountable? Was that not a paradox? He used alcohol to go to sleep, not as before to light the fires. And yet without the alcohol he could not go to sleep. The problem was, he did not take a specific dose. He just kept drinking. So, he supposed he did not really sleep. He merely ceased to function in whatever room or hotel, in whatever town or city, in whatever country he happened to be.

Nice young man, Timothy. Was not that what one was supposed to say, what was usually said? The truth was, first hand he knew little about him. Funny how one could still fall into that trap, at least momentarily, old ways of thinking, those cliches. And after all of these years and, even more, all that he, Cordon, had done. Actually, Timothy was a strange young man who did not appear so young. But, chronologically, he truthfully was fresh, at the beginning of time. Cordon had to believe that. Yes, it would be quicker, and shorter for him than he could possibly imagine at this time in his life but, nevertheless, he still possessed the illusion that he had it before him, that was the key, that burst anew. Ah, the marvelous youth with everything before him, the pure, white blank page, another chance, another life. Rubbish.

Yes, he must have forgotten something, but he knew he could not ask Timothy what it was. God knows what he would give away if he did that, although he was prepared to give away much. Why not? Why not do it, here and now. Thank heavens he remembered Timothy's name. It was certainly possible for him to have forgotten even that. What a silly predicament that would have been, to have blanked on that one, just as he was capable of blanking on anything, his own name included, capable of blanking on the fact that he had ever lived. What a mess. He was certain of that. And then something clicked.

"Did Klara bring you here or just send you? I know why she sent you. But she would not want to be here. Not that she would be afraid. Not Klara. Klara Blazek. Didn't I see Seema running in the park? I was looking out the window."

Cordon suddenly got up, pushed away from his chair as if he weighed one hundred pounds less.

"Of course I know why she sent you. But she doesn't, not really. She owed me this, even if it is too late."

That was the thing to say. Because that was what he had forgotten. Forgotten when he was someone else. And now he was not someone else, and never would be. Oh horrors. Oh horrors, indeed. Oh, Klara, oh beloved Klara, his last hope, and yet she rejected that.

"Oh, yes, she was born in Hungary all right, but she is as American as they come," he said, extremely agitated, "as American as Seema, although," he paused, looking away, looking reflective, "Seema is not very American, even if she was born in New York. Still," he turned back, "do not let Klara tell you otherwise. The truth is that she knows little about her past. She has no memory. She cannot afford it. Whatever she tells you comes from a fertile fear and a blasphemous imagination, although she fervently believes every word she invents. Oh well, it is the only thing one can do."

"The goddamned missiles will come and kill all of us," Timothy interrupted, blurted again, busted his silence as if from a deep slumber, his right eye beginning to twitch, "and that is the way it should be. Settle the whole thing. Mass suicide."

"What's that?" said Cordon, looking concerned and mystified. "You sound angry, young man. Perhaps you have reason to be, but it is all the same," he said, his emotions shifting quickly, waving his hand as if to dismiss the moment.

A young woman suddenly appeared in the doorway. Cordon had not shut the door. It was probably a scheduled appointment that he had forgotten. The student looked shy, tentative, unsure with Timothy's presence.

"Ah, pardon me, Professor Cordon. Were you going to bring that bookcase today?"

Cordon was startled, frightened even. It was as if he had suddenly awakened from a dream to wonder where he was.

"Oh, yes, yes, yes. No," he waved his hand again, "I mean no, Alexandra. Tomorrow night. I will bring the bookcase in tomorrow night. I have not cleared it off as yet. Call me tomorrow to remind me, if you would. Thank you."

The student nodded and left without a further word. Perhaps they had been through this before.

Cordon was breathing heavily, wheezing, which absolutely must have been from sucking a pipe, a cigar, must have been, it could not have been a signal of nerves, tension, pressure, not after all of the transformations that he had been through, God, no. Chameleons were nerveless.

"Let us go to my apartment," he said suddenly. "There may still be something, some way to say something, even at this late date, even if it does not matter. I suppose we must try."

walking along the street to the apartment, through Washington Square Park or around it, about it, all of it, everything abounding together, could not be everything ominous, as if the dark ages, nameless, forgotten terrors, shadows, as if the city the past the city is following ghosts they cannot escape never ever leaving Timothy everybody in danger always under the stars as they walked up the stairs of the brownstone, Cordon paused briefly and looked backward over his shoulder as if himself remembering another time who was following remembering everything possible the possibilities of other lives

Once inside the apartment, Cordon perfunctorily begged Timothy's indulgence for the apparent clutter, less obscure in the shadows now that he had drawn attention to it, asked that he be allowed to take a shower before anything further transpired, which was a request totally out of time, appropriate for the setting. He was perspiring profusely. He disappeared without a further comment.

Timothy sat in the quiet, having been left in the dark almost, not simply because Cordon had neglected to turn on sufficient lighting, sat in the large apartment, dark aged wood all around, another age, age obscured, Timothy could see that among the ghosts from the light of street lamps. The ceilings of the apartment were high, and the windows overlooking the plain of Washington Square Park were larger than paintings on the wall. A crystal chandelier dominated, glistened in the partial dark. Heavy brown dusty drapes were partially drawn. A variety of Asian, Middle Eastern rugs were everywhere on floors, everywhere flowing away like waves, some rolled away in corners, down hallways, pathways to other rooms of expansiveness. A large, golden candelabra was not lighted beside an inanimate bird on a long, polished dining-room table of many guests with stacked dishes as if from previous dinners, other occasions, spread in disarray, forgotten order. Perhaps the cleaning woman was on vacation.

Timothy stared at a bookcase until his eyes refocused, and then only to read title after title in rapid order, name after name, his mind's eye frozen. *The Sheltering Sky.* Huysmans' *À' Rebours.* Anais Nin. *Nightwood* by Djuana Barnes. Baudelaire.

The thought "God is evil" occurred to him. But was God dead, his mind wandered on playfully, playing with toys? If there is no God there must be a devil, because there had to be somebody. If there is evil there could still be a God unless he refused to be. If there is a Devil there might or might not be anything else. If there is evil there cannot only be a God. If there is Communism how can there be a triumphant God everlasting, lasting without a Devil? But we must have evil. Oh, Satan. The Prince of Darkness. Our horror films. And, most of all, Communists, we gotta have them. The Greatest American Mystery Ever Told. We outdid ourselves. The unknown fear. America desperately needed it. For some the existence of good necessitated the existence of evil. Or if it was necessary to have a God, must there not be a Devil to keep it interesting? And if there was no evil, why do we have to have a God? Therefore, the existence of Communism, playing in theaters coast to coast, proved the existence of God? Did J. Edgar know that? Of course, in a world of nothingness, perhaps one was free to create evil or good on one's own? And which choice was to be made? Which would be more fun, more enjoyable, more exciting? Who would you rather have pitching for the Red Sox, God or Satan? Satan would find a way to win. But could he win the big one?

Timothy started, shifting in his seat, rumbling within himself.

Cordon reappeared as if from the fog, his large barrel chest wet, dripping. He looked concerned as he looked at Timothy, actually seemed serious, not about to laugh. He appeared to have emerged from the sea, not from swimming, but as if he had risen from the bottom of the sea. He fumbled as he tied his faded crimson bathrobe around him, seemingly unaware now, unconcerned with his appearance, for he was, indeed, the man of his worlds. He had briefly exposed a hint of decayed muscles, his testicles hung. He was a different character from the one Timothy had accosted at his office at the university, the one that had disappeared in the walk in the park, a different man of Maine.

Cordon went to a glass-and-rosewood cabinet, snapped open the doors, and got the decanter. And then he spoke.

"You would like a whiskey, I presume? I think we could both use one or more."

He actually poured one scotch and one gin, kept the gin bottle for himself, and placed the decanter beside Timothy on a small table covered with journals and newspapers and letters and magazines and three pipes and some ashes. A bit of the scotch from Timothy's glass spilled onto a magazine.

"Ah, I am weary," Cordon said to the silence as he sat and stretched and collapsed in a large leather chair across from Timothy, who had slumped in a couch and was not speaking.

"Have you ever considered that life would be ultimately boring without death?" he offered as if gratuitously, as if it did not matter to whom he was talking, having given the speech before.

"I have lived long enough to be weary of life. I would not want another," he added, perhaps toying with Timothy.

The chair had sighed from Cordon's weight and he smiled, continuing to indulge Timothy's silence.

"So, a child of the Party you are," he began again after an extended period of heavy stillness. "Yes, we more or less adopted you as all of ours, like a mascot, which is what you were. You belonged to us all, to some more than to others, of course. Who knew? Things happen that way. You have been told all of this, I am sure. I remember you as a little boy, silent, sitting all by yourself, reading in a corner while all the talk and the planning went on. All of the organizing, the plotting, the recruiting, the strikes, the rallies, the picketing. I wondered then how much you were aware of, aware of what was taking place around you, of the activities, of the truths, of the lies, of the machinations, of that which was happening to you, being done to you, being determined without awareness of your little body. Aha. You did not play with the other children, not even then, when you were a two-year-old at the Party summer camp in Maine. You did not like to swim. I remember that."

Timothy took a healthy swig of his whiskey and tasted nothing. He felt as though it were a case of mistaken identity, that he had walked through the wrong door, that it was irrevocable, that he was about to be replaced. They probably wanted to insure his silence however they could, as preposterous as it seemed, for no known reason. Oh, Bela Lugosi, where are you right now? he asked himself. And he felt anger, anger at the gods. What in heaven and hell were they about? What had they intended? He would not commit himself now to anything, no matter what was said, because that, that would be making a choice for a life that was not his. Which meant that life would be over, JBK had said. And he was not ready, prepared, that was it, he was not prepared to make choices and he doubted that he ever would be, he would refuse. But it was true, nevertheless, that he would have to make career choices in the cosmos. Left face, right face, about face. But how could they take themselves so seriously? And yet that was the demand. You had to, they said, did they not? You were forced to believe. How else could anything be sustained? Sustained no matter how farcical. Yes, but what was it that they wanted to sustain? What did they want to believe? No, he could not take these people and these events any more seriously than Howdy Doody would take them. He looked down at them. He did not respect them. But why then was he afraid? Something primitive. No, no, impossible, they were stupid. Embarrassing. And yet they forced him to choose between dealing with them or avoiding them, hiding out, escaping. So he had chosen the latter and ignored and dismissed them, eluded them. No, he had not done any such thing. He had eluded nothing, not life. What life? He knew they had forced him to act. And he had hid only to seek. There was pressure all around. But he was not going to take the next step. He did not have to take any step at all. No goose steps for him. It was not his history. Rather, he would run after Hezekiah.

"She has totally denied that you are her child," Cordon was saying, certain that he was being heard, "as absurd as that may be, just as she claimed that you were his, which was ridiculous. She did not want to have you, you know? She was supposed to have an abortion. I do not remember who wanted this one. She probably did. It would not have been her first. And then she made you his child. In her mind, in her body, you became his child, like a miracle, as if one could do that. And that, too, was absurd, periodic, yes, yes, it was a phase, manic. Only as it could be for her. But, of course, that did not mesh with the possibilities, no matter what she insisted. After she allowed you to be born, odd, but that seems to be the way to put it, because she disappeared for months and then reappeared with you. I wonder if she even remembers the birth. But, still, she could not have you with him. Have you both, I mean. She knew that. He was married. And he would not leave Helen. He ended by being conventional in that respect. Even the Party did not want him to leave his wife. They had plans then. And then she was supposed to give you up for adoption. To an agency. A socialist agency, believe it or not. You might have been raised by one, anonymously. Imagine that? They actually exist, you know, although the Feds claim they are kidnappers. Baby snatchers. Hoover, of course. But she wanted you to be his, so she made the supreme sacrifice, she gave you to him and Helen, like a gift, and then as much as she could she repressed all memory of you for as long as she could. She was always good at that, denying reality. But not of him, of course. To be honest, I did not care. For me, it was as if you did not exist anyway. I suppose she did end by giving you up after all. Giving your life up. Aha. Actually, I did not even realize exactly who you were until recently. I had, well, forgotten even the possibility, if you will, that you existed. You do believe me, don't you?"

"I do not believe in anything," Timothy said, surprisingly. choking it off, "nothing you can tell me. Why should I?" he stammered, as if in forced response to a direct question from Cordon, as if Cordon had cared enough to ask him, no, was interrogating him, because it was nothing less than an inquisition. Or a sacrificial ritual.

He stumbled on.

"What is belief, anyway? I was without desire without knowing why. I did not want to see rhyme or reason to any of this. I see that now. But I thought I might as well get to meet the devil. Why not."

He was apparently rambling, but Cordon responded, as if to the point, as if it were still possible to pique his interest. As if there had been a thrust in his direction.

"The devil? Now, why that?"

Timothy did not miss a beat.

"I have been taught all of my life to believe that you are the devil, and somehow, emotionally, it took, even if I knew it was ignorant, primitive. Not just me, anyone my age has had that drummed into them. It does not matter whether or not one believes it. But, hell, all America believes it. It seems like the drums have been beating forever."

"So, what do you think . . . of your devil?"

"So far," he paused, "so far I am disappointed. A little frightened, I feel it. For some reason I still want to live in this stupid world with all of its monsters, although I do not know how or why. That is, I do not want to die. Don't ask me why. So, yes, there's some fear of you. It is as if you—he, someone—control my life, like . . . maybe I don't have a life."

Cordon drank and smiled.

"You know, the fact that I became such a satan was wonderful," he said in a distant, low voice that was almost imperceptible, spoke as if he were a man who had finally decided to confess because there was nothing else to do. It was a new mantle in life with intriguing possibilities.

"I never, ever dreamed that I would possess such stature in life."

He paused and then he made a decision to turn on a dime and head straight for Timothy, finish him off.

"When JBK decided to run for the Senate, he decided to leave the Party as well, or he intended to leave. Or the Party left him. It doesn't matter. The spirit left the body. But it would have been his candidacy, of course, not the Party's. American individualism. That's what it was with JBK. Sheer and simple unadulterated old-fashioned individualism. What great irony. The great idealist. He wanted to be the pied piper for the twentieth century, the American century. He wanted to be our leader, our heavenly father, bless him, the leader who would save us from ourselves, save the Party and America both, and doing that, of course, save the world. That followed. It was axiomatic. In the end I did not know what he was. It was absurd. The Party stopped him because he knew a great deal and he was getting close to a position of such power that with exposure he would have risked a great deal, and his ego would be tempted to go it alone. He was foolish. He wanted to expose us all as well as himself and then run for President. That's what it amounted to. He actually thought it would work. The incredible fantasy. The incredible campaign. Only in America."

Cordon paused to pour the gin.

"Funny, he was a hell of a shortstop in college, didn't you know that? A great American. Aha."

He chuckled.

"Didn't he tell you that? At Dartmouth. They played better in those days, too. They had a certain magic. Don't let anybody tell you differently. He played in timeless black and white. On the radio. Today they play in Cinerama. Yes, ironically the Party silenced JBK and it took him a long while to realize it."

Timothy choked.

"He was not my father. I never knew my father. I know that now. I probably knew it then. I never had parents. Just Hezekiah."

Cordon seemed mystified again.

"Your father? Oh, yes, I know, you think of him foremost as your father—he raised you, more or less—but really that is such a petty, archaic conceit. You know that, do you not? The literal truth about fathers and mothers?"

"But what am I to know?"

"What else would it be but that one has biological parents and who cares who it is. That's it. Fiction. And after that they are simply people, of course, who stumble and fumble through their own individual lives. And therein lies the problem. You can't trust people. People come and go, baaadly. They are not gods. But what would you like me to tell you about JBK? About your faaaather?"

Cordon struck with sudden, agitated impatience. He had moved to the edge of his chair.

"We knew all about your faaather, Jaaay Beee Kaaay, right from the beginning. I, of course, knew everything there was to know about him. We followed him all of the way. What fairy tale would you like to hear? I can tell you anything that you would like to hear. That he is involved in this Cuban missile business? Ah, daddy, the wonder of it all. That he is responsible for this entire Cuban/Russian mess? My, what drama. That it is entirely of his own doing, perhaps? Ah, such romance. I can spin those webs. That he's . . . he's an agitator, let's say? Yes, of course, how marvelous, JBK goes around the world in eighty days, creating or supporting or promoting or staging the unrest of the free world, of the entire uuuniverse for that matter, the problems, crises, imbalance, upset, all of that. Marvelous. Except, you know, as in life with that kind of thing you can never be certain whether or not events will turn in your favor, or for that matter whether what transpires is what you intended, or if it is real. If you are not careful, quite amusing, you might create a scenario that shall eliminate you, yourself. Invention is necessary but, take care, you might very well reinvent yourself completely out of existence. It is easily done, young man. Imagine, if you will, that JBK is persona non grata on both sides right now. That's amusing. That he is so notorious he is in the newsreel—read your newspaper, lately?—as a missing, mysterious person, under an assumed name, of course, so to read the newspaper would be tantalizing, but futile. Perhaps his plan, let us say, was to get the two sides to bomb each other back to the stone age. Perhaps he thought of himself as God ready to redo the world—oh, yes, there is a story to tell about that. Perhaps it will be the great untold story, that both the Soviet Union and the United States discovered this and figured out together or devised together a plan to extricate themselves together. 'He is a threat to both of our countries,' they tell themselves. Perhaps he is not just a Soviet agent, merely an American spy, a double agent, but an agent for the universe, for another unknown mysterious intelligence from outer space. We believe in that kind of thing, you know. 'We do not know with whom he is dealing,' they say anxiously among themselves, 'or how they are contacting him. But we do have reason to believe that their intentions are hostile,' aren't they always? . . . complicated by the fact, and this makes it interesting, that 'we know that he is not dealing with a full deck of cards.' We have always known that. Aha. That always gets thrown in. After all, he is a King, is he not? It is in the genes. 'We do our research. We know about that.' I know about that. I told them."

As if in conjunction, Cordon was laughing openly now and the shadows were lengthening, the ghosts encircling, closer and closer, nearer and nearer. He had slumped back into his chair as Timothy spoke.

"But, of course, I have always wondered about my father, so you could say almost anything . . . "

"You have always wondered about him," Cordon mocked, as if to heap scorn upon him.

And then Cordon caught it and snapped to again, surprisingly exasperated.

"Oh, please, will you forget the irrelevancy, the fiction that he was your father."

"Was my father? Have the stars shifted in the heavens?" Timothy snapped back, as if easily catching the manner. "What does this make me? Was his son?"

"Why not?"

"I know that you probably want to silence me, don't you? Since he died in the crash . . . "

"Nobody died in any crash. JBK went underground, which is what all good Communists have always done in America, which is exactly where they belong, where he was sent, off by himself, and he has not returned, which was entirely predictable to anyone who knew him."

Timothy jumped up.

"He died in the crash . . . a big fire . . . in the crash . . . "

"Fiction."

Timothy put his hands to his face and then he slumped back into his chair. He had read the paperback, bought it off a paperback rack in the drug store for 35 cents. As a teenager. And believed it all.

Killing, killing, killing, he wondered, who is killing whom? Should he kill Klara? Did he kill his mother? Would he kill Cordon? Did they plan on killing him? Would they? Should they? Killing.

"Underground?"

"Underground," Cordon spat. "We lost him in the underground forever. I don't think he could handle it anymore. He was already dead."

Again he waved his hands.

"They all went undergound and we do not know or care who came back or how. What an absurdity. Frankly, I am not certain who I am. Haven't been for the longest time. Aha. They all went undergroun' . . ."

Cordon filled his glass again. He did not appear as if he would ever stop pouring.

". . . and we don't know what happened to them. What nonsense. There is no Party. Never was."

"You don't know what happened to them."

"The more fanatical they were, the better it was for us. The more they believed the revolution was imminent, the more ridiculous, the more stupid their actions. Passion doesn't beget madness. They go together. It was so silly. It was better for us if they just became unavailable, however they managed it. JBK got some crazy ideas. Different ideas. That is what comes of believing in revolutions . . . and then not believing. Oh, revolutions are everything, everything unreal, every fantasy you can imagine, and isn't that too bad? But what did it represent? What did it stand for? What did it represent, I ask you? Have you no response? What fiction do they teach you nowadays? Why, people did whatever was asked, they always have, and what is that called? Blind man's bluff? Pin the tail on the donkey? It is called the loss of self in Communism and the loss of sight and mind in America. Except it did not work that way for JBK. He gained multiple selves, or he already possessed them. That runs in the family, too. Oh, I do not know what happened. He was supposed to be an agent for the Soviet Union. He had already left the Party, you know. He wanted to become President of the United States. Ridiculous. Wonderful. Institutions are full of those people. But he could have, too. That is the funniest part of all. I lied to him. I told him that we had worked out a deal with the Fabulous Bureaucracy International. In return for his going underground they would not expose him. That is what I told JBK. And he believed me, too. At first I think he thought he could beat us all."

"You told my father?"

"Yes, I told JBK. I told him many things in those last weeks, those last days, those last hours, those last minutes and seconds. He ended by not knowing who or what he was."

"What do you mean?"

"JBK was a creation. The reason that he can be alive and dead after being dead is that he never existed in the first place. We created him. We could uncreate him. He didn't exist. It does not matter whether he is dead or alive."

"The uncreated . . . "

Of course, Timothy thought, if you did not exist then you had no background, and if you had no background you had to at least have an underground. What was life without an underground?

"Yes, I made a deal with the FBI. Together we took away his existence, his being."

"The undead . . . "

"Sure, we sent him underground as we did hundreds of our agents. But we made it so that they, some of them, could never come back. When we sent them underground, yes, we sent them underground, we sent them away from their lives, their families. We were sending them off into nothingness. For all the significance it had, for all of its connection with reality, we might just as well have sent them orbiting into space. We imprisoned them in hell. The whole Party in space."

"Space? He talked about space," said Timothy softly, as if he were talking to himself, in a room by himself.

"We had to kill him because he was crazy. He had to die because he knew too much. Except we did not have to kill him. We merely removed him from life, from himself. We killed his existence. He did not die. He went underground. And then we lost him. He lost himself. He lost it on his own. He is out there somewhere. Doing what, I do not know. He is just a lost soul. A lost human being with plenty of company. We sent him underground with all the others. He will never come back. He is conveniently insane. I know that. He went underground just like Hezekiah, off the deep end. In the genes. Going underground was like death for him. He was a bon vivant, just like daddy Hezekiah. Why I wonder how many . . ."

"Hezekiah? I don't understand. Hezekiah?" Timothy repeated as if he had just reentered the room.

"You knew your so-called grandfather was crazy? That he was a disillusioned man when he died? Oh my, so he drank himself to death."

"You have no right . . . "

"I don't? I have no right? Well, let me tell you, he was my beloved father, too. My genes. Although, come to think of it, Grandmother Beatrice was not my mommy. And I don't even claim him. Aha."

Timothy started. Cordon was laughing, not smiling, staring at Timothy.

"Surely you will not pretend that you don't . . . oh, no, I cannot believe it. Yes, yes, Hezekiah was my father. Yes. Yes, yes, JBK is, was my brother. We were brothers, brothers in the revolution."

"Brothers in the revolution," Timothy managed to say weakly, he could not swallow, still trying to comprehend.

"No. Brothers in the flesh. We should have been, anyway, except I was the family secret, talked about in whispers. You must have heard about that, heard them whispering, anyway. They might as well have been whispering about you, my young man. Hezekiah's secretary was my mother. Yes. I was born in New York City. Like you. But I was raised by a branch of the Onward Christians in Canada, where our ancestors had been exiled originally, you know, from Ireland. But it was as if it had never happened. I had not happened. I was not the black sheep. I was the invisible sheep. I did not exist. I was the void. Until the end, when I told JBK everything and he went around the bend. And then he did not exist. Aha."

And then Cordon started . . . to chant, a welling, deep from his diaphragm. It became deafening. His mantra.

"God id dead
Is God dead?
The God is dead
Long Live the God
The King is dead.
Long Live the King."

A chill went down Timothy's spine. He knew something. Something horrifying. Oh, how liberating it is, he thought. If that man never existed then that man never died. Who is, was JBK? JBK, a myth? He was-is a shadow, a myth, a cause, a force, a mystery. A ghost.

"'I Am.' I am that I am," said Cordon as if from afar. "JBK's code name was 'God'—did you know that? Oh, how delicious this is," his familiar voice tuning in again, rising in volume. "And did you also know that after you were born, everybody knew you had been born, yes, there was a joke, supposedly unspoken, but it made the circuit of the apparatus, that, given that JBK was God, and Klara insisted that you were his son, why then you must be JC."

Cordon roared. And then he paused again, and again his voice lowered, almost to a murmur.

"I was 'Killdeer.' Appropriate for a son of Maine, don't you think? I am speaking of myself, of course. Maine was my country, too, you know. The old country."

JBK? Was this then the grand event? Was JBK dead? Had he, too, been cremated? Was this forever? Immolation.

"So, naturally, you do not exist either. You cannot exist if he does not exist. Nothing is the way you think it is. God was not your father and he was not your father."

"My father was God. And God is dead."

"Precisely. You are learning. God is dead, but your father is probably alive, if dead," and Cordon started laughing again.

"JBK was God, but JBK was not your father," he roared, laughed, coughed, spit, and cleared his throat.

"My father is not dead," repeated Timothy, tonelessly. "My father was not a Communist because the Party does not exist. And I am not his son, so I don't exist."

He realized that Cordon had changed before his eyes. And then he thought of the man, the force he had followed in the park or who had followed him. He was not certain that he could tell of the difference, tell of the man or of his father. In the beginning everything was indistinguishable. In the act of creation was the eye of the storm.

Cordon looked at Timothy for a moment and then he spoke with a different conviction.

"Yes. Maybe he is not dead. Maybe he just disappeared. Literally. Lives come and go. Sometimes they get crossed up, I guess, and somebody gets yours and you get theirs. I guess. But you have to follow somebody's orders. You have to step forward and not look back over your shoulder, because if you do you might be looking at yourself."

Cordon looked uneasy. He spoke again, apropos of nothing.

"I'm not certain of anything now. I have just heard that a good friend of JBK's is a close adviser to Kennedy. How odd life can be in its randomness."

Timothy blinked, in a daze.

"Yes. I know the man. I should be in his home right now."

"What you must understand is that he is alive, in a manner of speaking," said Cordon, as if he thought he had better insist upon it.

"I beg your pardon? What I must understand?"

Cordon turned and looked him in the eyes.

"Is there anything I can tell you? Where he is?"

Timothy blinked.

"Where he is," Timothy repeated.

"Yeees."

"You have just told me that he is alive when he has been dead for two years and that he does not exist and now you ask me, 'where is he?'? I don't suppose you would care to elaborate?"

Timothy paused.

"Actually, I am not certain I want you to elaborate."

"Perhaps he wants you to join him."

"Join him? . . . "

"At Anybodys. The bar. Didn't Klara tell you?"

And then Timothy remembered that JBK had not brought him to New York University at all. No, he had come to get him, to take him away from Cordon, who was drunk in his office. Cordon was drunk and JBK had taken Timothy to the bathroom. Taken him away.

"You are not his son. Klara lied to him."

The wild crazed lost look in Timothy's eyes suggested that he had ventured beyond his life. Who the hell did these human beings think they were, claiming and discarding him as if from their species. How could they presume to know when he did not know, when it was his right, first and foremost, to know, know himself. No, it had not been determined what he was, except Hezekiah was still his Grandfather. He had still dropped from the sky.

"You spoke of me as the Devil," Cordon said insistently, struggling to sit on the edge of his chair, trying to regain Timothy's attention, to screw it fast.

"Listen. If that is so, if I am the Devil, then you are not the son of God, but the son of Satan. Forever. You are my son, my bastard, Satan's bastard."

The instant after Timothy hit Cordon flush in the face he regretted it. He grieved. He hated himself for it. He despised the meaning. Hitting him was like putting his fist through a billboard.

"Go ahead and do it," said Cordon, who had fallen straight backwards over his chair. "I want you to do it. Finish me now."

Drunk on martinis, the dignified, distinguished André Cordon was drunk and dissolute, and did not care.

"Who are you? Don't you want to know?"

Timothy jumped on him and he hit him again and the blood started to flow. But then he stopped and he knew he would not ever hit him again. He felt incredibly calm. He walked to the window. He looked and imagined that the park was full of creatures, all exposed under the midnight sun. He stood and watched in silence for an hour.

And then the voice from the shadows.

"Wait, have I told you . . . I, I have been vilified in today's newspaper," said Cordon, finally, quietly, still spread on the floor. "You believe me, don't you? Do, do you read newspapers? But, I swear, I am not goooing to tell them you are my son. They will never find out if I don't tell them. Only I know. Klara doesn't know anything anymore. And she is really the only one who knows. Do you want me to tell them? Anything? Maybe I don't even know. I really don't, you know. Nobody does. But . . . he'll be there tomorrow night."

He was artificial, contrived, shoddy.

determining the story was the key to ever and ever although another way to put it would be to ask if there was a story is there a story if there never was was not another question but the same one was there a story what was the story he did not understand how it all started because they had not told him

But you could not ask. Because you would never know what happened. That was the nature of things. Even if someone presumed to be able to tell you, you would not believe what you heard. All you could do was perform and wonder as little as possible about what you had done, no matter the voices in the head.

14

The Party of Barmania

"Yes, but Jimmy and I play this war game with cards all the time. And he beats me. My son always beats me. He's relentless. Christ, sometimes I wish I could negotiate. Unfortunately, the game has no card for negotiation—you either defend or kill. And if you spend more time defending than killing, that's a sure sign you're going to lose. Except you do have to defend. You understand that?"

"Look, I don't know why you play the game with him. I mean, some father you are. Do you know what you're doing to him? You're screwing up his psyche, that's what, screwing it up for years. Down the road, he's going to remember his father was a loser."

"No, seriously . . ."

"I mean it."

"But it's a way to be with him. I have to get to know my son. It's the only time we're really able to talk with each other. Besides, it's fun."

"Hey, Cary, another Beefeater for Donny. He needs it. At least you drink good booze. Does Jimmy know that? Tell him. He needs all the help he can get, right Cary?"

Cary, the bartender of Anybodys, smiled reassuringly, and sang a song about love in the streets. From his open shirt he displayed black hair sprouting on his massive chest. He was a strikingly handsome man, except that there was too much flesh in his face, too handsome. Big chest, thick hair, and a resonant baritone voice. He served Donny his Beefeater singing of fools in love.

The large, gleaming, gold-trimmed mirror running the length of the bar was overflowing with people falling in and falling out, arms and legs, bodies and faces reappearing, disappearing from sight, long gone come again. The long string of brass lamps suspended in space, hanging and ever so slightly swaying from above the bar, stretched its light and shadow beyond the mirror's limitless expanse.

Timothy sat at the bar of Anybodys in limbo. He looked futilely for a static figure in the mirror, alas, an immutable cutout, looked for the center of life, a center that more and more did not exist, although he resisted the metaphysics, heard parts of conversations emanating around him, constant creations of phrases that bounced and lingered, began and broke off abruptly, sometimes extended monologues and exchanges that lasted for a limited duration, as if the voices could be heard only for as long as their owners appeared in the mirror, into and beyond being, beyond reach . . . reaching . . .

". . . if one group calls the shots for the entire world the danger of a nuclear war is almost . . ."

". . . of course, get him drunk, I don't care how you do it, get him drunk . . ."

"Where'd she go?"

"Home to buy water purification pills."

"Now . . . trying to lower our morale?"

"Nothing could . . ."

". . . improve it."

". . . never be a true intellectual until you have your self taken apart and . . ."

". . . the missiles . . . coming . . ."

"While it is true that experience is a factor, what most of those geniuses do not realize is that . . . is constantly unfolding, developing anew . . ."

"Bullshit. Experience is leftover life."

"What does that guy know?"

"So what? . . . They wipe out the entire South—they'll be doing us a favor. Kennedy should evacuate all the blacks on buses—the whites will think he's doing them a favor. Hey, you get it? . . . 'Blacks Only.' That's . . ."

"I see too many things I don't understand to be totally . . ."

". . . but you *can't* tell the dancer from the dance. You can't have one without the other. If you don't have a dance, you don't have a dancer. You know what I . . ."

"You have to look closely to think otherwise."

"Same thing happens on an elevator, except you look at the ceiling or count floors. No, I never leave this beautiful place under my own power. Out there we're all afraid of each other. In here everybody buys me drinks or makes passes at me or both. Both sexes. I quite like it. Why haven't you made a pass?"

". . . absolutely correct: there's something primitive and frightening about changing the spelling of a word, like 'a-p-e-a-k' as opposed to 's-p-e-a-k'. Absolutely short-circuited . . . prevalent affliction . . . tops of letters missing . . ."

Timothy remained silent and drifting, further and further apart, losing the desire to return, the whirl of words tossing, swirling round about him, buzzing, imploding. In separation, the apparent babble was at the same time strangely reassuring, inviting. There was the plausability of life and, at least temporarily, the illusion of a haven found. Or, perhaps, seeking to escape something, he had found an afterlife.

"You don't understand. We can't afford to be profound. People have to think they understand us. Glibness goes a long way. You know, short and sweet . . ."

". . . sweet smell, sweet world . . ."

"Yes, it does smell . . ."

"You have to keep it simple, make it look good—always that—and communicate wha . . ."

"Look, we are talking fifty years of foreign policy here. Except that, you know, there's the tip-off. We call it foreign policy when it is world policy. Why doesn't that penetrate? World survival. Earth survival. The planet. You and me. Maybe an implosion of the universe. More than you and me. It's not foreign. And if you choose not to do it for your own species, not to mention the birds and the bees, could we not at least be considerate, thoughtful, of the feelings of those creatures from other planets?"

"We have a lot of enemies out there, a lot of people would love to bomb the crap out of us."

"Well . . ."

Cary the bartender was singing again, a signal that he was serving another drink. Two voices seemed to rise in echo or answer, a man's and a woman's. A tenor and a soprano? Timothy was certain he had heard them. Was it a prelude or an echo?

". . . sell it back to Spain."

"Battle of the Bulge: General Motors and Khrushchev. Why I . . ."

With people singing and talking, shuffling and bumping, it did not seem possible for Timothy to be alone. Then why so alone? Why the cold and emptiness? The offer of secret companionship was present in abundance. The bar was an enclosed booth with drawn curtains. But he simply wondered why he was in the bar, why he had come to Anybodys, what the meaning could be. What could they, anybody, still want of him? Who? Was this merely a final moment of observation? He now knew that they had been watching him all of the time, all of his life. Why, had he not recently in this very life been observed while he was spending what he had taken to be a silent and eternal night dreaming among the blackmasked souls of the Hotel Sun, at what was indisputably the headquarters of the blackmasked arm of the American Communist Party, in broad daylight without, sinister darkness within him? Or had he not, was that not in his past, was that still to come in a vision? And how could he know? He could not remember if it was the past or the future; he had not desired to rearrange it in his mind. And then, Miss Klara America, no, Miss Mother Damnation of Souls, what promises had she foresaken? And more than that. Father Time, his father in time lost.

Was God the Father presently in Anybodys, then? Must be, that much could be ascertained, obviously in the house of ghosts, of final resting horrors, watched by millions of eyes that had gone before, waiting for Him to follow while He, apparently, had refused

and yet

the remainder of the world did not even know where . . . Timothy was. Incredible paradox. The truth was known that God was in Anybodys, but New York did not know who or what was Timothy. He did not exist. So how could he refuse life? He had ceased to be, lost fear, recognition, memory. Nothing touched him for a very few minutes or for eternity, periodically, and it was as if he could not will the space-gap even as he was, of course, in total control. Yes, his own god, without life.

A bar full of Communists? Was there such a thing? A Communist party in America? Here's to the Revolution, then. Of and by and for? Perhaps not. But while he was waiting he had to decide whether to order vodka or champagne, if he could remember what he had been drinking.

But wait. For what purpose had he entered this city? That would make a difference, provide a clue, settle everything. Had he forgotten, misplaced that thought as well? It was urgent that someone answer that question. He must ask for permission to ask. Waiter. The play must go on. Why, it must be his task to lead a delegation to the great beyond, to let loose a last religious revival, and, failing that, to assassinate or exterminate, always that, or, pathetically, to demonstrate for social reform, to make his bald fortune, to write the great book of a failed life, to stamp out callous corruption, worship at the silly shrine, find the hellacious holy grail. It was true. It was unavoidable. You had to make career choices in the cosmos. Who *would* cook your eggs?

He heard the whisper.

"Why are you here?"

It was perhaps an echo from his brain, a fly in his hearing, but he knew not how to respond despite being on guard for anything.

"I have come to join the Communist conspiracy," he thought he was saying, "or to betray it. I have had membership since before birth, apparently, before choice, before condemnation. I am the last of the Red agents. I am a double-edged spy for freedom. My uncle was Herbert, baby, Philbrick. They have already televised it and I want a leading part, I deserve it, because I watched the McCarthy peepshow as a kid. I know how it should go, I know what to say. I can tell them. I know everything there is to know about America. And I will, once and for all, I will tell all and be done with it all."

He liked not being understood. He liked not understanding. It was the American way. Always starting from ground zero.

The bartender placed a drink on a napkin in front of the man to Timothy's right. The man immediately moved it an inch. It struck Timothy as a stupendous act. The world had been transformed. He understood completely that this was not the first occurrence, that so with every subsequent drink the bartender served, the man would move his drink an inch away from himself or closer to himself, but always an inch from where the bartender had placed it on the bar, claiming it, claiming the world.

What was that? Had someone whispered in his ear again? Not again?

". . . just left . . . maybe he will come back."

Whispered in his ear and walked away. Just like that. Timothy looked over his shoulder. Had someone told him to look over his shoulder, to look away?

He heard the singing again,

". . . on the street where you live . . ."

And voices.

"If only everyone understood, knew our limits, our capacities, what we are each one of us capable of, what can happen. In some immense way . . ."

". . . do you know, because you see I disagree with you. We should never know our limits, we should never agree to limits, there can be no question of limits. That is non-negotiable. If we ever admit to such an unforgiveable thing . . ."

"It will be quick, right? Boom, just like that. I don't like pain."

"The missile attack or the revolution?"

". . . right. The bomb is the revolution. That's my announcement. Ranked as one of the all-time greatest in history. Descartes's thinking therefore I am, number one, of course, Sam Johnson's kicking the stone and farting in Berkeley's face, number two, because it will be ever so, and Anatole France, the whining adolescent, 'He was born. He suffered. He died,' bless us all, Tiny Tim, number three. I say the bomb is the revolution. It has happened. Number four. Let us pray."

"Absolutely. I think it would change things. If only we knew that we are all in it together, it might help. Camaraderie. Complicity. If we understood the latter we might truly have the former. But how can I know?"

"You know, the bomb could actually be construed as a religious act, a religious gesture. We can all die together in the one brilliant blast. We know all about that. We have already done it. We could manage it. We could have it again. Oh, let there be light, brother."

"Simply because we cannot forgive ourselves for the fact that we are capable of anything? To act, the Act, is, well . . . capability is sufficient for condemnation."

"But there is no credit for virtue. Being virtuous is a necessary sentence. . . . If our behavior is not governed by virtue . . ."

And then came a single voice:

"I can always tell when a man is looking for something," the voice said in low rumbling tones, as if asking Timothy from a distance to confide in him, asking confession in his sleep, the echo, looking to hypnotize.

The first thing Timothy saw when he looked through the clouds of smoke, when his eyes focused, was his own reflection straight ahead in the mirror of the bar, the bar, was he being watched in the bar, say, through the mirror, one way, staring back at himself through the mirror? He did exist. He had seen that face somewhere before. He had been followed. He knew it.

Cary the bartender broke his line of vision as he glided by, still singing of love in the streets as if nothing in the world had ever changed in Anybodys, serving drinks to the displaced—the man to the right moved his drink again. Oddly, the thought occurred to Timothy that you do not sell drinks in a bar, you serve them. People buy, but nobody sells. And then Timothy's mind shifted again, and he looked up and to his right in the direction of the voice and he saw the man.

"I can always tell," the man repeated, this time like beginning thunder from above.

The man was a giant, at least six feet five inches tall and well over two hundred and fifty pounds. If he had been sent to Timothy, if this was someone's courier—God's representative?—he might as well have moonlighted as the heavyweight champion of the world or hung around on the corner as a hippopotamus. The giant looked down at Timothy from under a large, wide-brimmed hat, and he sprouted a spotless, cream colored, vested suit that matched his hat, almost anyway, maroon scarf around his neck, maroon handkerchief in his front suitcoat pocket. It was his uniform. Massive head, ruddy face, peering, brimming with good cheer.

Actually, he was smiling as if he were commander-in-chief of the universe, as if he claimed more than authority, as if he were the afterGOD, self-discovered. Smug enough. He forthrightly took the maroon handkerchief from his front suitcoat pocket and wiped his massive forehead as if he had just completed recreating the world. Because it was not warm at Anybodys, he was, therefore, instead, if you will, his own source of heat in his own world.

"You are looking for something," he repeated, waiting patiently, knowing what was coming, assured of himself for no reason at all, speaking his lines into his handkerchief as if he were an actor attempting to hide the fact that Timothy had missed his cue.

"I am never wrong," he added matter-of-factly.

"The Square," Timothy said, feeling the pressure and having belatedly discovered his lines, taking what was there, all that he could retrieve, what was in his head, and then, remembering where he was supposed to be if he was to be found anywhere in the universe, in the bar, apparently, the bar, in **ANYBODYS**, the sign in lights at this entrance had said, **ANYBODYS,** he remembered that much, attempting to remember who had supposedly sent him or sent for him or sent him away, whichever it was, even if the ghosts of his lives, themselves, had disappeared and he had had the presumption, had dared to attempt to find his way on his own, because he thought he might yet be able to reassess history at any moment.

"I am looking for the Square," he repeated, as if that were it.

Timothy might or might not have smiled because he had not been told the strategy, what was required, did not know the endgame to be played in this new world, because no one had deigned to confide in him, but it did not appear to matter anyway, for the giant did not seem to mind himself, mind anything at all at the moment.

"But the blessed mother of muses did not show you?" the giant laughed knowingly but enigmatically. "'So blessed and beautiful that I asked her to command,'" he plagiarized, and then, inventing like a soothsayer, "But she was determined, hard, ruthless, and immoral. Was she immoral? And what was she determined about? Revenge? Against whom? And for what?"

Timothy involuntarily glanced in the mirror, as if compelled to look either for the answer to the question or for the fading muse, that is, for Klara's fading image, and he remembered, indeed, that she had moved bravely frightened bronzed smile, her own invention.

"But you must look no longer for her," the giant said, as if he knew, waving his hands as if in dismissal and rolling his eyes as if in pursuit of his voice.

"For you have found Anybodys. Yes, sir, Philly Morris at your service, on loan for this day and, what is your good fortune, for this day only. Light up and have a bit of good cheer," Philly Morris said, offering Timothy a Pall Mall.

"Surely we must observe the occasion today, for there may not be occasion tomorrow, which, as you surely know, is Halloween," he continued without pause, winking, "yes, it is my pleasure, my pleasure," he boomed, and, yes, yes, yes, his voice resounded, indeed, like rolling thunder, thunder that once heard is thunder you have heard forever, rolling thunder heard as a child.

Yes, sir, thought Timothy, the jolly Red giant had stepped down from the giant billboard on Times Square, USA, had stepped forth in a world where anything would be possible and nothing had happened, the Boss who smoked his cigarette over and beyond the people and poured his whiskey every day and night upon Times Square, the governor-elect forever of the world yet to come. An invasion was completely under way and it occurred to Timothy at that moment that he had not eaten, that he could not remember when he had eaten in this his hour of need, that he should have eaten at Nedick's in his dreams. He was moving further and further away from questions of subsistence in this life.

Philly Morris lit the cigarette that had found its way into Timothy's mouth and wrapped an arm around him. Sweet smell, indeed.

"Cary, two champagne cocktails for my friend and me. He has just arrived at Anybodys and I have asked him to join the celebration. It is my pleasure, my pleasure, my pleasure."

Timothy was experiencing vertigo. He suddenly could not remember to whom this giant was talking or if the giant had said that they were there to celebrate the revolution or the end of the world. And was the singing increasing in volume for the singing of the song? Was it near to closing time? Was the party over or had it just begun? Perhaps it was necessary to confide in Cary the bartender. Would he know where Seema had gone? Where had Seema gone? To her castle?

Philly Morris, of course, had no difficulty getting Cary's attention. Timothy perceived that had Philly Morris desired he could have reached over the crush of people at the bar in one easy motion and plucked the drinks for himself. Surely, he was king of this reestablishment, the producer of this last show of showing and he would know everything that had transpired in this and every last instance.

They clicked glasses in apparent joyous acknowledgment. The champagne fizzed and the Pall Mall burned in Timothy's nose and he understood that everything was . . . was an apparent illusion. Except the insistence of the voices of the people.

"But there is no connection with a million barrels of oil and my question."

"I made the connection. You understand that? You will understand it, I promise you. That is what it is all about, you know. Nothing is connected unless you connect it. If you connect it, it is connected. One has to insist upon connection. Connectedness. You, for example, had better insist upon the connectedness of your own life, otherwise there is no reality for you. Reality. There is not even chaos. Chaos. You are finished. No you . . . through our eyes we connect much of life . . . two incongruities, through thoughts . . . pressures, folds back, compounds, creates our own logic and thus our own history . . . our sense of history, our form if you will . . . is or gives us the necessary illusion of knowledge, of place . . ."

". . . the system—which we set in place . . ."

"That is an illusion."

". . . is independent of us."

"Now you are talking."

"It is operational because everyone or a majority of right persons acts as if it must be."

"Here is my card, for example, . . ."

". . . which shows that you have been identified."

"Because I have this card you must take me into the hospital . . ."

"Well . . ."

"No matter the expense."

"Certainly that."

"The system is in effect."

"For good or ill?"

". . . always look on the bright side of things, me boyo."

"True commitment . . . do anything ordered . . . horror of thinking for yourself . . ."

Did it matter whether or what he was celebrating, Timothy wondered. It mattered that he had been drinking, that he was now drinking champagne cocktails. It was a fact that he had never ever before drunk that magic potion in this manner. It was the elixir of the gods or the syrup of Satan and he had either mislaid the knowledge to say which or he had never possessed it.

"What is your name, sir, if I might ask?" asked the giant, indeed, obviously seeking to ascertain for certainty's sake exactly if Timothy was who he thought he was, whom Timothy thought he was, of course.

"Philly Morris, here," the giant repeated benignly, continuing to gently prompt Timothy, lead him, yet leaving him no recourse, no choice, like a relentless history, moving him along like a master of history.

"Timothy Brown . . . King," Timothy decided to say, pretend that he possessed the choice, having rejected in midname the idea of creating a new name as an absurdity, which, he also realized, might have justified his doing so, as was exactly appropriate, as was the absolute bent of his thinking in a brave new world.

"Well, Mr. Timothy Brown, do you live in a shoe? Ha, ha," Philly Morris boomed again, pleased with his little jest. "No, you are a Boston man, I presume? The accent, of course. Lovely town, Boston, the cradle of liberty, but now that you have come to the seat of the empire, you will never be the same, no sir, no liberty. This is not a sacred city, no sir, not a mecca, and nothing ever stays the same, mercifully, nothing ever is the same in Anybodys, you will be happy to hear, I am sure, it is my pleasure."

"No, not really," said Timothy, already beginning to let the champagne talk for him, he wanted it to, as if it were now his pleasure, his chosen intoxication for life.

"I mean, I am originally supposed to be from Maine, which has been an affront to me as well as a boon to my liberty, apparently, so some would say. That is, Portland, Maine, not Boston, Massachusetts, which was once a part of Maine, or vice versa, although I can understand your questions, that you would have them, your intense interest in saying that under the circumstances of my meeting with, as you say, my . . . muse, marvelous, for I have indeed met her, and she has left me. And it is, pardon me, not Timothy Brown, it is Timothy Brown King, son of a king, I was, not that it matters, because it is true what you say, that I will never be the same anyway. I never was, you see, I have been convinced of that. If you were talking of me, that is. Because I am not from Maine after all . . . you see . . . or Boston . . . although I came from . . . there . . . in a way . . . by bus."

He had stopped.

"King, of course it is King," said the giant, quick to reassure, "God knows it is King, and it is quite understandable that it would be so and quite reasonable that you would insist upon it. Forgive me for being overbearing, Mr. King it is, I should never have forgotten that even for a moment, because that moment could be forever," he laughed. "It certainly does matter, even if we do not say anything further about it. Unforgiveable, a man must know his own name if he is to be able to tell his own destiny from that of another," he laughed again. "Let us drink to it while we have time," he laughed again and again. "It is my pleasure, my increasing pleasure. Yes, sir, New York is a terrible town. It is not Boston, not that it really matters. And it is not Chicago, either, thank heavens for some. It is not even San Francisco, although that would suit others fine. But you play New York and you will get music, music of the eternal spheres, as the muse would tell us, music in a city of eternal anger. Yes, sir, indeed, they do not take prisoners in New York, my good man, Timothy, but you may take refuge in Anybodys. Say, I may call you Timothy, may I not? You may call me Philly, yes you may, for it is what I allow only a few to know me by, if they would know me at all, of course, for I was once from Philadelphia, once from someplace, like you."

"Well, Philly. Who is your friend of the evening?"

The questioner was a woman, and she was a woman obviously sent to match Philly Morris. She looked like a painted and adorned Statue of Liberty, oversized, bosomy, draped in a full panoply of gold chains that spread down and around the curves of her more than ample body, with more rings on the fingers of both of her hands than Timothy thought possible, more rings, more fingers. In the crush of people she must have moved like an ocean liner into the room, but Philly Morris did not act as if there were anything out of the ordinary about her size or her person in any dimension whatsoever. He was simply delighted.

"Gloria! Gloria! Hurrah! This is the man you will want to meet, the man you have been waiting for, the man I believe we have all been waiting for—I present Timothy Brown. Originally from Maine. Just flew in looking for the Square. Fortunately, I was here to greet him or he would still be looking, trying to find his way looking. Timothy Brown, this is Gloria Dehaven."

"Just flew in, Mr. Brown? Marvelous! Originally from Maine? How nice to be originally anything. And to what do we owe the occasion? Oh, yes," she paused, waving a long white cigarette holder toward Philly Morris, "you said he was . . . looking . . . looking about. How nice."

"I was told that was my mission," Timothy said, looking glazed, extending his hand, "but I did not fly anywhere, although I was supposed to, and maybe I should have. I took the bus because I was asked to, and I did. And I did not come from Maine, although it is true that I am originally from Maine, except that it has not been determined exactly where in Maine or why, for that matter, I am sure."

Gloria and Philly laughed together.

Timothy thought it was beginning to make sense, as the names Philly Morris and Gloria Dehaven did, made some kind of sense, there was a beginning ringing in his head.

Both Gloria Dehaven and Philly Morris laughed again.

"Oh, how nice," Gloria Dehaven repeated, taking Timothy's hand. "Yes, nice to meet you, Mr. Brown."

She was amused, but apparently friendly. Her hair was frosted and flowed up and around like an ice cream cone. If Philly Morris was the emperor of this carnival, she was its Dairy Queen.

Timothy thought to let his name stand, to let Brown be it but, thinking of her name, remembering his childhood queen of B-movies, he wondered out loud.

"Is your name really 'Gloria Dehaven'?"

"If you call me that, yes, if that is what you want, I will be Gloria Dehaven for you, and for you only."

Gloria Dehaven and Philly Morris were laughing in musical unison again, or perhaps they had never ceased.

Philly wrapped his powerful arm around Gloria this time, as if to link their massive humanities, and, like a bulldozer, the two of them wedged Timothy onto his stool at the bar, stopping only when Gloria's belly pressed into Timothy's knees. Timothy wanted to move but, remembering the hand of the black and white nun, and with the borrowed yellow belly of the red-haired woman of the street flashing in his mind, he did not have the inclination to break the contact of flesh, nor was he surprised when her belly did not give.

When Gloria Dehaven smiled at him with full red lips, he realized that she was inevitably the latest and the last in the long line of women in his yet young but nearly finished life.

"You do not mind calling me 'Gloria Dehaven,' do you, Timothy Brown?"

She looked at him like he was a cute teddy bear.

Timothy merely stared at her, because he realized it was beyond time for him to mind anything or to anticipate anything. He would simply let the world imagine itself.

"So you have come from Maine, is that it? Such a ways to come, I would think. I cannot say that I have ever had the pleasure of being in Maine. And perhaps you are tired, no, my young adventurer?"

"Indeed," a new voice interrupted. "He has come from the great dead beyond to be saved but, alas, we are not saviors."

"Dante Rossy," Gloria Dehaven said, feigning introduction, but for Timothy the name as well as the figure was overrun in a chorus of names spoken and in the rush of bodies now unidentified, as if the entire party had suddenly arrived from Broadway simultaneously, from all of the plays and musicals of New York daily life.

"This is Noel," he heard Philly Morris say, "and Molly . . . Edward . . . my pleasure, my pleasure," the names tumbling forth one upon the other, until Timothy felt as if the mirror of the bar had tilted and emptied all of the people all on top of him all at once.

"He has just left I heard . . . but get him back," Timothy thought he heard again, or he had heard it from memory, or it was an echo trapped in Anybodys, perhaps sounding before bounding from mirror to mirror.

In the jumble, he realized that he had finished his glass of champagne only when Philly Morris replaced it with another, full and sparkling. Were they simply talking and drinking simply to be talking and drinking? Only that? It appeared more and more as if much more must be taking place. Why such smiles? Loud bellowing? Why such posturing? The thought occurred that, at the very least, people disappeared in all of those clothes, particularly in Anybodys.

". . . his credentials, his resume, et cetera."

"Most of all, he holds a cigarette extremely well, can on command look people in the eye, and is an impeccable curser . . ."

"Do you think I should secretly write these names down or memorize them before I forget?" Timothy belatedly thought to ask, for no reason at all that he could think of, asked of no one in particular, as if he had been delayed, his life delayed by multiplying introductions to life, but Philly Morris and Gloria Dehaven had abruptly turned their considerable backs, pretending, as a sudden, surprising remaneuver, perhaps, to ignore Timothy, to leave him awash in introductions, thereby foreclosing any introduction at all to the people of Anybodys.

"Behold, a writer of names, then," said a man with a cigar, appearing out of a cloud of smoke that Timothy did remember remarkably as Dante Rossy, remembered maybe because he remembered that the cab driver in his dreams had smoked a cigar, a cigar Dante Rossy presently maneuvered to the right corner of his mouth, the better to speak his mind on his newly chosen subject.

"I am appalled that they have let you through immigration," he said, as if in mocking disdain. "We already have an undesirable surplus of writers in Manhattan. Writers are as plentiful here as I imagine potato pickers are in Maine. But maybe you have become a poet of last resort," he said in afterthought, the thought being to compose his poem on the spot, "because Maine is the last resort, a poet of the nearly dead yet though they would be undead. Maybe you have come to write about the end of the world, because you have come from the end of the world."

Dante Rossy's cigar was nearly pulp, mashed, chewed, as if he had eaten his words in glee rather than smoked his cigar to its present length.

"My good lad," he went on, "better to forget writing anything at Anybodys. Nothing verifiable leaves Anybodys anyway. Certainly not the truth. We are not interested in the truth. Only in beginnings and endings. For this is the first and the last stop."

"Now, Dante, you are not being nice."

It was Gloria Dehaven, who had magically reappeared. She was the stretch of her own horizon just as Philly Morris was the source of his own heat.

"Neither is it our mission to be nice, especially to you, my not so little Glorious one," said Dante Rossy, turning to face Gloria Dehaven as if eager to feast upon whatever lines were fed to him like so much raw bait, as if she would prove to be the juiciest morsel of all.

"Tell me, Timothy Brown," Gloria Dehaven asked, unoffended and unflustered by Dante Rossy, "do you have a local residence or are you visiting royalty, like most New Yorkers?"

"Did you not hear, Gloria?" said the undaunted Dante. "He came straight on his destiny express from Maine to Anybodys. It is a miracle."

"He's right," said Timothy, not certain if he was thinking of the Hotel Sun in a dim, faded light or of the Maine past, "I don't think anybody stays where I was, not for long, anyway, or having arrived they stay forever, but I don't think I was expected to leave, because I don't think anybody saw me arrive. I should probably report it to the authorities, although they would probably not be able to find it again. I cannot."

Gloria Dehaven slid down the bar with a smile that said that she recognized that all was not well, but the smile also promised that she would return, not to pursue the same conversation, but to pursue Timothy.

As if drawn there, Timothy was looking into the mirror again, although it was less crowded and he sensed a sharper focus beyond, as if he were being guided by the refraction of light to another stage. The volume of singing had indeed increased beyond, and then, in the mirror, he saw the immense figure of Philly Morris reappear, standing by a table like the master of these ceremonies, his arm extended, the palm of his hand open in pantomime. He could not hear, but Timothy was certain that Philly Morris was saying, "It is my pleasure, our pleasure," for there was the slowing growing music of the spheres and Timothy sensed that it would become stronger, overflowing with the voices of the people.

"Ahhh, New York on a Sunday morning. More than sanity . . ."

"It is Monday."

"Why should I talk about today? The trick is to avoid today."

"Actually, come to think of it, it may still be Sunday after all. Would we know the difference?"

"To demamnded patriotism is to impose a setted of values on the . . . my sensed that I should resisted that . . . freed to create my own . . ."

"What was it the man said? 'I have only one life to give'?"

"Precisely, but how many lives can you take?"

"You are wondering, of course, if this is legally legal."

Timothy turned away from the mirror to find that the single table had multiplied, tables surrounded by people singing, surrounded by the light of the bar. It was as if the last act had begun, more than that New York City was its usual party in progress. It was a rare, perhaps a divine moment. The people were beautiful, he thought, glamorous, men and women, golden creamy hair, black hair blacker and waved, clothes richer, imperious, a presence presumptuous, pre-emptive and predetermined, a separated breed with gilded voices for the closing act.

A woman, looking as if she had just emerged from a pool of water, wearing a glistening, sequined dress that clung damply to her thin body, tipped and teetered like a towering clipper ship on the top of one of the tables. Noel. The name of Noel floated through Timothy's mind. She was dancing by herself, with herself, dancing anywhere, everywhere, it seemed. And then she destroyed the illusion by bending at the waist in uncontrolled but silent laughter.

"They have been here every night for at least two weeks," a voice apart said, "after having performed elsewhere for years."

It was Dante Rossy.

"They have been singing in a musical they thought would never end. I was worried it would not end. They think they are celebrating their closing, but the truth is they simply cannot stop singing. Was it ever so? Celebrating? Ah, the indomitable human spirit. I suppose it is sad."

"What . . ." Timothy started.

"The only sad thing," a voice interjected, "is that the statute of limitations has long expired since you reviewed the musical, my poisoned-pen friend."

"Ahhh, Eddie . . ." began Dante Rossy.

"In the beginning, God created the statute of limitations," blurted Timothy.

He was high, suddenly very high, and instantly happy, which he knew was outrageous. Everything had melded. The walls had moved inward, the back of the room was closer. The world had shrunk and insisted upon its own meaning.

He could not understand why he was enjoying himself immensely. In fact he had never enjoyed anything so much. For just the moment he was in a reverie at the bar, utterly content to never move again, convinced it would be unnecessary at the end of the world. Yes, it was true. He was ready for it.

At first he thought he had imagined it, but, yes, someone had lit him another Pall Mall. The great socialist smoking state. And the singing, yes, voices singing, and he wanted to go in that direction, but he could not as yet move . . .

". . . Edward MacPherson," a man was saying. "Only the vulgar call me 'Eddie,' the great democratic unwashed. I do not bless them. I am Broadway's greatest character actor, which is a profound tragedy. I am too good to play the leading role. My performance would demand too much concentration for too long a period of time for the beloved American audience. You have seen me many times, young man, and did not know it. I do detergent, dog food, and diapers on the side. My only saving grace is that there are moments of greatness even when I do nothing."

Had MacPherson lit his cigarette?

"At least for your sake I hope you have seen me, in which case it may not be too late for you. This sweatshirt is my disguise," he continued, placing his hand over his breast, touching lettering that read "New York Giants."

"It is a necessary disguise, because I am so faaamous, it is the only way I can hide from my wretched fans."

There was something strange about the voice. Edward MacPherson's words seemed to follow his hands, as if the hands were doing the speaking. And the voice was not his. His lips moved but the voice was mechanical. Clean and perfect and recorded. Artificial. Separate from his person. The thought occurred to Timothy that, in the manner of a conjurer, the voice was in the possession of the hands entirely, that the hands had become the ventriloquist, the person the puppet. Surprisingly, Edward MacPherson abruptly offered his hand and Timothy boldly took it. It, too, was entirely of flesh.

"The voice, in case you were wondering but did not want to ask," MacPherson went on after pausing, perhaps having guessed Timothy's thoughts, or having learned from experience to aid each new audience in the comprehension of his oft-told story, "is part of my disguise. Except that I had to get throat cancer twice to make it work, which made the entire process excruciatingly messy. There was no other way. Some day I will play a role where I will wear my sweatshirt and talk and you will remember and say nothing of my character. You will remember, won't you, Mr. . . . Mr. . . .?"

"Timothy Brown, I believe," said Dante Rossy, as Timothy did not appear about to respond. "Exiled from Maine."

"I suppose . . ." murmured Timothy, speaking to no one.

"An innocent abroad," said Edward MacPherson. "How refreshing. Reminds me of other long-forgotten, humble beginnings in American history, long before your time, if not my own."

"An uncharacteristic moment of honesty," said Dante Rossy, moving closer as if in anticipation.

"Kansas," continued MacPherson, unfazed. "Not Maine. Like other great Americans, I, too, arrived untouched."

"That is surprising, or it is a characteristic moment of dishonesty."

"And I ended up here just like you. Right here in Anybodys, of course, in this very bar. First thing I looked for, and I have never been the same since."

"And he has not left since, either; of course, in his case only partly, because once one enters these gates one does not leave, one never sees light again, for there is no innocence in America."

"The time of night, which I have not mentioned . . ."

"You haven't?"

". . . was late. Had to have been, because the entrance to the bar was closed shortly afterward, locked, with me still inside. I was not alone. Surrounded by people. Feeling alone, of course. And frightened. The bar was on Eighth Avenue then, The Triple A it was called, I think."

"Remarkable memory. Knows every bar in town."

"Something like that. It was a rather undistinguished, innocuous bar, so . . . reduced."

"Exactly."

"Dingy, cluttered, drab. As I recall it now, it was surreal, surprising, that a child such as I should have appeared at that period of history at such a late hour in such a bar on such a street."

"Not really. In some things you were precocious."

"Unfriendly. Maybe hostile. No one could really have lived there, in that neighborhood, along that foreboding way. I was either naive or I possessed great courage."

"Neither."

"Or I was undefined, overlooked, a nonentity."

"Precisely."

"No, I was self-conscious, intensely self-aware of inquisitive eyes everywhere. Ah, that. How wonderful, thinking that everyone in the bar was looking at me . . ."

"Only make-believe."

". . . watching every step I took, the movement of every leg muscle, face twitch . . ."

"He does have a twitch."

". . . as I made my way, a long way, from the doorway to the bar stool . . ."

"To the bathroom."

". . . thinking, oh, why cannot I be there, why not be there with a glass of anything clutched tightly in my hand, sitting on the stool smoking, staring wistfully in the mirror . . ."

"At himself."

". . . having paid, for I knew not of tabs, and then, surprise, I was ignored. But, oh, the wretchedness of being ignored . . ."

"Poor thing."

". . . except I thought it was blessedness at the time . . ."

"Times change."

". . . make your entrance when you're ready, when . . ."

"If."

". . . it is a nuisance not being able to walk in a straight line . . ."

"He has that problem."

". . . from the doorway to the bar, having to bend around tables, twist around people. And not being able to see a thing in the darkness, just knowing that everyone was looking at me."

"You've said that."

"A simple bottle of beer is what I ordered."

"We were on pins and needles wondering."

"Light a cigarette, make believe you are thinking of something . . ."

"The grand illusion."

". . . wrinkled brow, look serious, nonchalant sip of beer, and, obviously I was waiting, trying to step into . . . something, but what?"

"I think Mr. Brown must have gathered by now."

"Ah, yes, Mr. Brown," said MacPherson, changing his expression if he could not change his tone, as he finally deigned to nod, almost imperceptibly, in the direction of Dante Rossy, "life is, indeed, a play, with playthings. Not altogether original with me, of course, but it does take too long to learn one's roles among the rabble, and there are so very many thoroughly unpleasant pitfalls. Or should I say, pratfalls? Take Mr. Dante Rossy here, please. I am afraid that you have fallen into the wrong hands. He feasts—I use that word advisedly—upon young playwrights in the theater in the same fashion that parasites feast upon mortal flesh. Yes, a preening parasite. Except that he is quite harmless, really. We tolerate him at Anybodys because he amuses us, although he would have it otherwise. Merely by being here amidst this august body, he thinks he will become. He has this quaint notion that such is creativity. By loitering at this establishment he expects revelations, believing, as he does, that unseen forces will deliver him from his unbearable nothingness, from his wretched state."

Dante Rossy was clapping, chewing on his stogie, his eyes still bulging. A trace of saliva appeared at the corner of his mouth.

"Another charming performance," he said, "from a representative of what passes nightly here as Anybodys' version of repertory theater, an overblown production if there ever was one. Oh, do not be misled by this pretense of the common man," he said, glancing at Timothy, but fingering MacPherson's gray sweatshirt, "for, behold, what you have before you is, indeed, a very common man at Anybodys."

"My role is to be here, just as you see me," responded MacPherson, turning totally on Dante Rossy, "just as I am, you wretched soul. I am here for you to see in your blindness. Now. If you were not looking at me, you would be looking at something else, and that would diminish your life, if that is possible. But how dare you profane this sacred garment, straight as it is from the fallen gladiator, from the shoulders of that tragic gentleman of the gridiron, Mr. Y. A. Tittle."

"Football!" said Dante Rossy with obvious disgust. "You see? You see? This is no actor. This is nothing but a frustrated, aged, adolescent jock-worshipper, nothing but, well, nothing but Eddie."

"Oh, but if you had seen his last performance. Tittle, Tittle, his broken body crushed again by those behemoths. Oh, every time Tittle gets hit, I get hit. I do not know how much more I can take. Monstrous. Frightening. Did you know that, alas, poor balding Tittle, the jock's Hamlet, had to leave the game Sunday?"

"That is very moving," said Dante Rossy. "Not very interesting, but very moving."

A renewed burst of song from the local company brought Timothy around. He had slipped again into darkness at the bar, unavailable even for his own private preview of the running performance of MacPherson and Rossy, twin jesters undoubtedly doing their best to obscure, to deflect his attention, to spare him a view of the developing party. Was it that people would perform like this forever if they could, for the sake of going on forever? Or was it just the time for it, because there was no guaranteed time? Was this the way it was, the way it would be, the way it would end, as it had begun? What he could not understand was the rush of the conversation, the cacophony of voices. Or was it not a question of understanding but merely that he was drunk? Was this Anybodys' opera company or a revolutionary rushing body rushing by his brain?

"Are musicals really real?" he asked suddenly.

"The most important philosophical question of the evening," said MacPherson eagerly, as if he had been waiting. "But is it not also a political question?"

"Yes," said Timothy. "Will there be musicals after . . ."

"Looked at in an immediate sense . . ." MacPherson said, pausing.

"Or in your limited time frame," Dante Rossy interrupted.

". . . much seems arbitrary, haphazard, uncontrolled, often destructive, and irrational . . ."

"Except that it is not that exciting."

". . . but from a long-range, chronological perspective, broad, powerful forces make a difference. Then, the impression is one of control, purpose, structure, and perhaps even rationality . . ."

"MacPherson's paradox."

Yes, mused Timothy, involuntarily drifting, increasingly borrowing from the flush of conversations, borrowed words, borrowed phrases, scattered writing to compose sadly without a pen on his mind's mournful notepad.

He mourned.
JBK's belief that revolution was waiting at the door———
The door of Anybodys, the door of opportunity
We have no time to waste, he must have thought.
We must do it, he must have thought.
We must speed up time, he must have thought.

Was that accurate, or was time accelerating to spite him, accelerating, that is—? was <u>that</u> possible?

Fly away

or

all fall down,

all fly apart

the revolution where we all turn against each other

in the dance of death and desire, yes, that was it

But, wait, Timothy was at Barmania Barmania Barmania, the voices said, where, he suddenly realized, he could have conversations with the voices, the voices that had escaped from his head, from the dearly dead, they had been waiting for his recognition.

And then the room returned and, Timothy marveled, was it because he had never seen such color or because he had never looked before?

or was he

drunk,

Party in Progress,

party in bar

Barmania Barmania

"Maybe it is because I never did it," he said out loud to somebody, returning to his conversations with voices. "Maybe the understanding is in the doing. Maybe something got incorporated in my genes."

"Which means that anything is possible for you until you are unidentifiable."

"Yes, until they are not my genes."

"Until proven otherwise, life may have meaning."

"I am," he said, "until I am not."

"Watch your mouth," a man said, laughing, folding in at the lineup of the bar beside Timothy to order a drink, his very own drink, his drink, and, fortunately, Timothy, believing himself to be in running conversation with the world of Barmania, remembered to ask the man, because you had to ask,

"How do you feel about dying?"

But when the man looked at Timothy, frowning, before walking away, the room had returned again, because it had its own voices.

A man coughed as if he had swallowed her whole.

". . . that will be the end of the species."

"What we are involved in is that there is not a reality in terms of consciousness. We are constantly putting such together and constantly dismantling it. There are 'physical' facts, not totally understood here, and there is death . . . burden of creation. The world was much more accepted before as is—to be entering another middle ages . . . well . . ."

". . . creating your own reality . . . retreating to it . . . imagine . . ."

"Flip the switch . . ."

Timothy heard the laughter and looked in the direction he thought he had been looking in for what seemed like hours, straight at the woman's green stockings, visible to just above her crossed-over right knee. She looked at him. Her coffee spoon stopped just above her cup. She laughed and drank her brandy. But Timothy knew that could not be so, because Klara always wore black, not green.

Was everybody dead or crazy? Or both? Not just Hezekiah. Or was everybody . . . alive . . . here in Barmania, and he was . . .

"They believe in the worker, don't you?"

"Yea, yea, but they don't believe in God."

"Why did they have to go and do that?"

"You mean be a Communist and simultaneously be a loyal citizen of the USA? C'mon. It is not possible. Noooo . . . that's like . . ."

"Trying to rub your stomach and pat your head at the same time."

"Impossible! Clearly, because before the first missile . . ."

"Revolutions do not happen, they are made because they are inevitable . . . the chosen can do nothing to bring that state about, but they should live saintly lives . . . to live a saintly life guarantees nothing . . ."

"You think everybody on the Bowery is a Communist."

"That is one of the main places they begin to surface. Harlem is another . . ."

"Where I live . . . you think the people of the slums . . ."

"And any, ah, others from such spheres of activity are red-blooded Communists."

"They're not Americans."

"Ah, no."

"Washington Square Park?"

"No."

"We do what we have to do to bring about what is perceived to be the next, immediate goal as one of a series of steps to the ultimate goal."

"What if your perception changes?"

"We cjhange."

"What about disagreements?"

"Part of the dialectactical."

Timothy was still listening, because he knew he was at the mercy of the voices. Not that he felt weak or weary. Not that he felt crushed, defeated. Or that he, as yet, wanted to walk away, to stop it. It was not an intolerable situation. It wasn't. No, no, no. You did not have to . . . just yet . . . discipline yourself to . . . for . . . what . . . end . . .

He was swept away in the waves of words again, loose in Anybodys.

"She had breasts like melons, firm melons," someone was saying.

"And you had a stiff banana . . ."

And then he had the premonition that it was almost over.

"It is all so temporary."

"Or forever. You have no imagination."

"I will have to think about it."

"You are probably wondering why you were brought here."

Out of the mist words continually filtered into his consciousness as if blown lightly into his ear. He did not ask who had uttered them but as if on cue, instinctively, naturally, from before birth, he responded.

"Yes, I want to be told about it. I want somebody to finally tell me just like anybody else, because I think I know about it already."

He was surprised to see Glo, bountiful Gloria Dehaven appear from out of the smoke, because he did not think she belonged here as yet. She looked stolid, immovable, and imperious. Indomitable Gloria of heaven had come to get him, and suddenly he knew why, he knew it was time to have the showdown with God the Father, who had undoubtedly cynically arranged the entire thing, because she had clearly been a kept secret agent for His sexual desires, although Timothy could not remember if He was JBK or Andre Cordon or whoever the Father was, himself, perhaps, because Timothy had been informed of nothing, the bastards, had been led to believe that he could never be told. They had insisted. That was what the man, his friend in the park, had tried to tell him, bless him. They had insisted that the world had been invented by secret agents for nothing because there were only people.

"Have you thought about what might happen to you," Gloria Dehaven asked, no, she launched in his face, bounced in the gut with her bowling belly, "if the identity of your fucking father becomes public knowledge?"

"Why should I? No one will tell me who He is, where He is, . . . if he is."

"You fool, if he comes here tonight, it could destroy your life even before it has begun."

Timothy mused.

"It hasn't . . . begun. My life."

It seemed like an answer. Despite the sense of urgency Gloria Dehaven projected, he was feeling wistful. He was beyond drunk. He thought there might still be time.

"Well, you are right about one thing," he went on, having reflected for just a moment for forever, "I have come to understand that life has not begun and it may not begin ever."

Where was memory?

"And, therefore," there seemed to be still more on his tongue that he had not known about, "death will probably come first and there will be no memory. But will you let me know if life has begun and I have forgotten? Please. God. I mean, my life is not my own if it has not yet begun."

"Whose is?"

"Is that the meaning? But, no, you do not understand. It is crazy. It does not mean anything. It could not have just happened. If somebody did it."

"Of course it just happened. What do you think life is all about, anyway? It just happens to all of us. Young man, the world is in disguise."

"But why should anything about him, whoever or whatever or wherever He is, become public? Is it because of Cuba? Is that the reason they won't let Him remain dead if He is? Is it necessary to resurrect Him if He is already dead?"

"But everyone has reason to think that your father is still alive, even if it would be better for all of us if he remained dead."

"Why would you think that He is alive?"

"He must be alive, otherwise why are you here?"

"Yes, I could not be here by myself, without Him, whoever He is."

And then he realized that he was possibly being made a fool of sexually, he realized that, because it had come to his dwindling attention that Gloria Dehaven was in gross, disgusting fashion flaunting her breasts at him, although Timothy would not acknowledge that she revolted him—she was flopping her breasts, flaunting them—perhaps he thought she would, like a drunken Irishman in America, drunkenly, his drunkenly, lure him home, collapse when she got there, but Timothy saw that she would become very old in the morning, become cold in the morning, finish him.

But he knew there was a connection between Timothy in the bar, and he had to tell Timothy that, he had to tell himself that, that some connection, being used, involved sexually, obviously a connection with André Cordon and JBK and . . . and . . . Him and their spy work which involved him in using and being used, because he had been used, no, he had used sex, too, and involved him if he could only figure it out sexually and that was the ultimate connection with the Father. Birth. He had been born. He had. That is what it was. He needed his notepad. The bloody birth. Born in the throes of the Party. A child of the Party, those mocking words. The womb, the womb, Mother Klara remembered the womb, she could not forget the womb, and she had tried to tell him. Where was his notepad? He and sexual passion and spying. All that spying, being followed, spied upon in the womb and the seed, the seed, everybody's seed, if he could follow the seed he would know the answer.

Barmania
My Grandfather's seed
seed, lose it, joking,
Drunk
Hezekiah was drunk
fantastic fright of FBI
friggin

"Get him drunk. I don't care how you do it. Get him drunk."

Somebody came up and whispered in his ear:

"He just left . . . maybe he'll come back . . . you must get him back."

It was ominous and unacknowledged and futile.

His father was alive, they were saying, dammit, in the translation of the living from the deaded at 4 A.M. in the morning. Had they found his father? Yet? They were behind the closed doors of Anybodys, the shades were drawn. It was better that he be beyond drunk to hear this. He knew that, especially when, as now, he could not remember how much time had passed since the spoken word, since someone had said something, said words, mine or thine, yes, there had to be a gap somewhere. You had to fill the gap.

And then he knew for a certainty, sudden knowledge, that he had moved miraculously from the bar stool to a booth, although he did not know how or when or who was responsible, whether he had been helped or led or forced or if he had simply wandered away.

He had slumped in the booth, crimson leather, he liked leather, he remembered that, his chin on his chest, one eye open when AP John Darnell Slamunster, squeezed from the crowd, in hysteria, hyperventilating, fell in his lap.

Timothy thought he knew the face, knew the man, his friend, he would help him.

"I know all about it," one managed to say.

"You know?" the other said.

"I sent the letters."

"You?"

"Yes, he left them with my father. I was told about them. I got involved. I wish I never did. So I sent the letters to you. What else could I do if I had figured it out?"

Timothy knew that this figure, whom he now recognized from the park, the park of creatures, spoke the truth, but he knew as well that it was too late.

"Did she know your father? Did she tell you?" Slamunster suddenly asked, as if in midstream, impatiently, as if he were continuing something left off, as if he were leaving off, looking more and more like the balding, sunken-eyed man Klara had once foreseen, looking like her wasted father.

"In the '30s? Meet him in Russia? Have an affair with him in New York? Like your grandfather in Boston? There's a connection, you know. My father told me everything. He took her groceries, too, the old Stalinist. He knew her father in Hungary. She will tell you she is not a member of the Party and that she doesn't even know if it is the Party that she occasionally does things for although later she will admit that she suspects that it is or that she has always suspected it, but maybe she really is, and because she does know your father and what his activities were, they have sent her to be with you in order to find out what you know about him, i. e., do you know anything that might implicate others, implicate him. It is a familiar pattern. She will say that she is not your mother and that he is not your father, but he is and she is not, or you would have neither father nor mother in the Party. But I am after him. I want him. I want them. She did the same thing with me, you see."

Timothy jumped to his feet as if aided by an unseen force and suddenly he found himself immersed in the crowd again, struggling to get through, away, when a voice whispered in his ear.

"The guy's a counter-revolutionary-subversive, you can spot 'em anywhere. Watch him. The dialectic as evolution rather than revolution. Remember that. Stall for time, it is all you can do . . . really."

"It's all fission, isn't it?" Timothy managed to say in the crowd, although he was not certain who had heard him, because his tongue stuck to the roof of his mouth, squeezed in the crowd.

The Absolute, absolute nonsense, he was pissed, because the key was to get away from so-called reality, he knew that, only in America, absolutely, and certainly the mundane palpability of human beings, horrors, fuck them, he was furious for what they had done of by and to him, *the fact was,* the more one could believe in and become absorbed by the idea, the image, the imaging in total isolation from people and events and act upon it on one's own—had he not acted upon it?—the greater the hope and paradoxically the risk. Create the romance. Fuck 'em. There was just the slightest chance.

No philosophy, no people, no father, no life and no . . . no . . .

And then he thought to ask:

"When did he write the letters? Did he write the letters?"

"The letters?" asked Gloria Dehaven, who was there again, suddenly there again. "Who's alive?"

"Who wrote them?"

"He just wrote them," interrupted Slamunster, having caught up with him, shaking his head, having pushed Gloria aside, which Timothy did not think he should have done. "I'm convinced of that. That's the ruse, you see? It's all an invention. Fiction."

"Yes, fission . . ."

"He does not know we arranged his death," Gloria added, back again. "He— got away from us. Honest. It would be better if he stayed dead. And then we wouldn't know. We thought you might think so, too."

"On the other hand, it would be better if he stayed dead," said Slamunster, more authoritatively, more and more officiously. "That's what they want."

"She . . . she told me that," said Timothy. "You just said that, I have heard it before."

"Of course I told you that. We thought you might think so, too. Stayed dead like God the Father. Isn't that what you want? Wouldn't you rather he remain a dead hero than become a living disgrace? You know what a Communist is in America? A Commie. They kill Commies, isn't that what they say? Well, don't you believe it for a second. You cannot kill 'em if you cannot identify 'em. And that is what they are. Unidentified. Impossible. They never existed at all. Which is why I had to get to you, to tell you that he never existed and they never existed and therefore you never existed. I think it is the best way. But I think you already know that for yourself, which is the worst way. I am so sorry. But I am sure you understand. But I thought that you might not think so as well, so I have taken the liberty to invite him here tonight, although invite is hardly the appropriate word. He just comes. God bless him."

"Invite?" asked Timothy.

And then Slamunster repeated it again, as slowly as one could repeat a single world in a crowded room.

"Invite."

Screams.

"It's him, he's back," somebody definitely screamed from the singing table, where there was now a naked chorus line, because no one had any clothes.

Timothy looked and, extraordinary, but there could be no question about it. There was obvious commotion at the door before a dog broke through, followed by the, followed by the furious frustrated force of the life of the man he had followed who had followed him in Washington Square Park, he had followed in life. No question. The Isolated Fury.

"It's him, he's back!" somebody screamed again.

"Behold, a true revolutionary," announced Philly Morris, hogging the spotlight, hugging Gloria Dehaven. "It is my pleasure, my pleasure."

Drunken Angus Anguish.

"Whoosh that?"

"Santa Claus."

"It is Angus."

"Who?"

"Angus."

"Whoosh Anguish?"

"Is that the same as 'Who is God'?"

"Whoosh God?"

"God is Dead."

"Yes, by all means," interjected Dante Rossy, calmly, "I think we should find out who God is, was. That is what we are all here for, is it not? That is reasonable."

Although Timothy was not sure what it was, yes, he did not consciously recognize the revolutionary. And he knew that what he could not decide was with whom Angus was suddenly dancing, because, of course, following his example, everybody was dancing by now, dancing with Seema, Seema had been found dancing with Angus, dancing with God, no, Seema would not be dancing with a bear, because she did not like bears but idiots, yes, Angus looked like a bear who could not be dancing with Klara either because she would not allow it and Seema could therefore certainly not be how could she be dancing with Hezekiah the great god gone before? But perhaps Seema was after all dancing with Angus and they were doing the dance of death and desire for with such a desire must there not be death desired? Did not death spawn such desire? Had it not come to this as well? So many conclusions, but he knew that Angus undoubtedly would be found to wear a wig and a moustache and that maybe they would fall off somehow, in some horrible way, because he had to be in disguise, he had to be a fraud. Because there was a question, increasingly Timothy felt that there was no question, that Angus was not JBK or André Cordon. Therefore, it followed accordingly, according to law, that thus, behold, Angus was the forcing of his creation. This was clearly a ritual about the beginning of the world. Or was it the end of the world? He could not remember which was the more important.

"He could have been a great man," somebody was saying, sobbing, a voice that seemed to be far away, "but this country will not let there be a great shortstop. It cannot conceive it."

Timothy lurched forward and grabbed him, grabbed Angus, struggled to hold him still, but it was impossible. The Fury. He looked into his eyes and made an effort to see with his life, but he looked forever and he could not see, from sea to shining sea. What could you see? How could you see a god?

He finally realized that his father was not there because the philosophy of life was peopleless. There was no place for God the father in life. Which was why he did not have one.

Ah, the kinship he felt. He knew the kinship he felt and he knew why there was no immortality, why there could not be, God no.

"But where are all the Commies?" he thought he suddenly screamed because he would not be silenced any longer.

"Don't you know?" the voices said. "We are all Commies, all of us one and all, and we are informing on ourselves because we are in search of ourselves."

What was that? Was someone making an announcement, giving a speech? Finally? Had they been introduced?

"We are all informers," they were saying. "Everyone in this room is informing."

"But what is there to inform about and to whom?" he asked, pleading to be informed at last.

"False identities to identify, that we are all refugees from ourselves. It is a miracle that we have escaped."

"Ah, I don't understand," he pleaded. "Didn't they . . . isn't he coming back?"

"We don't know. Nobody knows. We don't know where they are. We don't know if they came back or not or . . ."

"Or?"

"Maybe they did come back."

"When?"

"That's what we're worried about."

"Worried about?"

"We do not know where they went or who they are and, yes, we do not want to know."

"Means to whom? Or what?"

"To anybody. To anything."

Bedlam

Notepad. Nothing. Blank Page.

And there it was, naked human beings engaged in acts, flagrant acts, attempting to rise above their inherent limitations, of course, and risking everything.

"That is all we have," said Dante Rossy, putting his hand on Timothy's shoulder, "To Pretend, I was worried they would never close because

The Pretense is everything
AS IF""""""""""""""""""""""""""""""""

"I should have been a jet plane."

"And instead you turned out to be a guided missile."

"A man takes what . . ."

" . . . much to our everlasting regret. "

" . . . never done it, but I am going to try . . . "

"But it is all so temporary . . ."

"Or forever . . . you simply have no imagination."

"All right, someone call for my coach before I jump."

"Quite unnecessary."

the disembodied presences

"There should be no meaning in the context of death. It should be forbidden as an obscenity. No meaning . . . really no different than in previous ages . . . which is why there was once upon a time a god . . .

". . . no central beliefs . . ."

". . . cosmetics . . ."

". . . laxatives . . ."

". . . but where does morality fit in?"

Someone called for their coach to take them away.

Timothy attempted again to survey his newfound theater, but Gloria, back again, kept distracting him, flashing her ringed fingers, shaking her large bosom, blocking his view with her Dairy Queen, because she did not want him to understand. But he realized that all he had to do was keep concentrating.

"What?"

"Simply," Dante Rossy said, "that you are ignorant and paranoid. That is the worst combination there is."

He said it like a scientist revealing to the world for the first time the secret of the universe. He said it as if he knew what he was talking about.

"But I wonder what is attacking me, what holds me together?"

Everyone was gloriously happy. They were clearly here to drink forever. Socked in. An unlimited tab, unlimited money of one whose long shot of a lifetime had come in. Edward MacPherson was dancing with Noel who teeter-towered above him. He was the leading man.

"Angus, simply Angus. He always says he's hit the big one," said Dante Rossy. "It gives him an excuse to celebrate simply because he needs an excuse."

Unlimited enthusiasm of a minor character actor who was going to be paid more than the lead, as it should be in a play to run forever before generations to come.

"They're trying to forget, aren't they? They're trying to forget while they wait for the bomb to drop, because it is too late."

"I don't care if you are a Communist. I think it's silly."

"I thought he would come last night," she sobbed.

The whirling party. They closed in. Timothy felt the room closing in. Finally, Klara, Cordon, JBK, their faces appeared in the mirror. And then God. But he looked away quickly. And that was going too far. That was sacrilegious. Timothy wanted to walk away from it very quickly, disgustedly, purposefully, as if he had somewhere to go. That was exactly what Eddie, no, Edward MacPherson had said, that you should not be embarrassed.

Timothy wished he could rub his hand over his face and remove it. There was, as always, guilt. But there was more. Revulsion. Horror. A longing, intense, that it had never happened. He was trying not to think about it, to think back to the bus ride, which was away from him, a long ways away, as if he had taken a trip. But he had lost his ticket, panhandling for his ticket like a lackey. He knew that much. He might be twenty-one, but they did not have to tell him that. He had never done this, never before, he was doing it, he would forget as soon as he left. He would have to forget. That was the secret. If he forgot, it would be over.

But first it was time to choose the scripture while he sat down on the floor in memory of Hezekiah while everybody danced round about and they were sore afraid:

John 12:23–25—

23 And Jesus answered them, saying, The hour is come, that the Son of
man should be glorified.
24 Verily, verily, I say unto you, Except a corn of wheat fall into the
ground and die, it abideth alone: but if it die, it bringeth forth much fruit.

25 He that loveth his life shall lose it; and he that hateth his life in this world shall keep it unto life eternal.

And then Timothy arose and looked through the smoke, the stagnant, clinging smoke, and saw the figures of Klara and Cordon moving through the crowd, and he knew that he could not reach them in time, for they were going to do what they had already done. Perhaps it was time for him and Seema to go to her castle for the grand discovery.

This time when he started to climb the stairs he knew he would not stop until he had reached the heavens and only then would he return to the bottom. Philosophical certainty controlled even his legs. There was no weather, no time. But he wanted time to pass and have it not mean anything, even if it was raining.

His was a symbolic father, but he had slept with his mother. At least he had that. Otherwise, who were they? They had created a lie in the context of death.

His only hope was that he could still blow them all up even if they were all dead, ghosts. And then he thought of the obvious evidence, that he had read in the newspaper two days ago of the stabbing of the chess master (Hey, the game's over) by the suspect who had a record of mental disturbances

"You know, I've

never kept a record of mine," he said to no one in particular

and who claimed that he had attacked the chessmaster because the secret service had ordered his killing because he was a spy and Timothy knew that the connection was obvious. Not only that, but he had just read that very day, October 29, that a bomb toter had been shot in the IRT and Timothy wondered if he had a nuclear bomb and if it was his God the Father? Fortunately, he had not been identified.

When the blast came it shook the bar. The figures in the mirror rippled while the dancing, jostling lamps flickered light, and many fell to the floor. Timothy jumped only slightly. If he had not known when it would happen, he would not have known what had happened. Something had happened and he knew its impact. The explosion was so direct it seemed to come from inside his head. It had to be a direct hit and the only question they would have would be whether it had come from heaven or hell because that would be the only question they could have because there were limitations. And then another bomb exploded, exploded in his head, the bomb's last gleaming.

Death to all Commies! the voices screamed in his head. Death to all of the Commies within us.

He remembered the kids' game played in the street, the game where he had waited too long and everybody had gone home. And he knew why he had waited, why he could never ever come home. The problem was that he did not want to lose what he had. Forever. He knew he needed to find Seema, to grasp her and and the two of them run out of the bar before they called his name, before they were identified. He knew that much.

But why, oh, why then, were they insisting on carrying him feet first, as if he were drunk with alcohol—because of the bomb, of course, except they were not carrying him out to the sidewalk because he seemed to be having a fit, and he broke loose, free, and ran into the street where he feared that someone would run up and point a gun at his head, firing, because they could not let him get away with it, and just to make certain the green Cadillac whipped through sending him flying forever

Somebody ran out into the street, in the traffic, points a gun at him, about fifteen feet away, and shoots him in the head. (Points a gun at his head and shoots.)

but he broke away again and made it to the park just in time to see Hezekiah disappearing, running naked across the border and, looking backwards over his shoulder, he dared it, he saw Falstaff leaning against the world smoking a Camel

he knew

UNIVERSITY PRESS OF NEW ENGLAND

publishes books under its own imprint and is the publisher for Brandeis University Press, Dartmouth College, Middlebury College Press, University of New Hampshire, University of Rhode Island, Tufts University, University of Vermont, Wesleyan University Press, and Salzburg Seminar.

ABOUT THE AUTHOR

Born in Portland, Maine, ROBERT EATON KELLEY has a mythology that includes his present whereabouts, traces of which may be found in the Upper Connecticut Valley of New Hampshire, where he lives with his wife, the historian Mary Kelley; degrees from Dartmouth College and New York University; and his testimony that sometime in 1962 during the week of the Cuban Missile Crisis he stepped on a bus bound for New York City.

Library of Congress Cataloging-in-Publication Data

Kelley, Robert Eaton.

The first book of Timothy: a novel/by Robert Eaton Kelley.

p. cm.

ISBN 0-87451-725-7 (alk. paper)

1. Cuban Missile Crisis, 1962—Fiction. I. Title.

PS3521.E4322F55 1995

813'.54—dc20 95-17106

♾